THE BOOK OF WOLVES

THE DARK LIBRARY SERIES
BOOK FOUR

MORGAN REILLY

LIBRA'S INK
PUBLISHING HOUSE

ALSO BY MORGAN REILLY

Short Fiction

Secrets of Northanger Abbey

The Dark Library Series

Book One: The Book of Water

Book Two: The Book of Dreams

Book Three: The Book of Light

Newsletter: https://subscribepage.io/gQ6p2Z

Website: https://morganreallywrites.com/

To the ones who've felt left behind.
To the ones who've felt like "too much."
You are seen.
You are heard.
You are loved.
You are enough.

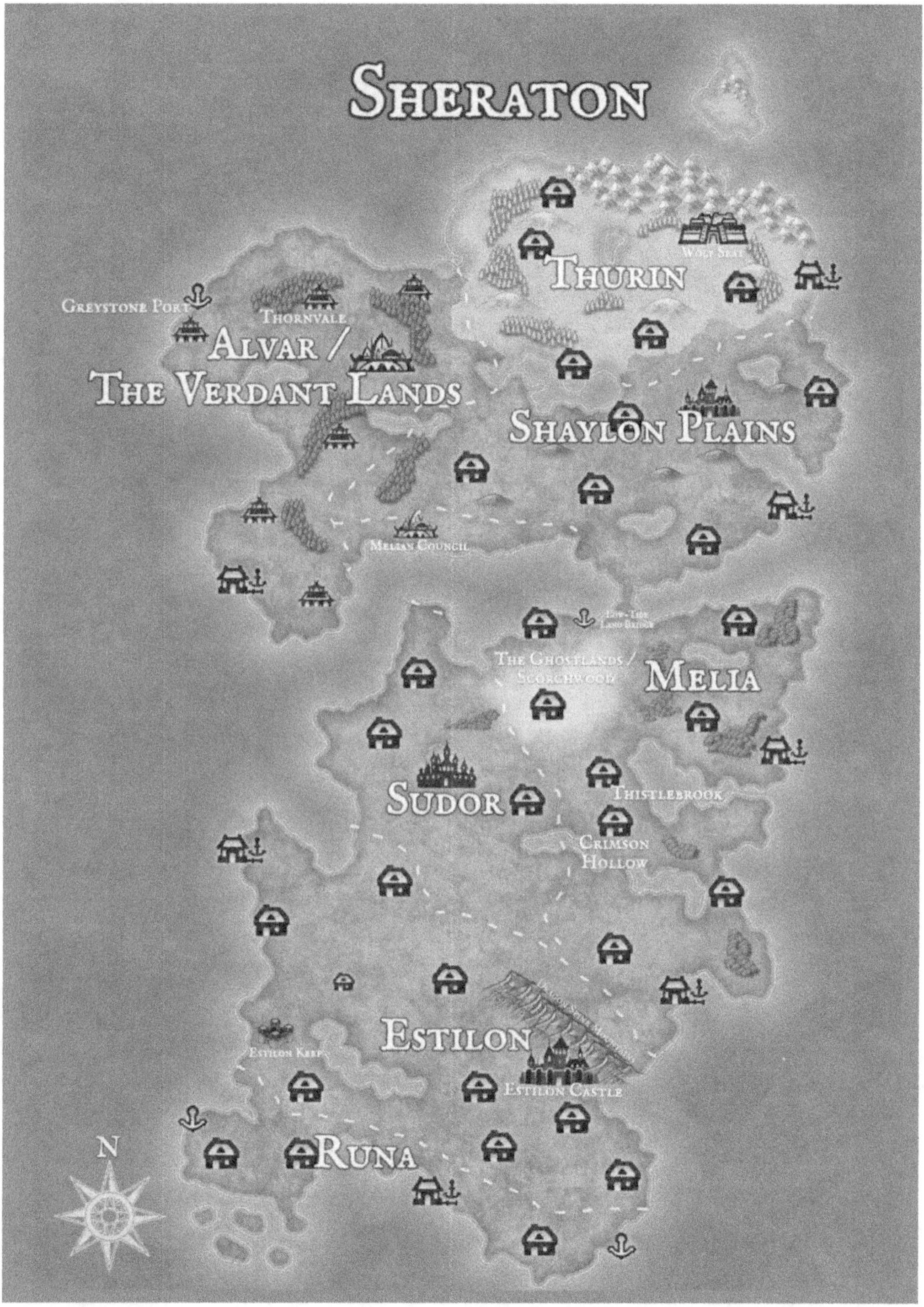

Sheraton
Thurin
Wolf Seat
Greystone Port
Thornvale
Alvar /
The Verdant Lands
Shaylon Plains
Melian Council
The Ghostlands /
Scorchwood
Low-Tide
Land Bridge
Melia
Sudor
Thistlebrook
Crimson
Hollow
Estilon
Estilon Keep
Estilon Castle
Runa
N

To Shanna, goddess of water, patron of sea and magic,
To Brena, goddess of fire, patron of artistry and creation,
To Erys, goddess of air, patron of storms and rain,
To Rhiann, goddess of earth, patron of land and fertility,
To Anya, goddess of order, patron of life and justice,
To Aishlin, goddess of chaos, patron of death and crossroads,
We swear our undying fealty.

CHAPTER 1

The black lining of Rowan's crimson cloak shrouded her face in shadow against the bright afternoon sun.

Crimson. The color of her choosing, though brown or green would have been more practical. The Watcher of Elderglen and Guardian of Rhiann stood out among leaves and trees as she protected Rhiann's woods.

Guardian. One of Rhiann's chosen. Only Rhiann hadn't chosen her. Rowan had collapsed to her knees, begging for the goddess's favor. In the wake of loss and grief, Rhiann had agreed, but Rowan often wondered if the goddess ever regretted her choice.

Rowan adjusted the hood, listening as two ravens chattered beside her. "You would like the forest back home," she whispered. "Dense trees, wolves to befriend."

Ravens found her no matter where she traveled, sensing the wolf dormant beneath her skin. Even in the back of the wagon, traveling home to southern Thurin, two ravens perched on the side, their glassy eyes fixed on her as they chattered and cawed.

The day passed quietly, her driver careful steering of the wagon as Rowan rested among his crates and barrels. Her feet dangled off the edge as the scenery passed in reverse, the world leaving as the cart wobbled down the uneven road.

A raven tapped its beak against the wagon, eyeing her.

"You hungry?" She couldn't understand them without shifting, her human ears unattuned to the language of wild things, but their behavior was obvious enough.

She fed them what remained of her rations, opting for the wildberries instead of jerky, and whispered what the deathseer had said.

A fortnight is generous.

If it hadn't been for the need of coin and medicine, she'd never have left. But none of that mattered if the deathseer was right. She'd held Rowan's cloak with respect and reverence, her white-blonde curls a stark compliment to the vibrant red, like snow among winter berries. And her voice had been soft when she unveiled the bitter truth.

A raven tapped its beak against the wagon again, sensing her thoughts and wishing to set her free. Or to receive more food.

"Thank you," she said, offering more berries. "We humans have a bad habit of building our own cages."

"Nearly there." Peeking over his shoulder, the lighter of his mismatched eyes regarded her and the ravens. "You're one of them elves from Alvar?"

"Thurin," she said, not bothering to correct him on being elven or how elves were actually earthborn. Wolfkind was enough. "Long may the wolves run free."

"Aye." Approval added a musical quality to his words. "Long may the wolves run free."

The ravens cawed before flying off, disappearing among the clouds and trees.

"The chosen of Rhiann can speak to ravens," Gran had said. "She blesses her guardians with the language of the earth, and ravens are close friends to wolves."

And the language of the earth had been an unexpected boon upon her blessing from the goddess of earth.

Thank you, she prayed, eyes taking in Rhiann's surrounding beauty. *Every blooming flower, every towering tree. Thank you for trusting me.*

Despite her desperation in grief. Despite her fear and her boiling anger. If her parents had had magic or Rhiann's blessing, would they have survived? Or had their deaths been a part of a design Rowan couldn't see?

Designed by fate or the product of chance, her parents were still dead, and Rowan's blood simmered at the injustice that followed. No trace or trail of who did it. No proof that they'd somehow paid for what they'd done. Rowan tried to console herself that they could have met their comeuppance in someone stronger and fiercer and angrier, but it didn't help. That someone hadn't been *her*.

A fortnight is generous.

Familiarity with loss didn't soften its blow. Loved ones left, whether through death or circumstance, while Rowan remained as though locked in place. Static. A still, quiet lake, while everyone else was a flowing river.

Every storm would pass, but the rain never failed to soak through Rowan's skin, chilling her to the bone.

Her eyes misted with eagerness to return home, to share in Gran's remaining days. To hold Gran's hand. To kiss Winter's crown. To run free with the wolves among the trees.

The coming days would be difficult, and Rowan could do nothing to change it.

"Speaking of Alvar, though," the driver said. "Heard there was a shipwreck west of there. *The Sea Phantom*."

"What caused it? A storm?"

"No one seems to know," he said. "But rumors say the crew marooned their captain on the coast before taking the ship. Word is the captain was devout to Shanna, and the goddess had her revenge on his behalf."

Rowan gave little to rumor and superstition. The goddesses didn't play revenge games among mortal grievances. The effort would outweigh the outcome.

"Captain of the *Phantom* was said to be ruthless," the driver went on. "Who knows if the crew did the right thing, only to suffer a worse fate."

"Devout to Shanna or Aishlin?" Rowan asked, amused. "If he was ruthless, perhaps he honored chaos more than the sea."

The driver chuckled. "Aye. Maybe." He paused before changing the subject. "I've never seen such a beautiful day this time of year. Autumn in Thurin is too much of a tease of winter, even this far south."

Perhaps he isn't used to silence. Rowan wasn't much for long conversations, especially with strangers. The quiet was a far more soothing companion.

"Rhiann is good to us," she said.

"Aye." She could hear his smile. "Long may the wolves run free."

She chewed slowly on what remained of her jerky as the sea of her thoughts grew deeper.

"Stopping here," the driver said, stopping at a crossroads several miles outside of Elderglen. "I'm taking the left."

Rowan hopped out, pulling the strap of her pack over her shoulder. "Thanks again."

He clicked his tongue, leading the horses left as Rowan took the path right.

A fortnight is generous.

Rowan uselessly smoothed the wisps of wild strands that had escaped her braid before adjusting her belt and walking faster, glad to have her body doing something other than sitting. Her two hatchets hung heavily at her sides, their weight familiar and reassuring while simultaneously burdensome.

The voice in her head repeated the words, an echoing cycle of anticipation, but her footsteps met the worn dirt path with rhythm, her blood flowing faster, her heart beating harder.

She shouldn't have left. Four days away from Gran when anything could have happened. What if Rowan came home to an empty house? What if Gran–

"No, my love," Gran had told her years ago, after her parents died. "The what ifs will kill you."

Rowan silently recited the words to herself every time the darkness whispered their what ifs, Gran's voice comforting even in memory.

"Don't go down that road," she said aloud to herself, the sound of her own voice helping to break the deluge in her head. In the distance, a raven called. "Keep your eyes ahead."

There wasn't space for the emotions that threatened to compromise her rational mind. Rowan knew grief already. She didn't welcome its imminent return.

So she walked with more determined steps, eager to return home.

CHAPTER 2

Rowan crossed through the wooden arch at the gate of Elderglen. Villagers moved through the heart of town, bartering and selling, some going to or coming from the tavern. In the distance, Rowan spotted Mayor Frederick and his wife, Suna, patronizing a vendor with fresh, stunning flowers. Rowan could smell them even as she turned down the path toward Sentinel Hill, their perfume the last lingering scent of summer.

Her home was a brick beacon on the hilltop, each red piece laid by her grandparents' hands, each wooden post of their fence cut and mounted, each garden plot tilled and nurtured. Rowan's life was in the walls and the earth, her eyes the windows, her breath the smoke from the burning heart of the fireplace. What her grandparents built, Rowan sustained with her life's blood.

Sentinel Hill. The Watchers of Elderglen. And she, Guardian of the Wood. Rhiann's chosen.

When Rowan was a girl, the forest edge was so far that she had to run at top speed, wind burning in her lungs, to feel the shadow cover of the trees and smell the damp, rich earth. But now, age had shortened the distance, and her grown legs quickly carried her to the thriving haven Rhiann had created.

In recent weeks, word spread grew of something monstrous lurking in the woods. Victims found bloodless, eyes wide as though they'd died from fear. Rumors in Elderglen spoke of a bloodborn threatening to devour every last one of them. But who stalks the woods to devour prey and leaves the animals unbothered? The only victims had been humans, left hollow in the unforgiving night. A dark appetite, indeed.

She pushed herself uphill, through the squeaky gate, and onto the even land of her farm. Chickens clucked from their coop, goats bleated from the grass, and a bark preceded the scratch inside the front door. Rowan smiled, relief easing the tension in her chest at the promise of Winter's joy on her return. If Winter rested on Gran's bed, situated between the front door and the hearth, would she leap into Rowan's arms? Or would she move to the floor first?

The bed was an antique and the only possession of value they owned, even though the value was entirely sentimental—handmade by her grandfather, as was most of the furniture in the house. The bed was a heavy ordeal to move, but the warmth of the hearth reached Gran better, especially with Thurin's winter already teased in the north.

Even after bracing herself, Rowan opened the door and nearly fell back from the pounce of her gray-white companion. Winter had been the runt of her litter, her mother worried over the pup's survival. The life of a wolf already bore difficulty, so when Rowan offered her home, Winter's mother was relieved. The natural world would not be a threat to her daughter with the Guardian caring for her. And in return, Rowan gained a friend whose love filled her.

"Oh, thank the gods." Gran smiled. "I was beginning to think you'd fallen for the Plains and deserted the village completely."

Rowan stood, brushing off her clothes as her eyes trained on the woman standing at Gran's bedside. Her hair was long, the shine from the sunlight glistening off the inky black strands that complimented her warm-hued tawny skin. And her eyes, as rich as wine, found Rowan's with a smile. She was tall, her slender body masking a lithe strength discernible in the way she carried herself. She was no stranger to a fight, and her grace could prove deadly.

"This is Mirelyn," Gran introduced. "She's one of the guild, just arrived from Alvar."

Patchouli, lavender, and citrus. Rowan took a deep breath, the fragrance like Mirelyn's fingerprint. She was lovely, with experience in her stature and gaze the only indication of age. "It's nice to meet you."

They shook hands, Mirelyn briefly glimpsing Rowan's scar. The soft pink line bore a significant contrast to Rowan's medium sienna skin, reaching from the inner corner of her left eyebrow, down the bridge of her nose, to her right cheek. Everyone looked at it, and Rowan was used to the normal path their eyes traveled when seeing. But Mirelyn's eyes didn't linger, her smile maintaining its warmth as they shook hands.

"Your grandmother was just telling me about your trip to Shaylon Plains," Mirelyn said, her voice soothing and maternal. "I haven't been that far south in a very long time."

"It was beautiful," Rowan said, removing her belt and setting it with the hatchets on the dining table. The absence of their weight was freeing. "I didn't venture far past the border, though."

Rowan didn't know what to expect from the conversation, her reserve of small talk nearly spent. She removed her cloak and hung it by the door, the red fabric complimenting the natural wood walls.

"I will leave you both to your reunion." Mirelyn squeezed Gran's hand, the pair sharing a look before their guest departed.

At Mirelyn's exit, Winter jumped onto the bed and settled by Gran's legs.

"I'd never abandon you for somewhere else, Gran." Rowan hugged her carefully, grateful for the strength in the arms that held her. "I'd happily desert Elderglen, but never you."

"All was quiet and well, my love," Gran said. "Winter missed you terribly."

"There's my girl." Rowan rubbed Winter's cheeks below her ears. "You've done well in your watch."

"Watch!" Gran snorted a laugh, her brown eyes gleaming as she smiled. "She slept more than I did, I'll have you know."

"Everything sold well," Rowan said, setting her pack on the bed by Gran's feet and rummaging through clothes and bundles of food. She found the sachets of medicinal herbs and showed them. "These should help you feel better."

"You are good to me, but what of yourself?" Gran regarded her knowingly. "You deserve care too, my love."

"I receive care." Though she focused her priorities outside of herself, for better or worse. "And I buy medicine for my favorite grandmother."

Gran touched each sachet, stopping at one. "What's this?" She brought the linen pouch to her nose, breathing in deeply. "Berries and rose?" She sniffed again. "Skydrop?"

The blend from the deathseer. A token of her condolence. "A gift from a friend."

Gram raised a thin eyebrow, nearly invisible but for the familiar pull of skin and muscle to prove it was still there.

Rowan opened a cloth bundle of fresh wildberries and laid and held them out, careful not to get the juice-stained fabric on the bed. "To hold you until supper. I'll fetch a bowl."

"Peter has seen to my appetite," Gran said. "Wil has seen to that damned fence, and Jean's seen to my company. All are following your instructions to the letter."

"They offered because they love you, and I happily accepted."

"Bah. You instructed, and they consented."

Rowan poured the berries into a bowl for Gran and prepared food for Winter, using her half-eaten oat bread from her travels with bits of carrot and peas. "Which tea would you like first?"

Gran chose the berry blend. Rowan set the water on the fire and inspected their food stores for supper. "I'll be at Wil and Jean's in a bit. Do you want anything?"

"Cinnamon whiskey."

Rowan burst out laughing. Winter wagged her tail. "Gran."

"You asked, and that's my answer. Peter and I share a common palette for well-made liquor."

"I'm sure you do."

Rowan unpacked other supplies—leftover rations and medicines— and pulled her clothes from her pack for washing.

"Rowan." Gran's serious tone made Rowan pause, turning from her open pack. "There's something with the guild that we need to discuss."

The guild. Feather and Claw. Gran's network of allies gathering information to protect magic folk from the Wandering Order. Missions filled with danger and stealth, protecting potential victims and rescuing all they could from those filled with hate.

Missions like the one that led Rowan's parents to their deaths.

Rowan worked to mask her loathing, her disgust for anything related to Feather and Claw. Her grandmother, as the Cornerstone, led the guild. And Rowan was a part of it by inheritance. A burden she didn't ask for.

"Have you heard of the cult experimenting on those with magic?" Gran asked. "With mist arcana?"

She bore no sympathy for those partial to the drug and the effects it gave. Those with magic experienced an incredible increase in magical power and output, and those without magic rode euphoria and wielded limited arcane ability. But the decline was steep, its cost great, its addiction heavy. Rowan's sense of disgust deepened.

"What about it?" Rowan asked, though she didn't want to know. Both Moonblade and the Wandering Order were up in arms over arcana crystal mines and the effects of mist arcana. And Feather and Claw tracked each one, marking them on maps to track and avoid Wandering Order activity as much as possible. But Rowan would rather watch every last crystal burn away to nothing.

Gran hesitated, the lines between her brows deep.

"This is serious." Rowan turned from her work to give Gran her full attention.

A knock came to the door. Three timid taps. If it was someone more familiar, their knock would be louder and faster. Rowan shared a look with Gran before answering. Suna, the mayor's wife, stood with pink and red peonies in her hands. Pale and thin, Suna appeared more frail than Rowan had ever seen her.

"Welcome back, Guardian," Suna said with a soft smile. She held up the peonies. "I brought these for your home. All was quiet in your absence."

"Thank you." Rowan accepted her gift. "Please, come in."

Their home was modest and cluttered, with Rowan blind to the mess until a guest arrived. There, with Suna in their home, Rowan noticed every piece out of place. Dishes, some clean, on the dining table and on the cabinet shelf. Clothes in from the line before Rowan left, still hanging on the backs of chairs. But Suna beamed at Gran as she crossed the threshold.

"She's returned home safe and sound," Suna said. "You look well, Cynthia."

"Well as can be expected." Gran eyed the flowers. "They are lovely, Suna. Thank you."

"I thought so, too. I like peonies best, I think."

Listening to them, Rowan set the flowers on the dining table, their vibrant reds and pinks brightening the room.

Peonies. An interesting name for a flower. Such delicate things in Rowan's strong hands.

The names of things were important, though wild things deserved to thrive. Names could be binding, limiting them to an identity that they may not care for.

Rowan. A tree, tall and impressive. She liked her name and all it represented. Protective, strong, unyielding.

Rowan.

Watcher.

Guardian.

She prayed she was enough.

"How is your son?" Gran asked, eyes focused on Suna.

The mayor's wife smiled with her lips pressed together, the expression full of strain. She was maintaining a facade Rowan saw through, though she understood why Suna tried. Emotions were cracks that allowed things in, when the body had to be impenetrable.

"We ask the goddesses for every mercy," Suna said, her voice wavering. "Derin is holding on, and we are grateful."

"Have the doctors learned anything more?" Rowan asked. The day he collapsed brought Elderglen to a standstill. Since then, he awoke only twice more before resigning to sleep. The outlook was grim, the clock ticking on as Derin's parents awaited the inevitable.

When Suna shook her head, Rowan's heart sank.

"There are no marks, no signs of illness. There are times when he is weak and trembling and others when he is in a deep sleep."

"Has the mayor sent for a healer?" Rowan asked. Mirelyn coming from Alvar, perhaps—

"He hasn't mentioned it to me, if he has," Suna said, "though I fear it may be too late for their aid."

"Rhiann and Anya are always listening," Gran said. "It's never too late."

The slight twitch of Suna's mouth was barely perceptible. Had Rowan's eyes not been trained on her, reading the anguish she was trying to hide, she would have missed bitterness, her well-contained rage. Two things Rowan understood.

Rowan bore the distinct impression that Suna wished to speak with Gran privately, though she was far too polite to say anything. The burden Suna carried was significant.

"I'm going to see Wil and the others before patrolling the forest," Rowan said.

"The woods missed you," Suna said with a kind smile, using the change in subject to her advantage. The weight around her eyes and mouth lightened, her practiced composure returning. "We could hear the cries of the wolves and ravens."

"Their Guardian has returned." Pride glimmered in Gran's eyes. "Go run, my love. I'll see you at dinner."

Rowan gathered her hatchets and clicked her tongue against her teeth, and Winter joined her, leaping from the bed to the front door threshold without issue. Suna cried out with a laugh, and Rowan offered a quick smile over her shoulder before taking her cloak and closing the door behind her.

"Leaving Gran feels wrong," she whispered to Winter, clasping her cloak around her shoulders. "But so does staying."

Winter answered by rubbing her cheek against Rowan's leg before trotting ahead.

"Dad!" A woman, her toddler clinging to her leg, walked the main thoroughfare that bisected the village. "Where are you? Dad!"

"Where has he gone this time?" someone asked, looking toward the field, squinting beneath the sunlight.

Rowan veered from the path toward Jean's home, heading toward them. At the sight of her, the woman looked relieved and hurried, picking up her child to walk faster.

"Watcher, please." She shook her head, on the verge of tears. "My father, he's gone missing. I haven't seen him since dawn."

"Missing?" Rowan looked from the woman to the field behind them. The expanse of tall grass led to the forest Rowan patrolled, keeping Elderglen safe from raiders and thieves. "What's happened?"

"He's loose in the head," the other villager said, their tone unkind. "Wanders off."

"Shut your mouth, or I'll make *your* head loose." The woman's daughter pouted at the sharpness of her tone.

A senile villager missing, and the wild wood was before them. Rowan's stomach tightened, her duty before her. "We'll look for him."

The woman choked a sob as she reached into the pocket of her skirt, revealing a sock. "You were my next stop, Watcher. Thank you."

Rowan hid her grimace, nodding. "I make no promise, but we will look." She took the garment and touched Winter's crown. "We'll return soon."

Both hurried for the trees, Rowan ignoring the sinking feeling in her core.

CHAPTER 3

At the tree line, Rowan crouched, dropping the sock onto the grass before igniting the magic to change her shape. Her muscles and bones realigned, her skin and clothes morphing to become crimson-hued fur. The auburn tones blended well with the brown earth and trunks of trees.

In the early days, shifting had been uncomfortable, though there was never pain. Now, with the seasons beneath her paws, shifting came as naturally as breathing. She and Winter sniffed at the sock, picking up traces of his scent.

"Old," Winter said. "But cared for."

Rowan sneezed, the sock reasonably clean despite having the man's scent on it. His daughter took care of him, loved him, worried for him. "Let's get him home."

The Guardian of the Forest, the Watcher of Elderglen, stepped into the trees with her companion, noses attuned and eyes searching.

"Friends," Rowan called, hoping for either wolf or raven to answer. "We seek one of our own, lost. Elderly."

"Guardian," the ravens called. "The guardian returns."

"Welcome home."

"She returns."

After their chorus of welcoming, the ravens guided them.

"Further north," they said. "He is slow. Confused."

"His mind falters."

Rowan and Winter hurried, the forest lending aid by carrying his scent to them, giving them a trial to follow.

"Mary Beth?" A man's voice, trembling with age and fear. "Oh, gods. Mary Beth?"

She and Winter moved faster before she shifted, her human form rising above the brush, moving to make enough noise so as not to frighten him. "Sir?"

He turned, his pupils pinpricks, eyes wide as his mouth formed words that didn't come.

"Your daughter is Mary Beth?"

He nodded, near to tears, hands trembling as they reached for his gray, wiry hair. He tugged at the strands, closing his eyes.

"Come with me." Rowan hurried to his side, taking his hands from his hair, holding his arms to steady him. "Let's get you home."

Winter's ears perked up as she looked beyond Rowan. Turning, Rowan's green eyes met the bright amber of the matriarch of the pack who called the forest their home.

Rowan eased him toward Winter. "Wait here. I need to speak with them."

"Watcher." The man gripped her hand. "Don't go, Watcher."

"I'm not going anywhere." She offered a small, reassuring smile as she peeled his grip from her hand. "I'll be right here, and so will Winter."

At the mention of her name, his eyes found the wolf's, and his expression softened.

"Winter." He smiled. "What a lovely name."

Ensuring he was steady on his feet, Rowan shifted, bowing to the matriarch and the two wolves at her flank.

"Guardian," she said, nodding her head in deference. "You've returned."

"How did you fare?"

"All is well." The timbre of her voice soothed Rowan's mind. "Some have found traces of the poison you watch for."

"Found traces? Where?"

"Northeast," she said. "Close to the road."

Along the road between Elderglen and the unsettled terrain further north, where Moonblade was known to linger. They had a hideout somewhere, its location unknown. Rowan and their leader had an understanding: Keep mist arcana away from Elderglen, and Rowan would not intervene with Moonblade's business. But they toed the line, testing the limits of her patience.

She was loath to reconvene with Valera, to connect with Moonblade more than absolutely necessary. But a reunion was close, with Rowan's temper a variable she would have to control.

"It's as though I'm not really here," Rowan said, frustration heavy in her voice. "They know how I feel. The lengths I will go."

"They also sense the goodness of your heart," she said. "And act as though goodness is a weakness to exploit. Humans have a tendency to believe they are stronger than they truly are. They are not invincible, but it is not until their blood is shed that they realize their frailty."

"Why must it come to that?" The very idea pulled her between two extremes, from furious rage to blinding exhaustion. "Why must my claws be my strength when my words aren't enough?"

"Your strength is not reliant on words or claws," she said. "And what others perceive of you is not the truth."

Aren't they? Aren't the impressions others have based on something true?

But Rowan didn't push, the weight of the question too heavy to ask.

"I am the matriarch to lead my pack," she said, "but I am not only a leader. I am a mother. I am a mate. I am a she-wolf. And I must run and thrive for my heart to sing with the trees and rivers. If I am unwell, my pack is unwell."

Rowan's heart tightened. "I, too, must run, but it's hard, Matriarch."

Wind swept through the boughs overhead, the trees whispering their consolation, the breeze offering comfort.

"The man there," the matriarch said. "His time is close."

Rowan didn't turn, didn't meet the old man's eyes, knowing what she would see. "His daughter is frantic."

"Her grief will come soon." After a pause, her eyes soft, she added, "So will yours."

The matriarch approached, nuzzling Rowan's cheek.

"She is strong," the matriarch said, "and so are you."

But strength came with a cost Rowan was tired of paying.

"Thank you for guarding him," Rowan said, glancing at the man with Winter.

"Thank you for guarding us."

The matriarch returned to her wolves, all of them giving her one final look before disappearing into the trees. Rowan shifted, patting Winter's head and taking the Elder's arm.

"Time to go," she said. "Are you able to walk?"

"Yes, Watcher." He took her arm gently, one hand patting her forearm. "Thank you."

They took their time, careful of the terrain. When they broke through the tree line, Rowan squinted in the bright sunlight, trying to focus on the part of the village road where Mary Beth, his daughter, likely waited. But a young man approached, his age near to Rowan's, his eyes keen and body sure as he moved toward the woods. His clothing was practical, the dark blue of his shirt faded, the deep brown fabric of his trousers worn.

When their eyes locked, her forest green met his deep sea blue, with the infinite ocean behind them. His hair, cut close at the sides, teased blond flecks that reflected the sun while the glimmers of gold rested against dark walnut brown. His beard was short, a shadow along his cheeks and jaw that captured Rowan's curiosity. What would it look like longer, fuller, smoother?

He was handsome, something in his presence calm and grounding. But the quiver at his back and bow at his shoulder raised her alarm.

"Please," she said, "don't hunt in the woods."

His brow furrowed, studying her and the man on her arm.

"There are wolves," she said. "Don't travel too deeply in."

"She is their Guardian," the old man said, patting her arm. "Our Watcher."

"I mean no harm." His voice, a low baritone, summoned a sensation through her eardrum, down her neck. "I'm looking for my brother. He's missing."

"Your brother?" She glanced behind, the trees a blur in her quick gaze. "And you think he's here?"

"It's been nearly a month," he said. "He was captured by the Wandering Order. Have you heard anything?"

"I haven't." The lines in his furrowed brow settled in the focus around his eyes. "He has magic?"

"Yes. Firecraft."

Firecraft? Who calls magic a craft?

"I can help you search." She extended a hand. "I'm Rowan, Watcher of Sentinel Hill and Elderglen."

"And Guardian of Elderwood," the old man added.

The stranger shook her hand, his palm and fingers calloused from work. "Fen. I'm grateful for any help you can give."

"I'll ask around," she said, thinking more of the wolves than of the villagers. "Are you staying in Elderglen? There should be room at the tavern."

"I am, and I will." His gaze lingered as though seeing her, understanding her. "I'll be careful in the woods. This place and those within it have my respect. Now you have *my* word."

He stepped past them and entered the forest, his posture sure and demeanor calm. A good hunter, one who could move through unfamiliar terrain with such a task as his.

A missing brother with fire magic. Fire*craft.* Taken by the Wandering Order.

"Dad!"

Mary Beth hurried down the path, but Rowan glanced behind.

CHAPTER 4

After seeing Mary Beth and her father safely reunited, Rowan attended a reunion of her own.

Further down Sentinel Hill were two homes belonging to the family she chose, relatives not of blood but of spirit. Wil and Rowan had grown up together, thick as thieves even well into young adulthood as they neared their twentieth year together. When Wil's mother, Jean, gifted him the cottage next door, Wil and his husband, Peter remained close as they built their new life.

Comfort swelled in Rowan's chest as smoke billowed from Wil and Peter's chimney, and after three knocks, the door flew open and arms surrounded her.

"Took you long enough." Wil's embrace tightened around her as Winter wove between their legs. "I'm going with you next time."

"It was four days." But Rowan rested her head against his shoulder, gratitude loosening the parts of her wound tight.

"He's talked about nothing else since you left." Jean rested her hands on both their shoulders, the crow's feet deep beside her brown eyes. "Did you find what you were looking for?"

Rowan regarded her with surprise. "You knew?"

"Specifically, no," Jean admitted, "but you had a gleam in your eyes."

"She said the same thing to me the day I met Peter." Wil smiled over his shoulder at his husband, who left the boiling pot of soup on the fire to greet her. "She knew before I did."

Rowan sometimes suspected that Jean's earth magic had tapped into light or chaos. How else could she read and understand them all so perfectly if she didn't glean their thoughts?

"A mother knows." Jean studied Rowan, her gaze discerning. "Well?"

Rowan stepped inside, Winter padding over to Peter. He kissed at her and gave her a piece of raw carrot. She crunched happily.

"I heard there was a deathseer not far from where I was selling," Rowan said.

Peter draped a heavy arm across her shoulders and kissed her head. "A deathseer?

"I was sick all those months ago. Gran took a turn after that."

"Blaming yourself is a burden you don't deserve," Jean said.

"What else could I think?" Rowan's eyes itched, but her emotions were far from surfacing. "It happened all so fast."

Winter leaned against her legs, looking up at her with her gorgeous gray eyes. Rowan rubbed her head behind her ears.

"It happened without you, my love," Jean said softly. "The cause is simply the way life goes on."

Rowan said nothing, grateful for the comfort, masking the guilt that churned within. "I need to patrol the woods. See what the wolves have to say."

"You've only just returned," Wil said. "Can't patrol wait so you can rest?"

"An old man wandered into the woods."

"Mary Beth's father?" Jean asked. "Bless him, his mind isn't as reliable as it once was."

"And you had to find him," Wil said, "not five minutes after your return."

"Closer to ten minutes," she quipped, though the joke didn't land.

"You are not the titles you bear," Jean said, her hand resting on

Rowan's arm, her thumb smoothing a line up and down, parallel to her wrist. "And you're not only worthy of love because you bear them. You can rest."

"Tell that to Braithen and Halie."

Wil scoffed. "The day I show politeness to them is the day Chaos comes to earth."

Then he hugged her, as he'd always done since their shared childhood. Jean joined, their shared breath triggering Rowan's claustrophobia. But it was when Peters' arms surrounded her that she nearly stepped back, recoiling from their touch. They offered comfort and love and family, but anxiety trembled within the deep chambers of Rowan's heart.

Not many were granted such proximity and contact. But Rowan understood how they each loved her. They, in return, understood how she received it.

"Don't suffer in silence," Wil said low in her ear before parting, his body prompting the others to loosen their arms.

"But the world is already too loud."

"Then don't listen." He tugged her braid. "Don't listen to the shadows, Ro. They have nothing of value to say."

"Make your mind a peaceful place to live," Peter said. "You will dwell there for the rest of your life."

Rowan continued to breathe, imagining what her mind would be like if light shone where shadows dwelled, what her heart would feel like if it wasn't overwhelmed.

Their words were a barrage of heartfelt kindness that piled in Rowan's heart, making it difficult to beat. She didn't know how to rearrange them, to place them in balance to set everything right, so they remained with all of their good intentions like a ball of iron weighing her down.

Rowan offered what she could of a smile, the result bittersweet sadness. "Thank you."

Winter vocalized a grumble, sitting with a humph until Wil scratched her head.

"We love you, Ro," Peter said. "And we're here."

"Not going anywhere," Wil added.

Jean kissed her cheek. "You're stuck with us, love."

Such reassurance surged a hope Rowan didn't have the words to express. She replied by squeezing their hands and slipping out the door, the four walls too close, the room too full.

The warm sun was a contrast to the cool autumn breeze blowing the frigid air from the mountains. Southern Thurin was spared her early winters, but not for long. Snow flurries would swirl in the coming weeks.

Cold. Lifeless.

Not yet.

Without ceremony, Rowan shifted, the magic that made her forming her body and garments without pain or stress. Rhiann's gift, one that came with responsibility.

Guardian of the Forest. Protector of life and defender of the wood.

But Rowan wanted nothing more than to *run*.

THE WIND COMBED through her fur as her paws thundered across the grassy plain before crossing the threshold of Elderwood.

"At last."

"Yes," Winter agreed. "At last."

Trees whispered greetings as their boughs waved overhead. The birds chirped, and insects buzzed. The ravens cawed a chorus of welcome that echoed off the forest walls.

Rowan ran until the world was no longer human, where the air was wild and the ground untamed. Four days was far too long.

They slowed, studying their surroundings. Crisp leaves. Squirrels. Wolves. And—

Rowan stilled, catching a foreign scent. Human. Recent. Leather, salt, and cinnamon. She breathed deeper, the notes delicious on her tongue.

"Who was in this wood?"

"A man," came an answer, the matriarch far from them. "Your scent mingled with his. Traces. Faint. He was cautious but did not hunt."

The man missing his brother.

The matriarch ran, two of her own at her side. Her mate likely hunted with the others. "Greetings, Guardian."

"Greetings, Matriarch." Rowan bowed her head. Winter moved beside her and did the same. "Was the human dangerous?"

"All humans are dangerous." Her amber eyes bore the weight of years, her power and authority strong. "But he passed through without issue."

"I'm relieved he listened. Were your patrols calm?"

"We tracked two groups of humans traveling east," she said. "Both smelled like magic."

"Magic." Wolves and other creatures couldn't smell magic, but their noses could pick up the traces left by mist arcana, bearing notes of sulfur and citrus. "And they were traveling east?"

"Two separate groups," she said. "One with two humans in a wagon, their load full. The other, more than a dozen humans, traveling on foot."

The trade in mist arcana had grown like weeds in an untended field, tangling in on themselves until nothing else could grow. And the poison reached more desperate or eager hands as the days passed.

Those with magic, hungry for more power.

Those without, desperate for a touch of something divine.

But this wasn't power. It wasn't divinity. Mist arcana burned the candle at both ends, spilling wax and cutting its lifespan, stealing years from your future as the present consumed it all.

And there were those who capitalized on it. Those like Moonblade. The first group the matriarch described sounded like a cargo shipment, two men guarding a load that would bring considerable gold. But the second group...

"The group with more humans," Rowan said. "What can you tell me about them?"

"The first tried to mask their scents with herbs," the matriarch said. "Typical of those dressed in black, who thrive in shadows. But the others had hungry eyes. Eager. Scents unmasked."

That didn't mean they weren't tied to Moonblade. But the distinction from the matriarch was curious, indeed.

"We will watch," the matriarch said. "And we will listen."

Rowan bowed her head, sensing dismissal. "Thank you."

"Thank you, Guardian." The matriarch's eyes alighted to Winter. "Her life thrives because of the strength of your heart."

"My life thrives because of her."

Winter nuzzled Rowan's neck.

"I am curious," the matriarch said. "Why is she named?"

Rowan understood the question. Wild things didn't bear the binds of a name.

"I named myself, wolf mother," Winter answered. "The humans I love say my fur reminds them of the snows and skies of winter. I am proud of my name."

The matriarch accepted with a wag of her tail, honoring her. "I am glad to hear it." She turned, her entourage following as they left for their den.

"Humans with that poison," Winter said, using Rowan's own term for mist arcana. "What do we do?"

"Watch and listen, as the matriarch said." But discomfort settled in Rowan's core. Waiting settled poorly inside her, leaving her anxious. "But I don't like how close this is to Elderglen."

Either Moonblade got brazen, or they had a reason to travel so close to their village. Rowan's disdain for mist arcana wasn't a secret, and her agreement with Valera made that clear.

"As long as our paths don't cross," Rowan had said, "your cargo remains unscathed."

A compromise she'd loathed, but one easy to maintain.

If they'd broken their agreement, Rowan would not hesitate, even if the fault rested on the shoulders of a villager bringing that poison into Elderglen.

Her stomach tightened. Could that be the reason?

Rowan would fight for her home to the very last, but she didn't want it to come to that.

I only want peace.

She and Winter lingered in the woods, rolling on dried leaves on the forest floor, reveling in its cool touch and spiced scent. *Rest.* That is what Jean and the others asked of her. She'd found a moment's peace to do just that.

Until cries pealed through the air, horror rich with agony.

Rowan and Winter ran without another thought, paws pushing into the earth to propel them at top speed. The voices continued, pleading with the goddesses, asking that this be a dream.

What nightmare had they stepped into?

It was further north from Elderglen, just inside the line of brush and trees. The man's body was prostrate as an old woman pulled at his arm, turning him over. Her splotched face glistened with streaks of tears, her agony echoing up to the late afternoon sky.

Others gathered with her, helping her to turn him over. Among them were Braithen and Halie, siblings who caused more trouble for Sentinel Hill than Moonblade and Wandering Order combined. Braithen, the village's tanner, held more self-importance than any other human Rowan had ever met, and that included their mayor, who stood at the fringes of the crowd.

Rowan shifted to her human form, momentum still pushing her into a jog until she reached them. "What's happened?"

"Gods, *finally*." Halie glared at her. "The Watcher finally decides to join her village."

"You didn't answer my question." Rowan met Halie's eyes. The other woman blinked before looking away.

"He didn't come home," the kneeling woman said, cradling his head in her lap.

There was no mark on his body that Rowan could see, but his mouth and eyes were open, agape in fear, his pupils pinpricks. His pale skin was beyond the pallor of death. It was as though there was nothing left. Gods, how old was he? Early 20s? Too young to have his light extinguished.

"A bloodborn?" Braithen asked, his side-look at Rowan serpentine. "Or something else?"

Others from the village joined, their confusion matching Rowan's. Their questions yielded answers as others filled in the gaps.

"Gods above." Mayor Frederick stared, brow furrowed. "What could have done this?"

Braithen crossed his arms. "The location suggests something from the forest."

"The blood's completely gone out," one villager said. "Gracious day."

"You said he didn't return from work," Rowan said, ignoring Braithen and speaking to the woman she presumed was his mother. "What time was he supposed to be home?"

"He—" She struggled to speak. "He said he met someone."

"Does anyone know who?"

"Isn't it obvious, Watcher?" Braithen sneered down his middle-aged nose at her. "He met a monster."

"Have some respect," another villager chastised.

"No one told you?" Mayor Frederick asked Rowan. "Anything strange has to be reported to the Hill."

The mother dissolved in grief.

"The wolves only reported peace," Rowan said to Mayor Frederick. "No sign of—"

"The wolves?" Halie almost smirked. "You're sure they didn't do this?"

"Don't be an idiot," Rowan snapped. "I know that's a challenge for you."

Several voices gasped. Mayor Frederick pinched the bridge of his nose.

Halie blustered, her string of angry defenses coming too slowly when a new voice spoke up. "Is there any drop of blood left?"

The stranger from the trees, the one searching for his brother. He approached the scene with scrutiny, one hand comfortably holding the strap of his pack as the other hung limp at his side. "Someone said the body is bloodless. Is that true?"

"It certainly looks that way," Braithen said, suspicion gleaming as he looked the man over.

"Last I checked," he said, "wolves didn't drain the dead."

"What, then?" Halie challenged. "A bloodborn, like the rumors say?"

"Has anyone investigated for clues?" He looked at each of them as though they lacked common sense and intelligence. A thrill hummed through Rowan's heart, vindication boosting her confidence. "Or are we going to wave burning sage to quell evil spirits like they do in the Ghostlands? *Wandering spirits, wander away.*"

Others agreed as Braithen and Halie seethed, the siblings moving closer to form a unified front. In any other circumstance, Rowan would marvel at their similarity in appearance—the way their brows furrowed over their scathing brown eyes, the unflattering twists of their mouths. But frustration dissolved any chance at amusement, the simmer within dangerously close to a boil anytime those two showed up. They had the maligned notion that, because they were decades older than Rowan, their authority was the natural order of things. But Rowan owed no one her respect.

"What's your name, friend?" Braithen asked, his tone devoid of amiable intent. "How long have you been in Elderglen?"

"Fen," he said, his name triggering Rowan's memory of their meeting. "I've just arrived."

"Then you are a stranger to this village, stepping in on village business."

"If someone's found dead," Rowan said, "I think that makes it his business. He has the right to know."

"I appreciate that, Guardian," Fen said.

If she hadn't watched him speak, she'd have missed the slight wink he offered her, the upward tug of his mouth revealing the shadow of a laugh line through his stubble.

"We will patrol the woods," Braithen said, his voice stern to rally the others. "This evil will be felled."

"Do not enter those woods with such intent," Rowan said, alarm lifting her hackles.

Braithen turned, his body squared and defensive. "The intent to protect what's ours?"

"The intent to do harm to what is innocent." She stood taller, confrontation prickling beneath her skin. The muscles in her arms and shoulders tightened. "If you harm even a single wolf, I will bring a reckoning."

"And she'll have help," Fen said. "They're not responsible for this, and you know it. Evil did this."

"I will protect what's mine," Braithen said, his voice raised.

Rowan didn't back down as light flashed in her forest-colored eyes. "I am the Guardian of the Wood, god-touched by Rhiann herself. Do you doubt it?" Her unblinking gaze moved from Braithen to the others. "Do any of you?" She waited through their silence. "Reckless acts make a difficult job even harder. Trust Rhiann. And trust me. Sentinel Hill is my home, and I know the responsibility it bears."

"Your grandfather would have had this nightmare quelled," Braithen said.

But Braithen cried out as Rowan closed the distance between them. "Did you know my grandfather? Do you know if he faced a darkness such as this?" At Braithen's quiet trembling, she said, "Do not compare that which is not the same. Your ignorance will be your undoing."

She turned, intending to leave him quivering and sputtering, words failing him again.

"Sentinel Hill is a privilege, Rowan," Halie said. "If your shoulders cannot bear the mantle—"

"Stop trying to take my home from me," she interrupted, her voice reaching every gathered ear. "Elderglen did not gift us Sentinel Hill. My grandparents offered it to you freely." She met the siblings' angry eyes. "You have no right to take what is not yours."

She left without another word, Fen and Winter falling in step behind.

CHAPTER 5

"Guardian."

She turned at Fen's beckoning, frustration mounting. She longed for solitude and quiet, for the expanse of the earth without watchful human eyes and grating human voices. But the stranger named Fen remained. Was it out of a sense of obligation? Or was he curious about how she would find his brother?

"Rowan," she said. "My name is Rowan."

"Rowan." The tingle returned, reaching deep in her ears, making her throat catch. The cadence and timbre of his voice changed when he said her name. "Like the tree. Strong. And lovely."

Her face warmed, the sensation strongest around her scar. And she was forest-laden, with leaves in her hair and dirt under her fingernails. *Lovely* wasn't a word she heard connected with her, though she wasn't heartsick over the lack of affirmation from others. Still, to hear it, to *feel it*, was altogether foreign.

What was he doing here?

"I saw you in the forest before," he said. "Wolfkind."

She waited, alarm rising up her spine. A stranger, learning she was god-touched. What would this mean for her? For Gran? For Elderglen?

Her ability wasn't a secret, but knowledge was power, and the wrong people could do much with it.

"Your warnings about the wolves make sense now, Guardian."

"Rowan," she corrected, though she didn't hate the way he said it. It wasn't attached to responsibility. It held reverence, like when the wolves spoke with her.

"I don't mean to make you uncomfortable," he said. "I only wanted to say you handled him well."

Him. *Braithen.* "He has a maligned belief that his grandfather should have had Sentinel Hill." Rowan chuckled, recounting the story from Gran, told with sarcasm and vitriol. "My grandmother spurned his advances, and he held bitterness up until his death."

"And passed it on to his grandson."

She walked slowly toward home. Gran was there alone. "Thank you for what you said."

"Logic can evaporate in the face of fear," he said. "But he seems determined to make your life hell."

Even a stranger could see it. "He and his sister both."

"Gods, they're *related*? How do you cope?"

She laughed despite herself, the sound low and quiet. She could feel his stare, the atmosphere pleasant between them. Almost comfortable.

"Be safe, Rowan."

"You too, Fen."

When they parted, Rowan watched the path pass beneath her feet as she crossed to Sentinel Hill and began her ascent.

"It feels like everything's different, Winter." Rowan rested her hands on the handles of her hatchets. She rarely drew her sidearms. Threats to the forest were mostly handled as a wolf, and threats to Elderglen were more political than violent. But her palms needed to feel their shape, to know their weight. They were a reassurance. "What are we in for?"

Winter looked up at her briefly before jogging ahead.

"Alright." Rowan smiled after her. "Keep moving forward."

Gran awoke as Rowan entered, blinking and smiling as she inhaled.

"Sorry," Rowan said. "I didn't mean to wake you."

"I was only dozing." Gran's hands lifted as Winter jumped onto the bed, her dirty paws leaving marks on the blanket. "There's my girl."

"The forest is calm," Rowan said, going to the bucket of water for a sip. "All is well."

Gran breathed in deeply, closing her eyes. "You smell of grass and sunshine. I can almost picture those trees now. Bright, brilliant green, just like your eyes, shielding us from the blinding sunlight and the crisp blue sky."

Gran must have rested well if she was waxing poetic. "I've never heard a sky described as *crisp*."

"But it fits, doesn't it? *Crisp*." Gran giggled. "Almost like a fresh, juicy apple. Perfect to sink your teeth into."

A quiet moment passed between them as Rowan removed her cloak and used the wash basin to cleanse her hands.

"Someone else died," she said.

"What?"

Rowan repeated herself and added, "They were killed."

"By the monster?"

Rowan could only nod, with no other term existing for what truly preyed upon them. Monster. Animal. Cultist. Witch.

Bloodborn. Rowan shuddered, her neck prickling as though bitten.

"Any more news from the wolves?" Gran coughed quietly into a handkerchief. Rowan passed her the cup of water from her bedside.

"Mist arcana," Rowan said as Gran sipped carefully. "Two groups. One is definitely Moonblade. We're not sure about the second."

"Moonblade and their vile powder this close to Elderglen?" Gran tsked. "Valera is either unaware, which I highly doubt, or pushing the limits of our patience."

"The behavior of someone bored."

"And one who likes to stir up trouble." Gran smoothed the blankets on her lap. "My money's on them planning something."

"Could they have found another crystal deposit?" Rowan asked. "They wouldn't risk my wrath without a very strong reason. Money or supplies?"

"Both, if it's Valera."

"That's even worse."

Gran hummed in agreement, thinking on Rowan's words amidst

the ambient quiet of their home. The hearth fire crackled pleasantly as Rowan assessed the chores to finish.

"You haven't said one word about your trip," Gran said.

Rowan smiled, pulling for something to say that wasn't about a deathseer. "I have returned home with a lighter load and a heavier purse."

Though *lighter load* was generous, considering the weight on her heart. Anticipation remained a brutal opponent, one built to withstand every possible blow.

"Well, Jean and I got a lot of time to review the latest goings-on in town."

"You mean the latest *gossip*." Rowan lifted the water bucket, its weight far too light. She poured what was there into the pot for boiling, having enough for porridge. She'd need to fetch more from the well.

"Six of one, half a dozen of the other." Gran's smile was relaxed. "How are things to the south of us?"

"Sunny. Warm. But nothing compares to our mountains."

"I'd love a quick getaway to the southern lands." Gran's expression turned wistful. "Even a trip to Runa. Flirt with a few pirates while I'm there."

She couldn't help but smile, imagining her Gran turning on the charm. "You scandalous old woman."

"Scandalous and proud." Still giggling, she adjusted her seat to rest higher. "Anything beats this confounded bed."

To take Gran out to the garden, down to the market in town, south to the Plains to see the wildflowers in the fields...

A fortnight is generous.

"Supper is already here," Gran said, glancing at the table. "Peter just dropped it off. They'll be here soon to dine."

"They are so good to us," Rowan said, relieved that she could eat and rest. She unraveled her braid and massaged her scalp. "I should take those wildberries and make them something. A cake?"

"Rowan in the kitchen," Gran said with a laugh. "Nobody panic."

But their brief amusement bled into a silence that harbored something unsaid, bringing Rowan to watch Gran expectantly.

"What is it?" she asked.

"You read me too well, girl." Gran adjusted her seat, grunting once more as her feeble strength pushed herself to sit up straighter. Rowan helped, hands and arms ready. "We will have another guest at our table. Someone from the guild."

"Oh?" Rowan tried to sound more enthusiastic than she felt. "Anyone I've met?"

"I daresay it's possible," Gran said, "though it was years ago. I doubt you would remember each other."

Only because Rowan tried to stay out of Feather and Claw when she could. But a member must have been hardy, indeed, to gain tenure within the guild.

Hardy or cunning. Likely both.

Two quick knocks at the front door were Jean's signature. Rowan and Gran shared one more look before bracing themselves for company.

"We've arrived at last." Jean hugged Rowan before going to Gran's beside. "Do you feel up to sitting at the table tonight, or shall I take up my perch beside you?"

"The table would be marvelous," Gran said.

Peter, upon entering, lifted Gran effortlessly and set her in the chair at the head of the table. She giggled, even kicking her feet.

"You've swept me away, young man."

Peter laughed, kissing the crown of her head.

Wil stood at Rowan's side, nudging her with his shoulder. "You alright?"

"Yes," she said slowly. "Why?"

"You look like you haven't slept." He gestured vaguely over her whole person. "Disheveled. Rough trip home, I bet. And you look like you rolled around on the grass."

She quirked an eyebrow, trying to mask the rising panic in her core. "Maybe I did."

"News is bleak," Peter said. "At least we can have a meal together."

"Rowan's just told me," Gran said. "Bleak is a good word for it."

"What are we facing?" Wil asked. "Could it really be a bloodborn?"

Gran shook her head. "I wish I knew."

Three knocks. Confident and assured.

"If that's Braithen," Wil said, "I will not be held responsible for my actions."

"It isn't Braithen," Jean said, moving to answer the door, but Rowan got up first. "We have a guild friend joining us."

Rowan opened the door, preparing her polite, amiable smile, only to meet Fen on the other side.

Someone from the guild. Fen was in Feather and Claw.

He offered a shy smile, running a hand through his hair, combed and clean. She felt the sensation between her own fingers, hands longing to know its softness.

Gods above. Her core wriggled as she caught herself staring.

"Hello again," he said. "Jean and Cynthia were kind enough to invite me to dinner." He held a small package wrapped in brown paper. "I've brought cinnamon bread for dessert."

Rowan stepped aside to give him entry, eyes tracing the line of his broad shoulders to avoid staring at the way his hair fell into his eyes.

"A kingly gift," Gran said, bringing her hands together. "Everyone, this is Fen. He's just come from south Sheraton."

"By way of Alvar," he said with a chuckle. "Thank you for having me."

Rowan led him to the only available chair at the table, between her and Jean.

"My," Gran said with a smile, eyes shining as she looked at each face. "It makes my heart happy to see friends old and new at my table."

"Here's to many more meals together." Jean raised her glass. "To family and friends."

Each echoed the salutation as they took their water cups and sipped.

Fen, seated by Rowan, set the cinnamon bread beside a basket of yeast rolls before reaching a hand to her hair, pulling a leaf free from the dark brown tangle of waves and curls.

Her hair wasn't in its typical braid. How she must look, mane wild and body holding evidence of her journey through the forest. With face flushed, she pulled her hair back, finding no more traces of the forest. "Thanks."

"Mayor Frederick was near the baker's," Fen said, "trying to reassure people that there wasn't a killer on the loose."

"But what if there is?" Jean snorted. "He's full of hot air and not much else."

"You've also just described Braithen," Wil said. "Too much air between his ears."

"Have you met everyone already?" Gran asked Fen. When he shook his head, she began with Rowan. "My granddaughter. Watcher of Sentinel Hill."

He offered a small smile as he nodded. "It's nice to see you again."

Wil raised his eyebrows, saying nothing.

"Jean, my dearest friend," Gran said, "and Wil, her son. This is Peter, Wil's husband."

"Nice to meet all of you," Fen said. "Thank you again for the invitation to dinner."

"And everyone," Gran said, her introductions coming to a close, "this is Fen. He is a Vanguard for the guild."

Vanguard. First responders to high-risk situations. They risked life and limb to stop the Wandering Order, to save anyone they could from the cult's dangerous intentions.

"Welcome to Elderglen," Jean said. "What sort of work do you do when you're not with the guild?"

"Odd jobs, mostly," he said, taking another sip of water. "I was apprenticed to a blacksmith, so I'm skilled in that trade."

"Was?" Wil asked. "What happened?"

Peter elbowed his side, muttering something too low for Rowan to catch.

"The Wandering Order," Fen said simply. "My brother and I managed to escape with our lives. Our loved ones weren't so lucky."

Images of fire and destruction flashed behind Rowan's eyes, with figures dressed in black moving calmly through smoke and flame, firelight glistening off their silver boot-laces.

"Your family?" Jean asked quietly, the horror on her face showing she'd guessed the answer. "Gods above."

"That was a long time ago," Fen said. "Seven years. My brother and I learned skills to work and survive."

Jean helped to dish mutton stew as Wil passed rolls.

"Where was this?" Peter asked, then quickly added, "There was a village completely razed to the ground where I grew up in Sudor. The Order and King Jesper had an alliance that cost people their homes and lives."

"Southern Estilon," Fen said. "Not far from Runa."

"Whose king had little tolerance for magic folk, too," Peter said. "I'm sorry, Fen."

"You and your magic are safe here," Rowan said, recalling the nearest safe house from memory. As Sentinel of Feather and Claw, she ensured all locations were guarded, as well as the people there.

At least, that was her task before Gran's health took a turn.

"Thank you," he said, "though I don't have magic. It's my brother who practices. He and my master were devout to Brena." He lifted a leather cord from beneath his collar and revealed two silver charms, their swirl patterns emblems for Brena and Shanna. Touching the charm for Brena, he said, "I made this while with my master. And this—" —he held the emblem for Shanna— "I made in Runa. I learned prayers to the goddess of the sea while I was there."

"Fire and water," Gran said with a smile. "Flame and sea."

"Like Wil and Rowan in Catcher's Lake," Jean said, mischief bright in her eyes. "Wil being the sea, of course."

"Making you the flame?" Fen asked Rowan, interest tugging at the corners of his mouth.

"She never backs down from a challenge," Wil said, an eyebrow lifting. "And she will likely win."

"I could tell that within five minutes of meeting you." Fen looked at her over his cup as he sipped water.

As her skin burned, she looked at her meal with focused interest. She wasn't used to so much attention, to so many eyes.

To his eyes, the deepest blue she'd ever seen.

"Back to the day's news," Wil said, unceremoniously changing the subject. "Braithen is a loudmouth, easily bored and easily entertained." He exhaled, closing his eyes. "The man needs a hobby."

"His words have been fast and loud in the tavern," Fen said. "His and his sister's."

Gran's easy smile shifted to a sneer. "Busybodies, both. They take after their mother."

"All he does is *talk*," Jean said. "If the man did a single day's work, the earth would fold in on itself."

"He will cause someone to do something foolish," Rowan said. "Or worse."

The wolves were at risk of human stupidity at the best of times. But with chaos brewing in the hearts of desperate people, Rowan questioned how long it would take before disaster struck.

More patrols, and not just to find the murderer. Rowan took a sip of cool water.

The meal concluded not long after, and Rowan and Wil collected the dishes for washing. Fen spoke softly with Jean and Gran, his demeanor gentle and respectful. His calloused hands and sun-kissed hair and skin proved his life was full of work and labor. By all accounts, Fen was kind.

Which made Rowan trust him even less.

"Let's go together," Wil muttered, his arms laden with plates. "We need to talk."

She tried to meet his stern look with a teasing one, but her stomach flipped just the same. "My four favorite words: *We need to talk.*"

They slipped outside while the others talked of life in Runa. The clay bowls clattered in Rowan's hands as she stepped down from the back door and reached their well.

Wil lowered the bucket quickly, the wood and metal squeaking until the bucket crashed against the surface of the water. He watched and waited for the vessel to fill before winding it back to the surface.

"Apprenticed to a blacksmith?" He scoffed. "Casting two goddess emblems? Does he think that will make him look more devout?"

Rowan raised an eyebrow. "You don't like Fen."

"I don't *trust* Fen." Wil shook his head and looked over his shoulder at Rowan's house. "His arrival is suspicious, Ro. A murdered villager. Raids every other day. Gran—" He stopped, but Rowan knew what his words would have been.

Gran *dying*.

Wil set the bucket on the edge of the well for them, and they took turns rinsing the dishes.

"Elderglen is compromised, especially with the likes of Braithen and

Halie causing trouble." He paused before adding, "It's not a secret we have a Watcher who's wolfkind."

"Jean and Gran trust him," Rowan said. "That's enough to share a meal."

Wil blinked slowly. "And he knows how to flirt."

"Pity his subject is a brick wall."

"Because of Avenith?"

She glared at him. "Not everything is because of her."

He lifted his hands in surrender. "I'm only making an observation. You haven't put yourself out there since she left."

"With what time?" Then she chuckled, her levity genuine. "And with what charisma? My winning personality seems to scare people off, not invite them for tea."

"You're not a wall, Rowan. But you're good at hiding behind one." With an eyebrow raised, Wil added, "Fen didn't seem scared off by your *winning personality.*"

"Because he wants something." She dipped a bowl into the bucket a little too hard, water spilling from the side. "Apparently, so did Avenith."

"I don't doubt anything he said." Wil glanced toward the house. "But that doesn't mean he's telling us the whole truth."

"He's searching for his brother." She rubbed food away from a bowl, the water sloshing. "He said he was taken by the Wandering Order."

Fen's melancholy confirmed as much for her. And there was a softness in his deep voice when he spoke to Gran.

"Gods. Those cultists with a fire magic in their hands." He shook his head. "Fen must be going out of his mind, looking for him."

"And it somehow led him here." Rowan massaged her hands, cold from the well water. "We'll play nice."

"Play nice?" Wil's forehead wrinkled as his brows rose. "What does *play nice* mean?"

"It means I won't tie him to a chair and question him."

Wil laughed, bumping her with his shoulder. "*For now.*"

CHAPTER 6

The clay road out of Elderglen sank beneath Rowan's paws as she patrolled, her steps taking her beyond the village perimeter toward the fields.

Tall grass and wildflowers swayed despite the still night, the overcast shielding the land from the white moonlight she loved. But even with the darkness, Rowan's keen wolf sight discerned shapes and shadows. She relished the solitude even as she missed Winter's company.

"Stay with Gran," she'd said before stepping out. Winter whined quietly, resting her head on Gran's leg while she slept, her gray eyes watching Rowan leave.

Her body moved in silence, the soft crisp of grass and flower stems beneath each step inaudible but to her ears. Her disturbance was minimal. She was a ghost passing over the landscape in pursuit of living souls.

She watched and waited for nearly an hour, the waning moon high in the overcast sky. Elderglen in the distance was barely visible, the few fires burning adding amber shimmers as she glanced back. But the rhythmic squeak of a wagon wheel cut through the night's quiet with a staccato, the creaking wood offering discordant accompaniment. Rowan shook her head against the sound, trotting forward to get a closer look.

Two men dressed in black sat in the wagon's front, one holding the reins to two horses while the other kept a watchful eye, his hand on the handle of a sword at his hip. In the back were two crates and one clay jar.

Rowan skirted around them, edging closer, nose working through the air to glean what she could of them and their loads. Oak, sweat, and—

She almost sneezed, catching the static burn of magic, its crisp sharpness almost like lightning. That's what discerned true magic from mist arcana. True magic smelled like electricity and energy, whereas mist arcana smelled like rotten eggs.

How frequently did they transport? Where was the node of arcana crystal, and where was their hideout?

Her paws thundered against the cool earth, moving as though to pounce the horses.

"You bring poison with you," she snapped at them.

The horses reared, kicking their forelegs as panic surged in their blood. "Don't kill us!"

The men cried out, the wagon losing control as it tottered with the imbalance of its load.

"I'm not here for you," Rowan told the horses. "Your lives are safe from me. I only want the cargo."

The human passenger pulled his short sword, crying out as he jumped from the wagon to face Rowan. But she leaped for the driver, causing him to yank too hard on the reins. The horses whinnied louder, their shrill cries deafening, and they galloped hard to escape. One of the wagon wheels rode over something, a hole or a stone, and the imbalanced load forced the vehicle to roll. The crates and clay jar toppled, Rowan's adrenaline surging at the sound of breaking and shattering.

The men bellowed curses, moving for Rowan as the horses fought to run faster, the wagon lumbering behind them.

"Don't hurt yourselves," Rowan called to the beasts, frenzied in panic. "You're not in danger!"

The horses were lost in their harried state, too panicked to respond.

A break in the overcast bloomed white moonlight over the landscape. One of the men, armed, kept his dark eyes locked on her as she charged. She feinted a lunge for his throat, aiming her back legs to kick his stomach. As he swayed, over-correcting in his balance, she bit hard on his wrist, tasting blood and sweat, forcing him to drop the weapon. She shook once before releasing, glad to see him clutching the injured arm against his chest as he staggered back.

When she turned for the other, she watched him try to sweep several arcana crystals into his arms before breaking out in a run in the wake of the horses. The other assassin followed, but not before his dark eyes studied her.

"You taste my blood," he said, backing away, "I taste yours. This isn't over, *wolf*."

She snarled, watching their retreat. She broke the clay pot further, revealing a considerable load of mist arcana. She backed away, careful of breathing it in.

"Rowan?" Wil carried a lantern in one hand and a sword in the other. Peter was empty-handed beside him, though his swords were sheathed in his belt.

"Winter was whining at our door," Peter said, looking at the disarray before them. "What happened?"

Rowan shifted, glancing where the assassins had run. "Winter came to you?"

"She got us out of the house," Wil said. "We checked on Gran, and everything was fine. But you weren't there. So here we are."

"How did she get out?"

"It looks like she opened the door." Peter used his hand to mimic the door's handle as his nose prodded it. "That's my guess."

"What the hells happened here?" Wil asked. "Are you alright?"

"I'm fine." She spat, still tasting blood. "I can't say the same for the two who have to report back to Valera."

"This was Moonblade?"

"That's my guess. They masked their scent. The matriarch noticed that about them too."

"The matriarch," Peter said. "This has been going on for a while."

"At least since I left."

"Let's get the crystal home," Wil said. "And destroy this poison."

He extinguished the lantern before pouring a stream of oil over the pile of magical powder. He used the flint and stone from his pocket, and flames soon engulfed the dangerous substance that made Moonblade a considerable profit.

"They'll be back," Rowan warned. "We should warn the mayor."

Peter scoffed. "Unless he's in on it. I'd be surprised he hasn't tried the venture himself."

"It's dangerous," Wil said, "and he's too much of a coward."

They worked together to carry the arcana crystal to Wil and Peter's home, where it would remain until Jean could have it moved. Arcana crystal was invaluable to the guild, with magical members and rescued survivors needing them to heal.

But before Rowan stepped inside with the task at hand, she glanced once more at the nighttime horizon, half expecting an army of assassins charging forward. But the land was quiet, as it should be.

For now.

CHAPTER 7

When Rowan reached the Hill, Winter trotted up from behind, the lights on in the windows of Wil's house.

"You clever girl." Rowan scratched behind her ears. "All this time, and doors couldn't hold you back."

Her temper had slowed to a simmer, her composure aided by the walk home. And upon entering her quiet home, Gran stirred, first by the sound of the squeaking hinges and then by Winter jumping onto the bed.

"What's the matter?" Gran rubbed her tired face. "Is it morning?"

"Not yet," Rowan said. "Go back to sleep."

"Hm." Gran's eyes closed. "Patrol?"

"I'll tell you over breakfast."

"Tell me now, granddaughter."

Rowan smiled to herself, going to the hearth to add another piece of wood. "Mist arcana. Moonblade had a transport too close to Elderglen."

"Moonblade?" Her breathing was slow and deep as she remained on the fringes of sleep.

"Right about now, they're likely licking their wounds."

"That's my girl."

Winter rested her head on Gran's thigh, watching her.

Rowan took up her spot in the cushioned chair by Gran's bed, eyeing the journal on the nightstand. It had been moved since Rowan last looked.

With a glance at Winter and another at Gran, Rowan lifted the volume and held it, the soft leather cover well worn by Gran's loving hands.

The last entry was a single sentence, scrawled in Gran's shaky, aged handwriting:

His brother has come to Elderglen, and I have no good news to give.

Rowan stared, rereading. His brother. *His brother.* "Fen?"

I'm looking for my brother.

He was captured by the Wandering Order.

Firecraft.

Fen. The Guild. The Wandering Order. And Rowan's sleeping grandmother, frail in her physical weakness while still undeniably the Cornerstone.

Rowan turned a page back, then another, and another, these filled with inked words of days passed. Months separated entries, but Gran maintained details of her days, of guild business, of Rowan.

"I shouldn't read this." Her whisper hissed in her own ears, even as her fingers flipped the pages to the beginning. Feather and Claw settled in a pool of bitterness in Rowan's heart, seeping into her core, but this...

Something about this was different. There was life in these pages, giving character and reason to the guild that took her parents, that took her grandmother while she yet lived.

Rowan met Winter's watchful gaze.

"Would she be angry if I read this?"

Winter blinked, the conclusion unsure.

Beneath Winter's watchful gaze, Rowan turned to the first page.

THERE HAVE BEEN rumors of an anti-magic group in Sheraton. Somewhere out in Sudor. That kingdom has been a blight upon the continent, poisoning it from the inside. Jesper, the fool, has squandered what was given to him, and the people suffer. His actions bear a ripple effect that have already affected Thurin, with citizens leaving Sudor in a steady trickle. The floodgates may open anytime if anti-magic sentiment gains ground.

Even in her journal, Gran reined her language and tone. Her opinions of Jesper were usually expressed with heavy, scathing sarcasm and threats of violence.

I can only guess what this will mean for Elderglen. The village is safe for now, but wary eyes find their way to the Hill every now and again as I patrol the perimeter and the forest. They don't view friendship with the wolves as the boon it is but rather a looming threat. Their foolish ignorance is half the reason the Hill exists at all. Sometimes, Johann and I regret that we offered the Hill to Elderglen. But taking it back would create a backlash so severe that, if the hatred from Sudor didn't tear us apart, Elderglen's retaliation would.

Vindication spread warmth through Rowan's body, her beating heart justified in her grandparents also hating Elderglen for their stupidity. But the Hill remained, as did Elderglen's entitlement.

"Something I could change," Rowan whispered to the quiet room, the firelight flickering with every inch of wood it devoured.

Nevertheless, we watch. And wait. I only pray people surprise me and do better than I expect they will. A group formed around hate has no place here. I can only hope Jesper doesn't feel emboldened by the citizens organizing their hatred against magic and those with it. His endorsement would only further the madness, and we've had enough of that already. This can only lead to darkness. Pray there is enough light.

Gran hadn't dated her entries. All Rowan had was the shape and curve of each letter, using Gran's handwriting to determine her age. She traced a finger along the last sentence—*Pray there is enough light*—hearing Gran's voice say the words.

She turned the page to the next entry and read.

The Wandering Order.

Pretentious as hell.

Sources say their leader is a man named Matthias. Some visionary with goals to eradicate magic from all known lands, to sweep the pestilence *from humanity.*

The only pestilence is hatred.

Matthias probably isn't his real name. The bastard probably sees himself as a prophet, and that name is as close as he'll ever be to one. And no, such irony is not lost on me.

The troubling part is that the Wandering Order has taken shape. It has a name. It has something of a hierarchy if there's a leader. Are there others within that bear titles? Gods, have they formed some sort of militia?

Why is nothing more being done to squash this group from causing real harm? Johann and I have sent word to other leaders in Thurin, including Wolf Seat. Others need to know the threat the Wandering Order poses. It will only get worse.

This was likely the beginning of Feather and Claw, predating Rowan by several years. She didn't know the Wandering Order was that old, that *established*. Knowing things as they've happened, reading about the past only makes the weight of what would come that much heavier. The world had a chance to rid itself of those rodents, but the cult thrived.

Shame on everyone who stood by and did nothing.

Rowan heard the words in Gran's voice, remembering the day the news came of where her parents were found, the fringes of grief mingling with shame.

Her eyes itched, but the tears wouldn't come. The ache was old, time-sealed and long-festered, and one that marked the height of Rowan's emotions.

She swallowed it down and closed the journal, guilt and unease sour on her stomach.

CHAPTER 8

Rowan carefully flipped the sizzling oatcake as Gran stroked Winter's head.

"You look like you barely slept."

Rowan hesitated before answering. "It was a long night."

Gran's entries remained undated, with months or years between them. The entry about Rowan's birth centered them within a frame that she could sequence, leaving around eighteen years passing between then and now.

She'd raced through the remaining pages, eyes trained to catch words and phrases relating to the Wandering Order and another burgeoning guild: Moonblade.

"Assassins and thieves," Gran had written as Moonblade began to take shape. "The only thing we have in common is our hatred for that damned cult and everything it stands for. The rest remains at odds."

And from Rowan's experience, anyone at odds with Gran would have their hands full.

Then, one entry in particular, written nearly two years ago.

"The worst news a mother could hear—"

Rowan had looked away, her tired eyes stinging, her face hot. She'd closed the journal and moved to her mattress on the floor, lying parallel to Gran. Closing her eyes had helped to assuage the discomfort, her eyeballs hot and dry, but she didn't feel the touch of rest until dawn came, proving that her body had shut down in the night.

"Rowan?"

She looked up, startled out of her thoughts. "Sorry." She flipped the oatcake again, that side a few shades shy of being burned. She slipped it onto a plate and poured more batter into the pan, sizzling pleasantly. "Did you say something?"

"What is it love? Tell me."

Her quiet, soothing voice invited Rowan to empty every chamber of her heart, and the temptation was strong. Turn over everything, empty every cavern, lose the weight of things that shouldn't belong to her.

But Rowan couldn't bring herself to say them. "It's nothing."

"You shouldn't lie to your grandmother."

Rowan almost laughed, the slight tug at her mouth the only amusement that surfaced. "The body found yesterday. The mist arcana cargo for Moonblade. And I need to speak with the mayor."

Gran scoffed. "What good that will do."

"He should know what the wolves saw."

"I suppose you're right, but that doesn't mean Elderglen can do anything to prepare."

"Elderglen *won't* do anything to prepare." She didn't look up, her voice savoring strongly of bitterness. "I hate how resentful they make me feel."

"I know, love. But if—" She hesitated. "You didn't ask, but if it helps, don't *let* them make you feel anything."

Unsolicited advice was Gran's specialty, but Rowan always listened. "I'm not sure how."

"You take things to heart. You take things personally."

The oatcake flipped easily, cooked to the right color. "It's difficult not to."

Elderglen is a privilege, Watcher. Or whatever Halie had said. Self-serving, entitled—

"Don't spiral, Rowan."

She exhaled heavily through her nose, giving her grandmother a wry smirk. "Yes, ma'am."

"Keep yourself busy. The barn needs looking after." After a pause, she added, "And Fen could use some work."

"Fen?"

"Traveling hasn't been easy. Finding Marc—"

"Marc. Is that his brother?"

Gran went quiet.

"Was I not supposed to know?"

"No, it isn't that. There are things I need to tell you."

Rowan put utensils on their plates, the clattering louder than it needed to be. "Fen needs us to give him work?"

Rowan's avoidance didn't escape Gran's notice, but she didn't push. "They're both in the Order, love. We look after our own."

Rowan didn't look up, something within her resisting involvement. But a man was missing, and Fen needed resources to keep looking. "I can't pay him, Gran. Not what the work is worth."

"So help him."

"I have to see the mayor."

"Which won't take the whole day."

Suspicious, Rowan side-eyed her grandmother while prodding the oatcake with her spatula. "Why does this mean so much to you? This is more than the guild caring for its own."

Gran pressed her lips together, using Winter as a distraction. She touched the wolf's paws, one toe at a time. "It's the right thing to do."

"What's right about it?"

"Rowan."

"Cynthia."

Gran gasped, prompting Winter to lift her head and watch the old woman with interest. Rowan chuckled.

"Proof that I'm your granddaughter." She slipped the final oatcake from the pan, cooked completely without catastrophe, and brought breakfast to Gran. "Tell me why you're so interested in Fen."

Gran's sigh of defeat reached deep as she deflated in compliance. "He was only fifteen when he joined the guild. The Wandering Order took everything."

"Except his brother. The one with magic."

Gran lifted an eyebrow. "What do you know, granddaughter?"

"I met him near the woods the day I returned."

"I see." Gran took a bite of the oatcake. She didn't grimace, so it must have tasted good. Rowan, as self-assured as she was protecting Elderglen, had little confidence in the kitchen. "Any other news you didn't tell me?"

Rowan pretended to pinch Gran's arm. "Hunters aren't newsworthy. I didn't know he was one of yours."

"One of *ours*."

Rowan took a bite of breakfast to keep from responding.

"He and his brother were children. Five years ago, with nowhere to go, they crossed paths with a ship captain in Runa."

"Quenvar?"

"That's the one. I'm impressed you remember his name."

"The one time he came to Elderglen, he left an impression. *'My name is Ken-Var, not Kwen-Var.'*" Boisterous, loud, charismatic. He'd managed, somehow, to be both difficult and easy to dislike. "He took them in?"

"Made them a part of his crew," Gran said, "and welcomed them into the guild after word reached me. But I..."

Emotion weighed heavily on her aged face. Rowan took her hand, rubbing her knuckles. "What is it, Gran?"

"I almost didn't let them in. I wanted them here, but how would I have cared for them? How would Beth or Simon? And no one in Elderglen had the means."

"Did Quenvar..." Rowan hesitated. "Was he cruel?"

"No. But he didn't raise those boys like a father. More like a friend who was also their employer. He probably loved those boys, but—" She winced. "I wonder if it was the kind of love they deserved. I'll never know, Rowan. And it wears on me."

What would that have been like, finding a caregiver who demanded you meet conditions to earn your place after losing everything?

"At least they had each other," Rowan said.

"It's one of my deepest regrets," Gran admitted, looking toward the window, her oatcake half-eaten. "I should have been braver, Rowan. Those boys needed a family."

"They have you now," she said. "That counts."

Gran said nothing, her sadness no lighter, her brown eyes misting.

A gentle knock came to the door, the same timid rhythm from their guest at dinner. Rowan eyed Gran with an amused lift of her eyebrows.

"I didn't send for him." Gran raised her hands in innocent surrender. "This is just divine timing."

"Is that what it is?"

Rowan rose to answer the door, seeing Fen as expected. His white shirt brought out the blue of his eyes, the richness of his tan, the golden shimmer in his brown hair.

"Good morning," he said. "Jean sent me."

"The barn needs some work done, Fen," Gran said, looking pointedly at Rowan.

Rowan stepped back so Fen could enter their home. Winter wagged her tail, glad to have his hand reach for her head and stroke down her neck. Everyone in the house was glad to see him, welcoming his presence. Everyone except Rowan.

He still wanted something from them. Of that, she was certain. But other than help finding Marc, she couldn't put her finger on what Fen was after and why his presence had already seeped into her skin.

Perhaps some time together wouldn't be such a bad idea after all.

CHAPTER 9

"The goats are escaping here." Rowan moved a loose wood panel in the barn, showing Fen. "There are other areas that need repair, but this needs it first."

"Holes worn through the walls," he said. "The hayloft railing broken."

"You get the idea." She pointed up. "There's wood in the loft. Tools on hooks on the walls."

Her grandfather's way of organizing—using hooks and nails to hang his tools within sight and reach—kept them out of drawers and off the floor. Rowan could almost see him moving to each one, eager for whatever project awaited his expertise.

"Shouldn't take long," Fen said. "I appreciate the work." After a moment, he said, "Being Watcher over a village is a heavy load to bear."

"It is. One that must be borne." She heard Wil's warning in her head. *It's not a secret we have a Watcher who's wolfkind.* "And as you've seen, recent events make that especially challenging."

"I'm glad to help," he said.

"The Hill is glad for it, too." She turned for the door. "You should have everything you need. I'll return soon to help."

"Where are you going?"

"To see the mayor about what happened."

She sensed another question but slipped out before he could ask, listening instead to the bleating goats and clucking chickens who sounded their chorus at her departure. Descending the hill never failed in giving Rowan a brief thrill, the closest she'd likely come to flying as the incline became steep before leveling to even ground.

The mayor's house was the largest in Elderglen, its two stories of brick and stone a sign and symbol of Elderglen's prosperity. At least, that's what the mayor likes to say in defense of his status and power. "From his home to his clothes, no one should question the validity of influence on the mayor's position."

But that only remained true if the one bearing the mantle could shoulder the weight. As far as Rowan was concerned, he'd been found wanting.

She knocked loudly, her knuckles smarting against the wood for three strikes, and she waited two breaths before one of the servants opened the door.

"Rowan," he said. "The master is taking breakfast in the dining room."

"This will only take a moment," she said. "I will wait for him."

"He dines alone. You wouldn't disturb him."

She retreated. "I'd rather—"

"He's given us instructions to grant you entry at any time."

Rowan didn't hide her surprise. "He has?"

"Right this way, please."

She followed him through the foyer to a short corridor that opened to a bright room. Tall windows, with curtains drawn, allowed natural light to pour in, and the mayor sat to breakfast, the meal surprisingly modest. Porridge, fresh berries, and honeyed toast.

"Rowan." The mayor wiped his mouth before standing. "Welcome. Pardon me for breaking my fast this late. I usually dine at dawn."

There was still much left of the morning, but Rowan understood the methods of early risers from years in Gran's household.

"I came because of what happened," she said. "I'm worried, Mr. Mayor."

"As am I." He moved to speak, sitting once again, but the entrance of a female servant interrupted him. "Yes?"

"My lady is unwell and will have breakfast in her chambers," she said with a slight bow. This was far from a royal house, but one wouldn't know it based on the behavior of the staff.

"I thought as much," he said with a reassuring smile. "Thank you."

Once the servant left, the door latching behind her, the mayor continued. "This threat to Elderglen is strange, indeed. I received news of a nearby camp of Wandering Order where two bodies were found, similar to the man from yesterday." He sighed. "I hate to admit that I'm relieved for the monster hunting monsters, but that foul creature doesn't discriminate good from evil when it is evil itself."

"I hadn't heard of murdered cultists, Mr. Mayor." She paused before adding, "You're certain it was the same attacker?"

"Positive. The manner of their deaths looked identical to the others. No one told you?" As she shook her head, he rubbed his chin. "I don't like that, Rowan. All news should be reported to the Hill."

"But it reached you." She considered, her skepticism rising. "Who told you?"

At this, he sighed. "Braithen and Halie."

Of course. "Their strength is in the truth they manage to find. Their cunning is how they want to use it."

"I couldn't have said it better myself."

Silence passed between them, both deeply set within their own minds as pieces of the puzzle came together. The images created were not as different now, and something akin to understanding began to form.

Or so Rowan thought.

"My concern is also for its people." Rowan straightened her shoulders, working to keep her face controlled and stoic. "Those like Braithen, specifically."

"Hm. Yes. He and others concern me, too." The mayor leaned back, thinking, his eyes focused on the wall behind Rowan. "If they do something reckless, I fear the aftermath that would follow."

"Sentinel Hill can't protect those who willingly put themselves in danger." She scoffed. "I hate that I feel the need to say that, Mr. Mayor. But my home is threatened. The very bricks my grandparents laid."

"It's a title you bear."

"A title my grandparents created." Her stare cooled. "Not you or anyone else. Sentinel Hill is a part of Elderglen, but it is not owned by Elderglen."

He tilted his head downward, meeting her eyes with concern. "What are you saying, Rowan?"

What *was* she saying? What accounted for the flare within, one eager to defend her place upon Sentinel Hill? But the words flowed from her as though divinely given.

But this wasn't divinity. It was fear, which Rowan was loath to suffer. She'd rather embrace her rage than allow weakness to settle in.

I am not the titles I bear, she thought, remembering Jean's words. But their truth hadn't reached her, not when anxiety caged her heart in bars of iron.

"Halie practically threatened my home, as though it was a seat of office to be voted on and filled." Rowan gestured to the mayor for emphasis. "I won't have anyone thinking they have a right to take what is not theirs."

"Rowan—"

"They did not create Sentinel Hill. They have no charge over the Watchers. Elderglen may refuse the gift if they wish, but my family and I are not subject to the village's whim."

"Whim?" He stood, his cheeks flushing. "This is not a whim."

"I will not be bullied out of my home by a team of loudmouths who refuse to help themselves." Her lips pulled back from her teeth, magic tingling beneath the surface of her skin. "You will have to kill me first."

"Rowan—"

She turned. "I've said all I came to say. Lead those people to common sense before someone gets hurt."

"We're not finished here."

But she didn't stop, even as his voice echoed through the hall, calling her name. Her clicking heels following the path out of his home was a glorious sound, punctuating her decision and intention.

But she froze as she saw Fen standing outside the mayor's home, eyes squinting against the sunlight as he looked up to the second story. She descended the front steps, securing the door behind her. "What brings you here?"

He held up a handful of iron nails. "I couldn't find any in the barn, and it didn't feel right going through your things."

"I'll pay you back," she said.

"No need." He glanced toward the blacksmith with a half-smile. "He knew my master and gave me a discount. They were old friends."

But something tugged at her core. She took a chance and a step toward him as she asked, "What are you doing *here*?"

His look sobered, though the kindness didn't leave his eyes. "The mayor." He flashed a wince before sighing. "I have a bad feeling, is all. I don't trust him."

"Over what happened yesterday?"

"That, and other things." He met her gaze with sympathy. "He doesn't respect the work you do."

Even a stranger can see it. Rowan turned for home, Fen walking in step beside her.

"Thank you," she said. "Let's hope nothing drastic happens for them to see reason."

"Let's hope."

Rowan climbed the hill, her jaw clenched and fists tight. The morning's beautiful birdsong did little to cool the heat within, but pushing against the hill's incline directed her energy.

"I'll be in to help soon," she said to him. "I need to calm down first."

"Understandable," he said. "That man would get under my skin, too."

It wasn't only the mayor, but his sentiment meant something, nonetheless.

She exhaled a quiet laugh as she pressed on, wondering if this was how Fen earned his friends and admirers.

Admirers? She shook her head to rattle the thought from her mind. *Where did* that *come from?*

Once inside, Rowan didn't waste time telling Gran the gist of the conversation.

"Dramatically expressed, granddaughter. *You'll have to kill me first.*" Gran said with a chuckle. "I'm proud of you."

"I wouldn't put it past Braithen and Halie to try," Rowan said. "They're variables, and that makes them dangerous."

Gran sighed, rubbing her knuckles and fingers. "I wish I had the confidence to say this will be enough. Trouble finds its way to our doorstep one way or another."

Rowan took a jar from the shelf by the dining table and unscrewed the lid. Its earthy menthol scent quickly filled her nose as she passed it to Gran.

"Thank you, love." Gran rubbed the translucent green ointment onto her joints. "I'm sorry, Rowan. My beautiful girl."

"Why, Gran?" She sat at her bedside. "Whatever for?"

"Sentinel Hill and the burden it's become."

"It's not—"

Gran interrupted by taking her hands, her hold firm. "It is, Rowan. It is a burden that we never intended. Your grandfather and I had such hope for Elderglen and what Sentinel Hill could become. But the Wandering Order made it more than a home for Watchers. And now, with that *thing* plaguing our village—" Gran stopped before going on. "The people here have hindered more than helped. My disappointment in them cannot be measured."

Rowan was more disappointed in those so easily led by Braithen and his ilk. But fear shrouded judgment, making it difficult to see things clearly. If his was the loudest voice, they would follow him in hopes of being led through the dark. But he would lead them off the edge of a cliff they wouldn't see coming.

"There is something I never told you," Gran said, her thumbs running over Rowan's knuckles. "It's about your parents. What happened the day they died."

The day they were found, miles from where they'd camped. Rowan's blood chilled in her veins. Two years had passed, but the gravity of loss continued to press its weight on her chest.

"Do you remember the map your parents had?"

Rowan nodded. "One of the guild's. The emblem in the corner showed it."

Gran took a deep breath, fatigue taking its toll. "Several copies exist among the guild members."

In spite of herself, Rowan couldn't help but tease her. "You don't have to say *guild*, Gran."

"I will say what I wish." Playfully, Gran pinched Rowan's pinky. *Guild* certainly was easier than *network of spies*. "The mapmakers are a couple in Shaylon Plains. Very skilled and fearless. They marked each safe house and hideout we have across Sheraton."

"And mines and nodes of arcana crystal," Rowan added.

"Those maps are valuable, as you know." Gran pressed her lips together, looking at their hands while she summoned the words. "And one was stolen in Runa five years ago."

Rowan blinked, understanding slow to come. "Five years ago?"

"I never told you because the matter was to be sorted quickly." Gran's lips twitched a she spoke, her level of control over her emotions wavering. "Jean knew, of course, but it didn't seem—"

"Gran, I'm Sentinel." Rowan rubbed Gran's hands, the ointment still on her knuckles. "Why didn't you tell me?"

"You weren't Sentinel then," Gran said, defensive. "And Jean and I were handling it. So—" Her breath hitched. "So were your parents."

Rowan's blood chilled in her veins as she sensed where this was leading. "What are you trying to say?"

"They had a strong lead," Gran said. "Trailing evidence north through Estilon and Sudor. And they reached a safe house there."

"In Sudor," Rowan said. "Where they were found." She paused. "But the map was stolen in Runa."

"We still don't know everything. But we have our suspicions."

"Tell me." Rowan fought the urge to tighten her grip on Gran's frail hands. "Just tell me."

"Moonblade."

Rowan's teeth bared briefly as her lips twitched back. "Those bastards killed my parents?"

It took Gran a moment before she said, "I have no proof, but I know it. In my heart, I know it."

"Valera," Rowan said, the pieces falling into place. "She came to us. *She* told us."

"I asked her, and she said her people thought Beth and Simon were cultists. She said it wasn't intentional."

"Bullshit." Rowan's teeth bared. "She's a liar."

"Valera wouldn't have done this," Gran said. "Of that, I'm sure. But she knows who did."

"Is that why she was so quick to agree to my terms about mist arcana? She felt guilty?"

"I think so."

"Only someone with that map could have found them." Rowan clenched her teeth, warmth spreading within her core as her anger sparked anew. "Whoever stole the map killed my parents."

"And one of our own was recently recovered from capture."

"Fen's brother?"

"He was tortured with mist arcana, and—" Gran stopped, emotion taking her voice. She exhaled, the sound rheumatic in her lungs before she continued. "He fears that he may have revealed sensitive information about the guild, and I think—"

Gran couldn't finish, stopping to press a hand to her mouth.

"Is someone in Moonblade giving our information to the Order?"

"I think so," she said. "Or Moonblade is allowing our people to be found so they can access arcana crystal, navigating around the Wandering Order by distracting them and taking what they can."

Winter crawled from Gran's feet to rest her head on Rowan's knee. Rowan closed her eyes, her breathing focused through her nose. "Why are you telling me this now?"

"Because the fight isn't over. And the map must be found." She touched her journal, Rowan already familiar with some of its contents. "More of ours have been found dead. Closer to Elderglen, here in Thurin." She paused. "The one who lost the map is trying to mend his mistake and—"

"*Mistake?*"

"Yes, Rowan. It was a mistake. An accident. One I could have prevented."

"You? How?"

Gran moved to speak, but a coughing fit seized her chest.

Rowan helped Gran sip water, blotting the drops that fell around her lips and fingers. Her mind raced as pieces fell into place and her future aligned in clarity.

Finding the map would lead to her parents' killer.

Gran's breathing leveled at last. Rowan stood, still holding her hands. "Rest. I'll see to Fen."

"Thank you," Gran said, tiredness taking her. "Thank you for helping him."

She watched Gran's eyelids close and her breathing deepen, Winter resting close beside her legs. Rowan's body ached with the mounting tension in her muscles as more questions swirled among her racing thoughts.

Two years, yet the grief continued to suffocate her, as near and as fresh as ever.

But Rowan would find the one whose hands were stained in murder, and she would become their burning redemption.

CHAPTER 10

Fen had patched the spot in the barn wall where the goats would slip through before he'd gone to fetch nails. The next repair would be upstairs.

"We should both work in the loft," Rowan said. "That would be safer, instead of only one person taking it on by themselves."

"The lumber still looks good," he said. "I climbed up to check. How long has it been up there?"

"Years." She shrugged. "I haven't made it a priority until now."

"Not until I arrived. Here I am to save the day."

Her sardonic expression met his charm, his broad grin disarming.

"After the loft, we'll see about the chicken coop."

"You go for something when you set your mind to it," he said. "I admire that."

She didn't look at him, instead taking the hammer from its place on the wall. He'd returned it to the right place after the morning's work, which didn't escape her notice. "Then let's admire that in one another and fix this railing."

She climbed up, and he followed, both of them reaching the stack of boards and posts. Whether for the loft railing or the fence outside, she kept lumber ready to repair herself.

"Rowan?"

Something in his voice gave her pause, though she forced a mask of nonchalance. "Hm?"

"Have I made you uncomfortable?"

She lifted one board, its grain and texture rough against her calloused hands. "No. Why?"

"I feel like I have."

"I'm not used to you, Fen," she said succinctly, taking the board to the railing and letting it drop on the pieces of hay at their feet. "Our acquaintanceship is new, and we're both undertaking a task to complete together."

"Acquaintanceship." He raised an eyebrow, the hint of a smirk toying with his mouth. She tried not to look, but a dimple presented itself beneath the stubble. "Are you sure that's it?"

She took a deep breath, the air cool through her nose. "I'm sure."

She aimed the hammer's claw and worked it beneath the first nail head, but her shirt sleeves hindered more than helped. She freed one nail, taking the rusted metal into her hand and setting it beside her. "Here." She passed Fen the hammer. "Do the others for me."

She rolled her sleeves as far as they would go, the fabric tight around her biceps. She felt his eyes following her hands, fingers rolling each sleeve until they could go no further. When she looked at him, he was staring, lips slightly parted.

"Fen?"

He cleared his throat, focusing on the task. "Right. Sorry. It's just…"

He didn't finish his thought out loud, working the hammer's claw beneath the nail head to pry it up.

"It's just what?"

"Farm work keeps you fit." He pried one nail loose, then started on the other. "That and patrolling the woods."

Her face scrunched, confused, but she let the matter drop. With one end of the board loosened from its post, she took the other end and pushed, testing the strength of the remaining joint. She patted her sides, lamenting not wearing her belt.

"My hatchets are inside." She pursued with her bare hands, pushing and pulling the board until the nails gave way, her muscles flexed and strained. Then, with one final shove, she finished the task, sending the board to the barn floor with a hollow clatter.

She reached for the hammer but stopped, caught by Fen's shocked expression. There was a slight upward curve of his mouth as his eyes followed the path from her biceps to her shoulders to her eyes. She braced herself for teasing, a reaction she was used to when men witnessed her strength. But the way he looked at her was different. The kind of different that made her insides shift. Some said they felt butterflies in their stomach, which would have been preferable to the squirming within her. This was somehow uncomfortable but not undesirable.

"What?" she asked, though she was afraid of the answer.

"How strong are you?"

She glanced down at her arms, self-consciousness urging her to hide them in her sleeves. "Like you said. Farm work."

"I'm sorry," he blurted, his tone genuine. "I didn't mean to embarrass you."

She scoffed. "Gods, am I that easy to read?"

"I was impressed, but I didn't mean to embarrass you." He rubbed the back of his head, his own chagrin flushing his cheeks a light pink. "And now I'm repeating myself."

The sincerity in his voice helped, though she was all too aware of her arms and shoulders and the power they would bring. "Let's finish up."

"I'll nail the board in place," Fen said, twirling the hammer. With a grin, he added, "You, my strong new acquaintance, can balance it."

"Or we nail one end in place." She took the hammer and didn't hesitate to pin one end of the board with one nail, taking three strikes to bury the iron into the grain before lifting the other end to do the same.

"Gods above, you're incredible."

"And you're a shameless flirt." She passed him the rest of the nails. "Don't drop these. Give me one at a time. *Acquaintance.*"

"Yes, ma'am." He was still grinning. "I like it when you boss me around."

"*Fen.*"

A S THEIR DAY of tasks progressed, Rowan was delighted to learn that chickens and Fen do not mix.

"Gods, they're everywhere."

"Ah! She just attacked me!"

"Stop flapping your wings! You're alright! You're not on the dinner menu tonight! Calm down!"

At last, Rowan laughed, the amusement deep in her core.

"Gods, she attacked me again!"

"Shoo." Rowan bent and ushered the chickens away from him, the sassiest of the hens nearly pecking Rowan's palm. "See if I give you breakfast tomorrow, you grumpy old hag."

"How do you bear it?" Fen used his forearm to wipe the sweat from his brow. "Gods be praised, this coop is finished."

Repairs were minimal, mostly on the roof and one corner where Winter had gnawed through her frustrations at Rowan's recent absence.

Rowan didn't bother hiding her chuckle. "I'll see to the coop myself from now on."

"At least you find this funny." A hint of his own smile returned, one that he seemed to carry often. A defense mechanism? Or a way to charm strangers?

Likely both. Useful when there's something you need to find.

Fen stepped back, the heel of his boot rolling on the crown of a smooth stone embedded in the soft soil. His arms flailed as he tried in vain to regain his balance. Instinct triggered Rowan's hands to grip his wrist and pull, bringing him toward her. Pivoting on the balls of her feet and widening her stance, her other arm braced his back. Neither fell, with Rowan's strength keeping them upright.

As the urgency of the moment passed, they stared, his hand on her bicep, his grip firm. His wide eyes trailed from her arm to her face.

"Gods above," Fen said, slightly breathless. "You really know how to sweep a man off his feet."

Her shock leveled to annoyance. "I will drop you."

She straightened, helping him stand before letting him go.

"Thank you," he said, looking down at the stone and giving it a small kick. It didn't budge. "Funny how I didn't notice that before."

She took the tools and turned for the barn, eager to change the subject. But the one thing she wanted to talk about wasn't easy.

"Not to bring down the mood," Rowan said. "I wanted to ask about your brother."

His expression sobered, the ebullient and even flirtatious glint fading to seriousness. "Have you spoken with Gran?"

"Some."

He nodded. "After dinner, when you and Wil were washing up. She told me the guild found him alive."

"Thank the gods. Have you—" She hesitated, hearing how forward she sounded. "Sorry. I'm prying."

"No, I wanted to ask." He paused. "You're busy with the duties of the Hill and your guardianship over the forest, but..."

"Tell me."

As soon as the words left her lips, she felt the trap give way. Fen's charisma, his easy smile and reassuring presence. They'd finally gotten to her.

So be it.

"Maybe I can help," she added.

"That's what I'm afraid of," he said with a quiet chuckle. "I don't want to be a burden, Rowan. Another person you have to take care of."

"But this will be different, won't it?" Her tone was firm, as though to exert authority over whatever situation Fen would reveal to her. "You won't let me face this alone."

When she met his gaze, she could see his resilience matching hers. "You're right. I won't."

"I won't force you," she said. "If Gran knows, then that's something. But if I can help you and your brother, I will."

"Thank you. I'll tell you everything, but the conversation won't be quick." He aimed a thumb toward Jean's home. "I'm going to see what she has in store for me, then I'll come by when I'm done."

"Alright."

There came that wriggling in her stomach again, her heart joining in on the nervousness. In the excitement.

Maybe Fen didn't set the trap for her to fall into.

Maybe she walked willingly in.

She didn't turn around as he left, focusing too intently on settling the coop and the chickens after their repairs.

Did he look back at her as he walked away?

Thanks to her stubbornness, she would never know.

CHAPTER 11

"Gran?"

But Rowan froze, wincing, as she watched Gran snore, her head lolling to the side as she slept sitting up.

"That's not comfortable." Rowan patted Winter's side before reaching for Gran, taking the woman's frail body into her arms. "Let's lay back, Gran."

Gran groaned, mumbling something unintelligible, her voice barely a hum.

"You can still sleep. I'll have dinner ready when you wake up."

Gran didn't respond, her breathing deep as Rowan settled her on her pillows and covered her. Winter rested her head on Gran's hip, looking from Gran to Rowan.

"Is everything alright?" Rowan asked Winter, stroking her head and massaging behind her ears. "You look troubled."

Rowan tried not to read too much into it. Animals could sense sickness, and Gran had been sick for a long time.

A fortnight is generous.

Rowan took her time washing up, even cleaning her clothing as her wild hair dried in the cool autumn air. Rowan shivered only once, the cold bracing against her warm skin, and ran the clothes through a wringer before hanging them to dry.

With more wood on the fire, she prepared mutton stew, steadily cutting vegetables and meat as Gran slept. Her aged, furrowed brow bore a sign of troubled dreams. Rowan watched and waited, stirring the simmering stew as the broth thickened. Still, Gran slept heavily, despite the noise and smells.

"Sleep should be your respite," Rowan whispered, remembering their conversation from before. Sentinel Hill. Feather and Claw. Wandering Order. "How dare your dreams trouble you."

Whatever Rowan's burdens were, they were also Gran's. She once heard that a problem shared was a problem halved, but the burdens of Sentinel Hill didn't lighten in their sharing. If anything, they were heavier, Rowan's heart weighted with sadness as she watched unease knit across Gran's brow.

Winter whined from her place by Gran's legs before three knocks came. It was Fen, sweat glistening on his forehead.

"I've finished for the evening," he said, aiming a thumb over his shoulder to indicate Jean's home. "Thank you again, Rowan."

"For what? Back-breaking labor and stinky animals?"

"The labor and animals, I can handle." A shadow of his winning smile teased his features. "Do you need anything else tonight?"

"I don't think so." Then, "Are you hungry?"

The question surprised her, but she didn't show it. Instead, she held eye contact, sense memory returning of her hands and arms saving him from falling.

Her insides tangled, the sensation somehow both pleasant and uncomfortable.

He half-shrugged, gesturing vaguely toward the village. "I can get something in town."

"That's not what I asked." She almost laughed at how much she sounded like Gran. "Are you hungry?"

"Yes." He smiled at last, traces of his laugh lines visible through his beard. "Do you have somewhere I can wash up?"

"The well is out back. And there's soap here." She waved for him to follow, leading him through their small living room around Gran's bed and Rowan's mattress and chair. Taking him to the back door, she pulled a honey-colored bar of soap from a shelf.

"Thank you," he said.

It was when she placed the soap in his hand that she noticed the small hole in the side seam of his shirt. But when she pointed it out, he only shrugged.

"It's nothing," he said. "I have coin for a new one."

"We still have some of my grandfather's clothes," she said. "We kept them as spares for Wil and Peter when they help."

"You don't have to."

"I'm giving you a shirt, Fen, and I'll mend this one." She tried to hide her smirk. "You said you liked it when I bossed you around."

He conceded with a quiet laugh, his shoulders relaxing. "Thank you."

"Go ahead to the well. I'll fetch a shirt and towel."

He closed the door quietly behind him as she stepped on tiptoe to her grandparents' room. It smelled like Gran—rose and black tea with traces of her grandfather's pine.

Absences left their marks, with loved ones lingering in shadows of memories.

Would that I could turn back the clock. She swallowed her uneasiness as her hands rifled through a drawer of her grandfather's clothes. *Would that I could stop time.*

She laid her hands on a gray-blue shirt with dark brown leather ties at the v-neck before reaching for the towels stacked in a linen chest. With the bundle in her arms, she crossed the house in silence to the back door. She took a small tin from the shelf, the coins tinkling and sliding inside. A few gold pieces and several silver. How much would be fair to give?

She left the gold and pulled ten silver. That would be plenty for several nights in the tavern with meals. At least he could travel as comfortably as he chose.

Water sloshed as Rowan opened the door. Fen had already soaked his hair, slicked by the water as the ends dripped on his shoulders and back. What drew her attention first were the scars that marked his back. One rounded the curve of his upper arm. Another sliced across his left shoulder blade. When he turned, other marks decorated his chest and stomach, including a recent bruise at his side.

She tried not to stare at the muscles that defined his form, making a conscious effort to look him in the eye. Deep, midnight blue, made more piercing with his wet hair combed back from his face. Water dripped from his hair and beard, beading down his shoulders and chest. He worked his hands over his long arms, corded muscles flexed as his fingertips scrubbed.

Scars marked his torso, several on his side and back, a few on his chest and shoulders. Rowan's eyes drawn to the darker lines. Newer, with evidence of a deep cut on the curve of his left shoulder reaching over the joint of his arm as though something attempted to cut it off. He'd already removed the stitches, the line straight and even as the wound healed, but it would leave yet another mark on his already lined body. What sort of hell had he been through?

"This soap smells incredible," he said. "Like jasmine and honey."

"You have a good nose." She laid the shirt, towel, and coins on a small table holding a flower pot full of blooming skydrop. The silver pieces shimmered pleasantly. "Do you like mutton stew?"

"It's one of my favorites." He massaged soap around his fingernails, the sun glistening off the beading water on his skin. "I'm nearly finished."

"Busy day?"

Rowan nearly jumped at Jean's approach. Jean's eyes went from Fen to Rowan, a single eyebrow lifting almost imperceptibly.

Almost.

"Just here checking on Cynthia," Jean said. "I heard you outside."

"Fen helped with the barn and the coop." Rowan hated how flushed her face had become beneath Jean's perceptive gaze. "We have mutton stew if you're hungry."

"I'm fine." Smirking, Jean nodded to Fen. "I've got your room ready."

"Thank you. I'll return after supper."

"No rush." Mischief toyed with the corners of Jean's mouth. "Take your time."

Jean met Rowan's eye with a wink before turning back for home.

Fen dried off, rubbing his hair and skin before draping the towel on the well beside his shirt. "Your kindness means a lot. Traveling hasn't been easy."

"Of course." She could think of nothing else to say, her eyes playing a dangerous game as they flicked back and forth to the scars and lines of his chest. "Let's eat."

Fen ducked into the borrowed shirt and followed her inside. Winter looked up from her place beside Gran, wagging her tail.

"Is she pure wolf?" Fen asked.

"She is." Rowan prepared his bowl first, setting it on the table. "She was the smallest of her litter and malnourished. The matriarch and her mother gave me permission to take her to save her life."

"Gods. That kind of trust is incredible."

She nodded, taking her bowl of stew and sitting across from Fen at the table. "And their trust is something I treasure. I work to earn it every time I enter the forest."

They took their first bites, the meal hot and savory and satisfying.

"This is good." With a smirk, Fen added, "I didn't take you for a cook."

"What do you mean?" Then, "Did Gran tell you?"

He pressed his hand to his mouth to keep from laughing louder. "I meant no offense. And no, she didn't tell me. Why?" His dark eyes shimmered in the firelight as he studied her. "Are you a bad cook?"

Her nose twitched as she stirred her supper. "This is edible, is it not?"

"It's good, Rowan."

She prepared a bite. "It's Peter's recipe."

"Truly, I meant no offense." Amusement flattered his eyes. "You're a fighter. A guardian. Domestic tasks are difficult to keep as a priority while balancing other responsibilities."

"You're speaking from experience." Rowan chewed a bite of mutton, glancing at Gran while she slept. Winter remained beside her but didn't break her gaze from the pair of them eating.

Gran's hand twitched, brows still knit together. Whatever she was dreaming hadn't relinquished its hold.

"Do you want to talk about it?" he asked.

"About what?" Though she had an inkling from the way he watched her.

"Everything is heavier when you carry it alone."

"Funny. I was thinking of that very thing earlier today." She stared into the stew, the rich brown broth swirling as her spoon moved among the carrots and onions. "Her last sickness took a lot out of her."

"You have a lot of herbs here. I assume you've given her gravebloom and hell's dagger?"

She quirked a brow. "You know those remedies?"

He half-shrugged. "I've learned a lot on my travels." He took another bite of stew.

"And where have you been in your life so far?"

After swallowing, a corner of his mouth lifted. "A change in subject." He leaned back, demeanor at ease. "Recently, Alvar. I'd never been before. It was so *green*." He paused. "I've been to Kema and Ashlands. East Ileden. And now, Thurin."

"If I'm prying, please tell me, but I'm curious about how you're able to travel this way. To see the world like this."

He didn't seem devoid of responsibility, but his obligations were different from hers. Even if, for a moment, she wanted to hear his stories to live vicariously.

"It's not prying, though my answer isn't exciting." He wiped his mouth and lifted his cup of water. "I'm—"

Gran groaned, shifting where she slept. Discomfort deepened the lines around her eyes and mouth.

"Gran?" Rowan rose, taking her hand and touching her forehead. "You're so cold."

Winter whined, edging closer.

Fen moved beside her. "Where are your blankets?"

"Linen chest in the room on the left. And I have one folded on the bed frame in my room, on the right."

Fen brought a blanket, and they dressed Gran's bed once Winter climbed down against her will.

"She senses something," Rowan said as Winter returned to Gran's side.

Fen didn't respond, resting a hand on the wolf's back. Winter sighed, eyeing Gran.

"Do you have lady's ivy?" he asked. "We could make a tea and help her drink."

"For the pain." Rowan's voice struggled, the tightness in her throat choking her. "Yes. Let's do that."

Grateful for a task, Rowan prepared the vine's leaves as Fen boiled water.

"How much should I use?" she asked.

"Here." He took the dried leaves and put them in the mortar for grinding. His actions were practiced and precise. Likely feeling her questioning stare, he said, "This is a necessary life skill when you're traveling and may not reach an apothecary."

Gran groaned again, mumbling incoherent words as Rowan took her hand, sitting beside her.

"What is it?" Rowan asked. "What's wrong?"

"Failed." Gran grimaced as though crying. "*Failed.*"

"Failed what?" Her hand was so cold. "Tell me."

Tears fell from Gran's closed eyes. She said nothing else, the discomfort holding strong.

"How do I reach you?" Rowan whispered. "How do I make it better?"

Pain gripped her. "Read—"

"Here." Fen held a steaming cup in his hands, a spoon resting inside. "We'll help her."

Carefully, Fen eased Gran upright, and Rowan fed her small sips of tea, blowing gently on each steaming spoonful. Soon, the herbal blend did its work, offering respite. Without being asked, Fen cleared the dishes and washed them at the well, bringing in a fresh bucket of cool water for the afternoon. He moved here and there, with Rowan staying by Gran's side.

"Read—"

Gran's journal was a small leather-bound book, its cover soft from age and touch.

"She wrote about Marc," Rowan said, showing Fen the page where the single sentence was written. "That's his name, right?"

"You remember." He looked over her shoulder, then at Gran.

"She carried a lot of guilt," Rowan said. "About the two of you."

"What do you mean?"

"She wanted you here." Rowan closed the journal, pressing it between her hands. "She regretted you staying in Runa. She said you were so young."

"Mark was fourteen," he said. "I was fifteen. I suppose we were just kids."

"And you were with Captain Quenvar."

"On the *Sea Phantom*."

Rowan knew that name, though she couldn't place where. She'd never known Quenvar's ship, nor had she cared to. So why was the name familiar?

Gran relaxed, her breathing deep, but Rowan didn't leave her side. Remembering Fen, Rowan said, "You're kind to stay, but you don't have to."

"I've been where you are," he said. "The waiting is agony. But I...I could go, if you would prefer to be alone."

No. But would he be uncomfortable? "Your company is appreciated, Fen, but I won't burden you with this."

"It's not a burden." Honesty carried his voice through the sadness that flooded her thoughts. "I know the depth of this sadness, Rowan. I didn't want to be alone, either." He paused, giving her time and space. "Would you like me to stay?"

"Yes."

He settled in the chair, quietly watching as Gran mumbled something in her sleep, her lips moving, barely shaping around whatever words she wanted to say.

Gran exhaled, the reach of air deep, her chest falling and falling and falling.

Fen stood as Rowan stared.

Gran's chest didn't rise again.

Gran. Rowan's mouth formed around her name, but no sound

escaped. Only the sob that choked her, seizing her chest, her breath catching.

Her parents, gone.

Gran, gone.

And Rowan, alone.

"Rowan." Fen rested a hand on her shoulder. "I'm so sorry."

Rowan buried her face in her hands and wept.

CHAPTER 12

Rowan stared, eyes bleary and unfocused, mind flooded with a single truth, washing away all other thoughts.

Gran was gone.

Rowan held her hand tighter, rubbing her aged skin, pushing in warmth, pushing in *life*. Futility gripped at her chest and throat despite her mind stubbornly rationalizing this wasn't the end, that her life wasn't over.

But her body was still, cooling as the seconds passed. Her soul had gone to be with Rowan's parents. With Rhiann and Anya. Her soul basked in the glory of light and radiance and love.

But the light that illuminated Gran's soul was the same that cast a shadow over Rowan, the tidal wave of emotion too large to escape, the impact inevitable.

A fortnight is generous.

Rowan choked out a sob, burying her face against Gran's body, her weeping muffled by blankets. Her chest seized, breathing a labor as the icy cavern within her chest ached. Grief swept over the gaping wound with an impartial hand, reminding her that no living thing was immune from loss.

When Wil's hand touched Rowan's shoulder, she gasped, eyes

meeting his, hers filling with tears. She hadn't heard him come in, hadn't heard their whispered voices or delicate footsteps. Emotion ran loud in her ears, blood rushing to keep the well of emotion from overflowing. Her face was too hot, her body too cold. She wanted to run, paws thundering against the earth, and never look back.

"All shall turn, and all shall fade," Jean recited, touching Gran's hand. "All things are, and all things will be."

At the tug of emotion in her throat, Rowan turned, giving her eyes and ears something else to focus on. Peter stood a few paces back, offering a tear-streaked smile. Fen lingered by the front door as Winter waited on the bed, alert to the emotions in the room.

"Thank you for coming to us," Peter said to Fen. Rowan hadn't realized he'd gone.

"Of course."

"The plot beside Grandpa," Rowan whispered, recalling what Gran had often said. "I have to plant daffodils. They were her favorite."

Wil hugged her, his warmth and pressure grounding her, reminding her she was still among the living.

"Cynthia, Johann, Beth, and Simon," Jean said. "Reunited."

It was a small comfort as Rowan pictured her parents and grandfather embracing Gran, their spirits together again in Anya's radiant light.

"We have to bury her," Rowan said. "Gran told us not to linger."

"And she'll have cross words if we disobey." Jean chuckled as tears fell, her mouth turned down with trembling lips. "Oh, Cynthia."

Fen whispered something to Peter before stepping out, closing the door silently behind him. Rowan knew his absence but didn't blame him for it. She couldn't imagine his discomfort around someone else's loss and grief, an outsider looking in. But his warmth had reached her.

Jean sniffled, wiping her eyes. "She never lived to see her work fulfilled. I think that's what has me so upset. All the work she's done—"

She stopped, steadying her breath.

"Feather and Claw will thrive because of her," Wil said.

"And because of you." She smiled through her sadness, tears filling her crow's feet and laugh lines. "Cynthia was so proud of all of you."

Rowan's eyes were sore and her head was pounding. The scents of home were too strong. The air, too warm.

Peter appeared beside her with a cup of water. "Drink, love." He spread a broad hand on her back. "Little sips."

She obeyed, the relief slow. "She wants us to help Fen's brother."

"Marc," Jean said. To Wil and Peter, she clarified with, "He was captured by a dangerous Preceptor for the Wandering Order."

"*Dangerous Preceptor* is like saying *wet water*," Wil said. Peter snickered. "He made it out alive?"

"He did," Jean said, "but far from whole."

Rowan imagined him missing limbs, his body mutilated by the maligned evil touch of the Wandering Order.

"He was tortured," Jean went on. "Forced to undergo experiments with mist arcana. His mind—" She stopped herself before continuing. "He barely survived, physically and mentally. One of our Phantoms is with him."

"You have a *spy* caring for him?" Peter asked. "How is that going to help him?"

"Mirelyn is gifted in many things," Jean said, "including shadow craft and healing."

"Mirelyn," Wil said her name with reverence. "The chaosborn."

"And her son has recently joined our ranks." Jean crossed her arms. "Marc is in good, capable hands, but his journey toward recovery has only just begun."

"Fen," Rowan said. "Has he seen him?"

Jean shook her head. "Upon Marc's wishes. He's afraid." Jean pressed her lips together, looking at Rowan. "May I speak freely?"

"Of course."

"I mean as the Veil."

The Veil, second to the Cornerstone.

The Cornerstone. *Rowan*. The title passed down from Gran to her.

When Rowan didn't answer right away, Jean added, "The guild falls to you."

"It shouldn't have," Rowan blurted, panic fluttering in her core. "You know more than I do. It should be you."

But Jean shook her head. "Cynthia wanted it to be you."

Disappointment furrowed Jean's brow before her expression smoothed. Rowan's chest tightened.

"Wil and Peter are in the guild," Rowan said. "Shouldn't they know?"

"I'm still an Acolyte," Peter said. "New to the group, still learning."

"But Wil is a Phantom," Rowan said. "Wouldn't he already know the members?"

"Only if knowing doesn't compromise them," he said. "Mom's the Veil, your second."

Your second. Second-in-command. Rowan's thoughts were swimming, and she nearly drowned beneath the shame of all she hadn't done. But Sentinel Hill was her task with Elderglen, allowing Gran and the guild to work. She'd had a job, too, all this time.

"Speak freely," Rowan said, "if you think it wise."

But Jean reconsidered, wincing slightly as she used her index finger to rub circles against her thumbnail, a nervous tic Wil had picked up, too. "He should tell you himself. I'll tell him to speak with you directly."

Wil sighed with a growl. "Leave it to Mom to dangle the carrot only to yank it away."

Hours passed, Rowan's body aware of its fatigue while her mind held it upright in consciousness, like a scarecrow attached to its poll with dry-rotted flannel and twine. Her loved ones moved around the room, speaking to her or to one another, Rowan vaguely aware of her own responses. Her thoughts swarmed around nothing and everything, sometimes taking the shape of people or things, sometimes adopting voices that echoed in whispers.

Warmth spread over her shoulder, reaching through muscle and blood, pulling her from untethered space to tangible freedom. She blinked slowly, her eyes hot and dry as though she'd slept with them open. Maybe she had.

Jean kissed Rowan's temple. "It's time, love."

Her touch was gentle, her words soft, but they slapped Rowan back into the present. Dawn had come, the arching sun peeking over the horizon.

It's time, love.

Time to bury the dead.

CHAPTER 13

By the time Rowan had made the arrangements, the sun had risen well into the morning. The lumber mill had a coffin ready, one of average height that would suit Gran. All that was left was the burial linen. Gran had chosen a deep forest green to match Rowan's eyes.

"I refuse the white they always use," she'd said. "So help me, Rowan. I will haunt you to the end of your days."

Being haunted by Gran wouldn't be so bad. But Rowan's rational mind won out, fulfilling Gran's choice to allow her spirit peace.

Her final errand was with the florist, who had a few daffodils for sale. Rowan bought them, as well as several seeds.

But with her buying both coffin and shroud, news traveled quickly. Condolences became a murmur of voices in Rowan's mind, leaving her unable to discern specific words, forcing her to understand nuance and intent. She hadn't had time to think of the next step, following the motions of what others had said, of what Gran had wanted.

She will be missed.

Burial beside Grandpa.

I'm sorry for your loss.

Forest green shroud.

My condolences, Rowan.

Daffodils.

She held onto concrete tasks leading up to the ceremony. Each one grounded her in consciousness, keeping her hands and feet moving lest she stop and allow her thoughts to surround her.

Why am I so calm? She'd expected more tears. She'd expected a hole where her heart should be. But there was only the next task. There was only moving forward.

Wil, Rowan, and Jean had wrapped Gran before Peter lovingly carried her out to the burial site, where Fen and the miller had dug. Her body looked so small in his arms, his wide shoulders broad as he stood tall with the honor of laying her to rest. There was a crowd surrounding the hill, all of them with lilies and poppies in their hands.

For remembrance, Rowan thought. She held the daffodils closer to her chest.

Winter stayed close, keeping pace with Rowan's every step. Thunder rumbled in the distance, and many remarked that Erys greeted Gran with open arms.

"A good omen," someone said.

"Rain blesses the dead," another added. "She's home."

Rowan stared, emotionless. *She's home.*

No. Home was what her spirit left behind. Brick and flower and flame.

And Rowan.

She closed her eyes, praying for forgiveness even though guilt hadn't touched her. Her mind would speak, for her heart could not be trusted. Gran had earned her passage home, but Rowan's heart longed to pull her back.

"Blessed is she whom the rain falls on."

"The goddesses welcome her home."

Another rumble of thunder, this time closer.

Peter laid Gran in the coffin, the ropes ready, and he, Wil, Fen, and Rowan all lifted them to lower her into the ground. The marker was wide and carved from stone, bearing her grandparents' names. Now, Gran would reside next to her beloved beneath the stone etching of *Cynthia* and her title: *Watcher of Sentinel Hill.*

She was so much more. Rowan lowered the coffin steadily, matching pace with the others as the rope burned her hands. *So much more than Watcher or Cornerstone.*

Mother. Grandmother. Friend.

Rowan's own guardian.

But that was over.

The coffin reached the bottom. The silence that followed was both a reprieve and a burden.

"Elderglen was blessed to know her." Jean's voice carried, the stillness before the coming storm lifting her words.

A few murmured agreement.

"Without Cynthia and Johann, Elderglen would not have Sentinel Hill. Without her legacy, we would be a very different village. And I would be a very different woman." Jean's eyes misted, and her voice struggled. "She was my dearest friend, and we all are better for having known her."

When Jean finished, the village looked to Rowan. A hush fell over them as they waited. Even with the expectations and anticipation, there was nothing that could have prepared Rowan for the swirling within her. The words were slow to come, her mind far too congested with images and feelings to give them voice.

She took a breath and recited,

The wind is the breath of the dead.

Sunlight, the warm touch of souls to soothe the living.

Thunder, the voices to beg remembrance.

Rain, their grief for those left behind.

Jean nodded. Wil and Peter touched her back before they each wrapped an arm around her. Fen stood with one hand grasping the opposite wrist, sadness heavy in his gaze.

"She was strong," Wil said, "and she was loyal. She loved Elderglen, and she would be honored to have you all here. Thank you for loving her."

Thank you for loving her.

Rowan's throat tightened, warm eyes itching.

Thank you for loving her.

This time, the thunder came with rain. Wil, Peter, Jean, and Fen moved handfuls and shovelfuls of dirt over the coffin. Rowan crouched to join them, Winter whining and shaking her coat as the rain fell.

Rowan's hands were red and raw and aching. Her back and shoulders were taut and tense, her body exhausted. But as they finished filling and covering the grave, Rowan stood and stared at the headstone, eyes tracing the letters of her grandmother's name.

The rain fell upon her, but it didn't touch her. Rowan's body was numb to every drop, her thoughts moving so quickly that the world stood still.

Watcher.

Guardian.

Cornerstone.

I'm not ready.

I will never be ready.

A hand touched her back, bringing her back to life. The cold of the rain reached her at last, making her shiver as she turned to Fen. Winter's head was tucked beneath his other hand as she leaned against his side. "It's done."

Rowan's mouth curved to a sad smile, meeting Winter's eyes. "She likes you."

"The feeling is mutual," he said. "Let's get you both inside."

Rowan let Fen lead her, his hand gentle as it took hers. Both were dirty with soil from the burial, the rain steadily washing them clean. The walk was brief, but her disarray slowed all movement. The events of the day blurred together into a gray haze.

Blessed is she whom the rain falls on.

Rain, the grief for those left behind.

But all the rain gave was a cold weight that made it difficult to move.

"Towels in the linen chest?" Fen asked.

"You remember." Still holding his hand, she led him around to the back door. Their footsteps sloshed in their boots. Rain tapped from the roof in a thudding rhythm, out of sync with the droplets from their clothes that pattered on the steps, then the floor as they moved.

Winter's paws tapped behind them, following them to the corridor of rooms. Rowan had the presence of mind to take another one of her grandfather's shirts and a pair of his trousers, though the waist was wider than Fen's.

Fen had two towels in his hands as Rowan laid out her grandfather's clothes. "We'll dry your clothes by the fire."

"You don't have to."

"I want to." She turned for the hallway again, eager to peel the cold wet fabric that tightened around her. "I'll give you some privacy."

Rowan slipped into her modest bedroom, a space lately only used for clothes since Gran—

She banished the thought with much the same avoidance as her eyes skimming past Gran's bed. Changing quickly, her trousers and shirt were soft and dry, offering some comfort as the numbness lingered. With wet clothes in her arms, she padded barefoot back to the fire. Fen had pulled the dry trousers to his waist when she entered, his upper half still bare. Scars painted pink lines across his chest and shoulders, the color bright against his cold, pallid skin.

"Sorry." She spun around. "I didn't give you enough time."

"It's alright." There was a hint of amusement in his voice. He tied his trousers in place. "You can turn around."

She did, face warming as he remained shirtless, passing her his wet clothes. "I'll add wood to the fire."

He ducked into the dry shirt before tossing pieces of wood into the hearth. Rowan pulled the drying rack from the wall and draped each piece of clothing upon it. The flame slowly grew taller, the room warming. She watched him, remembering his connection to Feather and Claw and why he was there.

"Jean told me about Marc," she said. "About what they did."

He didn't respond right away, locking eyes with her, concern heavy in his gaze.

"I don't know how to hold everything, Fen." She looked down at her hands, their rich coloring having paled from the cold. "Someone killed my parents two years ago, and we think it was someone in Moonblade."

"Gran said that?"

Rowan nodded. "The pieces fit, but there isn't much else to go on. And I thought I was alright. But now—" Her fingers curled, her fists tight, her knuckles going white. "Are they still out there? Is Valera protecting them?"

"Valera?" He stepped closer, taking her hands and gently urging her fingers to unfurl. "Is she involved?"

"She came that day. She said they thought my parents were cultists." Her lips pulled back, her anger surging. But a lick of cold swept up her back, startling her to the present moment. "I'm going to find them."

He held her hands as silence passed between them, gently rubbing her fingers to warm them. Fen took a towel and squeezed the ends of Rowan's braid, its length having soaked a stripe of moisture over her shoulder. "Would you like your hair undone? To let it dry?"

Rowan nodded, hands reaching for the tie, but Fen's fingers already tugged at the leather cord, the knot pulling free as the ends of the braid unraveled. He worked the braid loose carefully, Rowan shivering as the back of her neck tingled.

She regarded with him an unspoken question, their proximity closer than she realized. The firelight shimmered like liquid in the depths of his eyes, which held her without fear, as though willing her to show him every secret corner of her heart.

She opened her mouth to speak when two knocks came to the door. *Jean.* The rain had lightened as she let her in, Wil and Peter in her wake, all of them holding up cloth shields against the weather.

"How long will this storm carry on?" Jean smiled with her eyes. "Makes me nostalgic for noodles and gravy."

"We don't have—"

Peter touched the satchel strapped across his chest. "You do now. Oh, the fire's good and hot. Excellent."

Jean took Fen's hand in both of hers. "You'll join us, won't you?"

Fen glanced from Rowan to Wil to Jean. "I appreciate it, but I should—"

"It's not only out of the goodness of my heart, Fen," Jean said. "You're a Vanguard. The guild looks out for its own."

But Wil's frustration mounted, and Rowan understood why. She hadn't trusted Fen either, not when he first arrived. She could tell there was something more to him, aspects of his intentions that he was slow to reveal if he should reveal them at all.

"Supper, then." Peter gave Winter the nub of a raw carrot, looking at his husband and nodding once with quiet reassurance.

"I'll stay with you tonight," Wil said to Rowan.

But the idea made Rowan tense. Even as they were her loved ones, she wanted nothing more than quiet and solitude. Her home was already too full, the walls too close.

Guilt soured in her stomach. "You don't—"

"I was going to as well," Jean said. "I suppose we're all thinking the same thing."

Wil's gaze was steady. "We don't want to leave you alone."

"I'm not alone." Rowan reached to touch Winter, who still dutifully watched Peter as he cooked.

"Let's not crowd her any worse than we already are," Peter said. "And, at the very least, you're not sleeping on the floor."

Peter left the chopped vegetables and bent for Rowan's mattress where it lay by Gran's bed. Fen hurried to help and, with Jean's guidance, put the mattress on the bed frame in Rowan's room.

"The offer stands," Jean said from the bedroom doorway. Rowan listened to the sounds of Peter and Fen adjusting the mattress. "But we won't force you."

"We were thinking about you in this empty house," Wil said. "It's a different home now. It was like that when my father died."

She looked up at her best friend. "You really don't leave much of a choice, do you?"

He draped an arm across her shoulders and pulled her close, resting his head on hers. "We're going to love you whether you like it or not."

CHAPTER 14

Rowan awoke with a start, heart racing, fear and dread coursing through her blood. But she didn't remember the dream, only the dread it left behind.

Her eyes adjusted to the dark as she brought a hand to her forehead, clammy and cool. Winter whined, resting her head on Rowan's stomach.

"I'm alright." Rowan exhaled, stroking Winter's head and neck. "Good girl."

She closed her eyes, but rest would remain elusive now. The previous day filled her mind, sense memory conjuring the cold touch and hissing sound of rain.

Winter exhaled.

"You too, huh?" Rowan sat up, swinging her legs over the side of the bed. It was time for a midnight run. "Let's go."

Even with little sleep, the moon's touch invigorated her, sinking into her skin and soaking into her blood. When she shifted, her fur glistened with moon-white shimmers across the dark brown and black that covered her.

"Rowan," Winter said. "I miss her."

"I do, too."

"Her scent is everywhere." Winter uttered a quiet, mournful howl. "She's not there, but I can still smell her."

Emotion swelled within, and Rowan nuzzled Winter's ear. They slipped down the hill before breaking into a run, the cold air of night filling their lungs and combing through their fur. When they broke through the trees, the dense embrace of the woods sheltered them as they howled together in mourning. The wolves heard and joined them, their grief filling the night.

"She was strong," one wolf said, though Rowan didn't see them. "And she was loved."

The wolves granted Rowan and Winter solitude as they grieved and ran, pushing their bodies through the emotions they couldn't otherwise express.

Interesting that Rowan wept in front of Fen with no reservation or embarrassment. Interesting that a stranger seamlessly passed into friendship. Once distrusted, now accepted. A stranger who was not a stranger at all.

A Vanguard. One who moved in where it was most dangerous to help fight against the Wandering Order. It would explain the fearless way he met her eyes and held her with nothing but his gaze.

She and Winter ran among trees and brush until pleasant tiredness settled in. Both slowed, panting, the weight of the world much lighter than before.

"Home?" Winter asked.

"Home."

But they were slow to leave the shelter of the trees, the calls of the ravens wishing them farewell. But Rowan picked up a scent, now familiar. *Fen.* He was close, and Winter sensed him, too.

"Friend," she said, trotting toward him.

He was lying on his back, the blanket of stars above him shimmering as he watched. He sat up abruptly at their approach, his alarm easing to relief. "Winter?" Then, meeting Rowan's eyes, he recognized her. "And Rowan. The strongest woman in Thurin."

"Racing heart," Winter said. "Blood rushing. But he doesn't seem afraid."

"We did just scare the daylights out of him."

Winter chuckled, the sound a grumble in her throat.

Rowan shifted, closing the distance between them. "Can't sleep?"

"I was about to ask you that." Their gazes lingered before Fen gestured next to him. "Join me."

"I don't want to disturb you."

Moonlight shimmered in his dark eyes, their depths fathomless, a galaxy all their own. "Disturb me."

She stared, making him chuckle.

"You're welcome if you want to stay." He joined his hands behind his head. "The stars are strong enough to bear both our worries. I was just telling them about Cynthia."

She sat, nearly asking him what he'd said, but he continued without being prompted.

"I met her when I was a lot younger than I am now. Full of rage and nowhere to put it."

Rowan understood what that was like.

"My brother and I were glad to have an outlet," he said. "The guild gave us a purpose, fighting against the very thing that—"

He stopped, his demeanor changing while he tried to maintain nonchalance.

"Sorry." He tilted his head as he looked up at her. "I miss her. And I tend to over-share."

"You can tell me anything," she said, lying back on the cool grass. "Just like you said. The stars are strong enough to carry both of us." She added, "I, too, have a lot of rage and nowhere to put it."

Quiet passed between them. She nearly said, "Tell me what burdens you," proving her care to know, but etiquette kept the question hidden within herself.

Etiquette. *Propriety.* Words to cement the bricks in place as humans closed themselves within their walls of fear, keeping things out.

But Rowan's cage didn't keep things out. It kept things *in.* Even still, she allowed herself to relax, stretching out beside Fen as Winter joined, walking in the narrow space between them and lying down. She put her weight on their sides, unapologetic as they groaned and laughed.

Fen touched Winter's head, meeting her eyes. "Her heart is full of love, and I am humbled to receive it."

They rested in comfortable silence, the stars twinkling as the breeze whispered its cool, soothing lullaby.

"It's difficult for me to sleep indoors," Fen said at last. "I'm used to sky and stars and moonlight."

"Really?" Something he and Rowan had in common. "Why is that?"

"I worked on a ship for a long time. The stink of the crew below deck was enough to kill a grown man. Sleeping up top was for my own survival."

Rowan laughed, surprised by the lightness in her chest. She turned her head to watch his profile as he regarded the stars.

"And south, around Runa, you want the breeze." He sighed, his look wistful. "Those were some of the clearest nights." He swept a hand toward the sky. "You could see everything."

"Even with the smell of drying seaweed?"

"You get used to it." He rested his hand on his stomach, the other still behind his head. "When I smell it now, it reminds me of home."

The way he spoke, the way his eyes took in the stars, the way his mouth moved...

She studied the silhouette of his face, the plain of his forehead, the peaks of his nose and chin, against the dark background of night.

"I miss it," he said. "I wonder if I'll ever brave the seas again."

"Apprenticed to a blacksmith. Crewman on a ship." She tucked her arm beneath her head as a pillow. "What else have you done?"

He hesitated before answering, a note of sadness in his voice. "That sums it up. After our village was destroyed, my brother and I traveled until we reached Runa. Then we kept going."

Rowan perked up at the mention of Fen's brother. "He was on the ship with you?"

"For a time, with Captain Quenvar. Our paths separated and were reunited."

His brow furrowed as he shared the memory with the stars. Alongside his sadness was grief. And perhaps regret.

Rowan read the stories of the goddesses in the constellations—the burning of the Ashlands, the battle at Storm Seat, the union of Shanna and Brena. Connecting the dots to form lines in the sky brought the memory of Fen's scars to her mind, seeing them trace across his body with cruel reminders of past experiences.

"Before, when we came in from the rain—" She hesitated, cheeks warming against the cold touch of night.

"Yes?" He turned on his side. "When we were wet and freezing?"

"I saw…"

Embarrassed, she didn't pull her eyes from the sky, though she could feel the phantom touch of his gaze.

"You saw my scars."

She nodded, finally meeting his eyes. "You don't have to tell me, but I would lie if I said I wasn't curious."

"I don't mind you asking," he said, his voice quiet, almost personal. As though he specifically meant *her*.

He sat up and pulled his shirt over his head, his bare chest and shoulders radiant in the moonlight. She nearly gasped aloud, her mouth parting, but her intake of breath was quiet as the wind swept past them.

"This one?" He touched a horizontal line across his left clavicle. "A sword slipped while I was apprenticing."

"*Ouch.*"

"It took my master almost an hour to stitch it closed." He touched one near his heart. "This one was a bar fight in Kema. The bastard had a hidden blade in his fist. Luckily, he was too drunk, or that would have killed me."

"And this one?" Rowan reached a hand, pointing to a long line on his right side, reaching from his ribs around to his back, toward his hip. The end of it disappeared into the waist of his trousers. "What on earth did that?"

"Believe it or not, a grappling hook from the ship." He smirked, touching her hand. "Here. Feel it."

Her breathing caught as he guided her to the scar, pressing her fingertips to the beveled line that adorned his side. He guided her toward his back, following the curve.

Don't look in his eyes. Don't look in his eyes.

She kept her gaze trained on where he led her hand, her cheeks burning.

"Right…*there.*"

Something hard had embedded into his skin. "What *is* that?"

Gods be praised, her voice was somehow level and smooth. Her heart thundered within her ribs as though Erys's power fueled it.

"The tip of one of the hooks had broken," he said. "It was a long time before I reached a proper doctor to remove it. He said the scar tissue would stay like this."

"They healed well," she said, her mind and heart flooded with wordless emotions, manifesting in the warmth of her face, neck, and hands.

"But they're startling if you've never seen them before."

She knew he regarded her with a curiosity that, in her embarrassment, she ignored, averting her gaze as she turned back to the nighttime horizon.

"Rowan?"

"Hm?" She ran her hand down Winter's side, her fur soft.

"Have I—" He hesitated. "Have I done something?"

"No." She chanced a glance at him, risked a reassuring smile, but the light captured him—his eyes, his beard, his nose—making it difficult not to stare and trace every line and curve. "No. Why?"

He ducked into his shirt, the air thinning to normal. "I didn't make you uncomfortable? Because that's the last thing I want—"

"No," she said quickly, wincing as she interrupted him. "No, but I —I've never—"

When she struggled with the words, Fen asked, "You've never seen a man's bare chest before?" He raised an eyebrow in disbelief. "But your friendship with Wil. You know, summers at the lake, swimming. Meeting and beating every challenge."

"No, that's—"

That's different. But the words failed her.

"Was it my scars?" he asked. "I know they're upsetting."

"I'm not upset," she whispered. "You're not upsetting, Fen."

He leaned closer, one palm on the grass to steady him as he read her eyes. The star-studded sky became a magnificent backdrop for the man before her. She didn't breathe, didn't move. The cool ground beneath her was the only thing holding her in reality. Then, slowly, he brought a hand to her hair. Gently, he pulled a thin twig from the tangle of curls near her ear. Tingles cascaded down her spine.

"That's the second time you've removed the forest from my hair," she said with a quiet laugh. Her voice trembled only slightly. "You'd think we were the same."

"You are. All of its strength and beauty."

Heat flooded her face and neck.

"It must feel great to run," he said, leaning back, his hands propping him upright. "After the stress of recent days."

"There's nothing like it." After a moment, sensing his gentleness leaning toward her grief, she lay back down. "I promise I'm alright." She swept her hair from behind her neck and shoulders, splaying it over the ground above her head. "You don't have to worry."

"It's alright if you're not." His voice was warm, the sound equivalent of a soothing touch. "I wouldn't be. Far from it."

Gran. Elderglen. The monster that haunted their woods.

Fen lay beside her, Winter still between them. The silence carried them for a time.

Rowan breathed easier, something close to trust forging between her and this stranger from everywhere and nowhere.

"I'm torn between two worlds," she said. "One where I am Watcher, and one where I am wolf. I don't know how I can leave Elderglen." Her whispered confession carried up to the sky. "After everything—"

Her words stopped short, her breath catching in her chest.

"Not every villager here is a fool," he said. "But enough of them make an already challenging job even more difficult."

"Their stupidity only makes the burden heavier," she said. "What if..."

The words dangled, untethered, as Rowan nearly set adrift in the sea of possibility. Then, at last, she gave it voice.

"What if there was no Watcher?"

Fen turned his head. "They would have to bear the responsibility themselves."

So simple, and yet Rowan could already hear their protests, their swears and curses, blaming her for abandoning them. As she'd been abandoned.

But the idea held freedom, intangible and limitless. The longing touched her heart with its cold, bitter sting, leaving the warmth of hope to linger deep within.

"You shouldn't bind yourself to them."

"But I am bound, Fen. I am bound."

"You bind yourself." His words were soft while bearing the strength of belief. "No one else would dare to keep you tethered."

Freedom. Limitlessness.

Responsibility. Expectation.

Her heart, tugged by opposing factions, strained as it throbbed within her chest. They watched the sky together in silence, Winter's gentle snoring the only sound between them.

Sleep for her came softly, rest easing its way into her muscles and bones. The night soothed her. The night...and Fen.

When she awoke, Fen was gone. The quiet morning came to her in solitude with Winter's warm body by her side.

But the dawn breeze carried the scent of blood, sickly and sweet and metallic.

Rowan's skin prickled, her insides unsettled as she inhaled with focus. Something was wrong.

She shifted, sinking her claws into the cold, damp earth as she ran.

CHAPTER 15

Winter ran beside her, her tension palpable as their breath came fast and bodies sailed around the trees.

"Blood," Winter said. "It happened before the sun came."

"Did you hear anything?"

"Some. Distress from the wolves. But your sleep was troubled."

"You didn't want to wake me?"

Winter didn't get the chance to answer as a wolf's cry came from within the trees. They ran harder, the frigid breath of the woods entering their lungs as they navigated around trees and brush. The metallic perfume of blood was stronger, fresher.

It's close. Winter sounded as determined as Rowan.

Branches and broken stems, crushed leaves and flowers, disarray across the forest floor. Something fought the wolves, but there was no body.

"How did it manage to escape?" Rowan asked.

"Guardian." The matriarch's voice was distressed. "Please come."

"What foe did they face?" Winter asked as they moved toward the wolf den. "It must be formidable to survive the pack."

Formidable didn't feel enough for what Rowan feared they would find.

They reached the den to see the wolves pacing and nervous. Several whined in a blend of pain and panic.

"A fiend of dark magic came. None are dead, but several are hurt." The matriarch kept her worried eyes on her mate. "His injury is worse."

Rowan stepped close, hearing the patriarch's distress, his left hind leg not sitting correctly in the joint at his hip.

"It looks dislocated." Rowan held the wolf's brown-eyed gaze. "I can help you, but I must be human."

"Thank you, Guardian," he said, whining as he gave permission.

"It will hurt, but the pain will pass."

"I trust you."

Rowan shifted, hands trembling. *I trust you.* The weight she bore grew heavier with each passing day, even as pride warmed her heart and blood. She'd earned their trust, and she would honor it.

Carefully, she placed her hands on his hip, feeling through fur and skin. He growled in pain, teeth bared.

"I feel it," she whispered. "Brace yourself. On the count of three." She set her hands around his leg and hip. "One—"

She shoved the bone back in place, the pop sickening. The patriarch snarled and snapped, and successive shouts overwhelmed her.

"Hey!" From the trees, Fen raced through, arrow nocked and aimed at the patriarch.

Alarm resounded through the forest, the wolves gathering around their injured leader, his mate leading them.

"No!" Rowan scrambled to her feet, placing her body between Fen and the wolves. "No, Fen!"

She faced him, breathless, watching confusion pull at his brow, his defensive stance wavering.

"You're not in danger?"

"No. He was injured." Rowan glanced behind her, the wolves still snarling. "And in a lot of pain."

Winter pressed heavily against Rowan's legs, growling without showing her teeth.

"I'm sorry. He didn't know." She turned and settled to her knees before the wolves, laying her hands open before her. "I failed to tell him the rule of the wood."

Snarls continued, and Winter's growls deepened.

"Forgive me," Rowan said.

"I'm sorry." Fen knelt beside her. She stared, not hiding her surprise. "I thought she was in danger." He dropped his weapons and matched the position of her hands. "She cares deeply for you, and I am learning what that means."

The patriarch barked, moving to stand between the wolves and Rowan. His mate joined him, the leading pair meeting Rowan's gaze.

Rowan shifted, still humbling herself in apology.

"He stormed here with weapon drawn," one wolf said, their voice clipped with anger. "Just like the other!"

"Other?" Rowan searched their eyes. "What other? Did they do this?"

"No. Another human, days ago," the matriarch said. "A man. Old enough to know better. Stupid enough to believe himself invincible."

A villager entered the wood, armed? Why had no one told her?

Days ago…Had she returned from Shaylon Plains? Why would they venture here alone?

"His intention was clear," the patriarch said to the wolves, his patience thin. "Stand down."

Rowan locked eyes with the matriarch, the warmth in her heart faded to disappointment. "I have broken your trust."

"No, child," the matriarch said, her voice gentle. "He put his life in danger for you."

"A warrior's heart," the patriarch agreed.

"We understand what he thought he saw." The matriarch nuzzled Rowan's face. "Our pack is still shaken. Their hearts beat fast with anticipation of more danger to come."

"He is a new friend," Rowan said. "I was remiss in my responsibility."

The matriarch continued to nuzzle her cheek. "You have borne much, Guardian. We miss her, too."

The rush of emotion filled her throbbing heart, tears welling as she blinked through them. She howled quietly, the notes low and mournful. The wolves joined her, Winter moving to touch Rowan's side.

"We guard their graves," the patriarch said. "They were dear to you."

"Your new friend may walk the wood," the patriarch said, "and we honor his warrior's heart."

"He won't draw his weapon here again."

"No, child," the matriarch said, alarm in her voice. "We may have need of it."

"We will protect our own," the patriarch said. "You and he will protect the woods."

Though Rowan didn't foresee Fen lingering in Elderglen like this, having a presence at Sentinel Hill and being welcomed by the wolves, his recent companionship provided her unexpected comfort. As fleeting as it likely was, Rowan allowed herself to let the relief sink in.

She returned to her human shape and stood, surprised by Fen's hand as he helped her to her feet.

"Forgive me," he said immediately. "I acted without thought."

"It would have saved my life if I'd been in danger," she said, offering a small smile.

"Rowan, I—" He shook his head. "You said you were careful with their trust. I didn't mean—"

"You impressed them," she interrupted. "You were protecting me. They said you have a warrior's heart."

"I acted in haste."

"But you acted." She gestured for him to join her back to Elderglen. "Not everyone would have."

They navigated back toward the village, their steady footsteps crunching dried leaves and snapping twigs. Winter walked beside them, glancing toward the woods and treetops until they crossed into the open field.

"Your arrival in Elderglen." Rowan stopped, studying him beneath the morning sun. There were hints of copper in his light brown hair. "Was it only for your brother?"

"A trail led me here," he said. "I was with Moonblade on the heels of a high-ranking cultist, and our paths crossed through Elderglen."

"A cultist in my village?" Lightning flashed in Rowan's forest-colored eyes. "How?"

At this, Fen's look darkened. "I saw him speaking with the mayor. That's why I'm here. I think the mayor knows something."

"The one he spoke with," Rowan said. "Can you describe him?"

"Light hair," Fen said. "Practically silver, in the moonlight."

"You saw him at night." Rowan's mind worked quickly, piecing this information together with what she thought she knew of her village and its leadership. "Was he the one who took your brother?"

Fen considered his answer, the seconds passing in silence before he said, "I think so."

Various scenarios ran through Rowan's mind—the strange visitor being a Wandering Order cultist, high-ranking, if Fen's information was accurate. Speaking with the mayor while Fen's brother had been in danger. "What do you know?"

"About the mayor or my brother?"

"All of it." Protectiveness tingled in her bones, her muscles pulling taut. "Tell me everything, Fen."

He glanced around, ensuring their solitude. "Gran was the one who told me about Marc. About the experiments."

When Fen didn't continue right away, Rowan said, "Mist arcana."

He nodded, clearing his throat. "They experimented on him. Tortured him. A human with learned magic who is also a Harbinger for the guild. And he—" A muscle in Fen's jaw feathered. "It made his magic unstable."

A Harbinger. One who finds those with magic to protect them or recruit them. If Elias had tapped into the secrets Marc held, the guild would crumble. "Gods, Fen."

"He's working with Mirelyn. She's been a godsend, but she's only tapped the surface of his mind."

Rowan waited, hearing the unfinished thought in Fen's tone.

"I don't know what to do. I don't know how to help him. Unstable fire craft, mingling with everything he's trying to recover from." He shook his head, running a hand through his hair. "I didn't even know he was taken until I reached Sudor and heard from someone in the guild. A raid, and the Order killed so many of us."

"Sudor," she said. "You said you were in Alvar before."

"I was."

But there was more to the story. Fen was as guarded as Rowan. She recognized the walls that surrounded him, some of them identical to her own. "You're not telling me everything."

But slow footsteps approached, interrupting them. Suna's skirts were heavy against the delicate grass and wildflowers. "Has something happened?"

Rowan regarded her with a polite, strained smile, but Suna's state was drawn, even frail.

"Are you alright?" Rowan reached a hand for the mayor's wife, steadying her. "You look faint."

"A few restless nights," she said with a dismissive air. But weakness made her voice thin and her eyelids blink slowly. "It's difficult to sleep with the troubles we face. And Derin is—"

When she hesitated, Rowan understood. For all that Suna and the mayor had done—medicines, doctors, prayers—their son's condition worsened.

Suna's grip was both frail and strong, trying to prove to Rowan that she was alright. "No matter what, we trust in Sentinel Hill. We trust in you."

"I don't know if your husband told you about our meeting," Rowan said, seeing Mayor Frederick's flustered face in memory.

"He did." She smiled softly. "The Watchers are a gift to the village, not a requirement. And certainly not an opportunity." She quirked an eyebrow. "Braithen and Halie don't quite understand the task you and your family have undertaken to keep us safe."

"I appreciate that," Rowan said. "But I meant what I said. I'll die before I give up my home."

"It will not come to that." The firmness in her voice came from conviction, even in her weakened state. Rowan's heart beat with more confidence at the steady reassurance in Suna's light brown eyes. "I will make sure of it."

Rowan offered her arm. "Let's walk back together."

Suna smiled as she accepted, Rowan sensing her reliance through the weight of her touch.

"Some rest," Suna said, "and I will be right as rain."

Rowan heard Fen's steps behind theirs, noting his silence as Suna and Rowan continued to speak together. Without looking over her shoulder at him, she sensed him gleaning what he could from Suna's words and behavior. Rowan had only ever known Suna to be sincere, but with Fen's suspicion of the mayor, he likely didn't hold Suna above reproach.

"There's a blend of tea I picked up from Shaylon Plains," Rowan said. "It may help."

"I would like that."

They reached Elderglen, with villagers eyeing the trio and their wolf companion. Suna's serene expression didn't waver, nor did her acceptance of Rowan's arm, and the pair reached the front step of Suna's home.

"Thank you for checking on us," Rowan said. "I sought the wolves' counsel with a recent attack."

"Another?" Suna's brow furrowed, her smile fading.

"A wolf was injured," Rowan said. "They're on alert to keep the woods safe. They mentioned a human presence in the forest. A hunter."

"I'm sorry to hear that," she said, relinquishing her hold on Rowan's arm as she stood in front of the door. "If I learn anything new, I will speak with you."

"Thank you."

Did Suna already know something from her husband? Knowledge she hadn't been able to share until now? Could any of it somehow relate to the man Fen witnessed speaking with him?

But before Rowan could ask for more, Suna nodded her head in farewell and stepped inside.

"Rowan." Fen's voice was quiet, a low reminder of their conversation from before. "May I explain further?"

"Yes." She glanced at him before walking home. "Explain further."

"Feather and Claw," he prefaced, keeping pace with her hastened steps.

But she interrupted. "Start with Alvar. Start with where you've been and why you suspect that monstrous cult is in my village."

"I didn't lie about being in Alvar," he said. "I arrived in Elderglen and sought Cynthia's help."

Rowan's thoughts spun as she tried to make sense of Fen's timeline, to match up with the events stirring Elderglen to madness. "Where a cultist was seen speaking with our mayor?"

"I mentioned it to Cynthia when I arrived," he said. "She worried something was wrong in the mayor's household. Others noticed the mayor's behavior, asked about to what's happened to their son."

"She never said anything." Rowan's hurried steps reflected her frustration. "Not to me." She stopped, her gaze boring into him. "What others? And did she think they were lying?"

"She didn't have any specifics," Fen said. "And all this came from Jean."

Jean. With Rowan as the new Cornerstone, but nothing had been said. She stopped, both of them at the base of the hill. He moved to stand in front of her, though her eyes cast downward, the question a difficult one to ask. "Why didn't she tell me?"

"When?" His voice was gentle, even cooling, as frustration burned beneath her skin. "After your grandmother's funeral? Between your patrols and confrontations with Braithen and Halie?"

Her next inhale came as a sharp gasp. He said nothing else, his silence reaching deeper than any words could, his presence grounding despite the bottomless feeling she endured. If he hadn't been there, she would have spiraled into nothing.

"I can do this," Fen said. "I came here for guidance, but I didn't expect—"

When he stopped, Rowan turned, the plea for him on the tip of her tongue. But his sympathetic gaze stopped the acidic frustration from voicing itself as a pull of grief seized her heart, catching her breath.

"You're not alone, Fen. Not in Elderglen and not in the guild."

"You're not alone either."

She didn't look up at him, knowing what she would find if she did.

"I need to talk to Jean."

She climbed higher until she crested the hill, reaching the familiar ground of home.

CHAPTER 16

Rowan's knocks were timid, which was unusual when she stood at Jean's door. Sometimes, she didn't bother to knock at all. But the weight of the looming conversation.

Jean answered, a slight wrinkle between her brows smoothing as she met Rowan's eyes. "Gods, Rowan, it's you. I thought Halie had the gall to stop by."

Rowan managed a small smile despite the whirlwind in her core. "That explains your cross look."

"But not why you *knocked*." Jean studied her, leaning against the doorway without granting her entry. "Explain yourself, young lady."

"I've just spoken with Fen."

"About?"

Jean's face was a mask, altogether unreadable. If only Rowan had such control. "Marc as Harbinger. A cultist seen speaking with the mayor. Vague suspicions about the mayor's son."

Jean exhaled, slight disappointment settling in her eyes. "You haven't read your grandmother's journal."

She refused to lie to Jean, no matter how tempting it was to deny it. "I read the beginning before Gran passed."

"But nothing recent?" When Rowan didn't answer, Jean exhaled.

"I'll tell you a summary, but you need to read it." Jean stepped aside to let Rowan in. "Which would you like first? Marc or Derin?"

"What is there to tell with Marc? Fen said he was tortured."

"Maliciously," Jean said. "And he is worried he may have divulged guild information under the influence of mist arcana."

"He isn't sure?"

Jean shook her head. "Mirelyn is doing what she can to tap into his memories. She recently learned mindwalking from a gifted lightborn, but the skill is still new, and Marc's mind is delicate."

"Gods above."

"It doesn't seem like Marc gave away anything incredibly dangerous to us, but we won't know for sure until Mirelyn can break through the barriers in his mind. And from what they've told me, those barriers are *strong*."

Rowan imagined torment leading someone to close off areas of their mind, to build barriers even they couldn't penetrate. Marc had survived something horrific. It was a miracle he was functional, let alone living.

"As for Derin." Jean pursed her lips, thinking. "We—Cynthia and I —had a conversation once before about the timing of Derin's illness and the attacks on the village."

Rowan's gaze narrowed. "You think Derin's the one doing it?"

"I didn't say that." But her tone held little denial. "The timing was and is suspicious. No one has seen him in months, yet villagers and animals are attacked and even killed." Jean rubbed her forehead before sweeping away flyaway strands of hair from her face. "Could that be the secret the mayor and Suna are hiding?"

"That Derin is a monster?"

"Or at least bloodborn?"

"As though they aren't the same thing."

"They're not, Rowan." At this, Jean's expression turned stern, as though she would scold her. "Bloodborn never asked for what they became. And they endure so much simply to survive."

Rowan never took the time to learn about bloodborn or what dark magic created their existence. Her only concern as if one terrorized her village or Elderwood, how would she fight it? And if it came to it, how would she kill it?

"Nothing is set in stone," Jean said. "Nothing is conclusive. But that's the most recent news."

"The cultist seen with the mayor," Rowan said. "Fen described him. Tall, silver hair."

"Elias," Jean said. "A Preceptor."

"Of course a Preceptor would lead experiments with mist arcana."

They were ruthless. Monsters determined to train others in malice and hate. And they were eager to get their hands dirty.

"Fen must be so worried," Jean said. "Marc has refused to see him. He only sees the monster he's become, not as a man walking the long road of healing."

"But he's not a monster. He's a victim."

"And that makes it worse. His fire magic is on a hair trigger. He has to consciously control himself to keep from bursting into flames. And..." Jean hesitated, worry darkening her eyes. "Without mist arcana, he loses his grip."

"You mean he's addicted?"

"It's more than that. More than addiction. What those bastards have done—" Jean pressed her lips between her teeth, taking in a slow breath through her nose before releasing it. "Mirelyn is working on decreasing the amount he requires so that, eventually, he will be rid of it completely."

"His body *requires* mist arcana?"

Flashes of the wagon, of the men in moonlight, with their load of arcana crystals and mist arcana confiscated or destroyed.

They'd delivered to Marc. That was why they were so close to Elderglen.

"They must think I'm such a fool," Rowan muttered, pressing her cool hands to her warm face. "Gods, I *am* a fool."

"What do you mean?"

"Moonblade. Their delivery."

"Ah. That."

"You didn't say anything," Rowan said. "Why didn't you tell me?"

"And make you feel worse with everything going on around you? They should have been stealthier. There are different routes they could have taken while still obeying our agreement. They obviously used Marc as an excuse to cut too close to Elderglen on their journey back to their hideout. Why couldn't they have delivered the amount requested?"

Jean was kind to take Rowan's side, but Rowan would have to apologize to Valera. Her stomach flipped in discomfort. "Do you think she's heard?"

"Valera? Absolutely."

Rowan scoffed a laugh, anxiety tingling its cold touch through her veins. "Am I being punished for something?"

"You weren't Cornerstone then," Jean said with a simple shrug. "You were acting as Watcher, going off of information you knew at the time. As far as I'm concerned, that's all anyone else needs to know."

"It does make things simpler." Though Rowan wouldn't describe the storm in her core as *simple*. The more information she learned, the more questions she gained, compounding every worry and responsibility beneath another layer she didn't see coming.

"Go get the journal," Jean said. "We need to go through it together."

"Jean—"

She insisted. "At least the last few entries. There's a lot of moving parts, Rowan, and you're at the center of it. Whether you like it or not."

Decidedly *not*, but Rowan obeyed, taking the short walk to her home and returning to Jean's, this time with Winter.

"We're not going to go to the beginning," Jean said. "You can do that on your own, easily enough. But you need to know the current situation and where we stand."

Rowan sat with Jean at the dining table, the kettle over the fire and a plate of Peter's butter cookies between them. Rowan set the journal in front of Jean, who opened the soft leather and flipped to the last written page. She ran her aged fingers over the scribbled text, Gran's handwriting wobbly. But Rowan could only see the beauty in it, despite the aged hand that tried to keep the pen steady.

"She lost so much sleep over this last raid," Jean said. "And when we couldn't find Marc, we were scared to hear of more terror against our people."

"You suspected that Marc would talk?"

"We suspected they would beat it out of him, and we were right. But Marc has proven stronger than all of them. Even if he revealed details about our guild, about the people we're protecting, it was only because they pushed his body beyond its limit. Marc would never betray us."

"You sound so sure."

Jean smiled softly, sadness and grief in every line on her face. "Joining the guild gave them both purpose."

"Jean, I—" For all her bravado and stubbornness in keeping herself out of Feather and Claw, all that was left to Rowan now was regret. "I'm so sorry."

"You don't have to apologize to me," she said. "And you damn sure don't have to apologize to Cynthia. Only to yourself."

"I've been so stupid about all of this."

"With how much hurt you've endured, it's difficult not to see past that and join in a cause you've come to hate."

Rowan winced. *Hate.* Such a strong and passionate word when a more accurate truth would be *apathy.* She felt nothing about Feather and Claw and had never cared to until now when so many things tried to find their place on her shoulders.

Jean flipped back several pages. "Here." She turned the book to face Rowan. "This is when Marc was captured."

Rowan read,

The raid left a lot of our people dead, several others injured. But those damned cultists always manage to slip past unscathed. Would that I could get my hands around their throats. Goddess grant me the strength to breathe through the flaming rage within me.

Jean tells me Marc is missing. When the scout searched for survivors, he wasn't among the dead or the living.

"The scout was Peter," Jean said. "Wil had to investigate another problem to the south, so Peter had to go alone."

"I remember. Wil was furious that Peter went by himself."

"We weren't pleased with that outcome either, but it had to be done."

Rowan continued with the journal.

Does the Order know Marc's role in our guild? Do they know who they've captured? Or was it merely his fire ability that pulled their attention and curiosity?

They were last heard heading east. We'll know more soon, but I fear we might not reach them in time. Goddess be with them. Be with us all.

"Gods," Rowan said. "And this was before we knew about their experiments, wasn't it?"

"We knew they wanted arcana crystal," Jean said. "And we knew they had mist arcana, though we weren't sure why an anti-magic cult wanted a reagent that amplified magical power. Now we do."

Rowan looked to the next entry, Gran's handwriting just as urgent, the letters just as pinched and hastened.

Marc is safe now. He is with our Phantom, goddesses be praised. And I fear Mirelyn's new strengths will be put to the test.

"She means mindwalking," Rowan said, pointing. "*Mirelyn's new strengths.*"

"Yes, which is how we'll know what Marc may have said under torture."

Rowan's stomach twisted, touching the words inked on the page. She could almost feel Gran's worry come through.

Still nothing on the map. Still nothing on the monster who took my daughter. It's difficult not to lose myself in the anger swirling inside, like a mountain ready to erupt with fire. I would render Elderglen like the Ashlands, all flame and burning. The only consolation I have is assuming the person who took my Beth has already paid and fights for his soul in Chaos. But reality reminds me that, like every other injustice in the world, they are probably alive and continuing to terrorize others because of their insatiable greed.

Rowan stopped reading, eyes itching. Greed for arcana crystal, greed for resources, greed for information. The map held all of those things, and Rowan's parents paid the price. Them and others.

Jean glanced at the page, already knowing its contents. "You aren't the only one bathed in anger."

"*Bathed.*" Rowan scoffed a laugh. "That's an extreme description."

"It fits an extreme emotion."

Rowan couldn't deny Jean's observation. If anything, she found comfort in what Jean could see. Rowan didn't have to explain.

"Which leads me to Marc and the Order," Jean said. "But you're not going to like it."

"I already don't like a lot of this," Rowan said, her tone lightly teasing while she spoke the truth.

"The Wandering Order had the brilliant idea to experiment with mist arcana and arcana crystal, the idea being to amplify one or the other through magical processing."

"Amplifying through processing?" Rowan's face scrunched in confusion. "How would that work?"

"The requirement is someone with magic casting through to the arcana crystal while channeling their magic through the mist arcana. That's how Marc explained it."

"What else did he tell you?"

"*He* didn't," she said. "Mirelyn did."

"The Wandering Order forced him to push his fire magic through mist arcana to fill a crystal?"

Rowan had heard of arcana crystal as a sort of storage vessel for arcane power, though most of the magic folk she knew used the crystals to amplify spells, not to store magic.

"What he thinks happened is the mist arcana amplified his magic but pulled too much too fast, making it harder for him to stop channeling."

"Like a dam breaking."

"And Marc says the crystal used would help him to regain control. To give him back the dam to stop the river, to go with your analogy."

"Because he pumped magic into an arcana crystal?" Something still didn't add up. After a pause, Rowan asked, "May I ask an insensitive question?"

"Of course."

"Are we sure Marc isn't requiring this crystal as some sort of crutch? Could this be an excuse why he hasn't better fortified himself against his power after torture?"

Jean lifted a shoulder in a half-shrug. "I won't lie and say that question hadn't occurred to me, but none of us know what Marc endured and what the magic and arcana did to him."

"What does Marc remember?"

"Not much. The Preceptors, a few cultists. And there was one person who remarked on routes between arcana crystal caves, though he refused to show either Preceptor anything on paper."

Rowan's interest piqued. "Nothing drawn out?"

Jean shook her head. "He came twice, from what Marc could remember, saying the locations of two arcana crystal caves near where they were camped. He even recommended using the safe house where they found Marc as a temporary base of operations while they mined."

"And this person." Rowan edged closer, her body unable to sit still. "Any distinguishing features?"

Jean shook her head, regarding Rowan with a questioning gaze. "What are you thinking?"

"Could they be from Moonblade?"

Silence met Rowan's question, Jean blinking in stunned silence before she asked, "Are you serious?"

"Surely you know." Rowan spoke quickly, her nerves upset that she hadn't already burst through the door to run until she found the first Moonblade assassin to cross her path. "Gran suspected Moonblade's involvement in how...how they..."

"Your parents?" Jean reached for Rowan's hands, her warm maternal touch soothing some of the anxiety fluttering through her blood. "She told me."

"Where is the camp where they kept Marc?" Rowan asked. "How far is it from here?"

"They've likely already moved," Jean said, "but they would take the crystal with them. It's far too powerful to abandon, though I don't know how they would tap into its power without aid from someone with magic."

Rowan didn't care to understand how the Order would use the crystal. She only cared about how the crystal could lead her to the assassin feeding those cultist bastards information from Feather and Claw.

That assassin had the map.

"I'll find it," Rowan said. "I'll go."

"Not alone." Jean squeezed Rowan's hand, her word final. "You have a team, Cornerstone, and it is your responsibility to use them."

"It's too dang—"

"They're going with you." Her words were clipped with firmness. "As your Veil and as your friend, I will not yield."

Rowan bit back her retort.

"It will be Wil, Fen, and Peter," she said. "Peter and Wil are great with fighting, and Fen with subterfuge."

"And what am I great at? Clawing and biting?"

"Hunting." Jean's gaze didn't waver. "You accomplish everything you set your mind to, and you'll know how to keep the others safe."

Protector.

Hunter.

Watcher.

Guardian.

Cornerstone.

But after two years of grief, she would finally gain the closure her heart longed for, the tear in her soul close to being mended.

CHAPTER 17

Rowan studied the map on the dining table, the lines clean and landmarks clear.

Cultist camp. Moonblade base. Crystal mines. She traced her finger over each marking, forging connections between them.

The afternoon waned as they planned, Rowan listening to Jean and the others while her own thoughts ran scenarios of tracking the assassin who had the map.

This close to Elderglen, she thought. *All this time?*

"What exactly are we walking into?" Wil paced the length of the room, arms crossing and uncrossing.

"You're walking into the ground if you keep that up." Peter took his arms and stopped him. "Don't wear a hole in Rowan's floor."

"Will this really help him?" Fen looked from Rowan to Jean. "Have you seen him?"

"I haven't," Jean said, "not since we brought him."

Fen ran a hand through his hair. "It would make things a lot easier if I could talk to him."

Rowan didn't disagree. "We can only go on what we know, and what we know is they're experimenting on people *and* arcana crystal."

"Which leads me to my next question," Wil prefaced. "Is the crystal still there?"

"Meaning, what if they've already used the power they transferred into it?" Peter rubbed his chin. "The same thing occurred to me."

"And me," Jean said, "but we won't know until we look."

"Not *we*," Rowan said. "You're staying here."

"Rowan—"

"I'm not bringing Winter." Rowan's tone was firm. "You have to stay in Elderglen. You're the Veil. This is Sentinel Hill." She rested her hand on Winter's head. "I'm not risking either of you."

Jean didn't hide her displeasure, but she didn't argue.

"After we retrieve the crystal," Fen said, "I want to see my brother."

Jean could only nod. "I don't think that's an unreasonable request, but I don't get to decide."

He growled, nearly hitting the table with his open hand, but he held himself back, instead rubbing his face with rough circular strokes.

"The latest bit of news shows movement further north." Jean touched a path northeast of Elderglen. "It looks like they've set up camp between these two known crystal mines."

"There's a farm not far from there," Fen said. "Good people."

"You've been there?" Wil asked.

"On my way from Alvar." Fen didn't elaborate, only to add, "They're earthwitches. Very kind."

The story he wasn't telling tingled at the back of Rowan's mind. If they made it out of this mission alive, she would ask him.

"That puts something else on our list of responsibilities," Rowan said. "If they're northeast, not far from the mines..."

"Gods," Wil said, exhaling. "They're in danger from the Order."

"I can send someone to the farm," Jean said. "Let's focus on one thing at a time."

"Who are you sending?" Rowan's ignorance turned her stomach. "Someone from the guild?"

"From *a* guild," Jean said. "Our people are scattered at the moment, with the exception of a few scouts tracking the Order."

"So, it'll be Moonblade." Rowan liked that idea even less than running into a cultist camp to find a magically infused crystal that might not exist. "You can trust them to keep the family safe?"

"As far as I can trust anyone who's not us," she said. "It's a quick fix to a problem we've only just seen while we face another problem that needs our resolution."

"Aid will reach them quickly this way," Peter said, nodding at Jean. "Until we can go to them, ourselves."

Rowan took a slow, deliberate breath. Succumbing to the overwhelming shadow of duty and responsibility would be easy, but her stubbornness refused to yield.

"As soon as night falls," Rowan said.

But a series of loud knocks on her door rattled all thoughts and plans loose, pulling her attention in abrupt urgency.

Until she opened the door to reveal Braithen and Halie.

"Gods above," Jean said. "What are you doing here?"

"What a reception from the house of the Watcher," Halie said with a sneer.

"If you come expecting hospitality, get used to disappointment." Rowan squared her shoulders, not looking back as someone behind her stifled a laugh. "Why have you come?"

"The village is concerned," Braithen said, matching his sister's bearing while keeping his voice level with a false sense of authority.

"The village?" Fen asked. "Or you?"

"You know nothing of Elderglen, Traveler," Halie said, her tone venomous.

"Or of the troubles we face." Braithen narrowed his eyes at Rowan. "Do you even know what's happened?"

Suspicion lined her gaze, eyes flickering from brother to sister. "What are you talking about?"

"Another attack." Halie crossed her arms and jerked her chin higher. "Word reached us just now."

Rowan clicked her tongue for Winter, moving to leave. But Braithen squared his shoulders, resisting her exit.

"It's too late, Watcher."

"If you don't remove yourselves from my doorway—"

"You'll what?" Halie looked at her, satisfied. "Rip our throats out?"

"It's a pity she spends her energy protecting you," Fen said, coming up behind her. "Letting this nightmare devour you both would be the simpler option."

The room's collective frustration simmered behind her, with her own boiling hotter. "You disturb my time with loved ones while we still grieve to tell me of another attack that you won't let me investigate."

"If you'd done your job—"

Rowan's hand found Braithen's throat before he could finish. Halie screamed, hands reaching with nails like claws to peel back Rowan's grip. But Rowan pushed hard, causing Braithen to stumble as he struggled to keep the pace. At one step, his ankle rolled, and his legs buckled beneath him. But Rowan kept her footing, releasing his throat to let him fall. She towered over him as Halie screamed behind her. Rowan glanced back, seeing Fen's arms braced around Halie's in an unrelenting vise.

"You are a worthless parasite," Rowan hissed. "Do not disturb our doorsteps again. If you hear of news, send someone else."

"You dare—"

Rowan reached for him again, scaring him into silence.

"You will not see me fall, tanner. But you? You're on the edge of a chasm you cannot come back from."

His pupils were pinpricks. Sweat gathered at his hairline.

"The monster isn't the only thing threatening Elderglen," she said, looking from Braithen to Halie. "Its own people compromise its integrity from within. I am Watcher. I am Guardian. And I will not suffer threats to my village, no matter what form they take."

Halie sputtered, stopping only as Peter rested a firm hand on her shoulder.

"You knew better than to come here to provoke us," he said. "Return to your home while we investigate."

"The mayor will hear about this." Braithen scrambled to his feet, dusting himself off.

"I should hope so," Rowan said, reaching for her cloak. She draped it over her shoulders, the black side out to help her blend in with the coming darkness. "I'll happily tell him myself."

Halie rushed to her brother, tugging his arm and leading him down the hill. Rowan watched them with lethal anger boiling just below the surface, her balled fists tight at her sides.

"Let's go, Winter."

Rowan shifted and ran for the trees as the others called for her, but she didn't stop, and she didn't look back.

CHAPTER 18

The grass and soft earth, cooled by the touch of the coming night, softly succumbed to the weight and pressure of Rowan's paws as she ran. Winter kept stride easily, the breeze combing through their fur, noses keen to the scents of the forest.

Wolves. Wood. Flowers. Not a trace of human scent.

"Did Braithen lie?" Rowan asked. "Can you smell anything?"

"Nothing that shouldn't be here." Winter stopped, her nostrils working to catch any trace. "Nothing human. No blood."

Rowan stared without seeing, recalling the mayor's account of two cultists found dead, though no word had reached her. "What is actually going on?" Rowan grumbled a growl as she scoured the grass and brush. "They're causing more harm than they realize, and I fear they won't listen."

"And blame you for their misfortune," Winter said. "Foolish humans. Wolves are punished if they disobey their pack leader."

"No one has to obey me," Rowan said. "And I don't want to lead them. I want to be left in peace."

The silence that passed between them soothed the tension tightening Rowan's muscles and skin.

"Humans are punished, too," Rowan added, "but the law bends to whoever is in power." She stopped, pawing at a patch of grass, the scent comforting. "Humans know how to manipulate things to get what they want."

A sentiment Gran had often shared. Rowan hadn't continued her journal since her passing, fearful of what she would find.

"Failed," she'd said. A pang of grief stabbed Rowan's heart, imagining the weight Gran carried into her final moments.

How did you fail?

But Rowan wasn't sure she wanted that question answered.

She and Winter moved on, their steps quiet around the brush and trees, noses tracking the scents of earth and beast, the things that belonged in this world apart from humans. The forest soothed her in its simplicity, in the way it welcomed her into its embrace.

"I'd be happy to snap my jaws at them." Winter rubbed against a tree, shaking her head. "Make them afraid to come near us. Silly humans." She trotted ahead, then stopped, ears perking. "Rowan."

Rowan followed Winter's gaze, moving to her side.

"Do you smell it?" Winter took a long sniff. "It was in our home before."

"In our home?" Rowan searched the air for what would be familiar. Several seconds passed before she finally caught the scent of patchouli, lavender, and citrus. "That woman."

They moved forward, easing their steps across grass, twigs, and fallen leaves until human voices came, their scents borne on the air. Stronger patchouli, lavender, and citrus...and something else. A spiced musk not unlike Fen's. But sharper—closer to clove and bergamot, mingling with wood smoke.

"Kill every wolf," a gruff voice said. "Until we're sure it's her."

Rowan and Winter froze. The human scents they trailed were in the opposite direction of the voices that disrupted the natural sounds of the forest.

"Kill every wolf?" Winter bared her teeth in a silent snarl.

"They'll know we're close, idiot," another voice chastised. "We need to be smart about this."

"Wolf pelts sell, and they'll warm up our clothes. Win-win."

"Win-lose if they alert those assassin bastards."

Rowan edged closer but stopped as she heard a footstep snap a twig. The echo was distant, from the same direction as the voices. They were moving.

"Killing wolves," Winter said.

"One mentioned assassins," Rowan said, edging closer. But the footsteps moved faster into the distance, their sound fading. "Are they from the Wandering Order?"

Winter growled at the cult's mention.

"Targeting wolves *until we're sure it's her.*" Ice formed around Rowan's pounding heart. "They know I'm wolfkind."

"Everyone does," Winter reasoned. "It isn't a secret."

"No, it isn't."

Fen's voice echoed in her mind, recounting who he'd seen speaking with Mayor Frederick. Tall, silver-white hair, dark eyes.

The Wandering Order knew that the Watcher of Elderglen was wolfkind.

Rustling ahead pulled their attention. Rowan shifted, her form growing above the brush, her human eyes catching sight of a dark-haired human several paces ahead.

"I think they've gone," one voice whispered. A woman's. "That was close."

As she emerged from the brush, Rowan recognized her. Patchouli, lavender, and citrus.

"Mirelyn," Winter said. "She has a fierce spirit."

"I noticed that, too."

Both waited, listening to Mirelyn move alongside someone else.

"I recognized their voices," her companion, male, said. Fen's brother, Marc. "They're with Elias."

The shape of his brow and the bridge of his nose were both similar to Fen's. But he was taller, and his hands were as red as flame, the color inching up his wrists and forearms before fading to the natural color of his caramel-beige skin.

"Do they know we're here?"

"Not sure," he said. "What were they saying about a wolf?"

Rowan moved forward, purposefully stepping with sound, lifting her empty hands to show she was unarmed. Mirelyn relaxed, though Marc's body braced itself for conflict.

"She's a friend," Mirelyn said quickly, resting a hand on Marc's arm. "Cynthia's granddaughter."

"The Watcher?" He glanced from Rowan to Winter. "She looks like a huntress."

"You wouldn't be the first to say that," Rowan said.

"Did you see those men just now?" Mirelyn asked.

"I heard them," she said. "It would appear they're looking for me."

"You're—" But the man stopped, nodding. "Of course. Guardian of Elderwood."

"Marc," Mirelyn said, "this is Rowan. Rowan, Marc."

Rowan made no ceremony with introductions. "Your brother is looking for you."

"I heard. I thought he was headed north."

"Not since your capture," Rowan said, assuming that to be true.

"But his ship." His eyes flickered to Mirelyn, then Rowan. "Who's sailing the *Phantom* while he's here?"

"The phantom?"

Confused, Marc's brow narrowed as he studied Rowan. "You're Cynthia's granddaughter, right?"

"She's only just become Cornerstone," Mirelyn said gently.

"But how does she not know the *Sea Phantom* and what my brother does?"

A ship. *The Sea Phantom.* And Fen, lying on the deck to watch the stars.

"He was the captain," she muttered. "Captain—"

"Alden Fen," Marc said. "You didn't know?"

"And he hasn't told her," Mirelyn said, piecing it all together.

"We should go see him," Rowan said, eager to change the subject. "Explain what happened."

At this, Marc recoiled. "I—I can't."

He turned his face, his eyes lowered in shame.

"The Wandering Order," Mirelyn said, reading Rowan's worry. "He escaped with his life, but—" She hesitated, looking for Marc to tell her.

"Experiments," Rowan said. "My grandmother told me. And your fire magic—" Rowan's imagination ran with scenarios of Marc's magic raging out of control.

"It helped me escape," he said, his voice low. "There's nothing left of that place."

"Except the Preceptor who somehow has luck on his side," Mirelyn said.

"We've heard they've moved somewhere northeast," Rowan said. "Near a crystal mine."

Marc growled, balling his red fists. Flames licked at his skin, even as his shuddering breath tried to calm him.

"We're in the hunting lodge further in the woods," Mirelyn said. "Would you bring Alden with you?"

"Alden," Rowan whispered, the name foreign when thinking of the man she was getting to know. "He told us his name is Fen."

"Alden Fen." Marc nodded. "It was our parents' way of including their names with both children. Our father gave us our first names, and our mother is Fenra."

"That would be a beautiful thing if it weren't for them being terrible parents."

Rowan whirled. Fen, along with Wil and Peter, were behind her.

"Marc." Fen's smile wavered, worry and relief mingling over his features. It was the same for Marc, who stared at his brother with an imbalanced blend of happiness and shame. "I know you didn't want to see me, but—"

"I did," Marc said. "But I didn't want *you* to see *me*. Not like this."

"Like what?" Fen scoffed a quiet laugh, a thin mask against the hurt. "Alive?"

"We'll find the crystal you need," Wil said, stepping forward. "We cannot begin to fathom what you must be going through."

"Don't," Marc said quickly before wincing. "I'm sorry. But please, don't."

Wil straightened his shoulders, nodding.

"Thank you for whatever help you can give," Mirelyn said. "The crystal is somewhat of a last resort. Mindwalking has given us some insight, but the barriers in his mind are strong."

"And you think the crystal will help to break them," Peter said, though he didn't sound convinced that it would work. "I suppose we won't know until we try."

"A piece of me went—" Marc stopped, turning his face away. "I felt it."

"Did the Preceptor say anything about using it?" Peter asked. "Or anything about what it was for?"

Marc shook his head, not making eye contact. "I don't—"

"It's alright, Marc."

But Mirelyn's whispered consolation didn't reach him. Without another word, Marc turned and walked through the trees, his movements calm and slow.

"What have they done to him?" Fen's fingers flexed, likely wishing for the handle of his sword or the grip of his bow. Rowan recognized the gleam in his eyes. Any cultist who crossed his path would meet a reckoning. He looked to Mirelyn for an answer, but when she didn't speak, he asked it again. "What happened to him?"

"Cruelty happened to him," she said. "Unhinged malice and hatred happened to him."

She moved in Marc's wake, leaving Rowan to face the others.

"We move forward with the plan. The sooner we retrieve this crystal, the sooner we can make sure that family is safe."

"Is no one going to talk about how Braithen and Halie lied?" Wil asked. "There was no attack."

"Their comeuppance will show itself," Rowan said. "They'd better pray to whatever goddess they serve that it doesn't come from me."

She moved through the trees, heading northeast in the fading light of dusk.

CHAPTER 19

Night came in silence as Rowan and the others walked.

Rowan had been ahead of the group for an hour, each step carrying a thought that followed a chain of uncertainty and questioning. Soon, Fen jogged closer, though he didn't speak. His presence raised a new series of questions, those planted by Marc in their chance meeting.

"He called you Alden."

Fen nearly stopped mid-step, reading her expression.

"Your brother," Rowan needlessly clarified. "He said your name is Alden."

He cleared his throat. "It's not a name I like."

"Why?"

"Because it's my father's name."

Rowan's chest hitched as though a needle stung her.

"I'm sorry I didn't tell you," he said. "I didn't mean for it to be a lie. I go by Fen, but Marc called me Alden in Runa."

"And the *Sea Phantom*," she said. "You mentioned you were a sailor, but that isn't the case, is it?"

"It was," he said. "I was a sailor. Then, after Quenvar died, I became her captain. Captain Alden, a ruthless wretch at sea, fearsome and wicked." He laughed without mirth, his deep blue eyes looking ahead. "An act I had to maintain while working for the guild. I had to be a man that no one would cross."

Rowan's mind raced, trying desperately to grasp the underlying meaning. Proving himself to his crew, to Runa, to anyone at sea eager to test their mettle against the *Phantom* and those aboard her.

"I wanted to tell you," he said. "And there's still more to say. But I don't want you to think less of me."

"I won't."

He didn't look at her, glancing at his feet as they walked. "You will."

"Where is the farm from here?" Peter asked. "Could we stop by after?"

"It's a bit further south," Fen said. "I'll make the trip when we're done."

Rowan had to admire their optimism that there would be an *after*. They walked toward a camp of cultists who would find no greater joy than shedding their blood. An *after* would be a gift from the goddesses themselves.

"While we're close by," Wil said. "It would be a good idea to check in."

And alert the family to any potential danger if they weren't already aware of the Order's presence.

Fen remained close, walking in step with Rowan. Anticipation lingered between them, something unspoken sparking like the air before a storm.

"I want to ask," Rowan said, "but not if you don't want to tell me."

"Ask about what?"

"Why you think I won't like you."

He pursed his lips before beginning. "I hate that I'm telling you this now when we're potentially facing a fight with the Wandering Order. But the longer I wait, the worse it will be."

"Gods, Fen," she said. "Did you kill someone?"

He glanced at her before looking away, tension around his eyes and mouth. "I was fifteen. Captain Quenvar gave me a really important job while we were in Runa. There were cultists harassing sailors all over the port, looking for anyone working against them. They didn't know the name of Feather and Claw then, but they knew a group like ours existed."

A group like ours. Though Rowan didn't feel a part of it. The community fostered within Feather and Claw, one of subterfuge and sabotage, hadn't reached her, thanks to the length of her arm keeping it at bay.

"The short version of the story," Fen went on, "is that I was robbed when I had my guard down. I was playing cards and winning, and someone I didn't suspect snuck past me and picked my pocket."

"And the long version of the story?"

He sighed. "It involves underestimating someone who would prove me wrong and compromise the entire guild."

Rowan's stomach tightened, sensing the news he was about to tell her. In her memory, she saw Gran's worried brow, etching pain on her face.

"The map," she whispered.

With melancholy shadowing his already deep blue eyes, Fen nodded. "The map."

"Why—" Rowan's breath came short, but she forced herself to remain focused, keeping her body steady as step after step edged them closer to the Wandering Order. "Why did you have it?"

"I had to study it, memorize it, learn every detail about it before he locked it away. Or destroyed it. Gods, I remember the two of us studying it by candlelight, and Marc leaned too close to the flame, singeing the back." He took a breath. "Then the Order came, circulating among ship captains, looking for anyone willing to sail dangerously close to South Ileden Sound and the Midlands in Ileden. Quenvar's idea was that no one would suspect a kid. A young upstart with a big mouth and fast hands. And that was the point—draw attention to myself to lessen my chances of being suspected."

"But that person you underestimated…"

"An orphan who had faster hands than I did. And she was quick. Scrawny with a hunger that couldn't be sated."

"What happened next?"

"She sold the map for coin to head north, and I never saw her or that damned map again. And I looked, Rowan. I spent days scouring the streets of Runa, desperate for any word or sign. But there was nothing."

The storm within her core swelled, understanding what Gran had meant when she said she could have prevented the map's loss. She could have kept Fen and Marc in Elderglen. Brothers scarred by the actions of others when Gran could have taken them under her wing.

But how? And with what coin?

"Rowan?" Fen's voice was gentle, timid. "Please say something."

"You were a child." But the storm continued to rage within.

"I'm sorry."

"I know."

She moved ahead, grateful that he didn't pursue, keeping her eyes clear for changes in the landscape. And there, with the feathering of campfire smoke reaching over a copse of trees, Rowan turned.

"Stealth," she said. "I scout and see what I see. If we can retrieve the crystal and leave without any of them knowing we were there, that would be ideal."

"I agree," Peter said. "How will you know what the crystal looks like?"

Rowan tapped the side of her nose. "Mist arcana leaves a trace."

"That skill is both awe-inspiring and terrifying," Wil said with a quiet chuckle. "I apologize for all the times we scouted the forest together and I didn't bathe."

"Apology accepted." She winked. "Next time, I'll shove you into the river."

Lifting up her hood, Rowan shifted, trotting ahead as the others were careful to keep up. Camp sounds carried on the air, with the evening meal in full swing. Several cultists sat around the main campfire, the flames tall with large pieces of wood feeding them. Other, smaller fires dotted the impressive perimeter, its spread large and accommodating for dozens of people.

"Gods," Wil whispered from behind her. "There is a small army here."

"Likely for the mines," Peter said. "Some working inside while others process mist arcana."

"And others keeping watch and guarding in both places." Fen

ducked out of his bow, prepping an arrow. "On your lead, Rowan. We won't make a move without your word."

Rowan used the thin tree line as cover, navigating far from the tents until she reached the rear of the camp. Her dark fur blended beautifully with the dark, the warm lamplight from the camp still several yards away as she closed the distance between herself and the nearest tent. Human scents trailed to her nose, but no one was close. The large bonfire had them gathered, sharing the evening meal among them.

Sniffing carefully, the trail of sulfur and citrus pulled her further to the left, passing several tents before reaching one nearly off to itself. She remained behind its canvas, her approach slow.

"Their information has been good."

Rowan froze, the tent between her and a pair of cultists conversing well beyond earshot of the gathering at the bonfire.

The speaker, a man, sounded pleased as he continued. "I was worried that they were going to mislead us."

"That could still be the case." The other voice was female, and she didn't hide her skepticism in her tone or inflection. "They want something, whether it's from us or the people they're supposed to work for."

"We all want something." The man's voice was pleasant, its depth and timbre tingling in Rowan's ears.

"It's as though they're betraying them from the inside. I don't trust it."

"It's not a betrayal," he said. "It's sabotage. Using their own tools against them." He sounded pleased. "A monster after my own heart."

"Still," the woman said. "Something isn't right."

"Even if they think they're leading us to something terrible, we know better than to follow them exclusively to the ends of the earth."

"You sound more sure than you have a right to," she said, though there was some amusement in her voice. "How long before we kill them?"

"Let's see if they can show us another deposit," he said. "Their usefulness may be running out."

Another deposit. Arcana crystal?

But a shout from the fire pulled their attention, both cultists leaving. Rowan glimpsed but missed their forms as they rounded the corner of a tent, disappearing from sight.

A guide to a crystal deposit.

Someone betraying the people they work with. Or work *for*.

Rowan's hackles prickled as they rose, her movements slow and deliberate as she slipped into the tent, the stink of mist arcana accosting her nose. She nearly sneezed, her eyes watering while she trained her gaze on the crates. On a small table was a jar of mist arcana, halfway filled, with unprocessed crystal shards beside it.

And there, on the floor in the back corner of the tent, was a collection of crystals shimmering with power.

Normally, an arcana crystal farmed from the earth held a simple blue-green iridescence. But these shone in various shades, their colors moving like liquid within their thin, glass-like shells. On the top was one glowing orange and red as though it housed liquid flame. With ears attuned, Rowan waited before she shifted, quick to take the crystal and slip it into the pouch at her belt. The delicate glass singed her fingertips, its surface almost unbearably hot. She blew on her hand before eyeing the others, their colors a shimmering rainbow in variety and beauty.

Take another. But voices grew near, her hand recoiling in anxious fear. She returned to her wolf form and slipped out of the tent, careful to meld into the darkness upon her retreat before breaking into a run.

How many magic folk had the Wandering Order tortured to add to their crystal coffer? Rowan shuddered. Were there any captured here?

Don't do it, Rowan. Don't compromise the others.

But the urge to wreak havoc upon the cultists remained like an unreachable itch beneath her skin.

When she was far enough away from the camp, she broke into a run, finding the others where she'd left them. She shifted without a word and showed the crystal in a steady hand.

"Not a single alarm," Wil said. "Excellent job."

"I hope this helps him," she said, returning it to the pouch. "Let's hurry back. We have a farm to visit."

"How did you find it so quickly?" Peter asked.

"I smelled mist arcana." Rowan mentioned nothing about the pair of cultists speaking of their mysterious ally. "I stopped where it was strongest. And there were several other crystals with this one, all different colors."

"That's not good," Fen said. "How soon before they think to use all that power they've collected?"

"Let's hope they don't anytime soon," Wil said.

They ventured homeward, veering more to the south to cross the farm.

"It'll be late when we arrive," Peter said to Wil. "I hope we don't frighten them."

"We may," Wil said, "but keeping them aware of the Order is for the best.

"Was it really the mist arcana?" Fen whispered to Rowan as Peter and Wil spoke softly to one another, distracted.

"Why wouldn't it be?" Rowan touched her nose. "It has a unique scent."

"Something's changed." His eyes moved over her face, the strength of his gaze uncomfortable. It pulled back the layers, showing what truly lay beneath. And she wasn't ready for him to see. "Did you find something else?"

She walked faster, but Fen had no issue keeping up.

"What is it, Rowan?"

"Something that I'm still figuring out." She glanced up to meet his eyes before looking quickly away, their blue depths like orbs of black glass beneath the night sky. "I'll explain as soon as I learn something concrete."

But Rowan wasn't sure if she would, if the words would ever come to her to share with the others. Hunting her parents' killer was a darkness she hesitated to reveal. What would Fen and the others think of her, knowing she repurposed Rhiann's gift to pursue a human being with ill intent? For where else would a path like this lead but to somewhere dark? Somewhere Rowan couldn't come back from?

Fen said nothing else, maintaining pace with her as they hastened toward the farm. An hour passed with conversation light as they traversed the dimly lit terrain with care until something sharp reached Rowan's nose. She stopped. Something was burning.

Once she shifted, she heard the cries of wolves and ravens. Panic peeled over the air with shrill, pointed fear that pierced her eardrums.

"Gods!" Peter pointed to the west. "Is that smoke?"

With her wolf eyes, Rowan saw the feathering reach the darkened heavens, the gray smoke almost invisible against the dark of night. And there, in the treetops, something glistened like lamplight.

"That's close to home," Wil said.

"Oh, no," Fen said, breathless. "Marc."

But Rowan was already running.

CHAPTER 20

Flames had engulfed the heart of Elderwood.

Not every tree had caught fire, but a large area near the river burned. From her approach at the east, Rowan followed the path toward the wolf den. Panicked voices from wolves and ravens alike nearly disrupted her ability to track them, finding the wolves racing through the woods to escape the blooming flames steadily reaching them.

"Guardian!" One wolf reached her but didn't linger. "Guardian, our home!"

"Our home burns!"

Laments mingled with angered shouts and snarls.

"We have to go," came another voice. The matriarch. "It is unlikely that we can return."

"I am sorry," Rowan said. "I have failed you both."

"The error of others is not your burden to bear," the matriarch said, approaching with her mate. "But we, too, are sorry. We must go."

The pair departed with their pack, the baying of the wolves echoing in the distance.

Human voices reached her, several calling for water.

"I'm an earthwitch, not a seaborn!"

Jean. Rowan ran, unsure how she could help. But hearing Jean's voice, knowing she was trying to help—

But the flames spread too fast.

Finding Jean, Rowan shifted, frightening the older woman with her hastened approach.

"Rowan! By the gods!"

"Where is Marc?"

Jean's gaze told Rowan everything she needed to know.

"He can calm the flames," Rowan said. "Where is he?"

Jean looked over her shoulder, eyes studying the thickest part of the flames. The heart of the firestorm.

"He can't control it, Rowan."

But Rowan pulled the crystal from her pouch, her frustration leaving little room for patience and understanding. "He'd better, or he'll face something more frightening than fire."

She didn't waste time, even as the others finally reached her.

"Rowan!" Fen called.

"Gods, Rowan," Wil said. "What are you doing?"

She untied her cloak and ran, making a considerable leap over burning brush to reach the man engulfed in flames. He was on his knees with Mirelyn in front of him, cradling his face in her hands.

"Breathe, Marc. Breathe."

But Marc was beyond consolation. Panic made pinpricks of his pupils, his hands glowing with almost sun-like brightness. He kept them at his sides, away from Mirelyn, away from anything he could touch.

"I have the crystal," Rowan shouted over the tumult. "This had better work."

He met her with a terror-laced apology. "I don't know how it happened. My hands—"

"Tell me after you fix this." And she shoved the crystal into his palm, his skin searing hers like a brand. She screamed, recoiling, the red on her fingers and the heel of her palm already blistering.

Mirelyn stepped back as Marc took the crystal in both hands, focusing his unblinking eyes on its own internal swirling flame.

"How did you find this?"

"Just do it, Marc," Rowan shouted, her demand sharp in her lack of patience. "For gods' sake, do something!"

He closed his eyes, the crystal pressed between his molten palms, and the brightness in his skin dimmed. Breathing deeply through his nose, he extended a hand toward the surrounding fire, pulling it toward him, urging it into the crystal. His breathing graduated to a hum, the melody a few steady notes.

"Good," Mirelyn coached. "Just like we practiced. Focus everything through the song. Use the music."

Rowan had heard of music as a conduit for magic but considered it the primary method for merfolk and seaborn, not for a firewitch who might burst into flames at any second.

Marc kept going, pushing himself to consume the fire, channeling it through his skin until it fed the crystal. The glass-like surface glowed brighter within Marc's hands, amplified by the coming dark as the last of the flames diminished.

"Gods be praised," someone cried.

"Brena, herself, must have come to quell this disaster," another said.

But Rowan stared at the devastation around her. Trees burned, the brush reduced to ash. Though not every tree had been touched by fire, most of the forest suffered the aftermath of Marc's cataclysmic power.

She survived a brief infiltration into a cultist camp, only to find her sanctuary nearly decimated. The matriarch and her pack had gone, unlikely to return. The world Rowan knew, singed to cinders.

Her heart ached beyond reckoning, the cracks the deepest they'd ever been.

"I'm so sorry." Marc, breathless, met Rowan with guilt and shame in his eyes. "I don't know how it happened. Something flared within me, and I couldn't control it."

"Will the crystal help?" Rowan's voice was raw, burned by smoke and anger. "Should we seek another?"

"I don't know."

"We likely should," Mirelyn said.

The others rushed to them, questions flying around Rowan without reaching her mind. Tears welled in her eyes, though her lips did not tremble. Her sadness touched the floor of the Sea of Kings, surrounded by the cold, dark, unforgiving touch of loneliness.

"Marc!" Fen crashed to his knees in front of his brother, hands reaching for arms that recoiled. Hurt painted across Fen's expression. "Marc, it's me—"

"I could hurt you." Marc shook his head, moving to rise to his feet. "I could—"

But Fen wrapped his brother in a tight embrace, refusing to give him an opportunity to run. Marc held the crystal away from Fen's body, squeezing his eyes closed.

A hand touched Rowan's shoulder. She gasped, disrupted from her thoughts, pulled to consciousness by human contact. She met Wil's worried eyes.

"I'm not alright," she whispered.

"I know."

"Let's take you home," Jean said to her, taking her hand. "Winter is waiting."

Winter. Safe and sound. "Thank you for making sure she didn't—"

When Rowan couldn't finish, Jean answered by patting her hand. "I told her you would be home soon and that you needed her to stay safe. I think she understood."

Rowan would ask her the minute she could shift and run and flee Elderglen, never to return—

Only she would remain here. Her body, interred within these grounds, forever upon Sentinel Hill, where she would molder and decay until the earth reclaimed her.

She would never be free of it. Obstinate villagers who didn't leave well enough alone. The consequences of the Wandering Order and those who *meant no harm* but left Rowan to pick up the pieces.

So much of her life balanced on the whim and inconsistencies of others. So much of her life had her paying debts she didn't owe.

The fuse burned brighter, its length running short. Rowan's tolerance was dangerously low.

"Come, love," Jean said, guiding her. "Let's go home."

For the first time, those words brought no comfort.

ROWAN CROSSED THE THRESHOLD, glad to have Winter's crown beneath her hand, her sweet eyes filled with joy, her tail wagging in happiness. She was the soothing balm amidst the chaos in Rowan's core.

"Rowan." Jean paused, figuring out what she wanted to say. "I'm sorry."

"You didn't do this," Rowan said, her voice low. Her calmness was for Winter's sake, her wolf companion sensitive to Rowan's moods. "The person who should be sorry already is."

"It doesn't change what happened," Jean said. "It doesn't change the outcome."

"And it doesn't change that it has landed up on me." Rowan's sigh was cathartic, but there remained still more within that couldn't find its way to the surface. "Just like everything else."

"I've tried to shoulder what I can."

Rowan's lips pulled from her teeth, her impulsive, bitter response caged before a syllable could be uttered. *What have you shouldered? What have you carried?* But there were things Rowan didn't know. That much wisdom reached her despite everything.

"You take care of everyone," Jean said. "You're so young to have such things upon you."

"At what age would it be better?"

Jean didn't have an answer.

Rowan pressed her lips together, forming her words with care before she went on. "What happened to Marc is cruel, but I would be lying if I said I wasn't angry. It would be a lie to say I'm not burning with a fire of my own that no firewitch could put out. I don't know what he's suffered or how his magic has changed. I don't know any of that. Yet I am bitter and furious that it took my forest."

My forest, as though she owned every leaf and blade of grass. But it was hers, a refuge no one dared breach, a sanctuary for a select few. And she was among the chosen.

But no more.

"This was how he burned the cultist camp," Jean said. "He almost couldn't stop his magic then, either. Mirelyn entered his mind and forced him to sleep, which taxed her considerably."

"Gods," Rowan said. "That kind of magic is beyond what any living thing should do. Entering someone's *mind*?"

"I'm not exactly comfortable with it, either, but it's proven helpful and effective, to say the least."

Helpful, effective, *invasive*, and Marc had to endure that on top of everything else.

If Rowan were in his place, she would've burst into flames long ago.

"I hate that this happened," Rowan said. "And I hate that it came from someone I can't be angry with. Now that anger has nowhere to go."

Fen's voice returned to her. *Full of rage and nowhere to put it.*

"Who says you can't be angry with him?"

"My conscience."

Jean sighed through her nose but said nothing else.

Rowan stepped outside, Winter at her heels, and nearly bumped into Fen. He sat beside her door, his back against the house with an arm propped on one knee, staring into the distance.

"Sorry," he muttered. "I didn't want to be alone."

"But Marc?"

Fen stood, dusting himself off. "He's still ashamed. And he can't work through his mental barriers with Mirelyn if I'm there."

Rowan didn't refuse his company, the same despondency joining his heart with hers. They walked together down the hill, toward the field leading to the trees. But Rowan didn't go far, the desolation too tragic, the smell too potent.

"I'm afraid I'm not going to be good company," Rowan said, staring at the dark destruction before her.

"Me either. My brother is struggling, and I don't know how to help him."

She read his profile in the seconds it took him to meet her gaze, sadness lining his eyes.

"I was going for a run," she said, "if you'd like to join me."

A small smile tugged at his mouth, almost imperceptible with his facial hair in the dark. "I'd like nothing more."

"Let's see if you keep up. I won't hold back."

"I'd be offended if you did."

Even though Rowan preferred running on all fours, stretching her legs at their full stride was exactly what her body needed. With no proper home for her frustration and anger, the only recourse was to push her body to its limit. Winter zoomed ahead, encouraged by their unspoken challenge, choosing to race for the stretch of forest further north where the fire didn't reach. They didn't stop for nearly a mile, not until they reached the river. Panting, her chest aching, Rowan paced the river's bank before crouching to drink, the cold, sweet water offering soothing relief to the heat and tightness of her muscles.

Fen did the same before sitting beside the water, staring ahead as he panted, chest heaving.

"There's nothing I can do," he said. "I've always protected him. Been there for him. I..." He stared at his hands, palms open in his lap. "I've failed him, Rowan."

"Don't shoulder blame that isn't yours." She smiled to herself, imagining how pleased Jean would be to hear these words from her mouth. Saying them to Fen helped to soothe some of the ache in her chest. "Aim your anger at the monsters who did this to him. They're the ones who burned the forest. Marc was their unwitting conduit, forced by cruelty against his will."

"What is *will*?" Fen exhaled a quiet laugh. "What is *choice*? Is it the name we give to a world we think we have a say in? Is it an illusion to keep us in denial about the truth of all things unfolding in ways we can't control?"

"The interesting thing about choice and will is that every human has it."

"Every human," Fen repeated. "Like Elias."

"And any other who would choose hate over love."

"It helps some," Fen said. "But I don't know how to handle what I'm feeling." He pressed a hand to his chest, fingers played, palm firm against the rhythm of his heart. "I shouldn't wish ill on another living soul, yet I can think of nothing else. The silver-haired Preceptor in sight of my bow, arrow nocked, the aim right for his self-righteous throat—"

"You're struggling against yourself," Rowan said. "Your toughest opponent."

"You speak from experience."

With knees bent, she laid back, allowing the earth to form to the curves of her spine. She stared at the darkness above, the trees and branches of the canopy barely discernible.

"I do."

Minutes of silence passed between them, the night eerily quiet in the wake of the terror of Marc's power.

"The map," Rowan whispered, remembering their conversation from before. "Alden Fen."

He twitched at the sound of his full name.

"Why do you hate it?" She turned her head to face him. "You mentioned your father."

He pulled at a blade of grass and twirled it between his fingers. "The short version of events is that my parents joined the Wandering Order." He paused, absorbing Rowan's stunned silence. "The long version will take us into the dawn, which I wouldn't recommend. We both could use some sleep."

"Gods, Fen. Did they—" How could she ask this question without hurting him? "Did they know about Marc?"

"That's why we left. Ran away. Escaped. A pair of cultists came in the night, trying to steal him from his bed. Another one was in my room, ready to cut my throat if I tried to fight back."

Fen pulled at his collar, drawing his finger down the scar that reached from the center of his throat to his clavicle. "I fought back."

"And your parents—"

"My parents were earning their place. Their initiation."

Rowan had never understood the compulsion to reach out to someone, to extend her hands and arms to them to offer comfort, to ground them in a present moment where they could feel safe. She sat up, extending a tentative hand, but she recoiled, the offering too unnatural, the phantom sensation leaving her uneasy.

"You have my permission to touch me," he said. "If that's what you need."

"I don't normally do this." She smoothed strands of hair from her face, her tight braid holding well. "Jean and Wil both touch with affection. Peter, too. Not me. But I finally understand why they do it."

"You want to comfort me?" He smiled despite the weight of their conversation, despite the burden of the day. "I'm touched."

She scoffed, her own smile fighting for its freedom as she worked her lips to hide it. "Your pun is terrible." She ran her palms against her trousers, wicking the dampness that came with the fluttering in her stomach. "Is that why you chose that name while you were on the *Sea Phantom*?" She recalled some of the words he'd said. "Fearsome and wicked?"

"I had to play a role," he said, "and it couldn't be a good or nice one. So I modeled it after a monster." He swallowed, still not looking at her. "I've done terrible things, Rowan. Holding up the mask of Captain Alden of the *Sea Phantom* nearly consumed me." With a mirthless chuckle, he added, "And it almost killed me."

"What do you mean?"

With a flick, the blade of grass sailed nearly a foot in front of him. Winter followed its arc, ears perked, before relaxing once more.

"There were three ships in Runa called on a job, stopping at the Ghostlands before heading north into Ileden. The captains were made privy to the real mission, which was hauling arcana crystal to a cultist stronghold somewhere north in Storm Lands. But my ship didn't only have arcana crystal." He met her eyes. "There was an assassin. One of those cultist bastards. He'd pissed off a Preceptor, and word reached their High Arbiter. To redeem himself, he had to find a specific target, kill her, and bring back proof that she was dead."

"Gods."

"His name is Kieren. He told me the woman he was sent to kill was a chaosborn or a soulwitch. He wasn't sure."

"Not sure, but he had to kill her, just the same."

"As far as I know, he never made it. But I don't think he will go through with it."

Rowan blinked, waiting for him to explain.

"He doesn't strike me as the type."

"A cultist but not a murderer?" Rowan smirked, her sarcasm surfacing. "Those two can be mutually exclusive?"

"I wish I could ask him. The crew caught on that I was taking the long way to Alvar, using weather and tumultuous waters as my excuse. There was even a storm coming toward us, but they know something was off."

"You were trying to stall."

"As much as I could. Sending an assassin to Alvar, then reaching Ileden with a haul of arcana crystal for whatever maligned tasks those cultists had in store..." He combed his fingers through his hair. "Then one of them found correspondence in code in my quarters."

"Did they know what it said?"

Fen shook his head. "We guild members have a code we use, though we haven't settled on a name for it yet. I happen to like *featherspeak*, but others prefer *claw code*."

Rowan hadn't even considered that Feather and Claw would have its own written language to protect correspondence. "There is so much I don't know."

"Not every guild member knows it," he said, "if that helps you feel better."

"It doesn't." But she knew his story wasn't over. "What did they do after?"

"Staged a mutiny," he said. "The storm threw us all into danger, though. The ship wrecked off the southern coast of Alvar. I don't know who else survived."

She remembered the marks on his body, bruises and cuts still in the process of healing. "They nearly beat you to death, didn't they?"

He didn't answer right away. "The storm was what saved my life, looking back on it. Kieren tried, but they turned on him, too. None of them wanted to risk the payout the Order promised."

"And now they're probably in the belly of some sea predator."

Fen studied her, the overcast allowing limited moonlight to somehow find his eyes. "I'm sorry for everything, Rowan. The map. My role in the guild. The Wandering Order. Everything."

"Quenvar shouldn't have trusted the map to you," she said. "You were new to the guild. Fifteen. And used as a decoy?" When he nodded, she turned her gaze skyward. "Why?"

"Quenvar suspected someone was sniffing around the *Phantom*, suspicious of him. Taking in two orphans and raising them as crew on his ship. Some said he'd gone soft. Others wondered if it was something more. And the Order was in Runa." Fen paused, exhaling loudly. "So, I was a distraction for grown men and women who were keeping their eyes on Quenvar. An obvious distraction that they would ignore, believing they'd seen through a ruse."

"But a thief saw right through it."

"Or saw an opportunity," he said. "I doubt she had any designs upon what she'd stolen other than its monetary value."

Rowan didn't respond at first, breathing in the mingled scents of the forest, the freshness of the trees joined with burned wood. She would never smell hearth fire the same way again.

"Whoever has the map killed my parents," she said at last. "Something tells me they have it still."

"What do you mean?" He leaned forward. "Have you heard something?"

But a sharp crack pulled their attention, the sound echoing from the forest.

"What in the hells..."

Rowan stood, eyes searching in vain, finding it difficult to discern shadow from shadow. "Something's not right."

She shifted and jogged beside Winter, Fen keeping up as much as his stealth would allow. Voices echoed, both male, one of them laughing. The wind carried scents of body odor and burnt trees and sulfur. Then, as a tease on the wind, the faint smell of citrus.

Mist arcana.

"More of that poison," Rowan said to Winter.

"That wolf is close," he said. Large, slow movements, a strong body capable of immense leverage.

The other man was smaller but no less dangerous, his strengths more in dexterity and quickness. He said nothing, eyes trained on the trees as he held the opened vial of mist arcana in one of his hands.

"They wanted to lure me here," she said.

"Rowan!"

But Winter's cry came too late as the third appeared behind her and Winter, the faint scent of lilies masked by burnt wood and sulfur.

"Avenith?" Winter's curious voice showed recognition despite the years of her absence. Winter was only a pup when Avenith was in Elderglen—and in Rowan's life.

As Rowan turned, recognition smoothed Avenith's face, her brilliant blonde hair bound and hidden beneath the hood of her cloak.

"Rowan—"

The net found Rowan from behind, covering her before she discerned the man holding it had swung.

"Rowan!"

"Run!" Rowan's panic escalated at Winter's fear-laced anger. "Get Wil! Go! Don't let them catch you!"

Winter obeyed, though Rowan could feel her trepidation.

"Oy!" A stone sailed toward the larger man, hitting him against his cheek. Fen ran forward, hands preparing his bow after his warning. "Let her go!"

The second attacker corked the vial, slipping it into his pocket. "Her?"

"Is that you, Fen?" The man he struck rubbed his cheek, his look murderous. "She your pet?"

"She obeys no one but herself." Fen's arms strained as he pulled his bowstring taut, the arrow aimed at the larger man. "And your actions have sealed your fate. But it's good to see you again, Naelor. Thenik."

He said their names for her benefit. Rowan eyed them—Naelor, the large one; Thenik, the one holding mist arcana. She breathed carefully, learning their scents along with their faces.

"What fate?" The man chuckled, the sound raspy and rumbling. He smelled like ale, sweat, and leather. "One where I wear her fur as a cloak?"

"You'll be dead before you try," Avenith said, squaring up with her long daggers in both of her hands. Her floral scent clashed with theirs. Rowan nearly sneezed. "Let this one go, Naelor. Trust me."

"What do we have here?" His voice had a dangerous sing-song cadence as he eyed Avenith. "What will Valera say?"

He was smug. Was there some challenge between them? Avenith had that effect on people. Pushing them. Provoking them.

Rowan knew all too well.

"Maybe we should listen," Thenik said. Hay, horses, and soap, with mist arcana muddying the traces of him. "When has she ever told us to stop?"

"You've sealed your own coffin," Avenith said before slowly repeating, "Let. The wolf. Go."

Naelor responded by tightening his hold on the net line and pulling hard, yanking Rowan off her feet. Fen fired, but Naelor dodged.

"*She* comes with us," Naelor said.

Rowan thrashed, snarling and biting, but her brute strength and ferocity were no match for Naelor's.

"Gods above, she's strong." He chuckled. "I love it when they put up a fight."

Fen, screaming, charged him, his utility knife blade-down in his fist. Naelor dropped the net to defend himself, tasking Thenik with dragging Rowan to the wagon. But Avenith stepped in, sparring with Thenik to keep him from obeying.

"You're holding back, Av."

"Because I don't want to kill you."

Rowan couldn't find the cinch in the netting, so she resorted to biting through the hemp. But the make was good, the hemp thick and fresh. Her teeth and saliva only worked at felting what was there, making the weave somehow stronger. Was this magicked material? How in the seven hells—

Bones snapped. Fen cried out in agony, lying on his side at Naelor's feet, his body curling in on itself. Naelor stood victorious, his foot returning to the ground after kicking Fen in the ribs.

"Serves you right, you parasite."

The distraction cost Avenith, who suffered a blow at her temple. She crumpled in Thenik's arms, who took care as he carried her.

"Let's get them *all* in the wagon," Naelor said. "Valera will just love our little family reunion."

No amount of fighting helped Rowan as Naelor hauled her to the ground, dragging her through the trees where they had their wagon hidden. They'd even rigged a ramp out of fallen wood to drag her up to the cage. Thenik was ready, climbing up and settling Avenith beside the cage before lifting a hook to feed through the bars. Without having to touch Rowan and risk losing his hands, he hooked the net and pulled it into the cage before Naelor shut her inside.

Where Thenik was careful with Avenith, Naelor was cruel with Fen, throwing him into the wagon. Fen hit his head against the corner of Rowan's cage, groaning in a stupor as he weakly held his ribs. Rowan struggled with the net still binding her, and the more she moved, the tighter it became.

"Better rest while you can," Naelor said, reaching through the bars of Rowan's cage. "We'll be at the base in no time."

As he touched her fur, Rowan turned and snapped, sinking her teeth into his flesh. He cried out, recoiling his bloody hand as his other slammed the iron bars with his open palm.

Fen's grin was weak, his eyes blinking slowly. "Serves you right."

"I'll enjoy skinning you alive, wolf." Naelor climbed into the front seat with Thenik and clicked his tongue. The horses began to move, the wagon wheels squeaking as they bore their considerable load.

Thenik looked over his shoulder, meeting Rowan's burning gaze. "Gods, Naelor. She's going to rip our throats out."

Naelor chuckled. "I'd like to see her try."

CHAPTER 21

The wagon stopped in front of a dilapidated shack, an ideal place to dispose of someone. Quiet, out of the way, infrequently traveled.

Rowan's wolf eyes watched, ears perked, hackles tingling.

Fen and Avenith had come to during the journey, though Fen didn't bother rising, his breathing labored and face locked in tense agony. Avenith, too, suffered, with sweat gathering at her brow, and Rowan eyed the iron bars of her cage. Not many knew Avenith was stormborn, a secret Rowan told no one else. How long would she last before iron sickness would set in?

"How many are broken?" Avenith asked Fen, wiping a hand on her face.

Fen chuckled, wincing. "At least one."

Avenith cracked a small smile before looking at Rowan, eyes searching her wolf form. "Are you injured?" she whispered. "Gods, that net is like a vice around you."

"Here we are," Naelor said, climbing down. The blood had dried to rust on his tunic, his hand still useless against his chest. "Home, sweet home."

"Underground," Fen whispered to Rowan. "I hope you're not claustrophobic."

A few hours from Elderglen. Escaping would be difficult, with Moonblade likely knowing the terrain as well, if not better, than Rowan. If Mirelyn and Marc sought help, would they know where to go?

"What about the wolf?" Thenik eyed Rowan knowingly. "She won't let us lift the cage. She'll bite our fingers off."

Rowan growled to show he was right.

"She's bound up tight, thanks to her fighting spirit." Naelor grinned. "We can get her out, no problem."

"You already touched her once and faced a consequence," Fen said. "I have no qualms about watching her rip you to shreds. Don't lay a hand on her if you don't want to lose it."

"Who's protecting who?" Naelor's grin didn't reach his eyes, his challenging gaze predatory. "The bound wolf or the man with the broken ribs?"

"I'll bring Valera here," Avenith suggested, her movements slow and weak. "She should see this for herself."

Thenik relaxed as he nodded to Naelor. "That's the safest."

"Bloody coward. You're the one good with animals, anyway."

"I respect animals, Naelor, which is something you and I don't have in common." Thenik glanced at Rowan. "And this one wants to claw out my eyes."

Avenith slowly descended from the wagon, Thenik offering an arm to help her.

"Gods, Av. Are you alright? I swear, I didn't hit you that hard."

"Hard enough to knock me out, you bastard." She punched his shoulder, the impact weak even for a playful hit.

The men stayed at the cart as Avenith went inside. Rowan carefully moved within the hemp, trying to loosen the tangles around her limbs. Weakly, Fen reached through the bars to help.

"You sure this is the one?" Thenik asked, gesturing at Rowan. "Didn't want to ask with Avenith here, ready to run her mouth."

"I remember the scar." Naelor drew a line over the bridge of his nose to match the diagonal slash down Rowan's face. "And the fur—"

"No way you can tell the fur by moonlight," Thenik said, chuckling.

"Awfully thick, isn't it?" He stared at Rowan through squinted eyes. "Even for a wolf."

Rowan's growl was low as she studied him, trying to determine if he knew she was wolfkind, that he'd caged a human.

She couldn't wait to cross him again, this time with her claws.

The derelict front door opened, its squeaking hinges preceding the sharp-eyed woman who crossed the threshold with Avenith in her wake. Her dark brown hair was loose, framing her face with flattering waves that fell past her shoulders.

"Valera," Fen muttered to Rowan. "Leader extraordinaire."

"I hear there's a gift for me." Valera smirked as she moved to the back of the wagon, eyes running briefly over Rowan's fur before landing on Fen. "Oh. Has the wandering pirate returned?"

"Hardly." Fen held up his hands to show his manacled wrists. "I was just out for a stroll when your errand boys found me and kicked me in the ribs."

"And the beast that destroyed our haul," Naelor said. "It has the scar and everything."

"*She*," Avenith corrected. "Her name is Rowan."

Valera looked from Avenith to Rowan, discernment alighting as realization sank in. Her face slackened in wonder. "Release her."

Naelor coughed. "What?"

"Release her at once, you fools. Haven't you realized you've caught a guardian?"

Avenith stepped back, victorious eyes watching the men freeze beneath Valera's ire. Her color slowly returned. Rowan didn't like seeing Avenith like that. Weakness didn't suit her.

"What?" Thenik fumbled the keys, shock making him clumsy.

But Naelor sized her up. "That explains why Avenith was so protective of her." His brown eyes glistened in the dimming daylight, overcast shadowing the sun with intermittent passes. "Could she be the one who broke her heart?"

Rowan almost snorted. Had Avenith recounted events differently with strangers? Garnering sympathy? Emotions could be a valuable currency in the right hands.

Thenik, still clumsy, unlocked the door and pulled it open quickly. "I'll free you, Rowan. Please don't bite my hand off."

She growled, the sound low and dangerous.

"Perhaps we should do it," Avenith said, looking to Valera before meeting Rowan's gaze. "Would that be alright?"

"Will *you* be alright?" Valera asked, her voice too low for the others to hear. But Rowan heard every syllable.

Rowan blinked once, giving consent, and the women climbed into the wagon. Avenith and Valera's hands were careful with the netting, but Rowan yelped as the net snagged one of her claws and pulled.

"Sorry, love," Avenith whispered. "I promise I'm trying to be careful."

Don't call me love, Rowan wanted to say. *You don't get the right.*

Relief came in freedom, and Rowan stood, her aching limbs and joints grateful for movement. She looked from the men to Fen's manacles and back again, her growl a warning.

"Release him," Valera ordered. "Before she rips your throats out."

Thenik looked to Naelor, who didn't pull his gaze from Rowan. He watched her, waiting to see something spectacular.

"Why is Fen still in his manacles?" Valera's clipped tone was as sharp as the sword at her hip.

Frustrated, Thenik dug into Naelor's pocket and pulled out the key. Naelor nearly slammed his elbow into Thenik's shoulder but stopped as Valera cleared her throat.

Thenik missed the lock a few times before the key finally found purchase. Once the manacles released, Fen rubbed his wrists, his expression still twisted from pain.

"Here." Thenik offered his hands. "You'll need help getting down."

"Promise you won't throw me off the wagon?" Fen scoffed a laugh.

"I'm not Naelor," Thenik said, his expression serious. "You can trust me."

"Forgive us," Valera said, regarding Rowan. "We hold all magic folk in high esteem."

Rowan jumped down and shook before she shifted, the crimson tones of her fur becoming the red of the cloak. She dropped the hood, her dark braid falling over her shoulder. With three quick steps, she closed the distance between herself and Naelor and threw her fist against his jaw. Lightning shot up her arm, but the crack of her knuckles colliding with bone bloomed a surge of satisfaction through her. The force of the punch threw him, nearly shoving him from his feet. He stared at her, shocked, holding his jaw.

"What the hell are your bones made of? Stone?" He flexed his jaw, opening and closing it in a circle. "How can you be that strong?"

"A human blessed by Rhiann," Valera said for her, moving to stand between Rowan and Naelor. "Guardian. Protector." She studied Rowan's features with admiration. "You're the one who destroyed the supplies?"

"I destroyed poison," Rowan said, her look fierce as she met Valera's eyes. "And I will sleep soundly. But I admit that I did not know it was for a member of the guild."

"But you know now," Valera said. "Does that change anything?"

"Only that the path was still too close to the village." On this, Rowan would not yield. "I understand now why they were there, but there is another, farther path they could have taken. We suspect it was used as an excuse to shorten travel times between the mine and your hideout." She looked at Naelor. "Don't prove me right, and don't push your luck with Elderglen."

His expression hardened, lips poised to speak, but Valera stopped him.

"While we value and respect magic folk," she said, the deference in her voice somehow complementing the note of authority that came with her words, "we ask that you refrain from damaging our property."

Rowan sensed the shift in mood, tension mounting as Fen and the assassins watched with bated breath. The head of Moonblade, without naming her threat, had made her position with Rowan clear. And by the unwavering look in her brown eyes, Valera didn't seem the type to make light of her intentions.

"And we ask that you keep your *property* away from Elderglen. Knowing now who it is intended for, we can arrange for a meeting place beneficial to both parties as you provide the agreed amount. Not an entire haul."

Naelor blustered to speak up, but Valera held up a hand to silence him.

"The road traveled was outside of your town," Valera said. "We will transport our quarry as we please."

"At least give me terms I can agree to." Rowan showed no sign of acquiescing. No amount of flattery could bend her intention. "You insist on developing and selling poison, and I insist on keeping it out of my village. The wagon was too close. The drivers knew better but made their choice. And I made mine."

Valera's smile was broad and genuine, but Rowan knew well the predatory glimmer within it. "Then let us agree we will expand our transport routes."

"As I said, we will build something beneficial for both of us." If it weren't for Marc, Rowan would dump every grain of mist arcana into the sea and beg for Moonblade to retaliate. But she needed a compromise. For now.

Naelor grumbled, knowing better than to speak up. Rowan nodded once, the agreement amenable, though not ideal.

"That went better than I expected," Avenith said.

Thenik agreed.

"A meal," Valera said, "then rest. You both have been through quite an afternoon."

"A meal and a healer," Fen said, holding his ribs. "Naelor made his feelings known."

Snapping twigs and rustling leaves offered an ambient chorus as Wil rushed in, sword drawn and chest heaving. Winter was at his side, teeth bared, eyes locked onto Naelor. Winter edged to Rowan, pressing her body against her legs. The rumbling growl in her chest was constant and deep.

"Did he run all the way here?" Fen gasped as he marveled, blinking at Wil with mouth agape, his hand clutching his side. "Gods above, man, are you godborn?"

But Will didn't answer, his gleaming hazel eyes deadly as they looked from Thenik to Naelor. He closed the distance between himself and Naelor, sword rising, Winter's snarling bark adding terrifying cacophony to his aggression. "Give me one reason why I shouldn't kill you."

"Naelor is quite useful," Valera said, lifting her hands in surrender. "And I find swordplay to be a messy business. Perhaps we could air our grievances with words?"

Wil lowered his weapon but not his rage. "Starting with your little wonder drug? Or kidnapping my best friend?"

"Taking your friend was an oversight on their part," Valera said. "They thought she was a typical wolf. They didn't realize she was a guardian."

"Since you speak for them," Wil said, turning to Valera, "you'll take responsibility."

"No," Naelor said, stepping forward. "All responsibility is mine."

"He's right," Valera said to Naelor, that predatory glimmer returning as her gaze bore into him. "I take responsibility for my people. Their actions reflect on me."

Naelor winced, moving back.

"I understand his frustration over the damaged cargo," Valera said, "but I also understand your frustration over the attack on your friends." She gestured toward the shack. "Shall we break bread together and make amends?"

Rowan raised an eyebrow, impressed with her skill in diplomacy. She regarded Valera with more respect despite the leader's tendency toward flattery and thinly veiled threats to get what she wanted.

But Rowan didn't want to stay. The urge to shift and run surged in her blood, almost burning beneath her skin. She needed something stronger to hold her anger. Her skin and bones weren't enough.

She rested a hand on Winter's head, soothed by her presence.

"Accepting the invitation will help fortify them as allies," Fen whispered to Rowan and Wil.

"What is their definition of *allies*?" Wil eyed the assassins who'd gathered in much the same fashion as they had. "But I suppose it wouldn't hurt."

"So long as they don't poison the food," Rowan mumbled, conceding as she watched Fen struggle to remain standing. "A meal, healing, and rest."

In the distance, the sky rumbled its threatening roar.

"A storm headed this way?" Wil asked, not hiding his displeasure. "I'd prefer to be home before nightfall."

"I need to patrol the woods," Rowan said. "The villagers are uneasy."

"We heard about the recent death," Valera said. "Attacked. Left bloodless."

Rowan almost blurted out her question—*how did you know*—only to remember to whom she was speaking. The leader of a guild of assassins who valued information as much as any currency.

"If Elderglen has a bloodborn problem," Avenith said, mischief alight in her eyes, "that's more serious than a load of mist arcana."

"An opinion I don't share," Rowan replied with the same challenge from before. "Both are dangers to my village, and both will be confronted with force."

"We'll give you shelter until the storm passes," Valera said. "Even if it's overnight."

Defeat soured in Rowan's stomach. Staying in the Moonblade hideout was not the path they would have chosen for themselves. But Fen's injury and the looming storm left them with little choice.

"Thenik," Valera said, "help Naelor get inside. All of you need to see Carrie immediately."

Valera waved for Rowan and the others to follow her side once Thenik, Naelor, and Avenith crossed the threshold into the shack. Rowan didn't miss Avenith's lingering gaze as they stepped inside. Rowan's core squirmed with dread.

What were they walking into?

CHAPTER 22

A well-hidden hatch in the shack opened to a set of steps, sturdy and well-built, that led deep into the earth.

"Welcome to Moonblade," Valera said, standing with a hand of invitation aimed at the portal below. "This is the primary outpost in this part of Thurin. Watch your step."

After Naelor and the others went first, their injuries making them cautious as they stepped down, Rowan offered Fen her arm. "Put your weight on me, Fen."

He chuckled at her firm tone, though his mirth cost him. He winced in pain, draping his arm across her shoulders as she took his waist. "If you insist."

"It's better to comply," Wil said from behind them. "Trust me."

"So I'm not the only one you boss around?" But Fen's pain interrupted his grin, his amusement turning into a grimace.

He stumbled once. Rowan braced him against her, trying to be careful around his ribs.

"I'm alright," he said, panting. He focused his breathing for a few seconds before continuing. Sweat beaded at his hairline. "Gods, it hurts."

"Who did it?" Wil asked.

"The large one," Rowan answered.

"Naelor," Fen said. "The one who said your bones were made of stone."

Wil chuckled. "So that bruise on his jaw is yours?"

"It is."

"Good."

At the last step, Rowan's eyes traced the shape and structure of the carved walls, reinforced with wood and steel. Crates and supplies filled the expansive clay floor, assassins in black milling around with various jobs. Pictures and patterned fabrics decorated the walls, pinned in place with nails or knives. The patterned fabrics each bore rust-colored bloodstains, the hue varying depending on the depth of fabric dye adorning each cloth.

Trophies, by Rowan's estimation. Ones worth showing off, all marked with blood. Winter whined, staying close to Rowan.

The stink of mildew mingled with body odor, bringing Rowan to press her fingers to her nose. Too many humans in one enclosed space. Her claustrophobia tingled on the edge of triggering, but Fen's hold on her arm kept her grounded. She could focus for his sake rather than letting her mind acknowledge how far underground she'd gone.

"What is this place?" Wil asked, looking around. "How long has it been here?"

"Centuries, if the stories are true," Valera said. "A hiding place for the military groups when the Wolf Seat was won by blood far more often than it is now."

Rowan knew the tales, how houses in Thurin would attempt to lay siege to the fortress and take the Wolf Seat by force. Now, the sitting monarch had to die or abdicate before the feats of strength would decide the next ruler.

"Queen Glyni does the Wolf Seat proud," Valera said, with several voices agreeing. "It's good to see Prince Lachlan's return, but keeping Glyni on the throne was the smart choice. She's a powerful leader for our people." After a moment, she added, "We're proud of the wolf who leads her people."

Several members lounged at a large table, drinking from wooden cups and bronze goblets. Rowan's nose picked up traces of cheap wine and roasted meat.

And mist arcana. How much, she couldn't say, but Moonblade had a sizable load within their base.

Rowan adjusted her hold on Fen, resigning to keep the peace with these tenuous allies, their union conditional. He looked at her quizzically but said nothing.

"Carrie is here," Avenith said, waving for Rowan and Fen to follow. "She'll have her work cut out for her today."

They approached an alcove at the rear of the room, past one dark archway and one closed wooden door. The woman there stood in front of a tall shelf, pulling clear glass bottles from the top. Rowan breathed easier here, with freshly brewed tea and floral notes making the healing corner almost cozy.

"That hand looks nasty, Naelor." Her voice had a lower timbre than Rowan expected, the sound indicative of age and experience, though her face and body appeared young. An old soul, perhaps, or one who had seen much of life despite her years. "And one of you...?" She looked at Fen, curious. "Something broken or something sprained?"

"Broken." He rested a hand on his ribs. "The toe of Naelor's boot is sturdy. My compliments to their maker."

"What's for supper?" Avenith asked, she and Thenik still remaining outside of the makeshift clinic.

"Stew." Carrie nudged her head toward the tables where several assassins sat. "It's hot."

Avenith's eyes grazed Rowan as she turned and left for her meal. Rowan didn't engage further, supporting Fen as Carrie looked at Naelor first, the bite on his hand still seeping blood. The physician hissed, grimacing.

"What in gods' name bit you?"

Without missing a beat, Rowan said, "A wolf."

Beneath Naelor's glare, Fen chuckled, only to groan, clutching his side. "Gods, Rowan, don't make me laugh."

But her amusement didn't linger as Naelor stared at her. There was no challenge in his gaze this time. Only a promise, one that he would fulfill with vengeance.

Carrie, seemingly oblivious, was gentle as she applied medicine to Naelor's wound. She hummed softly, the melody faintly familiar, like a lullaby from childhood.

"How do you cook food here?" Wil asked, looking around. "How is there no smoke?"

"That's the secret of Moonblade." Carrie winked before finishing Naelor's hand. "You're done. Get some food and try to rest."

Naelor didn't look at any of them as he moved to the others, but Rowan knew their business was far from over.

Carrie studied Fen as Rowan helped him sit down. "This is going to hurt like the seven hells. I can give you a tonic for the pain."

"I've had worse," he said, lifting his shirt.

"Don't endure pain if you don't have to," Rowan said. "Take the tonic."

He smirked, ducking out of his shirt and taking a small bottle from Carrie. "I will follow your command."

He downed the medicine in one gulp as Carrie prepped the bandaging. Self-conscious, Rowan crossed her arms, trying not to stare at the bruises and scars that marked Fen's body. The bruise from Naelor was already a deep, agonizing purple.

She cleared her throat, ignoring the warmth that climbed up her neck. "I don't command anyone."

"That's not entirely true," Wil said, mischief gleaming in his eyes. "You're pretty bossy, Rowan."

"I'm not *bossy*." Her arms flexed. "I'm the boss."

Laughing, Wil mimicked her pose, making a show of balling his fists beneath his biceps. "So strong. So fierce."

She punched his shoulder, a smile breaking through. Fen laughed, only to groan again.

As Carrie wrapped him carefully, Rowan turned her attention to the camaraderie among the Moonblade assassins, though the golden glow of Avenith's hair drew her gaze first. Her demeanor bordered on bravado, her smile broad and laugh loud. But every gesture held intention, as though she knew Rowan would watch.

"You alright?" Wil asked, edging closer to her. "It's been a while since you've seen her."

"I am, which is surprising. I thought I'd have feelings about it."

"About *her*," he clarified. "And you don't?"

"She tried to help me," Rowan said. "I suppose I'm grateful for that."

"Mm-hmm." With his arms still crossed, he nudged her shoulder with his. "Great progress, Ro."

"Can I get away with saying *it's complicated*?"

"Of course. As long as you're not lying to yourself." His demeanor became serious, his hazel eyes filled with understanding. "Your feelings aren't wrong, Rowan. The only wrong thing would be to say they're not there when they clearly are."

"So you're calling me a liar." But the insinuation didn't hurt her. He'd caught her, rightfully enough. "And you would be right."

"Do you want her back?"

She shook her head. "No. That chapter ended a long time ago. We're both different people now."

"Would you be upset if I made an observation?"

She raised an eyebrow. "When has my being upset ever stopped you?"

"She still has feelings for you," he said.

Rowan's core tightened, the recent memory of *I'm sorry, love* echoing in her mind. "I was afraid of that."

"All I'm saying is to be honest. If you're honest with yourself, you can be honest with her. And you won't hurt her the way she hurt you."

"Which I would hate." Rowan took a fortifying breath. "Thanks, Wil."

He draped an arm across her shoulders and kissed her crown. "Always. And moving on to another topic…" He glanced around the room. "Why does it feel like we're in the lion's den, and they're all hungry?"

"Trust your instincts," Rowan said. "I'd prefer the lions."

"Be careful what you wish for." Valera approached, offering a welcoming smile. "Please, make yourselves at home. We have plenty of food and drink."

"We shouldn't linger too long," Wil said, bowing his head in respect. "Our families will be worried."

Thunder rumbled, the muffled sound almost indiscernible. But the assassins collectively silenced, their eyes roving over the ceiling as though to see the lightning flash.

"Not in this weather," Valera said. "We have plenty of bedrolls and space for you."

Wil and Rowan shared a look before complying.

"Thank you, Valera," Rowan said. "Your hospitality is appreciated."

"Anything for you, god-touched." With a broad smile, Valera continued, changing the subject. "I met the merfolk queen of Estilon not too long ago. A remarkable beauty. And I heard she's a damn good fighter." Valera sighed, her look dreamy. "It's a pity King Owen met her first."

"I've heard she and King Owen rule well," Rowan said. "I've certainly seen proof of their influence in Sudor despite the small pockets of resistance."

"No doubt led by the Order." Valera's eyes darkened for a brief second before her expression neutralized once more. "Have you noticed any growing threats in Elderglen?"

"Increased news of raids and fights in surrounding areas," Rowan answered.

"I heard." Valera touched Rowan's shoulder briefly, a sign of solidarity that tested an unspoken boundary. Rowan didn't shift away, but she stood taller as though to say, *Thank you. Once is enough.*

"Elderglen isn't a threatening place, as far as magic is concerned," Valera went on. "I wonder if it will remain unnoticed."

"Any village can be susceptible to capture," Rowan said. "Nothing sets Elderglen apart from places that have been overrun and turned into a cultist outpost."

"But they have you." A glimmer of wonder returned to her dark eyes. "That's something, indeed."

"I can't promise how far that will take them," Rowan said. "I'm only human."

"You're so much more," she said. "Don't let humility become your cage."

Rowan didn't react, though she flinched internally. *A cage.* One of her own making.

Her spirit was contained, controlled. Her wildness kept from reaching its maximum. It's *potential*.

Rowan blinked away the thought, turning to Fen as he stood with effort, hand pressed against his wrapped abdomen.

"Thank you, Carrie," he said. "I feel better already."

"The softest bedroll for this one," Carrie said to Valera, nodding at Fen. "Naelor broke two of his ribs."

"He'll be sad it wasn't three," Fen joked, carefully ducking into his tunic. Rowan helped to pull the fabric down. "Thank you."

Warmth tingled in her cheeks, and she looked away as the storm grew. Glancing at the ceiling, as the others had done before, gave her eyes something else to study.

"We shouldn't try traveling in this," Wil said, disappointment heavy in his voice. "Let's at least take them up on their promise of a hot meal."

"And soft bedrolls," Valera reminded. "You will be safe here. I give you my word."

"None of your members can scry, by any chance?" Rowan asked, her hope thin. "Send word to our family?"

"Regrettably, no." Valera chuckled. "Imagine what we could accomplish with that kind of magic."

At Valera's command, a man carried a small wooden table from the dark corridor on the other side of the room while two others were behind him with chairs. It was large enough for Rowan, Wil, and Fen to sit comfortably with Valera. Winter laid by Rowan's feet, her eyes and ears alert.

"While you are welcome here," Valera said, sitting down. "I only ask you don't go exploring on your own. This is the only space you have access to."

Intrigue feathered in Rowan's pulse, but she agreed. "We don't wish to breach your trust or hospitality."

Wil quirked a single eyebrow, saying nothing. Fen only nodded once, and Rowan suspected he knew more about Valera's reason for their limited access. Did he know what was behind every closed door? Did he know what lay hidden in the darkness she couldn't see beyond?

A familiar scent caught Rowan's nose—the warm spice of cinnamon whiskey. She inhaled slowly, savoring it as her heart ached for the woman who'd loved it. Several Moonblade members brought their steaming food to the table, one of them carrying the brown bottle familiar to Rowan's household.

"Cynthia's favorite," Valera said with a knowing smile. "I would make sure she had a fresh bottle every month. Sometimes twice, when the world was ending."

"My grandmother respected you," Rowan said. "The work you and Moonblade have done against the Order worked in tandem with us."

With us, even though Rowan's connection to Feather and Claw had been tenuous at best. Now she was bound, duty and obligation becoming strong ties to bind her there.

"Likewise," Valera said. "Feather and Claw is invaluable in the fight against that damned cult. I'm relieved to know it's passed on to someone capable and willing to fight."

Rowan offered a small smile at the compliment. *Capable* and *willing to fight* weren't what kept Rowan from taking up the mantle of Cornerstone.

Valera dined with them, the stew simple but savory and the ale cold and refreshing. Rowan tasted the cinnamon whiskey, imagining Gran's reaction to seeing her dine with the leader of Moonblade. What hell would Gran rain upon Naelor and the others for throwing her in a cage? The idea made her smile.

"We will work to keep Elderglen apprised of any Wandering Order activity that looms too close," Valera said.

"I would like to do the same," Rowan said. "I'm sure we can figure out a way to keep communication."

"One solution I've already considered." A corner of Valera's mouth tugged upward. "Avenith, Thenik, and Naelor need to work off their debt to you."

"Debt—"

But before Rowan could ask, Fen interrupted. "Is that really necessary?"

Valera regarded Fen with knowing. "Moonblade resources were used without express order or permission. The punishment for that is severe unless an alternative option is presented. That, and they attacked civilians unprovoked."

"My attacking the mist arcana cargo was provocation enough," Rowan said. "Our ledger is even."

But Valera shook her head. "Your friends weren't involved with that. My people don't attack others without just cause. Even going back to exact revenge on you isn't a valid enough reason for what they did. Gods be praised, you're all still alive, or their punishment would have rivaled the Chaos Realm in severity and nightmare." She looked at Fen, apology in her gaze. "Breaking your ribs was out of line. Your actions were in self-defense."

"Most of what Naelor does is out of line."

Wil leaned forward, curiosity shimmering in his eyes. "I have one question if you don't mind me asking."

"As you wish." Valera smirked, matching Wil's body language. "I reserve the right to refuse to answer."

"Fair enough." And, without missing a beat, he asked, "How do you cook food down here?"

Rowan laughed, wondering if that was the only thought consuming his mind since Carrie had remained elusive in her answer.

Valera grinned. "There's space with ventilation."

Wil persisted, his mind working to put the pieces together. "And the smoke doesn't draw anyone's attention?"

"We're very good at hiding."

Rowan leaned back, taking one more sip of whiskey, her eyes catching Fen's. Amusement flattered him, the lines around his mouth deepening at his soft, closed-mouth smile, and she enjoyed looking.

CHAPTER 23

Their resting space was quiet, the bedrolls comfortable, but Rowan lamented Fen's pitiable state of having to sleep on the floor. She said nothing as she offered her hands, helping him to ease down.

"They gave us a nice spot," Wil teased, eyes roving over the room as he situated his bedroll close to Rowan's. He intended to provide a physical barrier between her and the rest of the room, even while sleeping. "Right in the middle of everything while somehow keeping us out of the way."

"Almost like a guest room," Rowan agreed.

"Some of the closed doors are bed chambers," Fen said, keeping his voice down. "Some with bunks like a barracks."

Rowan sat on her bedroll with Winter settling by her legs, Wil on one side and Fen on the other. "And the others?"

"Supplies," he said. "Weapons. Resources." Then, after clearing his throat, he added, "One is where they refine mist arcana."

"It's like she knew I'd want to keep watch," Wil said, his voice disrupting the spiral in her mind as he sat on his bedding and surveyed the room. "Now I want to see who goes in and out of each room and how often."

"Get some rest," Rowan said. "Nothing is going to happen tonight."

Wil raised an eyebrow. "How can you be sure?"

"Because they don't know how we sleep," she said. "And they know we're watching them."

"She's right," Fen said. "They're as leery of us. But I don't mind taking a watch if that'll make you feel better."

"What will make me feel better is being home." Wil reclined against the wall. "Peter can't sleep without me."

"Neither can you sleep without him." Rowan's mild amusement helped her body to let go of the tension it held.

Quiet passed among them for several moments as they settled onto their assigned beds. Fen edged closer to Rowan as he muttered, "There's something—"

But he stopped as Avenith approached, a few extra blankets in her hands. "Comfortable?"

Avenith passed them to Rowan, who accepted them with a wary look. The room was mild and pleasant despite the lack of a breeze. The blankets were Avenith's excuse to come over.

"What do you have for a headache?" Wil asked her.

"Lady's ivy," she said. "Carrie always keeps a good supply."

"Here." Fen pulled a sachet from his pack. "I always keep some on me."

Grateful, Wil took two leaves and chewed carefully, grimacing before sipping from his water skin.

"Get some rest," Avenith said. "See you in the morning."

Then she disappeared behind the rightmost door.

Wil sighed as he stretched out on his bedroll, the fabric and padding several inches too short. "We're going to face hell from my husband tomorrow, and I'd rather not do that while annoyed."

"Sleep won't cure that." Rowan offered him a half-smile before curling up on her side. "You're irritable in the best of circumstances."

Wil chuckled. "I'm the grumpy one. He's the sunny one."

"He'll forgive you when he learns what happened," Fen said. Then, with a touch of mischief, he added, "We could just blame Rowan."

She whirled, her thick braid hitting her throat and chest to see Fen's teasing expression.

"Sweet dreams," Fen sang with a wink.

"Don't be so charming, you flirt." Wil rested his arm over his eyes. "I'm a married man."

Soon, their collective breathing soothed Rowan's busy mind. Fen shifted on his bedroll next to her before exhaling, and she turned to study his features in the limited amber light. How he'd looked that night under the stars, at peace with himself and the world as the night covered him. Here, it was different as they rested underground, surrounded by strangers with hidden agendas. The thin line between his eyebrows was the only sign of his ill-ease, the rest of his mask firmly in place. Rowan knew all too well the power of a crafted facade to hide the wild within.

The storm growled its thunder. The wild of the heavens met the wild of her heart in kinship, giving her space to rest.

THE STORM HAD CLEARED to give them a beautiful morning, but Rowan awoke to a dimly lit den of thieves snoring and grumbling as they slept.

Her corner with Wil and Fen remained quiet, and as she opened her eyes, she turned to see Fen already awake, whittling. His strong, calloused hands managed the knife with practiced skill, the veins trailing from his knuckles to his elbows as each muscle worked.

"Good morning," he whispered. "At least, I think it's morning."

She sat up, taking a deep breath before sipping from her water skin, eyeing the wood he shaped in his hands. "What are you carving?"

"Winter." He held up the crude shape, eyeing the wolf in comparison.

"She'll be honored." Rowan untied the leather cord binding her braid and worked her fingers through her hair, rubbing the nape of her neck in short-lived relief. Almost as quickly, she worked a fresh braid through the indomitable waves and curls. "How long have you been awake?"

"Maybe an hour?" He took care as the blade gently shaved a curve. "I was in and out all night."

"No stars to watch."

He hummed in quiet agreement. "Do you always keep your hair bound?"

Her hands stopped, surprised by the question. "Yes. Why?"

"It's flattering," he said. "Braided or not. But it's nice when it's free."

"Just like us."

There was the trace of a dimple, barely visible through his beard. "Just like us."

She finished, tying the cord in place, listening to the steady breathing of the sleeping assassins.

"You were talking in your sleep."

She froze, the rush of panic hitting quickly. "I was?"

"Something about too many people watching." He mused for a moment, studying her. "Did you have a dream where you were in front of a crowd?"

"I didn't dream." But she couldn't trust that, either. Not remembering a dream didn't mean it didn't occur, her mind defenseless against whatever scenarios her fears and hopes would conjure. "I don't remember."

"It would be difficult not to feel every eye on you. Watcher. Guardian. And now Cornerstone." The latter he muttered, barely a whisper. "How do you find peace in that?"

"In solitude," she said. Then, after a moment, she added, "And in select company."

He worked his knife slowly, fingers careful. "Am I select company?"

The room stirred to life with grumbles and voices, the loudest among them Valera. Rowan watched as she roused Avenith first, then Thenik, saving Naelor for last. The latter went for his pint, taking a swig of last night's ale.

"You're bound for Elderglen," she said to them. "Help the village. I don't care how. After three days, you may return."

"Three days?" Naelor looked from Valera to the others. "That's a little extreme, isn't it?"

"Your quarrel was with Rowan," she said simply. "But the aggression expanded to others who should not have been involved."

"They fought just as fervently as she did."

"My decision is made," Valera said, her tone firm. Power gleamed in her eyes, the dangerous kind that wouldn't let his backtalk slide. "After three days, you may return."

Wil sat up, his hair mussed from sleep. "That was bracing."

"Three days," Rowan said, her insides churning with an ill omen. "It's a punishment for us, too, isn't it?"

"Valera does nothing without intention," Fen said.

Wil scooted closer, leaning so that he could whisper with barely any sound. "If they're in Elderglen, and Marc is in the shack…" He let his statement hang unfinished.

"Assume Valera knows something," Fen said. "That's the safest course of action. Assume she already knows."

Naelor and Thenik were slow to prepare, with Rowan, Fen, and Wil ready to leave. Avenith hoisted her rucksack strap over one shoulder, egging the other two on.

"My grandmother can move faster than that," Avenith teased. "You know Valera will add on another day if you move any slower."

That motivated Thenik, while it posed a challenge to Naelor. When they finally ascended the steps to leave, Rowan allowed herself a sigh of relief.

Once daylight touched them, the crisp, clean air of morning filled Rowan's lungs with invigorating luxury. Dew dampened their trousers as they walked about tall grass and wildflowers. She shivered only once in the misty touch left behind by the dawn.

"Why so early?" Avenith asked, rubbing her eyes. "Gods above, you couldn't wait to get away."

"I have someone waiting for me," Wil said simply. "I'm the reason we rose with the sun."

Avenith yawned. "Oh, to have a love as enduring and strong."

Wil lifted an eyebrow, his amusement showing in his slight smile. "Something like that."

Fen seemed alert and clear, which Rowan quietly envied. She

blinked slowly, senses still coming to her as she squinted. As soon as she reached home, she would collapse onto her bed and—

But she couldn't. Not with Avenith, Naelor, and Thenik entering Elderglen. Valera had insisted, even as Rowan tried once more to refuse.

"What can we expect when we arrive?" Thenik asked, one hand resting on the pommel of his sword while the other held the pack strap on his shoulder. "Will there be work?"

"Plenty," Rowan said. "Craftsmen. Farmers and traders." She met Thenik's eye with hope. "The stables are always looking for hands who are kind to horses."

He nodded once, reassurance lifting his shoulders and his spirits.

Naelor ran his tongue over his teeth, the sucking sound tingling down Rowan's ear canals. She fought the urge to shake her head to rid herself of both sensation and sound.

"Blacksmith?" Naelor asked.

"We have one if that's what you're asking," Wil said, irritation sharp in his tone. "A blacksmith and a tanner, if either suits you."

Fen smiled to himself, and Rowan faced forward, keeping her own amusement hidden. Fen, having met the blacksmith, likely knew her temperament. Naelor would have his hands full if he worked for her. And if Rowan could read into Fen's expression, he wished he would.

"And what about me?" Avenith offered a playful smile, combating the tiredness still around her eyes. "Any old ladies need someone to make them tea?"

"Don't let her cook for you," Thenik said with a chuckle. "Unless they're someone you wish to see dead."

Avenith punched his shoulder, Thenik laughing as he took the blow. But her eyes caught Rowan's, the look they shared speaking of a secret without words.

Other than, Valera, did the rest of Moonblade remain ignorant to the godborn power Avenith possessed? Or were they protecting her from those who may not know?

"The tavern has an opening," Wil said. "Just stay out of the kitchen."

Avenith pursed her lips, indignant, but said nothing.

"You know," Fen said. "Valera could have let us borrow a wagon for the return journey. You know, since we were brought in one against our will."

He smirked as he glanced at Naelor, whose lips curled in disgust. Avenith giggled before trotting closer to Rowan, who kept her eyes forward.

"What should I expect when I arrive?" Avenith asked. "Will there be warm fanfare for three strong volunteers to work without pay?"

Naelor clicked his tongue, punctuating the part about their lack of a stipend.

"Elderglen's a quiet village," Rowan said. "You'll likely find yourself bored, just like before."

"So little has changed. I still have to make my own fun."

Rowan chanced a look at Avenith, who winked. Avenith's version of *fun* usually led to Rowan apologizing to someone on her behalf.

"Keep your head down," Rowan said, "and don't cause trouble."

"Oh, a tough promise to keep." The playfulness in Avenith's voice made Rowan want to walk faster, discomfort tugging at her core. "You'll have to hold me to it."

"I already have my hands full, Av. I don't need another job."

"Oh?" The song-like quality in Avenith's voice made it difficult to stop listening. "Care to elaborate?"

"Not in the slightest." Rowan took a steadying breath and pressed on, purposefully walking faster to give them distance, but she heard Fen jogging up beside her, his glance one of apology.

"Three days," Naelor said. "Three days of hell."

The feeling's mutual. Rowan pressed her lips together. *Will we come out of this unscathed, or will we try to kill each other before the week's over?*

Unease swirled within her core, her stomach muscles tightening as she waited for the sparks of conflict to catch fire. Any moment now, her world would go up in flames.

CHAPTER 24

The group crossed into Elderglen by midday. Villagers passed here and there among the shops and the tavern, some with carts of goods to sell or trade.

"Gods help us," Naelor said. "You didn't say the village was this small."

"I thought you had a firm grasp of it already," Rowan said. "You asked if we had certain trades in our village as if there was a chance we wouldn't."

He grumbled as Avenith grinned. She moved up to Rowan, her look conspiratorial.

"I absolutely love how you stand up to him," she said, her voice low. "He's not used to someone talking back."

"I'm not doing either of those things," Rowan said, but that wasn't true. Naelor presented a confrontation that Rowan itched to meet. His bravado and ego, his physicality and insistence to take up more space and push out others—

"If you go into the woods," Rowan said, forcing her voice to interrupt her cascading thoughts. "Stay on the path to the river. Don't go in too far and disturb the wolves."

Naelor chuckled but said nothing.

"The stable is further up the road," she said, lifting a hand to point. She nodded to Thenik. "Stable hand's name is Orin. Older, gray hair, mustache."

Thenik nodded in thanks and pushed on toward his destination.

"Blacksmith and tanner are there, of course," Rowan said with quick gestures to each, "and this is the tavern. If either of you prefer farm work, the tavern is a good place to ask."

"A bit too hot and smelly for me," Avenith said.

Naelor chuckled. "Is *tavern wench* more your speed?"

He laughed harder as Avenith gave him an icy look. "Don't order from me if you value your life." Then, thoughtfully, she asked, "What should we say when asking for work?"

"I was going to go with *lost a bet*," he said. "I'm sure you'll think of something." He eyed Rowan, glancing at the red cloak still hanging from her shoulders. "You're the Cornerstone now, right?"

She couldn't hide her reaction, taken aback by his question. "Yes."

"It's just that the red side is out, not the black." He raised an eyebrow. "Say, is that why your wolf's fur is that reddish color?"

She didn't want to answer. Something about the way he asked made her skin crawl.

"Of course," he said. "Magic makes you shift, and it will change depending on what you wear. Even your hatchets." He smirked, eyeing her in a way that made her skin crawl. "What would your fur look like if you weren't wearing—"

Fen and Wil squared up, each of them taking a step, but Rowan beat them to it, rushing Naelor with inhuman speed. The itch to shift was strong, the pull toward wild ferocity almost too much to bear.

"If that bruise on your jaw wasn't enough of a reminder, you would do well to remember what I'm capable of."

Provocation gleamed in his eyes.

A low growl threatened to rumble from within her chest. "Any crudeness or cruelty within my village won't be tolerated. Don't make me regret letting you enter my home."

"Or what?" A corner of his mouth flicked upward, the threat of a smug grin almost surfacing. "You'll rip the flesh from my bones?"

"Seriously?" Avenith asked. "*That's* the first thing you think of?"

"Gods, I certainly hope so," Fen said. "I have no qualms about watching her rip you to shreds."

"I agree," Wil seconded. "You have no friends here, Naelor, save those you came with."

"And even those seem thin." Fen crossed his arms. "This isn't the right place to cause trouble."

Wil and Fen had given Rowan time to breathe, her nerves settling as her tidal wrath ebbed.

Wil laughed, though, shaking his head. "It's your grave if you keep testing her."

"Who's this?"

Rowan slowly turned as Halie eyed the strangers warily.

"Newcomers?" Halie raised an eyebrow. "Who have you brought to Elderglen, Watcher?"

Rowan's lip nearly curled at the way Halie said her title. But Avenith spoke up first.

"I'm Avenith." She pressed a hand to her bosom before gesturing to Naelor. "And this is Naelor."

"Avenith," Halie said slowly. "That name..."

"So you *do* remember me?" Avenith offered Halie her sweetest smile, the veneer perfect. "I am pretty memorable."

But Halie wasn't impressed. "What brings you to Elderglen?"

"Work," Naelor said, his tone clipped.

Frustration simmered hot beneath Rowan's skin, the irritating presence of Braithen and Halie exacerbating the tense anticipation of Naelor striking out, whether figuratively or literally. The man was a loose cannon, but she didn't have enough hands to keep him on a tight leash. Valera, by trying to make good Naelor's egregious mistake, had only made things harder.

But Rowan suspected this act wasn't out of the goodness of Valera's heart. Nothing with Moonblade ever was, if their reputation was any indication.

Naelor nodded to Avenith once before turning for the blacksmith.

"I can't wait to hear how his day went," Fen mumbled.

"Why here?" Halie looked more to Rowan than Avenith. The

assassin took this opportunity to walk to the tavern, her movements easy and assured.

"Why does it trouble you? There are no rules about newcomers trying to find temporary work, and the farmers could use the extra hands."

Halie rested her hands on her hips. "Things are tense enough without there being dramatic changes to our village."

A side glance caught Wil rolling his eyes.

But there was a scent that caught Rowan's attention, faint but familiar. She inhaled carefully, discerning the delicate fragrance of sweet citrus. She edged closer to Halie, the smell getting stronger.

"What?" Halie took a half-step back, eyes wide as Rowan continued to follow the scent. It was far too familiar to be left alone. Sharp. Acrid. With the faintest traces of citrus.

Mist arcana. Rowan leaned closer to Halie and breathed in.

Halie scoffed, taking a half-step back. "Did you just *smell me*?"

Rowan met the indignant woman's eyes, not in the least bit embarrassed or nervous. "Where have you been lately, Halie?"

She retreated further. "Stay back, *dog*."

Rowan snapped. Her movements were quick, hands like claws, fingers and thumb poised to seize. Were it not for Fen bringing her arm down and moving between them, Rowan's hand would have learned the shape of Halie's throat.

"She's not worth it," Fen said quickly, looking at Rowan over his shoulder. Then, with glaring eyes focusing on Halie, he said, "Consider this the one and only time I save your wretched life." His gaze was lethal, the depths of his blue eyes fathomless. "Speak ill of her again, and you'll wish I let her throttle you."

"I keep telling you to leave her the hell alone." Wil pulled Halie back. "Why doesn't anyone listen to me?"

"She's insane!"

"The order from Rowan still stands." Wil bore down on her. "Unless it is official village business, stay away from Sentinel Hill."

"You can't—"

"We can." Wil didn't relent. "And we just did."

Halie, in a huff, turned on her heel and hurried home, likely to tell Braithen everything.

"Thank you," Rowan whispered, looking down at her hands as she pulled and twisted her fingers together, ashamed. "How long before she beats on the mayor's door to tell him everything?"

"Frederick won't listen," Wil said.

Though shame lingered, Wil's irreverent commentary loosened the tightness in her chest. "I love how you don't call him Mayor."

Wil shrugged a shoulder but said nothing else.

"She and her brother seem the type to bring out the worst in people," Fen said.

"They're going to get in trouble sooner or later," Wil added. "And I can't wait to watch."

"I hate that they get under my skin." Rowan clenched her jaw, disappointment souring her stomach. "I hate that I let them."

"They'd get under anyone's skin," Fen said. "Anyone impervious wouldn't be human."

"It's my temper," Rowan said. "*Mine*. I shouldn't let others control it."

"There, we agree," Fen said. "But a heart like yours doesn't rest in apathy."

His sincerity didn't waver. Quietly, she asked, "And what do you know of my heart?"

There was no sarcasm or defense in her voice. And in the presence of such vulnerability, Fen's look softened. "Enough that I want to know more."

"Alright, you two." Wil glanced toward Sentinel Hill. "Let's get this over with. My husband will have a *lot* to say."

He adjusted the strap of his pack on his shoulder before walking on, Rowan and Fen close behind.

CHAPTER 25

The firelight augmented Jean's silhouette, triggering Rowan's memories of discipline in her childhood.

"Captured?!" Jean stood in front of the hearth of Wil and Peter's home, the firelight illuminating her form in an impressive silhouette, one that highlighted the flash of anger in her eyes.

"They recognized me as a wolf," Rowan said. "I attacked their load of mist arcana, and one had a grudge."

"And they're in Elderglen," Fen said. "Valera is forcing them all to work off a debt for our capture."

Fen described Naelor, Thenik, and Avenith, as well as where they'd opted to volunteer their time.

Peter chuckled at Naelor's choice with the blacksmith. "Whatever hell befalls him serves him right."

"They know I'm wolfkind and Cornerstone," Rowan said. "Naelor brought up the way I wear the cloak."

She didn't say more, refusing to give voice to the reason why the cloak remained red. She had the words and the guilt that came with them, but she couldn't bear the disappointment that would follow. Jean, Wil, Peter, even Fen. She knew what they expected. What Elderglen expected. What Feather and Claw expected.

Winter whined at Rowan's side, pressing against her leg. Her gray eyes held knowing within them, as though she could discern Rowan's thoughts and fears. Rowan scratched lightly around her ears.

Three knocks interrupted the atmosphere, the five companions collectively alighting to who would be outside, bidding for their attention. Rowan answered, surprised by their visitor. "Avenith?"

She smiled at Rowan, a hint of a dimple toying with her cheeks, her hands clasped in front of her. "I'm sorry to disturb you."

Jean didn't waste a second, swooping upon her with such speed and force that Rowan almost didn't move aside in time to block Avenith from Jean's wrath. "You should have known better, Avenith. Or are you bitter even though you're the one who left?"

Rowan gasped as Avenith blinked in shock.

"That's not it," Avenith said. "I didn't realize it was her until I saw her face." Avenith met Rowan's eyes then, sincerity enriching their golden hazel. "I swear it. Naelor said nothing about your scar, only that he wanted to capture the wolf and bring it back. That's why I'm here." Avenith bowed at the waist. "You have my sincerest apology. All of you."

"Don't bow, Av."

Jean balked from behind Rowan, her breath hot on her neck.

Rowan took a step back, intentionally taking Jean with her. "Would you like to come inside?"

"I have to return to the tavern," she said, "but while the others were busy, I wanted to tell you how sorry I am to hear about Gran's passing."

Rowan's lip twitched, but the tingling sensation of grief didn't come. There was only numbness and fatigue...and apathy.

Winter whined again, her snout poking the back of Rowan's thigh twice.

"And I wanted to apologize. For leaving." Avenith glanced at Jean, her smile quick. "I'm not staying in Elderglen after our three days are up."

Rowan said nothing for a moment. "You should return before—"

"I don't want our actions to create a rift between our guilds," she said quickly, sensing Rowan's dismissal. "We've worked hard to form our alliance."

"If our priorities align," Rowan said, choosing her words with care, "then we have no reason not to get along."

Avenith held Rowan's gaze, familiarity softening the otherwise sharp lines of her features. The history between them had aged with the passing years, though its freshness had managed to linger. Still, that part of Rowan's life had ended. She wasn't interested in returning to the past when so much depended on the present.

"I'll take my leave." Avenith bowed her head, glancing at the others before locking eyes with Rowan again. "We should catch up. Over a meal, perhaps."

"If you'd like." But Rowan didn't budge, even as she suffered the burning stares of everyone in the room behind her. "Dinner tonight?"

Avenith's winning smile returned. "See you tonight."

Rowan waited until Avenith was down the hill before closing the door. When she faced the room, four pairs of eyes studied her in varying degrees of astonishment and wariness.

"I don't trust her," Jean said. "Not one bit."

"That's wise." Fen crossed his arms, not taking his eyes off Rowan. "She wants something, that's certain."

"Having dinner with her may reveal it. She might talk to me." Rowan looked at Wil, whose expression was a blend of emotions all vying for prominence. "What are you thinking right now?"

"You're having your ex over for dinner, and she's an assassin who still has feelings for you." He raised an eyebrow. "Either it's genuine, or she's using it as a way in."

Peter raised his eyebrows. "And you know this from experience?"

"I was her way to Gran," Rowan said. "At least, at first."

"Gran?"

Jean exhaled. "Avenith wanted information about one of the Preceptors. With Cynthia as the Cornerstone of Feather and Claw, Avenith applied some leverage to learn what she could. Then she left."

"*Damn.*" Peter shook his head, combing his hair back with his fingers. "That's cold."

"It was more complicated than that," Rowan said, "but that's the short version."

"Avenith likes power," Fen said, his expression sympathetic. "Her feelings are likely genuine, *and* she would use them as a way in."

"With others, maybe," Rowan said. "But not with me."

Jean gave her a look but said nothing, her silence speaking volumes. No one trusted Avenith. Rowan didn't either, but she understood her. At least, she hoped she did.

"Do the two of you have a past?" Wil asked Fen outright. No hesitation, no etiquette. Peter nudged his shoulder, but Wil didn't back down.

"No," Fen said. "I didn't have something she wanted."

Rowan opened her mouth but stopped herself, not exactly seeing Fen's reason as the basis for Avenith's lack of interest. But, perhaps, that was *Rowan's* interest. Fen was fearless. Or, if he had fear, he didn't let it become an obstacle. Rowan couldn't deny the curiosity within her, eager to learn the path of his life to make him this way.

Strong.

Resilient.

Few could meet her gaze and maintain it. But he did, without hesitation. Such fortitude was rare.

"We'll see you at dinner," Jean said to Rowan, her stern voice breaking through her thoughts. "No arguments."

"She won't—"

"I said no arguments."

But Rowan stood her ground. "She won't open up to a group of people. What's the point if I can't learn something out of this whole encounter? Why open myself up to dinner with the girl who broke my heart if she won't talk to me?"

Jean sighed through her nose, her lips pressed to pallor. "As the Veil, I respect your decision and will obey. As your *friend*, I will tell you that this is a mistake."

As the Veil. Rowan's mixed reaction bore relief at possessing respected authority while bitterness soured on her stomach. Jean only complied because of Rowan's inherited leadership, not because it's what Rowan wanted.

The cloak around her shoulders weighed heavier than ever before.

"We can hide in one of the bedrooms," Wil suggested. "Eavesdrop?"

"That's your line of work, love." Peter kissed Wil's temple. "I'm not the stealthiest agent."

"I could agree to that," Rowan said, the tightness in her chest easing at the prospect of not being alone. "You, waiting and listening in absolute silence."

And if Avenith brought up the past, Wil had been there at every step, even comforting Rowan through tears that hadn't come. Wil already knew everything.

"You have my word."

Fen watched and waited, though Rowan could see his desire to join them. The corners of his mouth twitched as though to speak, but he kept his words unsaid.

"What of Naelor and Thenik?" Rowan asked him.

"Gods, don't invite them, too," Jean said.

"A meal in the tavern," Fen suggested, understanding Rowan's intent. "It would be awkward, but that might make it easier."

"Make what easier?" Peter asked. "Getting information from them?"

Fen nodded. "Thenik is more reserved, but Naelor likes to brag. Throw his weight around." Perhaps unconsciously, Fen touched his side, his hand passing over his healing ribs. "I can use that."

"Don't do what you're uncomfortable with," Rowan said.

He shook his head with a half-smile. "I'll see it done."

"They haven't seen our faces," Jean said to Peter. "Fancy a meal in the tavern tonight? A few tables away from Fen and the goons?"

Peter chuckled. "*The goons.*"

CHAPTER 26

Wil slipped into Rowan's home an hour before they expected Avenith to show.

"Smells good," he said, eyeing the pot on the fire with suspicion. "Peter's recipe?"

"Of course. For all the strength and skills I possess, *cooking* was never one of them."

He took a long sniff, eyes tracing the motion of the spoon as it stirred the stew. "It's a relief to know you're not perfect, Ro."

Winter rose from her spot beneath the window, greeting Wil with a wagging tail.

"There's my sweet girl." He scratched behind her ears and down her back. "Keep an eye on Avenith for me."

Rowan eyed the folded blanket on the floor that acted as Winter's bed. The color and seams of the fabric had aged with love and wear. It needed laundering.

"Try to lead the conversation to Moonblade and mist arcana," Wil said. "And if she knows anything about the men who took Marc."

"Would you like to be present?" Rowan quirked a brow, amused. "I can set the table for three."

"You know what I mean. It's easy to get caught up in the moment and forget."

"What moment?" Rowan scoffed. "You think I'm going to get caught up?"

"Avenith doesn't strike me as the sort to go into things with no plan," he said. "Even if it's just dinner."

"It's not *just dinner*," Rowan said. "She suggested it with such nonchalance that it doesn't feel like the first time for her."

"But it's the first time for you." He rested his hands on her shoulders. "Interrogation is never easy."

She turned from her best friend to stir the pot over the fire. "This isn't an interrogation."

"What is it, Ro?"

"A conversation." After a pause, she added, "To gain a sense of who she is now."

"That's a lot to attempt over a single meal."

"If we're lucky, this won't be the only one."

She didn't look up as he disappeared around the corner, quietly closing her bedroom door.

Peter's recipe for mutton stew and oatcakes was straightforward, and Rowan looked at both finished products with a touch of pride. *Gran would have liked these.*

Rowan smiled to herself despite the pang that sent an aching pulse through her body. Of all that had left with Gran, the absence of her humor and laughter had left the largest hole.

Three quiet knocks noted Avenith's arrival, just past sundown.

"Best behavior," Rowan muttered to Winter, who watched with her bright, unblinking eyes as her mistress opened the door.

When Rowan received her guest, her guard rose to its peak. Her attempt at nonchalance was thin.

"Hi." Rowan stepped aside to grant Avenith entry. "Please, have a seat."

"It smells great." The assassin's eyes scanned the modest dwelling, the pass of her gaze normal for one new to its space. She lingered on Winter, lying on a folded blanket in front of the window near where

Gran's bed had been. Winter, ears perked, did not wag her tail at their guest.

"Has she forgotten me?" Avenith asked, following Rowan to the table.

"Wolves have a long memory. She may warm up to you."

"What about you?"

Rowan didn't take the bait, feeling Wil's piercing gaze as if it could go through the wall of her bedroom. She kept her eyes and hands busy preparing Avenith's bowl of stew and two oatcakes.

"To assuage any awkwardness," Avenith said from her seat as Rowan served her, "should we jump right into what we both really want to talk about?"

"Who said it was awkward?"

"Everything about you." Avenith didn't bat an eye. "You're pulled tighter than a lady's corset."

The hands of the goddesses were upon her best friend, who likely had to swallow his own fist to keep from laughing. "I don't normally entertain. Or cook." She gestured to the bowl. "I promise I tried my best."

Avenith reclined, watching Rowan serve herself and take her seat. "My brother was like you. Quiet, reserved. And the smartest, bravest man I've ever known."

"I'm sorry," Rowan whispered, pausing to read Avenith's face before dipping her spoon. "You never told me much about your family other than they were killed."

"And I'm still trailing the man who did it." It was Avenith's turn to work at hiding her emotions, her voice strained as she reined it into her control. "Don't apologize."

"We've both lost," Rowan said. "Time helps us live with the pain of it, but the aching never goes away."

"No, it doesn't."

Awkwardness passed between them until Avenith took in a spoonful of stew. She nodded, humming her appreciation. "It's good."

Relieved that she wouldn't be poisoning her guest with her cooking, Rowan ate as Avenith continued.

"I will be upfront and say that I have questions you, as Cornerstone, may have the answers to. In turn, you undoubtedly have things you want to ask me."

"That's fairly said, but I've only been Cornerstone a short time."

"And you've been Gran's granddaughter for—eighteen years?" She quirked an eyebrow. "There are things you likely know that are buried deep in that sharp mind of yours. If it won't put you in too much trouble with Jean, we can share as much information as we can."

"And what about you?" Rowan took her water cup, poised to sip. "Two years with Moonblade has likely yielded some interesting knowledge."

"*Almost* two years," Avenith corrected with a wink. "Or are you trying to shorten our time together on purpose?"

Rowan said nothing, using her food as a prop to help maintain her calm demeanor.

"If I can tell you, I will," Avenith said, taking another bite. "It wouldn't be anything Valera wouldn't say."

"You know her that well?"

Avenith held up two crossed fingers. "Thick as thieves."

The joke didn't strike Rowan's humor. "I wonder if Valera sees it that way. Does she know?"

Avenith opened her mouth, confusion framing her features until she understood. "Yes. She knows."

"Does the Preceptor?"

"Somehow, no." Avenith rubbed an eyebrow, a tell when she was thinking. "I haven't exactly been subtle."

"Shooting lightning from your fingers?"

"That was *one time*." But Avenith smiled.

"It's rare a stormborn crosses my path," Rowan said. "Elderglen is small."

"And most are in Ileden." She leaned back, thoughts running behind her hazel eyes. "I've thought about going there. Seeing if I have any family roots in Storm Seat."

Rowan opened her mouth to ask, but Avenith shifted in her seat, grinning. In less than a second, her veneer returned, the mask firmly in place.

"I was hoping you would ask about Fen's brother," she said, eyes alight. "Marc Fen, wayward son, accomplished spy."

Accomplished spy. So she knew about Marc's ties to Feather and Claw. Either that, or she was fishing.

"Would you like me to?" Rowan leaned back, showing eased composure even as her heart thrummed in her chest. "What do you know about him?"

"That depends on what Fen's told you." Avenith watched her, searching for any clue in Rowan's behavior and expression. "Not much is my guess." She stirred her stew and took another bite. "Everything's connected. Moonblade. Feather and Claw. Fen and Marc." She blinked, the firelight dancing across her eyes and bared teeth. "*You.* The wolfkind Guardian of Elderglen, now Cornerstone of Feather and Claw." Avenith tilted her head. "One who hasn't put on the cloak."

Rowan leaned forward, mirroring Avenith's posture. "What does that have to do with Marc? What does that have to do with Moonblade?"

"All they need is an opening," she said. "Any sign of weakness to exploit."

"*They?*" Rowan thought quickly. "The Wandering Order?"

"News of Gran's death has likely traveled far, reaching ears eager for what they hope is a weakness. She had a reputation, which you know."

But Rowan only knew pieces, the journal still on the small table waiting to be read.

Gran was Cornerstone. The strict leader of a guild determined to rescue those with magic from the hateful eye of the Wandering Order. The crux of a group willing to do dangerous things to keep hope alive.

Rowan looked down at her hands, seeing her nails like claws. What would she do if faced with the choice?

Cornerstone.

Guardian.

Shifting was easier. Her wolf form made everyone hesitate before approaching her. It gave them pause before they burdened her with words and expectations.

Yes, they would hesitate, but they wouldn't stop. It would never stop.

Cornerstone.

Guardian.

"Rowan?" Avenith's voice broke through the cacophony of whispers circling in her thoughts. "Are you alright?"

"Of course." She attempted a small smile. "I still feel Gran's presence."

"Of course you do." Avenith glanced around the home, her expression almost serene. But serenity in the assassin's demeanor added to the alarm within Rowan. "She'll always be with you."

Rowan accepted the kind sentiment. Gran's imprint upon her would stay—

"You're one of the haunted."

Rowan blinked at her, processing her words individually, then together. "I'm what?"

"Things that have passed stay with you." She spoke as though she'd said nothing mildly offensive. "You're offering a home for things that can't move on."

Rowan's brow furrowed before she could control her expression. "The dead linger sometimes."

"Only when the living can't let go."

Heat flared within Rowan's core, but she fortified the cage walls around her heart, even as the beast within thrashed for freedom.

Rowan leveled her gaze at Avenith. "What can you tell me about Marc? Has Moonblade picked up any leads? Any details about his captors? You've been so busy speaking in riddles that you haven't told me the truth yet."

"I'm flattered you think I'm clever enough for riddles. And by the way you're asking, you already know he was captured." Avenith finished her stew and sipped water. "And he burned his way out."

Avenith knowing this much meant Rowan wouldn't accidentally reveal sensitive information or something Fen would wish to keep hidden. Moonblade—and Avenith—already knew.

"There's been movement to the northwest," Avenith said. "They're toying with the border of Alvar, but those cowards know better than to tempt a place full of magic."

"Some say the same of Ileden," Rowan said. "But they're pushing their way through."

"Only certain areas. They've yet to cross the witches in Storm Key." She laughed to herself. "My guess is that Marc is northwest. Still on the continent. Still close by."

"To what end?" Rowan asked, not letting on what she knew about Fen's brother and his escape. "Are they toying with him? Or us?"

"Always." Avenith smirked. "They only need reminding that they're not the predator in this relationship."

Relationship was an interesting way to describe it.

"In the name of fairness," Avenith said, eating more of her stew. She took a moment to sweep a bit of her oatcake around the inside of the bowl, taking a large, luxurious bite. "I have questions about your mantle and why you hesitate to wear it."

"I don't hesitate," Rowan said, though she feared she'd spoken too quickly. Unease churned in her stomach, knowing Wil heard every word, knowing Avenith could read between the lines. "From your perspective, I should already step into the role and the cloak, but, as you said, I am one of the haunted."

Avenith waited before asking, "Have I offended you?"

Rowan was tempted to say yes.

"Suffice it to say, the colors bear significance, and I am more often the Guardian of Elderglen than I am the Cornerstone of Feather and Claw."

"And you weren't exactly prepared to wear both."

Rowan wanted to retaliate, to correct Avenith in her presumption. But she was right. Even with Gran's decline, Rowan was far from prepared when the time came to become the Cornerstone.

"It shouldn't have been me," Rowan muttered. "I'm the last person who—"

"Don't say that," Avenith said. "You're the only person this could have fallen to."

But those words didn't bring comfort or confidence. They were a burden, just like the rest of it.

"Why not green or brown to match the colors of the forest?" Avenith asked, changing the subject. "The guardian's cloak stands out."

"Red is my favorite color," she said, insecurity and vulnerability mingling dangerously within her. "Not everything is coded or complicated."

"On that, we disagree." She winked before sipping more water, her demeanor at ease. Quite the opposite of Rowan's, who felt whatever hold she'd had on the conversation had slipped through her fingers. "Everything has intention and meaning."

"What would red mean, then?" Rowan prodded. "What would it mean that green and brown don't?"

"You're in the woods but not a part of them," she said. "You stand out as the human interloper among the wild, untamed forest and all its creatures."

How could Avenith find the words so easily when Rowan had lost herself in the feeling of it? *You don't belong here.*

But the forest was home, as much as the surrounding brick and wood of what her grandparents built.

"I see I've offended you again, but I would like to see you wear the black."

"Because you do?" Rowan asked, her tone sharper than she'd intended. "As Moonblade?"

"Black is neutral," Avenith said. If Rowan's tone had affected her, she hid it well. "Both in nature and among humans. Moonblade uses it to blend in with the dark. We can pass through shadows completely undetected once we've trained enough. The Cornerstone of Feather and Claw is a neutral entity, guiding the members to meet their goals while working with allies."

Neutral would *not* describe Gran. But Rowan's vision cleared, her mind quieted, and she could read into Avenith's words, as well as her delivery of them.

Like the way she told people what they were like and what they should do because Avenith needed something to fix.

Rowan followed the lead, sensing a path to understanding her guest a bit more. "And what would we aim to achieve?"

"Resources, squashing that pesky cult, broadening our reach beyond Sheraton and Ileden."

"Like Kema and the Ashlands?"

"Anywhere there's land, our guilds should exist. Because the Wandering Order and their ilk will exist in one form or another."

Rowan's own pessimistic outlook saw the reasoning in Avenith's words, but something about them reached a depth that made her uncomfortable. It was more than killing the spread of hate and ignorance. For Avenith, it was personal.

"You said you had a lead on the Preceptor," Rowan said. "Can you tell me anything?"

"Some." Avenith shifted, a thin sign of discomfort showing through. "There are actually two Preceptors. They work closely and share the same maligned vision for experimenting with mist arcana."

Rowan hadn't expected two. She avoided looking at the journal, the tome holding judgment in its eyeless gaze.

"One was injured pretty badly in Ileden," Avenith said. "The other —" Her voice caught. "He's the one who took my family."

While Rowan no longer harbored romantic feelings for Avenith, her heart ached with shared anger and grief. Hatred orphaned them both, with murderous hands stealing their families away. But Rowan had Gran and Jean and Wil. Avenith had no one.

"What do *you* want to see come out of this?" Rowan tugged this thread carefully. "What are your goals now?"

"The honest answer? My goals haven't changed." Sadness lined Avenith's expression, though her poise maintained his casual confidence. "I'm closer than I've ever been. Years of working toward finding him..." She let the statement dangle unfinished. "I can't stop now."

Avenith rose, the meal and conversation concluded.

"Thank you," Rowan said. "I know that wasn't easy."

"Spending time with you was always easy." She nodded toward the stew. "And your cooking's improved."

"Does the tavern have a room for you?"

"Yes, though—" She wiggled her eyebrows. "If you're offering better accommodations..."

"Our tavern is warm and welcoming," Rowan said, gesturing toward the door. "I know you will rest well."

"See you tomorrow, then."

Rowan ushered her out, closing the door. She counted to ten, measuring her breath, before glancing through the front window. Avenith's form retreated down the hill before disappearing out of sight.

Wil emerged seconds later, unblinking eyes watching her. "Interesting."

"That's one word for it." She crossed her arms, overexposed from Avenith's watchful eye and Wil's discerning mind. Never had she missed shadowed solitude more than in this moment. "What do you think?"

"She absolutely wants something, which we already knew," he said, rubbing his chin. "But how you fit into her plan is the question. Because you do. Another key question is, are you in her sights because of the guild?"

"Fen said Avenith followed power."

"No." He chuckled. "He said she was *attracted* to power. She doesn't strike me as the sort to follow anything or anyone. And while we're on the subject…"

Rowan's core clenched, waiting for Wil's question about Avenith's interest in the Cornerstone. In *her*.

But he surprised her by saying, "I wish Fen would be more forthcoming about what he knows about her. His insight would be invaluable."

Rowan didn't stop the grin that emerged, levity easing the anxiety tightening her insides. "You sure it's for the good of the guild and not your own curiosity?"

He quirked a brow, smirking. "Why can't it serve for both?"

CHAPTER 27

Avenith was out of sight when Jean stepped in through the back door, Fen and Peter in her wake. Wil waited with Rowan at the dining table, the tea already steeping in their cups.

"How did you do?" Jean asked. "Is she crawling back on her knees, begging for forgiveness? Or is it much worse?"

"I'm afraid I don't have much to tell," Rowan said. She shared information about the Preceptors and Avenith's questions about the Cornerstone.

"So, she's still out for revenge." Jean shook her head. "Does she think you can help with your newfound leadership?"

"It's not a question of *if* she wants something." Rowan rubbed her forehead, the pressure of a headache forming. "Our relationship has gotten more complicated."

Wil nodded slowly, eyebrows reaching for his hairline. "That's an understatement."

"Naelor wants something, too," Fen said. "I'm not sure how his goals align with Avenith's. Naelor and Thenik are friends, but Naelor and Avenith? Theirs is a relationship of convenience. Has to be."

"Which would be mutual on her part," Rowan said. "How did the conversation go?"

Fen shrugged. "The ale helped. Naelor gets chatty with enough drink in him. Poor Thenik was too tired to give a damn about anyone or anything. After two pints, he went upstairs. But Naelor kept going, talking about Moonblade focusing their efforts on arcana crystal." He sipped his tea, nodding in approval before going on. "He was kind enough to say that several mines near Elderglen proved more abundant than initially thought."

"That explains why they were so close the other night," Wil said. "The mine *and* Marc."

"I've already apologized to Valera for my interference," Rowan said, "but I've also made it pretty clear that proximity to Elderglen is still an issue. Our agreement with Valera is present but delicate."

"Unless Naelor decides to see how far he can go."

Peter chuckled. "Let him go right off the cliff if he's determined to test his limits." He looked at Rowan with a glimmer in his eyes. "It's his own fault if he does."

But Rowan wasn't so sure of her success. If anything, Naelor wouldn't fall without taking her with him.

THE NIGHT WAS young when Rowan stepped out her door, Winter at her side and Fen at her heels.

"You don't have to come," she said. "We're all exhausted."

"And you still have a duty to complete."

He was as resolved as she was, which was both comforting and annoying. "Suit yourself."

They walked through the field toward the forest, the night bugs and birds offering their melodies as dusk diminished what sunlight remained, giving room for the moon and stars. The overcast was thin, allowing natural light to shimmer against the darkened landscape.

It was Rowan's favorite time of day. The transition into evening with the world turning dark and quiet. Nothing compared to the cool shift in tone and temperature, with the world whispering its way to sleep.

If only she could spend all her time in the dazzling embrace of midnight.

"About Avenith."

Rowan looked at Fen from the corner of her eye. "Just like that? *About Avenith*?"

"I thought you would appreciate straightforwardness."

"You would be correct. What about Avenith?"

"You likely know her better than I do," he said. "My time with Moonblade was extremely limited, and couple that with an extremely limited *person*, there isn't much I know."

"What *do* you know?"

He waited before speaking. "I'm not sure what she wants or what she'll do to get it. And I worry what she'll leverage along the way."

"You mean me."

His silence was her answer.

"We've only known one another a short time, Fen." Her emotions were teetering between offense, amusement, and appreciation. "I know where this concern is coming from, don't get me wrong, but—"

"I've overstepped."

Her tone remained kind as she confirmed, "You overstepped."

"I'm sorry, Rowan."

She touched his shoulder in a gesture of comfort, the urge within her simultaneously strange and fulfilling. But her hand didn't linger, only offering a moment's contact before returning her hand to her side. "I don't know what she wants from me or from anyone, but I know she will steer her path toward a Preceptor for the Wandering Order."

Surprise mingled with awe as he furrowed his brow. "Gods, why?"

"She has her reasons." If Fen didn't already know about Avenith's family, Rowan would protect that. "And they are not mine to tell."

They crossed into the forest, the smell of burned wood and flora present, though diminishing.

"She's right to trust you," he said, "but I worry about trusting *her*. She met me because Valera learned I was a Vanguard. Before, if I was anywhere near Avenith's awareness, she didn't offer me the time of day. But after? I became one of the most fascinating people in Sheraton."

"Did you know anything about the Wandering Order?" Rowan asked. "Specifically about a Preceptor?"

He nodded. "That information wasn't confidential. Part of the reason I allied with Moonblade was because of cultist movement and aggression. Valera and Cynthia both knew why I was there, but I can't say the same for the other members of Moonblade."

"I always assumed Gran and Valera had an alliance out of necessity. But now I wonder if they were close, somehow."

"I don't think that's an unfair assessment—"

But Fen was cut off as a low rumble pulled him to silence. A growl, dangerous and feral. Winter pushed close to Rowan's legs, protecting her as her growl vibrated through her chest.

Rowan shifted without a word, using her goddess-given language to communicate.

"He's not a threat. He's—"

"What have we here?" The wolf voice was unfamiliar and sinister. "A human who plays at being wolf?"

Rowan's hackles tingled, everything in her core activating toward a threat.

"She is god-touched," Winter said, her tone sharp. "A guardian. You're not of the pack."

"No." The wolf laughed, the sound grating and unpleasant. "No pack for me. And no pack for this forest. So beautiful. So full of meals to keep me satisfied."

"This territory is marked," Rowan said. "If you're not joining the—"

"The pack?" The laugh came again. "What pack? All I smell is ash and sulfur. The burned wood still weeps in its sundering."

"This place is a haven for those who do not cause harm to others," Rowan said. "No violence is accepted without provocation."

"Is that your rule, *Guardian*?" He said her title like a swear, drawing out the vowels in mockery. "Your rules mean nothing."

He pounced, his growling bark amplified by the snapping of his jaws. Rowan and Winter dodged, and Fen aimed a hastily nocked arrow. The shot went wide as the wolf adjusted and aimed for Fen, moving with impressive dexterity to bring him to the ground.

"No!" Rowan barked, but the wolf's claws ripped through Fen's arms as he guarded his face and chest from the attack. Fen screamed, turning and kicking. The smell of fresh blood reached her as Fen fell.

Their enemy salivated, moving to pounce again, but Rowan slammed her paws into his side, jaws snapping for his throat. Winter snapped and clawed where she could, taking up the offensive when their enemy rolled Rowan off and tried to pin her.

Fen pulled the short sword from his belt and swung, blood splattering across the forest floor. The tip of the blade met the wolf's flank. When the enemy cried out and recoiled, Rowan struck, sinking her teeth into his throat.

"Guardian!"

"*Guardian!*"

Familiar voices and the thundering of paws.

"Rowan!" Fen, breathless, his voice laced with pain. "More wolves!"

But they were allies. Trusted friends. The matriarch and her mate had returned.

"Leave these woods, interloper," the matriarch said, her voice charged with lethal anger. "Don't make us kill you."

The lone wolf yelped as Rowan let him go, and he limped toward the burned woods, likely toward the river.

"Guardian." The matriarch and her mate approached, careful as they surveyed for any wounds. "Are you alright?"

"I am, but my friend—"

"He bleeds heavily," the patriarch said. "Take him to your healer now."

Winter approached with reverence, bowing her head. "You've returned."

"We were not far," the matriarch said. "We are establishing our den further east, where the woods were untouched by flame."

"That wolf was a fool to come here with such bravado," the patriarch said. "My heart aches when one wolf attacks another."

"Take care of your friend," the matriarch said. "You must hurry."

"Thank you," Rowan said before shifting, her hands already reaching for Fen.

"Is all well?" His breathing was labored and shallow, sweat gathering at his hairline. "Gods, this hurts."

"They're deep," she said, her hands framing the gashes down his forearms. Blood flowed along corded muscles, channeling down veins toward his knuckles, dripping from his fingers. "Have you ever been stitched up before?"

"On the ship." He winced at the memory. "Caineth didn't have the steadiest hands."

"I can't do anything here." She ripped the hem of her shirt, the linen frayed to threads as the strip dangled from her hand. She gave the fabric a strong yank to sever it completely, leaving her with a garment that hung just above the waist of her trousers.

"Gods, Rowan, you could have used my shirt."

"Another shirt ruined because of me?" She smirked, slowly wrapping the gash with a careful touch.

"You're..." He hesitated, watching her hands.

"What is it?"

She stopped as he looked up to meet her forest green gaze with his deep sea blue. "You're not a healer?"

"No." With a chagrined smile, she returned to dressing the wound. "I don't have magic."

"But you can shape-change." She felt his focus studying her, reading her, confusion trying to reconcile what he knew with what she'd just said. "That's magic."

"I begged Rhiann," she said. "I'd never worshiped her in my entire life until the day I learned my parents were dead. Then I begged her for something, anything, to make me stronger. Something I could use to fight back."

He said nothing as her work continued, nearing the end of the makeshift bandaging. Then, quietly, he asked, "Why didn't you ask Aishlin?"

"Chaos?" She quirked an eyebrow, tucking the end of the strip into the wrapping. She ripped off one of her shirt sleeves to wrap the other arm. "I considered it. Darkness for darkness. Death for death."

She met his eyes, realizing what she'd said, realizing it was true.

Death for death. But there was no judgment from him, no recoiling or disgust. Only understanding.

"But Gran worshiped Rhiann. Jean is an earthwitch. She was the first goddess I thought to turn to."

Blood soaked through the thin fabric, feathering through each thread as the wound continued to gush.

"Speaking of Jean." Rowan helped him stand. "She can heal. And she'll do well with your stitches."

"From your lips to Rhiann's ears."

Heat bloomed on Rowan's cheeks at his mention of her lips, the flush spanning wider as his eyes looked from her cheeks to her mouth, then her eyes.

"The way you ripped your sleeve just then—" He chuckled quietly, almost to himself.

"What?" She looked at her bare arm, sweat and dirt highlighting the definition of muscle.

"It's very flattering."

She was waiting for the joke, for whatever punchline he'd come up with. But there was only the glimmer in his eyes, despite the pain in his arms. There was only the light smile shaping his mouth.

He leaned close as they walked, keeping his voice low.

"The color red suits you."

She elbowed him in the side, his grunt leading to laughter.

"Is that any way to treat an injured man?"

"Hurry before you bleed out." She walked faster, pressing her lips together. His laughter followed her.

CHAPTER 28

There was so much blood.

Fen growled through the leather of his belt as Jean carefully sewed the deepest wounds closed. Some claw marks were shallower, his blood already sealing them, while others required needle and thread.

Jean's healing magic coursed through her fingers as she hummed quietly, and Rowan busied herself by keeping her in clean water and linen.

"That's the last," Rowan said, bringing a roll of clean fabric.

"It will have to do," Jean said. Then, to Fen, she added, "Lucky for you, I'm an earthwitch that heals and not one that likes to throw rocks at people."

"Though she *does* throw rocks sometimes." Rowan smirked over Jean's shoulder.

Fen chuckled before groaning, the sounds muffled by leather.

"There." Jean finished the last stitch, the surface of her table bloody with droplets and soiled fabric. "Rowan, here's the salve. Bandage him up while I wash my hands and get more linen from Wil."

Rowan helped Jean with the back door, keeping her bloodied hands from having to touch the handle, and then she took up Jean's seat as Fen removed the gag.

"She works quickly," he said. "And it was not nearly as painful as when Caineth did it."

"You did very well, which helped her work. You didn't recoil once."

Rowan imagined the sensation of a needle passing through her skin like fabric, prompting her to fight off the urge to scratch a phantom itch down her arms. She'd busied herself with water and linen to assuage the distress, and now she would help seal Jean's hard work with medicine and bandaging. This wasn't easily placed in Rowan's realm of tolerance.

"You alright?" He asked. "You look a little green."

"Stitches aren't pleasant, even if you're not the one getting them. But I'm fine."

Rowan took one of Fen's arms, the wounds fevered beneath her touch, and carefully smoothed transparent green salve on the first cut. He winced, controlling his breathing, but kept his arm still.

"Has that ever happened before?" Fen asked. "A lone wolf causing trouble?"

"Not since the pack built their home there," she said. "It's not uncommon for lone wolves to join packs, so long as they don't challenge the hierarchy. But that was..." She hesitated, searching for the word. "That was unfamiliar."

"I'm glad the others aren't far," Fen said. "From what I've gathered, they had to be close by to hear the trouble. The ravens were cawing like crazy."

"Were they?" Rowan began wrapping the linen around his forearm, using the salve to help the fabric stick. "I was so focused on the wolf, I didn't hear them."

She worked carefully, a moment's silence passing between them.

"What are you thinking about?" Fen whispered.

Without hesitation, Rowan said, "The lone wolf, seeking trouble." Then, "Avenith's return."

He raised an eyebrow. "An interesting parallel."

"I'd be a fool not to worry about her intentions. About what her plan is."

"Do you think there's a reason Avenith wants to get close again?"

"My shining personality?"

Rowan teased with a small smile, but the sting was there. Reuniting with Avenith wasn't what she wanted. The relationship ended where it should have, and Avenith was the same person who left her. But Rowan had changed. Life and circumstances had shaped her, putting knowledge into her mind and heart that could never be unlearned, making a young woman who had been reborn several times over.

"I didn't mean that," he blurted. "She'd be a fool not to reconcile. I only mean—"

"It's alright. I'm not interested in rekindling anything. And I, too, find her outspoken interest opportunistic."

"I'm sorry for prying," he said. "This is very personal, and I know I'm still a stranger."

"You helped me fight off a wolf and made sure Winter and I didn't die." Rowan squeezed his index finger. "I think that makes you more than a stranger."

This made him smile, even as he flinched as she applied medicine to his other arm. "Even though our *acquaintanceship* was not your idea," he said. "I'm still glad we met."

She didn't look up from his arm, feeling the warmth of his eyes as they studied her face. She liked the way he looked at her, even though she found it difficult to reciprocate. Warmth bloomed across her cheeks. "I am, too."

The back door opened, but Rowan remained composed despite her nerves wanting to jump as though caught. *Caught doing what?* But her fluttering heart knew the answer.

"More linen, and I'll fetch more water." Jean glanced from Rowan to Fen. "Everything alright?"

"Yes," he said. "I can't thank you enough."

"You're welcome, Fen." But Jean focused on Rowan as she went to the bucket of water by the fire. "I'll be right back."

Rowan said nothing, finishing Fen's other arm with a careful touch.

"Your ears turn red when you're embarrassed," he whispered. "I think she noticed."

"I'm not embarrassed."

"Then why won't you look at me?"

Stubbornness derided a challenge unmet. She looked into his eyes with false fortitude, feeling the pleasant tremble within her chest rattle down to her core. How had they gotten this close? Mere inches separated them. If Fen leaned but a little closer...if Rowan met him halfway...

"I don't think I've ever seen the true color of your eyes before," he said, his tone calm but serious. "It is the deepest green, as though the forest lives within you."

Words failed her. She looked away, taking the soiled linens to clean the drops of blood from the table, but Fen gently touched her chin, turning her to face him once more.

"You are remarkable, Rowan of Elderglen."

She froze, his touch no longer unfamiliar. Now she knew the gentleness of his thumb as he traced the curve of her jaw, of his fingers as they curled around her neck, tucking into her hair.

"Thank you," he said. "For saving my life."

"Thank you," she echoed, her voice barely above a whisper. "For saving mine."

Jean's footfalls hit the back steps before the door opened. Fen drew back, his motion natural and nonchalant as he looked at each forearm to admire Rowan's work with bandaging. As though he hadn't just touched her face. As though he hadn't been so close that she could have kissed him.

She'd learned the touch of his hand.

What, then, of his lips?

CHAPTER 29

Sleep came early but didn't stay long.

The world was dark when Rowan opened her eyes, a cold sweat lining her brow, her breath coming fast. But she couldn't remember the dream that shook her to waking, only the feeling that lingered in her quivering heart after it was over.

Winter whined, her head resting on Rowan's stomach, ears perked as she watched her mistress press a palm to her clammy forehead.

"I'm alright." Rowan stroked Winter's head, exhaling in catharsis through her parted lips. "I'm alright."

She stared at the ceiling, the moonlight peeking through the drawn curtain, painting a streak of blue-white light over her. Winter sighed, prodding Rowan's side with her nose before lifting her head, her gray eyes almost glowing in the dark.

"You want stars, too, huh?" Rowan patted her side before rising, her bare feet touching the cold floor. "Let's see what we can find."

The night was cool as she slipped outside, shrugging into her cloak with her boots unlaced and loosely sliding over her feet with every step. Her hair was unbound, the wildness of it a mantle of ferocity. Untamed. Untethered. And for a while, she allowed herself to feel such freedom as the night enveloped her.

Insects buzzed beneath the cloudy night sky, streaks of gray-white moving steadily across the moon and stars. The cool, crisp night was perfect.

And there, in the field beyond, between her home and Jean's, was Fen.

Winter caught his sight and scent and trotted over to him, tail wagging. He sat up at the sound of stirring grass, and his smile was bright as he greeted her with sweet words and warm hands. He glanced up at Rowan as she followed behind.

"Can't sleep?" he asked.

"Something like that." She sat beside him, Winter lying between them and rolling on her back. "You?"

"Something like that."

"Another dream I can't remember," Rowan said. "I'm considering it a blessing."

"It probably is."

They laid back, staring skyward. Winter snorted once, kicking her feet, and Fen laughed.

"I should patrol," Rowan said, though she didn't move an inch. "The Wandering Order. Moonblade. Foolish hunters." She exhaled, her breath a plea to the sky. "And we still don't know what killed the villager. There has been nothing since."

Silence passed between them before Fen said, "You deserve to rest, Rowan."

"When the world is falling apart?" Her laugh was a quiet exhale. "Braithen and Halie would burst into flames."

"Let them." He turned slightly to face her, grunting quietly, trying his best not to wince.

"Fen." She nearly reached for him, alarm sweeping over her. "Your stitches."

"I'm alright. Jean's healing and that salve have done wonders. She healed my ribs some earlier, too." He rested his arms carefully across his stomach. "But everything's still tender."

Broken ribs, his arms nearly ripped open. Fen had been through several layers of hell in a matter of days.

"No one person can save the world," he went on. "And they would be foolish to try."

"And trying would only lead to heartache, but the world doesn't see itself that way. The world demands a hero to pull it from a hell of its own making."

"Since we're a pair of restless souls," he said. "Do you want to talk about what's troubling you?"

She turned her head, regarding him in the dim moonlight, his eyes like black and white glass. "But I don't remember the dream."

"That's not what I meant."

Several seconds passed before she answered. "The wolves noticed activity northeast of here. Avenith mentioned the Wandering Order is moving around. And Moonblade has moved into Elderglen." She pursed her lips, tension wrinkling her brow. "I feel like a tidal wave is consuming the horizon, but I can only stand and watch."

"How would you stop it if you could?"

She considered her answer, imagining what superhuman power she would need to save the earth from destruction. But fatigue pushed her toward apathy, the only conclusion being to let the world drown.

"I'm not sure I would do anything," Fen said. "Like you said, the world demands someone save it from itself. Maybe the tidal wave *is* its salvation."

"That's dark, Fen." But Rowan smirked, relief easing the muscles in her chest and shoulders, comfort allowing her to breathe easily. He understood, and he didn't apologize. She shouldn't, either.

"When do you want to visit the farm?"

Her relaxation was short-lived.

"Damn." She sat up, disappointment souring her stomach. "I can't believe I forgot."

"The forest fire, the wolf, and everything else."

"I should've gone. I *should go.*"

"Not alone," he said. "We go together."

She opened her mouth to object, thinking of his injuries, but stopped herself. "We'll take Wil. And the others, if they're interested."

"You sure you want Naelor to go?"

She turned her head back to the stars, the earth soothing her with its touch. The mist of the night sky limned the speckled lights with an ethereal glow. "I'm sure we'll do well with numbers in our favor. Especially if the farmers are in danger."

And I don't trust them in my village without me here.

"The family has magic," Fen said. "They're earthwitches."

Earthwitches at the mercy of the Wandering Order. Gods, how could she be so careless? "We should leave now."

"Where?"

Both Rowan and Fen started, eyes alighting to Wil's stealthy approach. They sat up, though Winter remained where she was between them, tail wagging.

"Gods above, Wilhelm." Rowan pressed a hand to her heart and looked down at Winter, who was still on her back with her tongue lolling out from her open mouth. "You could've told me he was here, you know."

"We're going somewhere?" Wil asked, looking from Rowan to Fen. "After a bit of stargazing?"

Ignoring his question, Rowan brought up the farm.

"We're at an advantage if we go at night," Wil said. "But we're at a disadvantage not knowing how many cultists are there."

"If they're there," Fen said. "That camp wasn't far."

Wil and Rowan shared a look of mutual understanding. The Wandering Order may have left the farm alone, knowing it would draw attention. But greed and opportunity rarely left things well enough alone.

"There are two children," Fen said. "A teenage boy and his younger sister."

What if they're already dead?

Wil rubbed his chin, pacing a few steps back and forth.

"And the arcana crystal mine," Rowan said. "The camp and the farm, together, would give them an outpost."

"Right next door to us." Wil combed his fingers through his hair. "This has gone from bad to worse, hasn't it?"

"They'll experiment on anyone, depending on who they can capture," Fen said. "One story came through of a chaosborn in Ileden nearly leveling their entire camp."

"Gods." Rowan exhaled, imagining what those shadows must have done.

"We should go," Wil said. "I'll tell Peter."

"What about Avenith and the others?" Rowan glanced toward the tavern. "Additional hands wouldn't be a bad idea."

"I'd rather they be hands I trust," Wil said, "but I leave that decision up to you."

Rowan nearly objected until she remembered. *Cornerstone.* Wil's declaration to leave agreed with her choice. He hadn't decided for her or anyone else.

"Mom and Peter are both still awake," Wil said. "You'll want to tell her."

Jean. Her second-in-command. The Veil. "And I'll leave Winter with her. We don't know what we're walking into."

As though understanding, Winter whined. Rowan scratched behind her ears. "I know, sweet girl, but you have to be safe."

She rose, meeting her best friend's look. He studied her with a hint of a proud smile.

"What?"

"It's nothing. Just—" He nudged her shoulder with his. "The cloak looks good on you."

***

ROWAN KNOCKED on Jean's front door.

"I'm up, Ro. Come in."

Surprised, Rowan obeyed, the hinges squeaking quietly as she entered. Jean's home was warm and savored of soothing spices from the tea she'd made. Cinnamon, clove, dried apples. Rowan took a long, luxurious breath.

"I noticed Fen had walked to the field," Jean said with knowing in her voice. She took a cup from the shelf and poured tea for Rowan. "Did you find him?"

"I did, and he told me about a farm to the northwest."

Jean looked up from the steaming cup, teapot still in her hand.

"According to Avenith and the wolves, the Wandering Order passed that way a few days ago." Rowan sat at the table, letting the tea take her focus. She couldn't explain why, but she found it hard to look up at Jean, to let her see the questioning vulnerability. "Wil, Fen, and I are going to see if the rumor is true."

Jean nodded. "Isn't there a mine close by?"

"That's what Fen said."

"Moonblade likely has it handled," Jean said, "but I would want to be sure."

Moonblade. Funny that Rowan hadn't considered Valera already scouting them.

"Fen said there are children." She sipped, the brew too hot and burning the tip of her tongue. She winced and blew gently, rippling the surface of the brown liquid.

"Did Avenith mention Moonblade getting involved?"

Rowan cupped her hands around the warm cup. "There was a lot she didn't say."

She sipped more, the cinnamon soothing with the light notes of clove soaking through.

"Will you invite them to join you?"

"Yes. Perhaps that will lighten their sentence if Valera hears they've done some good with the guild."

Jean nodded, then shrugged. "I wouldn't want to leave them here unsupervised either."

Rowan hummed a laugh. "Mind reader."

"I know this has fallen upon you." Jean rested her hand over Rowan's, her warm touch gentle and achingly maternal. "One thing that Cynthia did I disagreed with was that she tried to bear it alone after Johann passed."

"I could have done better. I could have tried to work with the guild. To learn all I could."

"Feather and Claw led to your parents' deaths," Jean whispered. "I'm amazed you're here at all."

Tightness threatened to seize Rowan's chest, even as she inhaled to physically push through it.

"I don't—" Rowan winced, the truth hard to admit. Weakness.

Vulnerability. Rowan couldn't give an inch, or the world would eat her alive. "I don't know how to share something like this."

"By trusting those you love." Jean's thumb rubbed the curve of Rowan's hand to her wrist. "No matter what decision you make, you are loved."

Rowan closed her eyes, a cold pocket of her heart knowing warmth again. She hadn't known its emptiness until Jean filled it with her touch and her voice. "I do trust you."

"We are here, and we love you." She took Rowan's hand and kissed her knuckles before pressing her fingers firmly between her palms. "No one's shoulders are strong enough to carry the world in solitude, my love."

Rowan held her breath, her throat tightening as her eyes burned. Jean rose, pulling Rowan to her feet and wrapping her arms around her. It was a relief to let Jean care for her, but Rowan hadn't prepared for the strength of Jean's embrace, for the welling of emotion that surged to the surface. She waited in vain for the tide to ebb, but the wave only grew, threatening to crash any second. Rowan's lips quivered, eyes welling.

"The hole that Cynthia left behind will never be filled," Jean said softly, stroking Rowan's hair. "It would be foolish to try. But we go on living because she loved us too much to let the world win."

Rowan buried her face in Jean's shoulder, letting her shirt soak what tears fell. Rowan collected herself, breathing carefully to will the emotional swell into obeisance. Jean smelled like warm spices and fresh flowers.

"There's still so much I don't know," Rowan said, her voice muffled. "I'm going in blind."

"We are with you."

Gods, Jean was so *warm*. Rowan hugged her tighter.

"We are with you at every step, and our eyes are open, same as yours. Trust that you'll know what to do. That you'll do the right thing."

"How do you know?" Rowan squeezed her eyes shut. "How do you *know?*"

"Because I know you." Jean kissed her head. "And you are strong. But your strength should not cover everyone else's weakness, my love. Your boundaries should be firm and your load shared."

Easier said than done. Rowan heard Braithen and Halie's voices echo in memory. The Wandering Order. The dead villager left unavenged. Moonblade interfering in Elderglen—

Suspicion poisoned any chance of peace or respite.

"I should go," Rowan said, though she was slow to rise from Jean's embrace. "Would you mind watching Winter?"

"She's always welcome."

"We'll return soon."

"You will. I'll take care of Winter. You take care of yourself."

Jean squeezed Rowan's hands before letting her go.

CHAPTER 30

As though conspiring with their stealthy journey northwest, thicker overcast swept through the sky, shielding Rowan and the others from the thin moonlight and star shine.

With her cloak turned to the mantle of Cornerstone, Rowan blended in seamlessly with the dark landscape, the shadowed flora barely creating contrast against her covered form.

"What would it take to have a forest planted here?" Avenith trudged as tall stalks of weeds and grass clung to her shins, her leather boot buckles snagging them. "Some additional cover would be nice."

"It's potential farmland," Wil said, "but you can take it up with the locals. Maybe they'll like the idea."

"*Locals.*" Avenith chuckled. "One family for two miles."

Naelor and Thenik said nothing, the former grumbling while the latter walked in silence among them. Naelor had tried to make this venture his portion of the apology Valera had insisted upon.

"That's up to her," Rowan had said. "Even in the short time we've met, I know better than to make a decision that should be hers."

"We'll put in a good word for you, big guy," Avenith had said with a wink. "You're too eager to leave this town, but it's kind of growing on me."

"Like a fungus?" Naelor's gaze fell to Rowan. "Or a rash?"

But rather than show offense, Rowan nurtured a small victory in his hatred of serving Elderglen and its Watcher.

"How'd you earn your scar?" Thenik asked, the change of subject abrupt. "I got mine from a bar fight." He tugged his loose sleeve up and extended his left arm, the scar trailing from shoulder to elbow. "Broken bottle."

"A hunter," Rowan said. "He ventured too close to the den."

"That's no hunter," Thenik said with a quick, unapologetic laugh. "That's a fool."

"You don't even know if he won," Naelor said, shaking his head. "He probably survived and tried again."

"He didn't," was Rowan's reply. "I almost lost my eye, but he lost his life."

She glanced at Fen, determining his reaction to the whole truth this time. She wanted him to know he wasn't alone in the burdens that weighed on his soul. He deserved to know who he trusted with his life as they moved to confront a looming, dangerous threat. But the night shrouded his features. She couldn't read his eyes or his mouth clearly enough to determine an outcome. Still, the truth was there for him to take. That had to count for something.

Nearly an hour into the journey, the expansive farm came into view. Light flickered from the windows in the house, dim but present.

"Either no one is sleeping," Fen said, "or they're keeping a very watchful eye."

"The barn too." Wil gestured a hand, tracing the window where a faint orange light flickered.

"Looks like they have unwanted guests," Avenith said. "We should help pack their bags."

"How many, do you think?" Thenik asked.

"Let's plan for at least two dozen." Avenith's hands rested on the pommels of her daggers. "And hope for three."

Rowan shared a look with Wil and Fen. Then, to the latter, she said, "After I shift, watch for my eyes. I'll do my best to communicate."

She moved forward without another word, her wolf form the color of midnight as the cloak of the Cornerstone became her lupine mantle.

Wil briefly explained what she meant to the assassins as she stepped in silence, the hum of the natural world singing its pleasant, soothing song. The contrast of the peaceful night with the urgency of their mission made Rowan's heart thrum as she watched and listened through each agonizing second.

Rowan chose the barn first, her nose and ears catching traces of livestock and humans within. Two men, as far as her nose could tell.

Her green eyes met Wil's and blinked twice.

"At least two inside," he whispered to Fen. He waved to Avenith and Thenik, holding up two fingers.

"Let's check the house," Naelor said, flexing his hands. "I'm getting antsy."

Rowan grumbled, blending a growl with a whine.

"That's a bad idea," Wil said. "Wait until—"

"Then *you* check the house." Naelor approached the barn, shaking off Thenik's hand as he tried to stop him. "Don't tell me you prefer your new friends over me."

"Don't be stupid." Thenik didn't back down. "There's a family here. Haste could mean death."

"Listen to him," Avenith said. "They have children."

But Naelor persisted, moving to round the corner, but Rowan jumped into his path, teeth bared.

"Tame your beast," Naelor growled over his shoulder to Wil. "I can't promise I won't mistake her for something other than human."

Rowan dug her nails into the soft, cold earth, but a hand gripped Naelor's shoulder and turned him. The large man lost his balance, falling to the ground as Fen knelt on his chest, a knife pressed against Naelor's throat.

"Disrespect her again, and I cut out your tongue."

Fen's voice was barely audible, yet the intensity of every syllable struck like a blow. Naelor struggled, but Fen pressed harder with the knife as he leaned against the pressure point of Naelor's shoulder. The large man groaned through clenched teeth.

"She insisted on bringing you," he said. "We told her it would be a bad idea." Fen exhaled a quiet chuckle. "I suppose I owe you my gratitude for giving me a chance to say *I told you so.*"

"He'll stop," Avenith said. Rowan caught the worry in her eyes as she stared at Fen. "Don't kill him, Fen."

"He needs to give me a reason not to."

A moment of silence passed between the two men before Fen stood, stepping back as Naelor rose swinging, but everyone froze as the voices in the barn spoke to one another. Wil, his furious gaze lethal, bore an unspoken reckoning on Naelor with his sneering mouth soundlessly telling him to stop. Everyone drew their weapons, their steel sliding in ominous whispers against their scabbards.

Without a word, Avenith, her blades still at her sides, mussed her hair and clothes before pinching her cheeks and tugging the side of her shirt free from the waist of her trousers. She climbed through the barn window with urgency as the others watched in frozen silence.

"Oh!" Avenith said. "I didn't..." She laughed nervously, the notes of her performance impressive. "I didn't know—"

"What's the trouble, lass?" He sounded pleased to see her.

Then, a second voice. "You running from something?"

"Some*one*," she clarified. "I stayed too long in the woods. Some men were there..."

Emotion thickened her voice, and she shuddered a gasping breath. If Rowan had the opportunity, she'd be impressed. But as it stood, Avenith's distraction was enough to allow her and the others to round the corner to the barn entrance and prepare their ambush.

Amber light flooded them as Naelor burst in, Wil and Fen following close behind. But a twig snapped several feet behind Rowan. She stepped back and watched a shadow move toward the barn's light, the orange and yellow firelight dancing across his silver hair. But his eyes were the color of night, as though chaos welled within them. His tall form cast a long shadow over Rowan as he moved closer.

"Hello, wolf." His low voice was smooth. "What beautiful eyes you have."

Traces of mist arcana feathered the surrounding air...coming from him.

"Elias!" But the voice from the barn choked, the sound sickeningly wet.

Elias. *Preceptor*.

"And here I thought this place would give us the rest we need." Elias chuckled, his amused look more sinister in the firelight.

Rowan snarled, ears perked to the sounds of quick movements behind her coming closer.

"Good evening, Preceptor," Naelor said with a broad grin. The blade of his short sword glistened red and orange as the light shone off of blood and steel. "I haven't seen you in a while. I wondered if you'd finally met your end."

"Not as yet." Elias's eyes gleamed with eagerness—no. It was hunger. The sight of the assassin triggered his eyes to wander over the others, lingering longer on the two faces he didn't recognize. "Have your numbers increased?"

"New acquaintances," Naelor said. "A common goal can forge alliances almost anywhere."

"It's not like you to make friends, assassin." Elias studied them, eyes flickering down as Rowan growled louder.

Look at me, you filth, she urged, knowing his eyes had studied Wil and Fen's faces. But she learned his scent—pine, sweat, and sandalwood. She could find him in the dark.

"Easy, pup," Elias said. "You're too beautiful to slaughter."

She feigned a lunge, bringing Elias to move in defense. Naelor struck, pulling his attention too late to the blade that aimed a swiping arc at his chest. His movement's momentum helped to assuage the potential severity of the wound, but the blade still cut through fabric and flesh. He cried out, and Rowan's ears alighted to sounds stirring from the house. Voice cried out in panic.

"Sarra! Gods, Sarra!"

A child screamed.

She ran, paws thundering against the earth, someone falling in step beside her, but she slid to a stop as the front door opened with a rush.

A man emerged, his murderous scowl searching the near distance as he clutched the squirming child in his arms. His footfalls were heavy on the wooden porch before he stopped, his dark gaze brimming with an unspoken challenge.

Those inside cried for the girl who froze as the villain brought his knife to her throat. He set her to stand in front of him, his hand heavy on her shoulder. The man stood tall, grinning, daring anyone to make a move.

The mists in the sky parted, unveiling moonlight that glittered on the child's wide, panicked eyes.

"Move," the man said, eyes falling to Rowan, "and she dies."

The fighting behind her ceased, the quiet eerie as the night, too, had silenced her voice in the face of such a threat.

"You were fools to come here," Elias said. Rowan's eyes remained trained on the man holding the girl while her ears listened. Elias didn't move closer, but neither did the others.

Magic and fear tingled beneath Rowan's skin, urging her to shift back to human. *Offer yourself. Save her.*

"This one has magic." The villain ran a lock of the girl's hair between his fingers. "It breaks her heart to see flowers wilt and die."

Rowan began, the pull of magic starting at the tips of her paws—

A whistle pierced the air before an arrow pierced the villain's chest, just left of center.

Fighting burst behind her, thuds and grunts filling the air as fists punched and weapons clattered.

"Preceptor!"

More cultists, perhaps from the fields. Had they brought a small army?

The man before her stared down in bewilderment at the arrow's shaft, lips slightly parted as he weakly formed words that wouldn't come. Keeping her wolf shape, Rowan lunged, Sarra screaming. Rowan's wide jaws gripped the man's arm that held the knife, and the girl scrambled back to the corner of the porch, cowering with her arms over her head, her body trembling.

"Sarra!"

"You monsters! Sarra!"

Rowan didn't let go, her teeth tearing into his flesh, the hot copper and iron of his blood covering her tongue. The knife clattered against the wooden porch as the man died, his ragged breath wet in his throat.

Rowan stepped through the front door, hackles raised, eyes and ears alert to whatever terror she was about to witness. The cultist guarding the family within stood from his stool, his short sword already in his hand.

"A stray has wandered in," he said with a quiet laugh. "I've never had *wolf* before."

Her growl rumbled low, studying his shape and movements. He favored his left leg. His breath rattled in his chest, audible even from this distance. Rowan braced her body before aiming for his left, his body weight faltering as he overcompensated. When he hit the floor with a resounding thud, Rowan took his sword arm into her mouth and shook. More tearing flesh, more hot, coppery blood. Steel clattered against the wooden floor, and the father took the cultist's sword and cut his throat. Rowan watched the flash of metal before meeting the father's eyes, burning with rage.

"We are not victims in our own home." He grabbed the dead cultist by his collar and dragged him through the front door, throwing him down the front steps.

"Daddy!"

"Sarra!"

But one cultist abandoned the fray at the barn and charged for them, bloodied sword in hand.

Rowan surged with a running start, pushing herself off and extending her claws toward the assailant's face. At their collision, Rowan flowed with the momentum of his body falling, bracing herself for the landing as he crashed to the ground. She rolled before bracing herself in another defensive stance.

"Two more upstairs!" the father called, taking his daughter into his arms.

But they were already thundering down, their dark garb a contrast to the warm, inviting light of the home.

Fen and Wil were ready, the former running at a distance as the latter rushed forward, armed and bloody.

"They're trained better than I expected," Wil said, breathless. "The Preceptor left them to deal with us."

He got away? But Rowan lacked the time to follow his scent.

As one cultist appeared in the house's doorway, an arrow met him, piercing through his skull. Rowan glanced behind Wil, seeing Fen using the barn for cover, his bow and arrow visible from the window. Even with his injury, his aim was impressive.

The second cultist was Wil's target, and Rowan provided an excellent distraction as their opponent struggled against two antagonistic forces. Wil dragged him outside before finishing him, allowing Rowan to stay with the family huddled together in their modest kitchen.

When she shifted, they cried out. But wonder replaced the shock and fear in their eyes, and their breathing came easier.

"Guardian?" The mother wept openly. "Gods bless you, Guardian."

"Are any of you hurt?" Rowan quickly surveyed them, seeing only bruises. "I know someone who can help heal."

"We're mostly unharmed," the father said, trying to embrace his wife and both of his children. "Gods, thank you."

"What made you come?" The wife wiped her eyes. "How did you know?"

"Rumors of cultist activity, and one of us was here—"

There were slow, polite footsteps, and the family glanced past Rowan.

"Fen?" The boy smiled despite the tears filling his eyes. "Is it really you?"

"You can't get rid of me that easily."

The boy rushed to him, hugging him around his waist.

"I'm glad you're alright, Henry." To the parents, he said, "Don't let the children go outside."

"I can—"

But Fen knelt in front of Henry. "Sarra is too small to see what's out there. I need your help to make sure she stays inside."

Henry pressed his lips together, nodding, putting on a brave face.

"Thank you, Fen," the father said. "You knew to come?"

"I had a feeling." He looked at Rowan, nodding once with satisfaction. "Only one escaped."

"The Preceptor," Rowan said. "Wil told me."

"Hell-touched, he is," the mother said. "There is naught but darkness in that man's soul."

"None of them have souls," the father said as Sarra hugged his neck.

There was more he wanted to say, but he held his words and anger within, embracing his daughter as she cried against him.

"We'll make quick work of what's outside," Rowan said. "Is there a shovel in your barn?"

"That and more," the father said. "I'll help you."

But Sarra cried louder, holding him tighter.

"We have it in hand," Fen said. "You're safe now."

The mother reached for Rowan's hand. "Thank you, Guardian." She kissed Rowan's knuckles. "Thank you."

"I wish I could do more," Rowan muttered. "I could stay—"

"No," the mother said. "You do enough. We need to pick up the pieces. We finally have our home back."

Rowan nodded once, offering a reassuring smile, and stepped out with Fen to the grisly aftermath that awaited them.

"He just slipped past everyone?" Wil was saying as they approached. Naelor, Thenik, and Avenith finished searching the bodies, pocketing whatever valuables they found. "The *Preceptor*?"

"Things were busy," Naelor said with a sneer. "It's not like I wanted him to leave the party so soon."

Fen didn't engage, instead heading straight for the barn. Rowan followed, finding tools easily enough and helping to drag the bodies far from the home.

The work was tiresome, their muscles aching as they buried each cultist in the cool, soft earth.

"All this, and we still have to walk home," Wil said, leaning on a shovel. "Gods, I don't know if I'll make it."

"We can make it," Rowan whispered. "Staying here will only put the family out, and they've been through enough."

Naelor opened his mouth, likely to say something caustic, but Thenik punched his arm, shaking his head.

"What?" Naelor rubbed his arm. "I wasn't going to—"

"You were," Thenik interrupted. "You always do."

They put everything right before they left the farm, Rowan kicking dirt over the bloodstains marking the earth where the fight had been.

"We'll need to check in," she said to Wil and Fen, knowing the others were listening. "The Order might come back and do worse."

"Moonblade can help," Avenith said. It didn't escape Rowan's notice that Naelor and Thenik shared a look. "Valera will want to know about this."

"Any eyes against the Wandering Order are a good thing," Wil said, but Rowan spotted the tension around his mouth and eyes.

Their walk home was mostly silent, the tired group eager to fall into their beds and sleep for days. But with Rowan's approach to the Hill, something was different. Something around the forest—

A yelp echoed in the distance.

She shifted without a word and raced for the trees, catching sounds of distress from deep within.

The wolves were in danger.

CHAPTER 31

"Help!" a man screamed, his footsteps thundering. "Gods, somebody help me!"

Rowan raced around the trees, over moss and roots and shade-growing flowers.

"Coward!" roared a voice, one Rowan recognized. The Patriarch. "Killer of the innocent!"

Howling and snarling wolves nearly overwhelmed the breathless cries of a man running. Rowan feared the worst, her heart pounding in her ears as she moved closer to the sounds of distress and anger.

She saw him, his bow in one hand as his quiver bobbed on his back as he ran.

Braithen.

"Gods!" He pivoted away from her, flailing in terror, his voice high-pitched from fear. "Not another one!"

Rowan turned human, reaching to steady him. "What are you doing in the woods?"

"They attacked me!" He turned to show his back, where blood oozed from three long gashes caused by claws.

"You killed one of them?" She looked from him into the trees where the sounds of baying howls called for him. "You know better than to tread too far into the woods."

"You're blaming *me*?"

"Rowan!" Wil and the others, closing the distance.

"Here," she called. "Be on your guard. He killed a wolf."

The matriarch and patriarch rushed in with more of their pack behind them. There was blood on their fur and seething rage in their eyes.

"They don't attack unprovoked," Rowan said, turning back to Braithen. "What did you do?"

"What did *I* do?" He edged closer to Rowan, a threat in his gaze even as he grunted and groaned from pain. "Only what our Watcher will not."

"And what's that?" Wil asked, breathless, appearing with Fen and the others. "Get themselves killed by being a complete fool?"

A scream pealed through the air as Halie approached, her wide eyes flickering from her injured brother to the snarling wolves.

"Gods, save me from this madness." He hurried to her like a drowning man reaching for a lifeline to shore.

"Gods above!" Halie looked from the wound to the wolves. "They did this?"

"And she's blaming me!" Braithen screamed.

The wolves snapped a cacophonous bark, jarring even Rowan's nerves.

"He went too far," Rowan said. "The rules of the forest are clear, and he violated their trust."

"I did no such—"

"You killed one," Rowan interrupted. "You moved into their home with murder in your heart and expected them not to attack? They are not the monsters, Braithen."

"Rowan." Mayer Frederick moved forward, having just arrived.

"She thinks I should die for trying to protect the village," Braithen said, wailing.

"You walked into a wolf's den of your own conscious choice, you absolute idiot." Wil shook his head. "She just saved your life."

"Who goes into woods at night on his own?" Avenith asked. "This feels like a setup."

"A setup for what?" Braithen challenged. "Getting one of our own killed?"

"Or making people doubt Rowan because you can't keep yourselves alive."

Rowan stared at her, shocked by Avenith's defense.

"Leave it to a newcomer to spread lies," Braithen said. "You know nothing of Elderglen or its *Watchers*."

"She knows plenty," Frederick said. "Enough not to go into the woods alone."

Sick of all of them, Rowan shifted, hearing a voice cry out at the suddenness of her change.

"Halie, for gods' sake, *shut up*."

"Wilhelm! What would your mother say—"

"She would say the same thing," he replied. "Now, for the love of all things holy, stop bloody *screaming*."

Rowan moved to the wolf pair and bowed her head, hearing the elegiac howls echoing from the trees.

"Do not bow for him," the patriarch said, rage still deep in his rumbling voice. "He is a murderer."

"One of our own died in pain," the matriarch said. "The arrow is still in him."

Rowan's heart ached, anguish and shame heavy on her already burdened mind. "My spirit is low. My faith in them is weak. I can't trust them, but I cannot always be here to watch."

"You were northwest," the patriarch said. "One of ours was not far. They could smell the blood."

"That was fast," Rowan remarked.

"As are wolves." The matriarch nuzzled Rowan's cheek. "We must see to our dead."

"If he reenters the woods, he will die." The patriarch didn't break his gaze from Braithen. "I will only allow him this one warning."

"I will see he gets it," Rowan said. "My heart aches for your loss."

The pair left, and Rowan shifted back, her shoulders sagging and muscles weak. She was too tired—too *exhausted*—to carry the dead weight of Elderglen.

"Having a single coherent thought must take every ounce of energy you have," Fen was saying, towering ominously over Braithen as he cowered behind his sister. "No sane person would traipse into a forest filled with wolves. You either have no intellect, or you have a death wish."

"I vote for the former," Thenik said. "I've heard him bragging in the tavern."

Naelor remained silent, watching the drama unfold with amused eyes.

"You're forbidden from the woods," Rowan interrupted, glaring at Braithen. "The wolves have marked you as a threat and will not suffer your return."

"Animals don't tell me where I can and can't go," he said with a sneer.

A growl escaped her as she stepped to him. A soft touch grazed her back, giving her pause. Fen, his deep blue gaze full of knowing, bidding her to remain calm.

"If you value your life," Rowan said slowly, "you will never return."

"Are you threatening me?"

Halie squared her shoulders as though posing the same question. Mayor Frederick, ever-present and ever-useless, remained silent.

"Do I have to?" Rowan didn't blink, almost willing her consciousness to bear into his. "Or will you listen? You are a threat to them, and they will not hesitate."

"Neither will I."

"Do as she says," Mayor Frederick said at last. "She is the Watcher of Elderglen and the Guardian of the Wood. When she tells you your life is in danger, you'd do well to listen."

"In danger from *her*," Braithen said as he turned to go.

"If you spread lies around the village, Braithen," Wil said, "any damage it does will be on your shoulders."

"It wouldn't be necessary if Sentinel Hill fulfilled its duty."

"That's enough," the mayor said, his eyes full of warning. "Goodnight, Braithen. Halie."

Braithen sneered. "Goodnight, Mayor."

The group remained silent in Braithen and Halie's retreat, the tension easing as they gained distance.

"I didn't know he'd gone," Mayor Frederick said to Rowan. "I admit to ignorance that anyone would venture in on their own, with the threats being as severe as they are."

"They're compromising the village with their stupidity," Rowan said. "Has there been another incident?"

"Nothing that's reached my ear," he said. "Though we still haven't found the creature responsible."

Creature, said in the thin hope that what killed the villager wasn't human.

"You all look like you've been through hell," Mayor Frederick said.

"There were cultists at a farm northwest," Wil said. "All but one are dead."

"Gods above." Mayor Frederick's shoulder's slumped. "And you return home to this."

Rowan read an apology in the mayor's eyes, and her burning heart cooled to a tolerable heat.

"Try to get some rest," he said. "I need to speak with Braithen and Halie, but heavens, let me have breakfast."

Rowan chuckled, surprised by the mayor's levity, and watched him take the long walk back home.

"We know so little," she said. "And people like Braithen act without thought."

"What do you know about the murder?" Avenith asked.

Naelor and Thenik grumbled to one another but said nothing aloud for the rest of them. Rowan ignored them and answered her.

"The corpse was bloodless when we found it," Rowan said. "There were no clues about how he died or who might have done it."

"Who?" Naelor asked. "Not *what*?"

"Some think it's bloodborn," Fen said. "I've heard whispers in the tavern. But there hasn't been another attack since."

"A traveler?" Thenik offered. "That would limit their chances of being caught."

Wil worked his tongue over his teeth, thinking. Then, with a pointed exhale, he said, "The man's mother said he didn't go home after work because he was meeting someone."

"A romantic meeting?" Avenith asked, no sign of teasing in her tone or expression. "Or something else?"

None of them knew.

"We should ask his mother," Rowan said. "Who he was meeting, and where."

"What are the odds they're still in Elderglen?" Naelor asked. "If I'd killed someone, I wouldn't stick around."

"Any information is useful," Fen said. "It's more than we have now."

Dawn was still hours away, but Rowan's tired body wasn't eager for rest. At least, not yet.

"I'll need to patrol," she said, moving as though to usher the others out of the trees. "I have to make amends, and gods above, I want to run."

Fen offered a half-smile as he glanced over his shoulder. "I'll see that no one disturbs you."

The lingering cover of night hid the blooming heat that flushed her cheeks, but she didn't miss Avenith's eyes darting from her to Fen.

"If anyone needs the Hill, send them to Jean," Rowan said.

As they broke through the trees, Rowan shifted, running on all fours toward her home where Winter waited. It took no time for the pair to reunite in peaceful relief and to run as fast as their legs could carry them.

THE WOLVES GATHERED around their fallen, the air heavy with grief and anger. Rowan helped them dig in the earth as Winter joined them, confusion leading to sadness.

Rowan explained what had happened, Winter's anger flaring.

"No respect for the woods, the wolves, or the earth." She snorted, digging faster. "Stupid, foolish human."

They ushered their dead to his grave, their mournful howls crying a lament to the heavens.

"The village does not deserve you," the matriarch said to Rowan. "I share your anger."

"They're fools," the patriarch said, his voice heavy. "They believe themselves invincible only to be surprised when our jaws break their bones."

Rowan winced, her sense memory conjuring the touch of flesh and the taste of blood.

The wolf pair held no grudges against Rowan or her allies. They held no grudge against Elderglen, save for Braithen and Halie.

"Halie," the matriarch said. "Nosy. The woman lingers on the edges of the forest with mischief in her scent."

Gran would say *I smell trouble*, but Rowan had never thought it anything more than a silly idiom.

"I think she watches the woman who weeps," the matriarch said. "She is full of sadness and mourning."

"A woman who weeps?" Rowan looked from the matriarch to Winter, who had no idea.

"Grief has reached deep within her," the matriarch said, "just as it has reached within us."

A woman who weeps...

Rowan knew no one who fit such a description. Unless it was the mother who lost her son to a mysterious attacker.

"There's another scent," the matriarch said. "One mingled among yours." This time, her voice warmed as she watched Rowan's with keen interest and intelligence. "The man who has joined you."

"Man? What man?"

"He has a lovely voice and kind eyes."

"F—Fen?"

"You have found another who cares for you, Guardian," the patriarch said. "And his feelings are growing."

Rowan shook her head. "He was seeking his brother, and the Wandering Order threatened a family. He found help with Feather and Claw. With me."

"Even still," the matriarch had said. "We see what we see. We smell what we smell."

"His heart races," the patriarch said. "As mine does for my mate."

"But he and I are still strangers," Rowan said. "We've only known one another for days."

Rowan recalled moments with Fen, from their meeting to the leaf pulled from her hair to the way the stars reflected in his eyes.

We see what we see.

Each memory came through a different frame, as though the images were as they'd always been but with renewal, her eyes fresh and clear, seeing them as they were meant to be.

"Rest, Guardian," the patriarch said. "We will mourn our loss and guard the forest."

Rowan and Winter bowed in respect before parting, giving the pack several paces before jogging faster through the trees. Even as exhausted and burdened as she was, running released every tension, every aching weight. Simplicity. *Freedom.* There were no cages among the trees.

But when their run ended and Rowan began to scout through the woods, tightness returned to her back and shoulders.

Winter remained silent, sensing her companion's unease, and Rowan was grateful. No explanations needed. No conversations or definitions or discussions. Only *presence.*

The pair finished patrol close to dawn, their muscles pleasantly sore and breath misting in the cool damp of morning. Fen was there, sitting outside the reach of the trees, whittling a small piece of wood with a pocketknife.

I'll see that no one disturbs you. He'd meant it.

We see what we see.

Before Rowan shifted, she drew a long, deep breath. Leather, salt, and cinnamon. She drew another, the tightness in her heart loosening, and returned to her human form.

He turned at her approach, and she knelt beside him. "You're here."

"And you've returned." He reached a hand for Winter, who nuzzled his palm. "Anything?"

She shook her head, resting on her heels. The stretch in her leg muscles pulled taut before relief settled in. "Quiet."

"We'll need to do the same again tomorrow, won't we?"

"And call for aid to watch the farm and the lands near it." Such an undertaking lay before them. "But you don't have to, Fen. You're not the Watcher of Elderglen."

He smirked. "That rhymed."

She scoffed, cracking a smile as she shoved his shoulder. "Is that Winter?" She gestured to the carving in his hands. "The one you were working on before?"

"It is." He showed the piece, still crude in its early stages, the shape faintly resembling a canine creature. "I hope she likes it."

The wolf sniffed at Fen's hand before snorting. He chuckled, glancing toward Jean's home. "Do you reckon you'll get any sleep?"

"Knowing my luck?"

Even with the tiredness in her body, sleep would only come with the tiredness of the mind. And hers was far from fatigued.

"Then let's see about preparing breakfast for everyone." Fen stood and offered his hand to her, which she accepted, warm and dry and strong. "What do you have at home?"

"A few wildberries and some grain." She pinched her fingers together. "About this much."

He looked toward Wil's house, the lights dark. "What are the odds we can pilfer some of their ingredients back to your place?"

She grinned for the first time in ages, her body relieved to feel mirth again. "We can certainly try."

CHAPTER 32

Rowan and Fen crept around the back of Wil and Peter's home, the world still dark and quiet.

"You sure it's unlocked?" Fen whispered as they approached the back door.

"Everyone is afraid of Peter," Rowan said with a slight chuckle. "They wouldn't dare breach his home uninvited."

"Peter?" Fen cocked his head as he wrapped his hand slowly around the door handle, turning it carefully. When it gave away, he moved with caution as the hinges groaned. "I would think they'd be afraid of Wil."

"Wil's temper flares but calms quickly," Rowan said. "But Peter's burns for a long time."

"Should we rethink our plan?" Fen, holding the door open, regarded her with barely any moonlight to see.

"I know where everything is," she said, inching closer. "We won't be inside long enough to get caught."

"As you say."

Carefully, they stepped inside, and Rowan took the lead toward the food stores near the back door. Wil had fashioned a beautiful cabinet for their first anniversary, his skill in carpentry passed down from his father. Peter cherished it, putting it in the part of their home visible from any point. Rowan opened the two front doors and pulled a small sack of oats.

"There's fruit here," Fen whispered from behind. "Wildberries, by the smell."

"Perfect."

"Does he have honey?"

"I think so." Rowan reached for a dark brown glass jar, sealed with a hinged lid of wood and wax. "This could be it."

Fen took the jar and opened the lid, releasing its delicate smell. "These are going to taste incredible."

The pair set everything else as it was before slipping out, latching the handle in silence behind them.

With quick steps, they hurried through the dark as dawn's light began its delicate glow on the horizon. Once inside, Rowan added wood to the fire and kissed Winter's head as Fen made preparations for cooking.

"Let's make flour from these oats," Fen said, pulling Rowan's mortar and pestle from the shelf. "We'll make the best oatcakes they've ever had."

Rowan worked steadily, grinding oats to flour as Fen prepared the wildberries with fresh water from the well.

"A cook, a blacksmith, a hunter." Rowan watched as Fen worked. "Any other surprises?"

"Don't forget sailor and ship captain." He half-smiled, emphasizing the deep lines around his mouth. "I grew quite accustomed to life at sea."

"Even with the ever-present threat of grappling hooks?"

He laughed, its sound deep and rich.

"Why did you leave?" It wasn't until the question left her lips that she felt its weight. "I'm sorry. Don't answer that."

"Why?"

"I don't mean to pry." She kept her hands busy, grinding the oats to dust. "The reason might be personal, and I don't want you to feel forced to say something."

"How about this?" Fen stepped closer, his shoulders back as he looked down, meeting her upturned gaze. His expression was soft, bordering on amused. "I'm the sort of person who will tell you if I'm uncomfortable. I don't do anything I don't want to do." He paused, the corners of his mouth curling up. "I know we're still new to one another, but I think we can afford to give one another that kind of respect."

"I agree." Warmth bloomed in her core. "That kind of honesty is…"

She struggled to find the word until he said it for her.

"Comforting."

She nodded.

"I'm going to be straightforward with you, Rowan." He didn't falter in his stance or proximity. If anything, he leaned closer, leveling his gaze with hers. "There's nothing you could say or do that would make me uncomfortable."

She didn't back away, something akin to pride holding her spine straight and eyes steady. "Because of your life on a ship?"

"Among other things."

Playfulness touched her mouth and her eyes. "Would you find it amusing if I made a game of it?"

"What kind of game? See what you can say to make me blush?"

She quirked an eyebrow. "It could be fun."

"I remember what Wil said." Fen poured the ground flour into a bowl with the berries and worked them together with his hands. "You don't back down from a challenge."

"And I usually win."

He grinned, flames sparking within her heart.

"Well, then, Rowan of Elderglen. *Challenge accepted.*"

"*ROWAN* COOKED BREAKFAST?" Peter blinked in shock as he entered behind Wil and Jean.

"Stop sounding so surprised!"

"I'm more impressed the house is still standing." Wil grinned, wrapping his arm around her shoulders for a small hug. "What brought this on?"

"Fen's idea." She nodded toward him as he added wood to the fire. "But it was mine to take your oats and berries."

"I knew it!" Peter broke out in a laugh, pointing at Wil. "Didn't I tell you?"

"You knew?" Rowan looked from Wil to his husband. "How?"

Peter opened his mouth to answer, but Wil spoke first.

"He knows every inch of our home." Wil smirked at him. "You noticed the berries first."

"I didn't take that many!" Fen said.

Peter raised an eyebrow. "You took enough."

"But the mystery was solved as soon as we received your invitation to breakfast." Jean eyed the wildberry oatcakes. "They look delicious, by the way."

"You did well, Fen." But Peter watched Rowan, his smile widening at the light flush on her cheeks.

The question showed on Fen's face, glancing at Rowan before understanding sank in. "I see."

"One hell of a fighter," Jean said, nodding to Rowan. "Not the most adept when it comes to cooking."

"Now that everyone has had a giggle at my expense." Rowan gestured to the dining table. "Fen *and I* have prepared a lovely meal."

Wil and Peter took turns kissing Rowan's head before taking their seats, side by side across from Jean and Fen. This left Rowan at the head of the table. Gran's seat.

In the span of a quiet breath, Rowan allowed her heart to miss her, to whisper her name in her mind as a remembrance. The small, quiet moments remained the heaviest, but the love surrounding her helped to carry the grief.

Through some magic or spiritual knowing, Jean reached for Rowan's hand and squeezed. Wil nudged her arm, his expression matching his mother's.

"Would it be strange to ask how you both came together with a plan for breakfast?" Jean took a bite of an oatcake as she looked from Rowan to Fen, then to the oatcake. "Oh, my, this is excellent."

"I had the same question." Wil quirked an eyebrow as he glanced between them. "Out for a stroll?"

She shrugged. "It just worked out that way."

Saying nothing of midnight conversations and stories about scars.

Of stargazing and shared secrets. It was the lightest her body had felt in months—*years*.

Three knocks came, pulling every eye to the front door. Rowan answered, the lightness she'd enjoyed evaporating like mist in the dawn.

"Avenith?" Her body was a silhouette against the daylight until Rowan's eyes adjusted. "Good morning."

"Good morning. I'm sorry to interrupt. I wanted to see if you were free to visit the farm this afternoon."

The forest. The village. And now the farm. But who else did they have? Rowan had yet to write to the nearest stronghold for aid.

"I can," Rowan said. "Unless you and the others would like to take the trip yourselves?"

Avenith shook her head with a slight wince. "They don't know I'm here."

"Why not?"

But she didn't answer, peeking over Rowan's shoulder at the breakfast gathering.

What is she hiding?

But that question would take days to answer if Rowan's suspicions were correct. Avenith was a woman made of secrets. How many did she keep, and how many kept her?

"Have you eaten yet?" Rowan stepped aside, inviting her in. "We have plenty."

A smile dressed Avenith's face, and Rowan tracked the connections it made from her mouth to her eyes. It was an expression long practiced and beautifully executed. Giving her access served a purpose, but what?

Avenith took the next empty seat beside Fen, the end seat giving her full eye contact with Rowan.

"Thank you," Avenith said as Rowan served her two oatcakes and a cup of water. "That's very kind of you."

Wil gave their newcomer a side-long glance. Though he wasn't smiling, amusement framed his eyes and mouth. Amusement and interest.

"I don't see you for years, and now you grace my table twice in as many days." Rowan held Avenith's eye before returning to her seat. "Don't tell me it's because you missed me."

"What if I did?"

Peter glanced from Jean to Rowan before returning to his plate, acting as though he hadn't noticed the collective shift in mood.

But Fen's discretion wasn't as fortified, for the faintest flush brushed the peaks of his cheeks and ears.

When he caught Rowan's eye, her smile bloomed.

"*I won*," she mouthed, touching one of her cheeks while eyeing his.

"No," he said audibly, trying not to smile. Then, eyeing the others, he cleared his throat, the flush deepening.

"No?" Avenith looked from Fen to Rowan. Her polished veneer hadn't wavered, so Rowan couldn't tell if her interest and mirth were genuine. "No what?"

"It's only a joke," Rowan said, smug. "Isn't it, Fen?"

He said nothing, looking at her through his lashes as he took a large bite of breakfast.

"I hope I'm not prying," Jean began, looking at Avenith. "You said before that the others don't know you're here. Has something happened?"

"No," she said. "But I wasn't sure if either of them would be receptive to visiting the farm. Just to be sure everything is alright."

"I'll send word for help," Rowan said. "There should be someone soon."

"We hope," Peter said. "With the raids from the Order, resources are thin."

"Moonblade has helped," Avenith said, "but we face the same challenges. There aren't enough of us."

"We're all fighting," Jean said. "But why does it feel like it's not enough?"

Because it isn't. Rowan didn't look up from her breakfast, embarrassment crawling through her veins, making it hard to look any of them in the eye.

"Hate feels insurmountable," Fen said, and the direction of his voice found Rowan. He was speaking this to her. "But our hope is bigger."

Hope versus hate, with an invisible clock ticking down to a deadline Rowan could feel.

But I'm not alone, she reminded herself. *They are with me.*

"Breakfast was good," Will said, "but Avenith's got a point. We should check on the farm and if anyone's coming."

"I'll help clean up," Avenith said, standing, her plate and cup empty. "Do you have a stream where I can wash these?

"We use the well outside," Rowan said.

We. The cold sting in her chest pierced through bone, straight to her heart. *We.*

But no one noticed, busying themselves with tidying breakfast.

"I'm going to freshen up," Fen said. "See you on the road."

"I'm healing your wounds once more, Fen, before you go." Jean's tone was resolute. "That wasn't a request."

Concern focused his gaze on her. "It takes a lot from you."

"It wasn't a request," she repeated slowly, though a smile teased her mouth. "See me before you go."

"I should freshen up too." Rowan gathered her hair into a mass in her hands, tying it quickly at her neck. "See you on the road."

Avenith stepped out with the dishes, and Rowan and the others straightened the room.

"So," Jean said, a quality in her voice that Rowan recognized.

"You have that tone. What do you want to know?"

"What tone, young lady?" But Jean was half-smiling.

"You and Fen," Wil said for her. "We're all curious. Or didn't you see the way he was looking at you?"

"And you at him," Peter said, nodding slowly. "Something happened between you."

"Nothing happened."

"Define *nothing*."

Rowan pushed Wil's shoulder. "Nothing. Happened."

"You two have an inside joke," Jean said. "Something happened."

"We won't leave you alone," Wil said. "Not until you tell us."

Rowan glanced at each of their faces, their interest both annoying and endearing.

"I'm not sleeping," Rowan said at last. "At least, not well. I don't remember the dreams, but I wake up in a cold sweat, my heart racing like I've been running for my life." She paused, allowing their silence to give her space to breathe. "Fen isn't used to sleeping indoors, so it seems. Stargazing helps. The first time, I—"

Wil's eyes widened. "The *first* time?"

"Two night owls, finding each other under the stars." Peter rested his chin in his hand. "I love this story already."

Rowan's sigh was deep, her catharsis ending with a quiet laugh. "I'll return soon." She crouched to Winter, stroking the wolf's cheeks with her thumbs before rubbing behind her ears. "Take care of Jean and Peter for me, love."

Winter grumbled a response but didn't argue further.

"If only she could talk," Wil said with a grin. "She strikes me as someone with a lot to say."

"She does." Rowan winked before stepping out the door. "She has a lot to say."

CHAPTER 33

Rowan wrote a hasty letter to the nearest Thurin stronghold, paying the courier an extra five copper for speed. After a moment's consideration, she penned a note to Valera, detailing their worries and asking for any help Moonblade can give.

"Even if it's changing a travel route to keep the farm in your sights." She hated that compromise after swearing to destroy any mist arcana cargo that edged too close, and she hated the smug look Valera would wear after reading it. But it was a family's life, traded for Rowan's pride. An easy choice. "I fear what the Wandering Order will do."

To Rowan's surprise, Naelor volunteered to deliver the letter and bring back Valera's answer.

"It will give me time to consider a new assignment in Elderglen," he said, taking the note. Rowan noticed several red spots on his forearms, likely from recent labor. "The blacksmith's forge isn't for me."

"Interesting." Avenith cocked her head to one side. "What's he up to?"

She and Thenik shared a look before the party began their trek to the farm.

"Jean is a marvel," Fen said to Rowan, extending his arms to show the crisp bandaging beneath his rolled-up sleeves. "She removed the stitches, and everything's healing well."

"Are they still sore?" Rowan poked his arm.

He grunted, eyeing her with playful annoyance. "*Yes.*"

She smiled to herself. "So you're not god-touched, then?"

"Why?" He lifted an eyebrow, his smirk flattering. "Do you see me as something divine?"

Wil cleared his throat. "We'll probably walk faster if we're not flirting with each other."

"I can manage both just fine," Avenith said with a wink.

Travel progressed quickly, the group moving with no concern for stealth as daylight shone its golden hue over them.

"Will this be quick?" Thenik asked. "One horse needs new shoes."

Avenith smirked. "You're enjoying your assigned post, aren't you?"

"Animals are easy. It's people that make life hell."

"Hear, hear," Wil said. "And I think Rowan would agree."

She hummed in validation before saying, "I'm not in wolf form nearly often enough to suit me."

"What's it like?" Avenith asked. "The transformation."

"What do you mean?"

"Does it hurt?" Avenith curled her fingers like claws. "Your body is changing its shape, your bones and organs realigning."

Thenik grimaced. "Gods, Avenith. You don't have to go into detail."

"You've given it some thought," Fen said, eyebrow raised. "Are you considering Rhiann's blessing for yourself?"

Avenith half-shrugged. "More speed and dexterity wouldn't be a bad thing in my line of work."

"It doesn't hurt," Rowan said, trying not to imagine a Moonblade assassin with the powers of wolfkind, though it wasn't out of the question. The goddess would choose whomever she deemed worthy. "What changes me is magic. I don't know how to explain or describe it. It's as much a part of me as my blood or breath."

"Do *you* have magic?" she asked. "I've never seen you use it other than shifting."

Rowan shook her head. "No."

"I thought..." Thenik paused, as though to choose his words with care. "I thought all wolfkind were earthwitches."

"Most are," Rowan said. "But I never learned."

"Then how did you find favor?"

Thenik's question came with genuine curiosity, a tone of reverence in his voice. But Rowan's muscles tightened, the walls around her heart and stomach fortifying. All the parts of her were too soft, too vulnerable.

But the conversation faltered as Rowan's nose picked up the smell of smoke.

"Do you smell that, too?" Wil sniffed the air. "Where..."

There. Wisps of black feathering up past the horizon. The smoke was thin, which could mean—

Rowan shifted and ran, voices calling after her before running in her wake.

She sneezed against the acrid traces of death, burning wood, and flesh smoldering, but the blaze had long been over. She didn't need to see the catastrophic aftermath to know, but she pushed herself harder, faster.

There was no need for reinforcements now. The Wandering Order had come.

I should have stayed.

The farm was in cinders, the home and barn rubble where embers chewed on the blackened remains of wood.

The family was in front of the house, clothes and skin burned, dried blood staining the clay road.

"Gods—" Wil stared, awestruck. "What have they done?"

What have I done?

"We finally have our home back," the mother had said, embracing her children.

Rowan was a fool to think the Order wouldn't retaliate this quickly.

The Preceptor. Hell-touched.

What have I done?

"They killed them." Avenith didn't tear her eyes away from the family, horrified. "They—"

Thenik ran from the group to retch upon the roadside.

"Rowan—"

She ignored Fen, spotting Sarra's doll in the middle of the road, filthy with soot and dirt and blood. But one scent pulled Rowan's nose with traces of sweat. She studied it, pressing her lupine nose against the doll's fabric. Pine and sandalwood. *Elias.*

And his trail led north.

She shifted, her legs faltering to carry the weight of her anger and shame. Her limbs quivered as fire coursed through her blood. Fen caught her as though he knew, his arms ready as he held her from behind.

"They're north," she said, her voice raw, her body desperate to revert back to claw and teeth. Her human skin was too delicate for the rage within. "I don't know how far or how many, but he's with them." She took a breath, ragged and knife-edged, tearing into her throat. "The Preceptor."

Fen tightened his arms around her. Her shaking hands pressed against his forearms, his strength the only thing keeping her from losing herself to blinding red. She stared at the family through welling tears, at the house, at the feathering smoke trailing to the sky before Fen turned her and pressed her face against his chest.

"Rowan—"

"I didn't stay. I—"

He held her tighter, not letting her move. "No."

"Let go, Fen."

But she struggled in vain, his arms a vise. Fighting him scratched an itch beneath her skin, one longing for something physical, but his soothing voice pulled her from the brink. She would have lost herself, were it not for him.

"We will care for them," he murmured, the words only for her. His lips touched her ear. His breath swept over her skin. An anchor in human form. "We will honor them. And we will make those monsters suffer for what they've done."

"Monsters," Rowan repeated, forcing her breath to come slowly through her nose. Fen's scent soothed her even as the rage continued to burn. She groaned in agony as the latest flare of anger ached in her chest. Her lungs struggled to accept the cold, smoke-laced air. A string of curses welled in her tightened throat, but there was no room for their escape. She growled instead, holding Fen tighter.

"Oy!" Thenik, having recovered, kicked aside a fallen panel of wood from the barn, one of its walls having covered the body of a human form clad in black. "It's one of ours!"

The man lay suffering, his breath shuddering against agony as he gazed at Thenik.

"There were so many—" He shuddered, grimacing, his bloody hands pressed to the oozing wound at his stomach.

Thenik knelt beside him. "Cultists?"

He nodded. "We got word. But everything was burning. They were —" Pain took him as he groaned. "They were out for blood."

"How did they get word?" Wil asked.

"Me," Avenith said. "I sent a message to Valera last night."

"How?"

"Moonblade has ways."

"Then why did Naelor leave?" Fen asked.

"To get the hell out of Elderglen," Wil said. "I doubt we'll see him again."

Rowan couldn't say she disliked that outcome.

"We think they went north," Thenik said to the dying man before them.

He nodded. "They were looking for someone. '*Where is she now?*'" He coughed, blood staining his lips. "Something about a guardian. They laughed over the bodies. Then everything was on fire."

Fury bloomed in Rowan's core, igniting every inch of her as she shifted. Retribution would be swift in arrival and slow in resolution. She would make sure of it.

The dying man's breath shuddered before it passed from his parted lips, the exhale too deep to leave anything behind.

"I'll rip them limb from limb," Thenik said, rising, fists tight at his sides. "Every last one of them."

But Rowan was already running. She howled her anger, her voice screaming retribution, begging the wolves to listen.

In the distance, they answered, meeting Rowan in the trees as she reached the edge of the field, her lungs burning with the cold, smoky air. She slowed, panting, hearing the ravens calling from overhead.

"Murderers!" The ravens cawed, their voices bouncing off the trees. "Murderers!"

"We smelled the smoke and burning flesh, Guardian," one wolf said. It was one she didn't recognize, though they acknowledged her god-touched form. "We've tracked them to a camp and are waiting for nightfall."

"We want their eyes," the ravens cried. "We want their eyes!"

"They murdered innocents," Rowan said. "Because I protected them, they killed them."

"The earth weeps from tasting innocent blood," one wolf said. "Its sadness reaches deep within us."

Sadness had buried itself into every grain and fiber of muscle and bone. She would never be whole after this.

What have I done?

"How many are there?"

"Ten. Armed with swords and arrows."

Ten. After those they'd killed the day before, more waited to strike.

"Leave none alive," another said, snarling. "Corrupted. Depraved."

Rowan dug her claws in. "Waiting for nightfall is wise, but—" She hesitated, a snarl pulling her lips from her teeth.

"The anger burns," one wolf said, understanding in her amber eyes. "Like the farm and the one who set it ablaze."

Hesitant steps and whispered voices pulled every wolf's ear, turning their gazes with alarm.

"Friends," Rowan said quickly, smelling Fen and the others. "They were with me when we found them."

"Friends," another wolf said. "But they come too close."

Without another word, Rowan hurried toward them, shifting so that her human feet carried her. She walked several steps before calling their names at an elevated whisper. "Wil! Fen!"

"We're here," Wil said, jogging with Fen beside him. "What news?"

"The wolves know where the cultists are. They're waiting for nightfall."

"And do what?" Wil asked. "Murder them in their beds?"

"It isn't murder." Rowan held onto a lifeline to keep from being consumed, gripping the promise of vengeance like it was air as she drowned. "Not after what they've done. What they'll continue to do."

"It's *life*, Rowan." Wil's position didn't waver. "As wretched as they are, they're living things. We aren't the ones to decide if they have the right to breathe. That's not for us to judge."

"Then where are Anya and Aishlin?" Rowan's whispered voice nearly ripped through her throat before she reined it back, caging her anger within the depths of her chest until she could use it. Now wasn't the time, and Wil wasn't the target. "How could they let such darkness spread across the earth that Rhiann took such care to make? What about *us*?" Her eyes turned up, itching even as she blinked over and over. "We're the ones left picking up the pieces."

"We don't choose for them," Wil said. "They wish to spread darkness because darkness is within them. But we have something they lack, something they're desperate to touch."

She waited for him to say *love* or *hope* or some other sentiment. But he didn't.

"Power." His hazel eyes were bright. "And what they did to the farm is supposed to make you feel powerless. But you're not. *We're* not. That's the thing they fear the most."

Rowan's heart simmered in her lingering anger, Wil's point sinking in.

Until a woman screamed. A voice she recognized.

She shifted and ran toward the sound, toward the cultist camp.

"Rowan!"

But she did not turn.

CHAPTER 34

The terror of the woman's cry scaled down Rowan's spine as she ran, the wolves snarling in her wake.

"The small homes," one wolf said, speaking of the cultist's tents. "There are three. One large one, closer to the stream."

The larger tent was likely the Preceptor's. Room enough for whatever cruelty he would unleash on those he captured.

"Wood burning," one said, a low rumble in his throat. "And meat."

Rowan caught the scent of the woman who screamed. Lillies, her sweat laced with the sharp touch of fear.

Avenith.

Rowan ran harder, paws thundering on the soft forest floor until the wolves urged her to slow.

"Their camp is here," one said.

They stalked the trees, watching movement around the fabric tents and campfire. Avenith struggled against the iron grip of the cultist who brought her before the man Rowan had seen at the farm. His silver hair shimmered as his dark eyes siphoned light, the world darker as he glared with eagerness at the captured woman.

"We meet again, assassin," the Preceptor said, his deep voice melodic. "It's lovely to see you."

Other cultists had gathered to watch. Eight...nine...ten...and a Preceptor with murder in his abyssal dark eyes.

"Nice to see you, too, Elias." Avenith's smirk was strained as she grimaced, fighting the grip of her captor. Her wrists were bound with rope. "Though you look a little tired. Having trouble sleeping?"

With every cultist distracted, the wolves moved silently around the trees, edging closer to the camp.

"You and your allies have kept me on my toes." Elias's smile was composed and relaxed, as was his demeanor, walking steadily toward her. The man who held her squeezed her arms, making her cry out.

"Easy," Avenith said, looking over her shoulder. "I'll need my arms later."

"For throwing knives at me?" Elias chuckled. "I would be honored to be your target practice."

"It wouldn't be practice."

One wolf growled before rallying the others. "Now!"

They struck, moving fast with claws and teeth. Rowan shifted before emerging through the trees, hatchets in her hands and fury in her eyes. She ran hard as the wolves dove for their targets, the cultists shocked by the ambush. Their round of surprise had given them an opportunity for advantage, but Rowan wouldn't leave anything to chance. She met a cultist with furious intention, blocking his hasty swing and countering with her own arching strike. He dodged the hatchet at the sacrifice of his weapon, which slipped from his fingers.

Another rushed her, screaming as he held his daggers poised to strike, but an arrow whistled through the air, its iron head piercing the center of his chest. She looked over her shoulder at Fen, who was already nocking another arrow.

"Foolish girl," Thenik said, rushing to Avenith. "Where has your patience gone?"

"With the family at the farm," she answered, her eyes never leaving Elias's face.

Thenik faced the man behind Avenith, his grip forfeiting her arm in favor of his sword. He blocked Thenik's first swing on pure luck, the timing a near miss. But his second attempt didn't succeed, the force behind Thenik's hit bringing him to his knees. Thenik's sword blade finished the task quickly, cutting through the man's chest and stomach without mercy.

"They wouldn't tell me anything about the person who protected them," Elias said, looking from Rowan to the others before landing on Avenith once more. "I have to admire their loyalty."

Rowan's grip tightened on her hatchets, her eyes narrowing at the Preceptor. To aim with a steady grip, the sharpened edge sailing head-over-handle until it met his skull—

A cultist raced for her. Her hatchets met a new target, though their blades hungered for the Preceptor.

Elias. Would that she could haunt his dreams.

Thenik made short work of the rope around Avenith's wrists, and she wasted no time in filling her hands with the handles of her daggers. She faced Elias, who stepped away from her.

"Fall back!"

But Rowan and the others would not let them go. Each cultist took on either human or wolf, none having the opportunity to disengage and flee.

Avenith lunged, but Rowan couldn't watch as her target refused to stay down.

"All life is precious," Rowan said, frustrated. "Yet you all seem very eager to die."

"I know my calling," the cultist said, a young woman not much older than Rowan. "Those with magic stain the earth. We will purge every last ounce of it until these lands are free again."

"Magic isn't an oppressor." Rowan sneered, too angry to suffer pity for her. "Hatred is."

She cried out as she lunged an attack, but Rowan blocked and struck, her aim and actions swift and true. But the weight of death bore heavily upon her heart. These fools didn't have to give up their lives for this. They didn't have to die for a cause that would abandon them.

All life is precious. Yet, they threw it away as though it were a commodity worth spending. A hollow, meaningless death.

Avenith cried out, blood staining her clothes as she clutched her forearm, her legs wobbling as she struggled to remain standing. Blood oozed from between her fingers as Elias grinned, malicious glee shining in his dark eyes.

Rowan threw a hatchet, the blade nearly finding purchase in his chest, but he swung his great sword at the last moment, metal clanging as the blocked weapon landed hard on the blood-stained ground.

"And who do we have here?" Elias eyed her with curiosity. "A new shadow for the guild? First a firewitch, and now a huntress?"

"Firewitch?"

Elias grinned, bearing his broadsword with practiced ease. "Who do you think burned the farm?" He shook his head, delight enhancing his malice into mania. "He wanted to ensure we couldn't access that particular resource, and I have to say, I would do the same."

Marc. He'd burned the farm to keep it from the Wandering Order, swallowing everything in flame.

"It's amazing what mist arcana can do," Elisa went on. "What that incredible powder is capable of."

Without another word, Rowan picked up a discarded short sword and closed the distance between them. Elias engaged her immediately, his skill with such a massive weapon impressive. But he was slow, tactics focused on strength more than dexterity.

Rowan pivoted quickly, the balls of her feet aching as she danced around him, moving to strike and counter as he blocked her at every turn.

"No formal training," he said, "but I admire the fire that burns within you."

She said nothing, a touch envious he hadn't shown signs of exertion.

"Survival," he said, pivoting as she attempted to disrupt his movement and make him stumble. "And a touch of rage?"

She struck, the handle of her hatchet landing a hard blow against his left thigh. She felt the impact against his femur through the weapon, the vibration through the wood mirroring what he'd felt through the bone. His resulting cry sent encouragement surging through her blood.

"More than a touch." He laughed, the sound low, almost seductive. "You intrigue me, Huntress. Are you the one I've heard so much about? Protector of the Glen?"

Searing heat surged beneath her skin. She made a conscious effort to control her breathing, but rage boiled to the edge. The slightest act, and it would spill.

"You're the one *they* were protecting." His smug expression was unnerving. "The protector's protectors."

Rowan feinted a swing with her hatchet, exploiting the pain in his left thigh to force him to overcompensate. As he took the bait, she ran the sword through his side. He dodged, but not before the blade sliced skin and muscle. His shout of agony was deeper than before—deeper and angrier. He hadn't expected such an injury, least of all from her.

"Preceptor!"

But the cry of the cultist was muffled before his screams dissolved in the blood that flooded his throat, Fen's arrow sticking out.

Elias's gaze flitted from Rowan to her allies, who'd remained alive and full of fury. The cultists were not winning this fight.

"He's mine!" Avenith's cry ripped raw from her throat, her voice clawing its way out. "He's mine!"

The distraction cost Rowan as Elias struck her hard against the temple. She fell, no strength left in her bones, the world flashing between light and dark. Thundering footsteps retreated.

"Rowan!" Hands touched her face and shoulders. "Gods, Rowan, are you alright?"

Fen, his hold on her strong enough that she allowed herself to fall. He caught her effortlessly.

"Gods, her head." Wil, his voice too far, floating in the distance. "What did he hit her with?"

"Easy, Av." Thenik, using a voice that would soothe a spooked or furious animal. "Easy."

"He's mine to take." Her breath came in desperation, shredded gasps teetering between low and high pitches. "His blood is mine."

"You want to murder the Preceptor?" Wil asked, his tone full of sarcasm. "Then why did you toy with him before? Is this some sort of game to you?"

"It's not a game. And it's not murder." The restraint it must have taken Avenith to speak without screaming. "It's a reckoning."

Fen lifted Rowan, his breath cool and delicate across her face. "I've got you. Can you open your eyes?"

Her eyelids obeyed, but not quickly enough. The sun was far too bright, the weight of consciousness far too heavy.

"Look at me, Rowan."

She blinked, her mind returning in small doses.

"You need to stay awake," he said. "That blow was nasty."

"Hm." Speaking required too much effort.

"Let's loot the camp," Thenik said. "You need to do something other than stew in your anger."

"Stewing suits me," Avenith said, but Rowan heard her leave with Thenik.

"We'll see to the family," Wil said. "Get her home."

"As fast as I can," Fen promised before walking away.

"You're warm," Rowan muttered, her eyes closing.

"Stay awake, love."

She would have smiled if her body still belonged to her.

"Did he say anything?" Fen asked. "That look in his eye..."

"He knows I'm guardian," Rowan muttered. "He knows."

Fen held her closer, listening. "Is that what he said?"

She nodded, which was a mistake. An iron pendulum swung against her skull, back and forth, booming thunder as it struck bone.

"Easy," Fen whispered. "Are you alright?"

"I'll be fine," she said, wincing against the pounding in her head.

"Liar." He kept his tone light, thinly masking his concern. "Jean will know what to do."

"Oh, gods, she'll be furious."

Fen chuckled, and Rowan's own smile tugged at her lips despite the pain, despite how near sleep felt.

"We're almost home," he said.

"Liar." Her reply was quiet, sleep nearing closer with its comforting embrace.

But Fen's was stronger.

"Stay with me, Rowan. Open your eyes."

Her eyelids peeled back, Fen's head and shoulder shielding her from sunlight.

"Stay with me," she repeated. "You said—"

"I'm not going anywhere." He held her closer, helping her head to rest against his chest. "Let's get you home."

CHAPTER 35

Rowan knew the moment she returned to Elderglen by the sound of shocked gasps and voices.

"Gods above, what happened?"

"The Watcher's hurt!"

"Gods—"

"Rowan?" Suna approached, basket in hand, worry augmenting the severity of her pale, exhausted presence. "Who did this?"

"Wandering Order," Fen said. "At the farm to the northwest."

"What do you need?"

Rowan appreciated Suna's firm voice and unwavering control. Even with her own trials, she was there, steadfast and ready.

"A bed," came Fen's answer. "And Jean. Do you have an apothecary?"

"I'll fetch her. What should I tell her?"

"Blow to the head," he said. "She's remained conscious, but it isn't strong."

"And she can answer these questions herself," Rowan mumbled, stubbornness surfacing. But she groaned as she turned her head. The pendulum had snapped from its chain, and the giant iron ball rolled around within her skull at the disturbance.

"You can rest," Fen whispered. "I've got you."

The temptation to let go had never been greater.

"What the hells happened?" Peter hurried toward them, Jean in his wake. "Where's Wil?"

"Burying the dead," Fen said before repeating what he'd told Suna.

Peter took Rowan, the men careful with the transfer. "The dead?" he asked, but silence answered him.

"Take her to mine," Jean instructed. "I've got everything she'll need."

As Peter walked with Rowan, she made out Jean's words before the distance grew between them.

"When we're safe, tell me everything."

"Of course."

"Who did this?" Peter asked, glancing down at her as he walked her toward Jean's home.

"A Preceptor," Rowan said. "Elias."

"A *Preceptor*?" He exhaled, his cool breath laced with wildberries and mint. "They're ruthless, Ro. Sadistic."

"This one proved as much. That family—"

She grimaced, the words hard to say.

Bile rose in her throat. She held fast, swallowing it back down.

"He escaped," she said.

Her stomach flipped.

"Put me down." She tapped Peter's arm. "I feel—"

The gag pulled at her stomach and chest. She pressed a fist to her lips, tight against her teeth. Peter was careful to keep her standing and help her to the grass at the roadside. He swept loose strands of hair away from her clammy face as she heaved.

"Gods," Jean said. "What darkness created their souls?"

"Darkness that reclaimed them," Fen said. "Would that I could be there at their judgment."

As Rowan's body calmed, she stood with Peter bracing her against his legs, steadying her.

"I'm alright," she said, breathless.

"I know." But he didn't loosen his hold. "Let's get you home."

He lifted her easily. Suna returned as they ascended the hill, the apothecary beside her with her basket of herbs and tinctures. Glass bottles tinkled as she hurried to Rowan's side, helping with the door as they entered Jean's home. Peter navigated the small dwelling easily, despite his size, carrying Rowan down the small hallway toward the guest room. He kept her from collapsing on the mattress, easing her to the pillow.

"Winter is at our house," Peter said. "I'll fetch her."

"Please." Relief soothed every muscle in her body at the thought of holding Winter, of smelling her fur. "Thank you for taking care of her."

Peter kissed her clammy forehead. "I'll be right back."

Rowan closed her eyes, focusing on her breathing, trying in vain to distract herself from the sense memory of blood and sweat. But she smelled and tasted warm, salty copper. If her stomach had anything left...

"That's perfect," Jean said from the other room. Other voices came quietly, their words indiscernible.

"Thank you, Suna," Jean said. "I hope you're feeling better. Have you been able to rest?"

Fabric rustled in the quiet, and Rowan opened her eyes to see Fen standing near the bed. His clothes and skin were stained with dirt and blood.

"What do you need?" Fen asked, his brow furrowing as Rowan brought a finger to her lips. She glanced toward the door and tapped her ear.

"Some," Suna said. "Though it could always be more."

"I hope the tea helped," Jean said. "I would be more than happy to come by and try something stronger."

Jean's gift with healing earth magic had often soothed Rowan to sleep when the vise grip of grief held her consciousness in a waking prison, though it took a lot out of Jean each night. Offering it to Suna was no small thing.

The apothecary entered the doorway, and Fen stepped aside to give her room. She bent over Rowan with a kind look.

"Gods above, that looks nasty." Her cool fingers were delicate against the fevered wound, but Rowan flinched before her touch came. "I've made a quick paste that will help. You'll want to reapply it every few hours. It will help prevent scarring and help the wound heal faster."

"Scarring doesn't matter." Rowan meant for her light laugh to sound amiable, even teasing, but the notes in her voice were too sad. "Thank you for coming so quickly."

Jean and Suna filled the doorway, their shared expressions showing concern.

"Of course." She applied the medicine, her touch practiced and gentle, and left more medicine in a small brown jar. "Let me know when you need more."

The apothecary didn't linger, giving everyone space to recover.

"Let me know how else I can help," Suna said, bowing her head in farewell. "Food, supplies. Anything. Please."

Jean walked her out, leaving Fen and Rowan together in the temporary silence.

"At least the bone isn't broken." Fen crouched at her bedside, his voice above a whisper. "There was so much blood."

"I keep ruining your shirts. First, the snagged seam from the barn. Now this." She looked down at herself, seeing the blood on her clothes, now dried to rust.

"I don't care." His fingers slipped beneath hers until they reached her palm. His hold was gentle, as though she was fragile. No one had ever touched her that way before, like she was breakable. "Ruin all of them. Just get well."

Jean cleared her throat from the doorway, eyes trained on their hands before looking at Fen. "I need to speak with Rowan. Alone."

"How much trouble am I in?" Rowan teased, releasing Fen to sit up. But Jean's hand stopped her.

"You're not in trouble," she said. "You're Cornerstone, and you're injured."

"I'll be outside," Fen said. "The others are returning soon."

He slipped out quietly as Peter returned with Winter. Rowan made out Fen's words carefully—*Jean is healing her*—before hearing him leave.

"Stay here, sweet girl," Peter said to Winter, giving Jean time and space to see to Rowan's injuries.

Jean touched Rowan's head, her fingertips cold. Emotion welled in Rowan's chest, feeling Jean's healing magic soak into her skin, soothing the congestive ache behind her eyes until it dissolved to nothing.

"Tell me what happened," Jean said, her voice quiet. "Every detail."

Tension subsided in the absence of pain, and Rowan breathed easier. She sat up, her head no longer pounding, her body no longer teetering on the edge of consciousness.

Rowan told her everything, from blinding anger to rescuing Avenith.

"You both are quite a pair," Jean said. "Prone to impetuous action."

Rowan couldn't argue with her. "If it weren't for Fen, I would have ripped their throats out."

"Hm." Jean massaged Rowan's neck and shoulders, healing steadily coming through her hands. "He does have a calm spirit, doesn't he?"

"But there's something else," Rowan said without thinking, the words flowing out of her as easily as breathing. "It's not weakness when it's with him."

"What's not weakness?"

"Feeling." Rowan closed her eyes, Jean's touch reaching deep into her tight, aching muscles. "Allowing my emotions to come to the surface. He doesn't shy away from them."

Jean said nothing at first, the silence in the room broken only by Winter's sigh from the living room.

"Your grandmother was much the same," Jean said. "Stubborn. Wrapped her feelings in layers of iron and thorns."

Iron and thorns. And a furnace that was always burning.

"Don't be like her," Jean said. "Caging your heart only makes the hurt sink deeper, with no hope of healing."

Rowan didn't look up. Not when her eyes itched and stung at Jean's words, her voice and touch soothing.

"The infection will set in, making it harder to set yourself free when the time comes to deal with the hurt."

She wouldn't have to deal with the hurt if it stayed buried.

But it won't stay buried.

"You have to let them go, Rowan."

"Them?"

But she knew. Gran. Her parents. Even Avenith, for what tethers remained.

A fresh wave of grief crashed through her body, freezing her core and making her heart jump. Guilt-laced rage made its home in the tundra within.

And today. The family who died protecting her.

"The cage that holds your feelings keeps the dead with you," Jean said, "instead of rightfully letting them go. They were never meant to stay."

"How can I?" Rowan's words came as a whisper, not trusting her voice to carry them without breaking. "When it feels like a betrayal?"

"Betrayal to them?" Jean shook her head. "You haven't betrayed them, Rowan. But I think you're afraid of betraying yourself."

Jean stopped moving, her hands remaining still on Rowan's shoulders. Warmth seeped in through her skin to her muscles as though radiant light sought to make a home within her.

"The only way you can do that," Jean went on. "The only way to betray yourself is to abandon what makes you *you*."

"But what am I?" Rowan asked. "Cornerstone? The Watcher of Sentinel Hill?" She scoffed. "Titles I neither asked for nor wanted."

Jean said nothing, her disappointment likely locking her words in place. Rowan's throat tightened, anger stirring. Frustration and guilt had created a dangerous combination that her heart pumped through her blood, reaching the ends of her limbs.

"I bear it because I have to," Rowan said. "Not because I want to."

"Rowan—"

"The village. The farm. The *guild*." She stood, the bed scooting on the wood floor as she left Jean's grip. "The only title I sought was Guardian. Even that has been swallowed up by the responsibilities thrust upon me by others." With every word of truth spoken, Rowan couldn't face her, shame far too heavy. She paced the short width of the room, too much anxiety feathering her nerves beneath her skin. "A part of me is tempted to give Braithen Sentinel Hill just to shut him up." Rowan's laugh was bitter, tears welling threateningly behind her burning eyes. "Then he'll see that one of Aishlin's layers of hell is *here*."

"Rowan—"

But Rowan stepped out, moving past Winter and Peter without a word. Winter followed, her paws quick against the wood floor. Together, they walked in silence across the small field toward the trees. Rowan didn't shift, the wolf form far too holy for the guilt and anger that still simmered within her.

She didn't go far into the trees before stopping, her body a foreign entity as she stared at the surrounding natural beauty still healing their burned scars from Marc's fire.

The day flew through her mind behind her eyes, everything in memory scarier, the terror reaching deeper.

"What do I do?" She touched Winter's head, the warm softness of her fur grounding her in reality. "What do I do?"

Winter leaned against Rowan's leg, whining quietly.

The family, dead.

Elderglen on the brink.

The Wandering Order.

Feather and Claw.

"I can't do this anymore."

The truth slammed into her, the impact taking her breath. Her stomach soured as the world unraveled, pulling at everything within her she tried to safeguard. She wasn't untouchable, after all.

Her heart reached its breaking point at last as Rowan fell to her knees, wrapping her arms around Winter's neck. She sobbed into her fur.

I can't do this anymore.

CHAPTER 36

Despite Jean's healing, a headache teased Rowan at her temples, the thrumming a steady pulse that reminded her she was conscious, that she was human.

She sat with Winter at the edge of the forest, her back against a tree as her hand absentmindedly stroked Winter's fur. The day passed to afternoon, the busyness of Elderglen on the periphery of Rowan's sight and mind. Jean and the others had left Rowan to her peace, her solitude a stronger balm than any remedy from the apothecary. But her hand remembered Fen's, his warmth offering quiet assurance she longed to feel again.

Avenith, Wil, and Thenik came down the path, their bodies bloody and dirty and visibly tired. Wil caught sight of Rowan first, then Avenith. Both stopped, waving a quick goodbye to Thenik, before walking the length of the field between the road and where Rowan waited. She stood, sitting far too casually for the weight of what they were about to say.

"You're awake," Avenith said, touching her head. "You alright?"

"Jean's magic is strong," Rowan said. She looked up to Wil. "I'm sorry you all had to do that without me."

"Don't be sorry that a madman nearly broke your skull." Wil embraced her, his hold almost too tight at first. "I'm going home. What about you?"

"In a little while," she said. "Home is too claustrophobic right now."

He understood, looking to Avenith to join him as she walked toward town.

"I need to speak with Rowan for a moment," she said.

Wil sought Rowan's consent before turning to leave.

"I'll be quick." Avenith held up her hands in surrender. "No funny business, I swear."

"Get some rest, Wil," Rowan said. "We've been through the hells today."

"Every layer."

He took careful steps through the tall grass toward home.

"Let's sit," Avenith said, moving to sit cross-legged on the grass by Winter.

"This must be serious," Rowan said. "It's almost like the night you broke up with me."

"And you will *never* stop bringing that up." But Avenith exhaled a quiet laugh, though her eyes held sadness.

A breath of silence passed between them, Rowan finding her patience as Avenith found her words.

"What I did could have killed us all," she said, looking down at her hands. She tugged at a blade of grass. "I'm sorry."

"Elias," Rowan whispered, knowing his name bore power. She remembered Avenith's voice and the desperation it carried. "He's the one you've been looking for."

"He took something precious from me." The words escaped from Avenith's mouth as she stared, as though the confession was an unconscious reaction to the question in the confrontation's aftermath. "Nothing I can do will bring them back."

Rowan swallowed, her saliva passing down like shards of glass. "When did they die?"

"Three years ago. He killed them for their magic."

"You never told me about them." Rowan fought the urge to reach for her hand, fearing that her intent would be misread. "You told me they were killed, and a Preceptor did it. But you never spoke about them."

"Were you too afraid to ask?"

Rowan nodded. "You were there for me when..."

Her statement remained unfinished, the experience between them speaking for her. Rowan had already accepted Rhiann's gift when Avenith crossed her path and when their mutual interest grew into mutual affection. And Avenith had been there when the nights were the longest in Rowan's unresolved grief.

Rowan rested her hands on the cool grass. "How did you survive the attack?"

"I was a coward." A tremor came into her voice, slight and fleeting. Avenith sat up straighter, steeling herself as she continued. "I obeyed when they told me to hide. And I will have to live with that for the rest of my days."

"They wanted you to live." But Rowan knew a fraction of Avenith's guilt in surviving. Rowan lost countless nights to wandering thoughts. Would her parents still live if Rowan had been there? Would Rowan have joined them in death?

A stabbing pain sent a rippling wave of guilt through her body at the thought of Gran going on alone.

"You're an orphan too," Avenith said, meeting Rowan's gaze for the first time since sitting. "Living feels pretty empty without love."

Avenith pulled a small flask from her belt, the bottle only large enough for one shot of liquor. She unscrewed the lid and passed it to Rowan, who took the first sip. Cinnamon whiskey.

"You remembered." Rowan nodded to the flask as she returned it.

"Your grandmother was furious when she found us with one of her bottles." Avenith laughed at their shared memory. "I thought it seemed appropriate, with her passing. A way to quietly remember her." Avenith sipped before screwing on the lid. "She was fierce and strong and one hell of a woman."

Rowan couldn't have said it better. The night was calm as she heard Gran's laugh in memory, the notes of her voice like a melody of joy.

"The wind is the breath of the dead," Rowan recited, just as before when putting Gran to rest. "Sunlight, the warm touch of souls to soothe the living. Thunder, the voices to beg remembrance. Rain, their grief for those left behind."

Avenith weaved her hands toward the sky. Lightning forked through the clouds, the rumble of thunder soon following.

"You could have taken out that entire camp," Rowan said. "What happened?"

"Iron," Avenith said. "Those bastards have weapons made out of it."

"Gods, do they know?"

She shrugged. "I didn't use any power. I cursed them for what they did to that family. They likely thought they were exploiting my emotions, not my physical weakness to iron."

A pause passed between them as they sipped more whiskey.

"It's hard to find peace," Avenith whispered. "The soil is barren. The seeds planted dry up before they can even take root."

Avenith's words sank deeper than Rowan cared to admit. "I am one of Rhiann's guardians, but I sometimes find my faith thin and starved." She brought her hands to her lap, looking at the lines in her palms and fingers. "Magic exists. All-powerful deities exist. Yet the world suffers because of the humans created by divine hands."

"Order brings chaos," Avenith said. "There is balance in everything."

"This isn't chaos," Rowan said. "It's malice. It's hate. Chaos is the opposite of order, but hate is not the opposite of love."

"It's not?" Avenith asked. "Then what is it? What is hate?"

"Hate is love turned dark. It's tainted with pride and greed. With jealousy and anger. Hate and love are the same, only one is touched with selfishness."

"And what is the opposite of love, then?"

"Apathy." Rowan stared ahead, the movement of the village giving her eyes something to follow. "It hurts more when someone you love doesn't care. But if they hate you? That means feelings remain. That means you're still coursing through their blood, filling their pounding heart. But if it's apathy, if they don't care, then you don't fill a single thought, let alone a heartbeat."

"I never thought of it that way." She looked at Rowan with a side-glance. "Is that the way it is with us? Apathy in place of love?"

Rowan shook her head. "It's not apathy. And it's not hate."

But she didn't elaborate, and Avenith didn't ask.

CHAPTER 37

Vengeance burned deep within Avenith's words.

He took something precious from me.

The assassin had left hours ago, leaving Rowan in peaceful solitude. So much of Avenith's own experience matched Rowan's, from family lost to family found, with anger simmering within.

Bitterness and resentment found ways to bury themselves within a human heart, tainting the blood with its ichor.

The darkness that stained Elias's hands soaked into his blood, tainting his entire soul, and it spread like sickness to all he afflicted with his malice. Avenith was no exception, and now, neither was Rowan.

She stroked Winter's fur, lying on her back beneath the cover of the trees. The forest ceiling shimmered with daylight shining through the boughs, the branches long and thick as they granted Rowan and Winter a canopy while the floor was cool and soft. When the twig snapped behind them, both looked up at the approaching shape of Fen, hesitation weighing on his brow.

"Join us," Rowan said without thought. "It's not the same as stargazing, but it'll do."

He scratched behind Winter's ears before moving beside Rowan, laying his tall frame to be level with her head and shoulders. The silence that followed gave the breeze a chance to whisper through the branches before Fen said, "I've just been to the tavern. Everyone heard about what they did."

What they did.

Monsters in human skin.

"There are some wanting more protection from the Wolf Queen," he said. "Others are driven to take matters into their own hands."

"It took a family's murder to see them give a damn." She turned her head, seeking the comfort waiting for her in his deep blue eyes. "Will they actually do what they say they'll do?"

"Do you want them to?"

"No." She turned back to the boughs overhead. "And yes."

His fingers grazed hers, but he didn't take her hand. Perhaps he thought the gesture too intimate or too selfish, his own want for contact potentially in conflict with her desire to remain in solitude in every sense. But her palm itched, wanting the sensation of his fingertips tracing her heart and life lines.

"What are you thinking about?" he asked.

"Are you sure you want to know?"

"Yes." His index finger extended down the length of hers. She responded in kind, both of them teetering on the edge of what they both wanted. "Tell me everything. I can take it."

"I fear what you'll think of me if I do."

"Don't." He exhaled, his finger moving over hers. It would curl any second, linking them, joining them in this quiet moment together. "We all have light and dark within us, Rowan. Your dark won't scare me away."

"I'm too much for some. Too much wild. Too much anger."

"It doesn't mean you're too much. It means they're not enough."

She couldn't tell if she took his hand first or if he seized her at last, the agony of waiting finally too much to bear. But now, palm-to-palm, their grip anchored her beside a man who hadn't shied away from her, who'd held her when her rage blinded her.

"How are your arms?" she asked. "You've used your bow twice since being injured. I'm sorry I didn't ask before."

"They're fine, and don't be sorry." He massaged her fingers, his rhythm slow and gentle. "It was a miracle you remained conscious until I brought you to Jean."

She fought the urge to stay something scathing about *miracles*, the wishes of fools who waited for gods that would never come. But her frustration manifested in the answer he sought before, the one where she would reveal darkness she never shared.

"I want to feel my claws tear through Elias's skin." She paused, the words out in the world, unable to take back. She didn't look to read his face, to determine his reaction. A touch of fear tingled over her heart. "I want to sink my teeth into his throat. I want the ravens to eat his eyes."

"Would you believe me if I said I shared your desire?" His hold tightened, thumb working over the curve of her hand. "To feel his bones break within my hands? To rip him limb from limb for what he's done? For what he will do?"

"Is this why I was changed?" she whispered, the question half aimed at Fen, half at Rhiann. "Why have the blessing of guardianship if I can't wipe such evil from the earth?"

He didn't answer, knowing the truth would further fan the simmering flames within her. All life was guarded by wolfkind. *All* life.

"As wretched as they are," Wil had said. "They are living things."

As wretched as they are.

"We aren't the ones to decide if they have the right to breathe," Rowan said, echoing her best friend's wisdom. "That's not for us to judge. But my anger is hungry for it."

Fen turned, regarding her, but her head didn't budge. She stared at the shimmering sunlight, at the gently waving boughs, wishing the wisdom would reach her aching heart. But it didn't. It couldn't breach the wall of flame that thrived with every breath.

"I feel guilty for the gifts I've been given."

Another confession, this one just as deep. Just as disappointing. Innocents dead while monsters roamed free. If only Anya's white-hot wrath or Aishlin's chilling dark would swallow them whole.

"Sentinel Hill isn't a gift," he said. "Except for the people there who love you, it isn't a gift. It's a responsibility."

"The home my grandparents built." She allowed her lips to quiver, fatigue and apathy overriding any desire to slip into her mask. "I want to run from it all." She imagined closing the door to her home on Sentinel Hill, never to return, her feet and hands never touching the floor or walls again. Her throat and chest tightened. "Gods, I'm so ashamed."

"You shouldn't be," he said. "There's nothing wrong with feeling like you're on the edge of something alone."

His grip remained firm, grounding. Warm, calloused, strong. Somehow, through the life Fen had lived before meeting her, he'd come to the same place where she found herself drowning, and he was ready to pull her from the threatening current to get her to shore. All with the touch of his hand.

He edged closer, his cool breath sweeping over her cheek and neck. "You shouldn't be ashamed for wanting to live your life."

"The day I became Guardian..." She paused, her statement dangling unfinished. "We'd just learned my parents were killed. Gran had tried to shield most of the truth from me. She tried to make the news less than what it was. Someone sought them out and ended their lives. It felt—"

Her throat tightened only slightly, but enough that she paused from fear of sounding broken. The cracks within ran deep, and the balm she'd applied for healing did little to repair and restore.

"I'd never realized the depth and darkness of *murder* and *death*. My grandfather's passing had been expected. His decline led to his death in a way that I could understand. But this?"

The emotional tidal wave within her chest grew to colossal proportions.

"Murder. *Intention.* And there was nothing I could do but listen to Valera tell my grandmother what her people found and how they think it happened. Cuts on their arms and necks. Their bodies found near a mine in Sudor."

She closed her eyes, grateful for his hand to keep her in the present moment.

"A mine?" Fen asked, his voice barely audible.

"Valera came. She said her people found them." She nearly swallowed the words back down her throat, but it was too late. The dam had broken. "But Gran and I think Valera covered for the ones who killed them."

"Gods, Rowan. I never knew."

"Gran told me her suspicions before she died." Rowan stared at the forest ceiling, the shadows of the branches blending with the dark of the night sky, their shadows blurring together. "Someone in Moonblade murdered my parents and used the Wandering Order to cover it up."

She waited a beat before going on, Fen's thumb rubbing a soothing line against the curve of her palm.

"After Valera told us, I ran into the forest that night and begged for something, *anything*. I'd heard of wolfkind from Gran's stories, from things I'd seen in her books."

"You thought you had no power," he said, "so you took some for yourself."

"With both hands."

She turned her head to face his, quietly acknowledging the dark corners of her heart freshly laid bare.

"What do you remember?" he asked. "Of Rhiann and becoming wolfkind."

"Not much. I remember being half-blind with tears, then I woke up in the woods as a wolf. I ran for hours, elation overshadowing the fear of not being able to change back."

"Did you want to change back?"

"Eventually." She paused. "I didn't want to leave Gran."

They rested in the quiet for several minutes, Rowan stitching together the fragments of that day. But there was nothing save the *before* and *after*.

"No one can ever take your strength, Rowan." His voice was confident. His gaze, unwavering. His hand, strong enough to hold hers. "Damn the fool that tries."

"That day on the road," she said. "You saw me change."

"I did."

"You weren't afraid. Seeing a wolf become human."

A corner of his mouth curled up. "I was too captivated."

Confidence surged as she turned, relinquishing her hold on his hand to bend her arm beneath her head. "Did you know who I was?"

"Cynthia's granddaughter? The Watcher of Elderglen?" When she nodded, he shook his head. "No. I learned that later."

"When you spoke with her." Rowan's question was on the tip of her tongue, the words nearly escaping as Fen matched her pose, his lips parted to speak. But neither did.

"Go ahead," Rowan whispered. "You wanted to say something?"

She watched him study her, self-consciousness worming its way to the surface as she felt the phantom touch of his eyes reading her face. Absent-mindedly, she reached for her scar.

"I told you about mine." His look softened, his voice low and warm. "Would you tell me about yours? You mentioned a hunter before."

"It wasn't long after my parents died when I was more wolf than human."

Their hands found one another's again, and Rowan traced the peaks and valleys of his knuckles, the action giving her something physical to do while she found the words to tell him.

"I was with Winter. She was still a pup then. The hunter's knife went for her, but I got there first." The sensation of the blade cut through her skin all over again, the sense of the memory still close. "I was lucky not to lose my eye."

"Where's the bastard now?" Fen interlaced their fingers. "Six feet under, I hope."

"I didn't kill him, though I made it seem like I did with Naelor." She chuckled. "Bravado goes a long way with men like him. But I wanted to. He came into the forest and *took*, thinking—no. *Believing*. Believing he had the right to whatever he wanted, to whatever hadn't already been claimed by human hands."

"You saved her," he said. "And yourself."

"Sometimes I forget it's there." She lifted her hand from his arm to touch her scar, fingers familiar with the difference in textures in her skin. "Until I watch someone's eyes when they look at me."

Fen wrapped his fingers around her wrist, his touch gentle as he pulled her hand away. He leaned closer, Rowan staring with wide eyes as his lips touched the end of the scar on her cheek. Her gasp was almost silent, her body stilled as his kiss lingered. The pleasant tingle of his beard, coupled with the softness of his lips, fed sensation through her skin, and her curiosity piqued. She wanted to know more, to *feel* more. Her palm found his cheek, fingers trailing along the arch of his cheekbone as her skin learned the texture of the beard that flattered him, that brought out his remarkably dark blue eyes. Their parted lips inched closer, the warmth of their breath mingling against the cold touch of the forest's shade.

The brush shifted, something moving along the forest. Both started, separating, eyes searching for human or beast but finding none.

The demands of everything she needed to do came crashing upon her, and she was here on the forest floor, nearly kissing him. A family had died. The monsters of all types waited where she couldn't see. And she was here, doing nothing.

"I should go," Rowan said, standing too quickly. The world spun for but a moment before her vision righted itself. "Winter and I should patrol."

She shifted to her wolf form and ran further into the trees, Winter's confusion filling her mind with questions left unanswered.

Rowan's nose picked up the trace fragrance of lilies as she ran.

CHAPTER 38

The quiet world was a stark contrast to the whirlwind that raged in Rowan's mind as she ran, Winter keeping pace beside her. The breeze against her face did little to sweep away the sensation of Fen's lips on her cheek, with gentle pressure against her scar.

Her heart fluttered, even as it raced from running.

She and Winter stopped, the forest wild and deep around them, a welcome haven from humans and civilization.

"Your heart hears him," Winter said. "His hears yours, too."

"You know?"

Winter snorted before panting a grin.

His heart hears mine. Even the mention of such intimacy ignited anticipation in her core.

"He's strong," Winter said. "Strong like Wil and the others."

Rowan understood. Wolves had a sixth sense that could read the spirits of living things, or so Rowan believed. She'd longed for such insight. "Strong like Gran?"

"No." Winter sighed. "There were few strong like that. You are."

Strong like Gran. The blooming warmth battled the familiar tingle of grief. In one of the rare moments since her passing, Rowan nurtured pleasant remembrance instead of bitter loss.

"You would have liked my parents," Rowan said.

"What were they like?" Winter nuzzled Rowan's face and neck before trotting around to smell the surrounding flora.

"My mother was a fighter," she said. "My father was a healer. And he would tell jokes to make her smile."

Her mother would roll her eyes, laughing quietly despite herself at whatever he'd said. Then he'd wrapped her in his arms and spun her, their sounds of joy warm and full of life even in memory.

"He thought his title made him untouchable."

Rowan and Winter stilled, hearing Avenith's voice before her footsteps, which were quiet against the forest floor. Then Naelor's came after, his lumbering gait far less graceful.

"A street urchin bested him." Naelor chuckled, the sound gravely. "How untouchable could he have been?"

"Hide," Rowan said, taking refuge in the brush. Winter obeyed.

"Why are they here?" Winter asked. "This feels wrong."

"It *is* wrong," Rowan said. "They know the rules."

"I heard she was exceptional, to be fair," Avenith said. "I heard she made a lot of coin when she sold it."

"And thank the gods it was to one of us," he said. "Imagine that map in the hands of those dirty cultists."

The map.

Thank the gods it was one of ours.

A flare of anger ignited the furnace in Rowan's core. Moonblade had the map. From the mouth of Naelor, himself.

"Fen certainly did." Avenith laughed quietly. "It kept him up nights. His crew lost faith in him."

"And here endeth his reign aboard the *Sea Phantom*. The mighty Captain Alden Fen hath fallen." Naelor's smug expression was clear, even through the branches and leaves Rowan hid behind. He smelled strongly of ale, roasted meat, and sweat. "Serves him right, the pompous bastard."

The way their words flowed, with ease and practice...

They knew she was there. They knew she was listening.

But the story they told was wrong. Fen wasn't the captain of the *Sea*

Phantom when the thief stole the map. It would be years before he would be captain.

Unless...

How much of this was the truth, then? Were they twisting facts to force Rowan to jump to conclusions? To create a rift between her and Fen?

"He was a good captain," Avenith defended. "We all have bad days, Naelor."

He chuckled. "Some worse than others. But I haven't had one that's haunted me for five years."

"That could be your lack of conscience talking," Avenith teased.

Naelor's laugh bounced off the forest canopy. "Fair point."

They moved deeper into the woods, Rowan's thoughts moving fast.

"Rowan?" Winter nuzzled her again. "What's wrong?"

"What they were saying—" Putting her fears into words, making emotions comprehensible, proved to be difficult. "Were they telling the truth?"

Winter sniffed in their direction.

"They knew we were here, didn't they?" Rowan asked.

"They didn't look at us." Winter snorted. "They didn't say our names."

But worry gnawed at Rowan's insides. Their conversation was staged, a performance just for her.

The details about Fen and the *Sea Phantom* were all true. Did that include Moonblade having the map? Did Naelor say that to hurt her? To drive the thorn deeper into her heart, forcing her to endure her own grief as well as Gran's?

"Naelor thinks he can use this as a weapon," Rowan said, turning his words over in her mind. "But I'm not the one getting hurt."

"What are you talking about?" Winter nudged her cheek. "What is Naelor doing?"

"He said Moonblade has the map Fen lost," Rowan said. "He wanted me to know that. He thinks it'll affect me."

"Won't it?"

"It would have, if I hadn't already suspected them..."

Rowan didn't finish the thought.

"Let's go," she said. "I need to see Fen."

———

FEN WAS AT JEAN'S, running a small rake over a dark patch of soil, preparing the earth for cold weather crops. Sweat dripped from his forehead, a flush painting his cheeks as he worked the soil for seeds. He glanced at Rowan, Winter at her heels, the softness of his gaze shifting to concern as he read her expression.

"What's wrong?" He let the rake fall as he approached her, wiping his arm against his forehead. "What happened?"

She stilled, the urge to pace strong, but she met his eyes and relished the safety there.

"Rowan?" He reached for her but stopped himself, glancing at his dirty arms and hands.

"Naelor and Avenith, just now." She took a slow breath, allowing her emotions to calm so that her mind could organize her thoughts. "They were talking about you losing the map as captain."

His brow furrowed. "But that—"

"—was the wrong time." She nodded. "Why would they say that in the woods, the two of them together?"

"Unless they knew you were listening?"

"What does Naelor want out of it?" She crossed her arms but brought one hand to her mouth, rubbing her bottom lip with her thumb. "He made sure to say things so specifically."

"Naelor?" Fen quirked one brow. "Not Avenith?"

"She was never one to hide jealousy well."

"And that's what this is?"

Rowan said nothing at first, her familiarity with Avenith recalling the days before her heart healed. "From her, I think so. But Naelor?"

He winced, a muscle in his jaw feathering. "Last I checked, he didn't have any vested interest in either of us. Or Feather and Claw."

"Shouldn't he?" Rowan tugged at her braid, twirling the end around her middle finger. The sensation was pleasant, giving her a physical action to balance the force of thoughts racing in her mind. "Feather and Claw has become a thorn in his side."

"And causing you to break trust in someone within the guild..." Fen didn't have to finish his thought.

"I think she saw us in the forest," Rowan said. "Though I can't imagine her asking Naelor to take a stroll with her just to spout nonsense to hurt me."

"That is a curious pairing." Fen rubbed his chin, scratching at his beard as he thought. "Which makes me question how much of it was planned and how much was opportunity."

A cacophony from the forest broke through, their heads and bodies turning toward the sound.

"Did a tree fall?" Fen moved to Rowan's side.

The wind swept over them, Winter's nose working as she read the scents it carried. Then she ran.

"Go." Fen freed arrows from a makeshift target beside Jean's house before lifting his quiver and bow. "I'm right behind you."

"It's dangerous," she said, already following in Winter's wake.

"That's why I'm going with you."

Winter was already several yards ahead of them as Rowan raced for the trees. Fen's athleticism was impressive, his running stride almost as fast as her god-touched speed. She shifted, her paws carrying her across the field toward the trees.

Blood, the scent growing stronger as she ran faster.

Winter howled a cry. "Wolves! Matriarch!"

They waited for the reply only to be met with silence. Rowan's pounding heart faltered against her ribcage. Then, their answers came.

"Guardian!"

"Dark magic!"

"Guardian!"

Rowan pushed harder, her throat and lungs burning with the cold air that filled them, her body eager for a fight. She and Winter broke through the tree line, following the scent of death mingling with blood, sharp and metallic. Wolves snarled and barked, the sounds full of distress and anger. Fen didn't falter, his agility put to the test as he maintained pace through the brush, navigating around trees as he kept up with her.

"Guardian!" One wolf, its voice panicked. "The witch flees!"

Witch? Someone with magic?

"There is one dead," another said. "A villager."

"Gods—"

Rowan maintained the trail, racing toward the river. "We'll lose them if they reach the water."

But her fear met hope as she made out a shape among the trees. "There!"

Fen saw it, too, as he fired an arrow without hesitation. The weapon met its mark, and the scream that followed pierced Rowan's ears in agony.

A scream that was human. Female. And afraid.

"Winter, can you catch her scent?"

"No. Something masks it from us."

"She knows." But Rowan's thoughts froze in the urgency of catching their target, one that was somehow eluding them. "She knows we'll find her."

A great force splashed water, swimming hard until the sound faded. By the time Rowan and the others reached the river, the woman was gone.

"Gods damn it all!" Rowan sniffed around the bank, she and Winter desperate for any trace. She bolted downstream, following the flow of the water, but caught sight of nothing.

"Guardian!"

Rowan turned to the wolves who approached. She glanced at Fen, who stowed his bow and arrow and stepped back at the wolves' approach.

"That fell creature. She dares to wear human skin." The wolf snarled as it spoke, lips twitching over its bared teeth. "One of yours and one of ours are dead."

"Its soul and life consumed," another wolf said. "Inhaled like breath."

"Gods—" Rowan's stomach soured in grief and guilt, even as her anger burned. "A soulwitch?"

But there were no soulwitches in Elderglen. Rowan would have known.

"The forest has been too quiet," the first wolf said. "We were complacent."

"This is my fault," Rowan said. "I allowed other things to get in the way of my duty."

"No." The patriarch approached, blood on his fur. He limped, his front left leg raised. "You are Guardian and Watcher. You are human. This domain is ours. I am the one who has failed."

Rowan disagreed, and other wolf voices sounded with hers.

"No."

"No, Patriarch."

Winter whined, lowering her head. "You lead with strength. Great evil brings only destruction and death. We fight for and defend life."

"Yet one of my pack was taken." Sorrow softened his voice. "Murdered by darkness."

"I will find who did this," Rowan said. "And I will end this."

"We harmed it," one wolf said. "Us and your archer."

Rowan looked back at Fen, who watched them with calm focus.

"I ripped into its leg," another wolf said. "Disgusting. Meat that tasted like death. Tainted with dark magic."

"That will make it easier to find," Rowan said. "I am sorry for what this has cost."

"We grieve, and we fight," the patriarch said. "My mate is with the others, recovering. This is far from over."

Rowan shifted, though her legs quivered beneath her weight. Fen's arm found her waist, steadying her on her feet as her adrenaline dissolved, leaving fatigue in its wake.

"Two are dead," she said. "One human, one wolf. But she's injured."

"She?"

"A woman. Human. Someone from Elderglen. A villager did this."

"You're sure?"

She couldn't nod, couldn't speak. She could only breathe as she tried to sort through the cacophony cascading down her mind, rattling her bones.

"I'm sorry, Rowan."

She shook her head, trying to offer a smile that was far too weak. "The wolves were impressed by your marksmanship."

She refrained from using their words—*your archer*.

"Let's go back," Fen said. "Jean and the others will need to know."

"You tell them." Rowan moved a half-step back. "And find the person who was killed. I'll check the river one more time. And I'll think of something to tell the mayor."

She shifted without another word, running further downstream with Winter at her heels. She could feel Fen's stare following her until she was out of sight.

CHAPTER 39

Running the length of the river offered nothing. Any trace of the killer had washed away, leaving Rowan to sit at its bank and stare into its calm and beautiful blue surface. Did she find her way south to Shaylon Plains? Or did she continue west all the way to Alvar?

"We should return," she said to Winter. "This won't resolve itself."

They didn't hurry as they moved across the landscape, the warm fragrance of umber leaves faint with the cool, crisp breath of winter.

"Autumn is leaving us," Winter said. "My namesake will be here soon."

Her namesake. Winter's pure wonder soothed any ache that found its way into Rowan's heart. It made each step easier as they neared Elderglen, giving Rowan the strength to fortify her heart against what she was about to face.

She would start with Jean and the others. Fen had likely filled them in, leaving Rowan the task of developing some kind of plan. What could they do? The killer had no discernible pattern or method other than blood and death.

Consuming the wolf, devouring its soul. What of its blood? Did it drain the wolf as it had the human?

The human. Which villager had died? Rowan hadn't located the body. She would need to bring it back to the village.

"The human." Rowan reached out to what wolves and crows were close by. "Where is the body?"

"Here," came the crow's calls. "Here. Here."

The remains were bloody, the attack likely in haste. He was face-down, his red plaid shirt stained dark crimson. But Rowan recognized him as soon as she saw his aged hands in the grass, reaching out.

Mary Beth's father. The man Rowan had helped to find when she returned from Shaylon Plains.

The monster had taken him.

Rowan shifted, falling to her knees beside him, turning him over. Soulless eyes met hers, his mouth agape, fear freezing his pupils to pinpricks.

"No—"

Winter whined beside her, sitting with a mournful look. Rowan's hands, stained with dirt, swept bloody hair from the old man's face.

"She shouldn't see her father like this." Rowan glanced over her shoulder toward the river. "Gods, what have I done?"

Winter whined again, and Rowan could hear her gentle scolding. *No, Rowan, not you*, but Rowan's heart struggled to beat within the vise grip of failure. Because she'd failed him. She'd failed Mary Beth. She'd failed all of Elderglen.

Footsteps, voices, and Rowan froze in guilt-fueled shock before Fen and Wil appeared.

Their shocked whispers met her ears as she stood, lifting the man in her arms. He was thin and frail, his weight regrettably easy for her to carry.

"She shouldn't see him like this," Rowan muttered, unable to string together anything else comprehensible. "Not like this."

"Rowan—"

"Dad?" Mary Beth's voice carried through the trees. "Gods, not again. Dad?"

Panic flowed through the three friends. Wil nodded and turned toward Mary Beth, Fen not far behind. Rowan, then, turned for the river, her movements careful through the brush until she reached the cool flowing water. She was careful as she laid him in the cool grass.

"Where is he?" Mary Beth's voice was panic-laced and violent. Wil and Fen did their best to stop her, to warn her, but she wouldn't listen.

"I'm so sorry," Rowan whispered to the dead man in her arms.

With handfuls of water, she cleaned his face and hands, combing her fingers through his bloody hair until the gray strands rinsed clean.

"Dad!"

Mary Beth rushed over, her shrill voice tearing through the air. She crashed beside her father, taking him into her arms and wailing. Rowan sat back on her heels, powerless, defeated.

She stared down at her hands, the blood diluted with water as it coursed through the lines of her fingers and palms. She put them in the river, watching the blood leave her skin.

"I was afraid this would happen," Mary Beth said, holding her father close. "My worst fear..."

"I will find who did this," Rowan said, her voice low. "The wolves injured it. Fen shot it. But it escaped up-river."

It. Not *she*. *It* was easier to avoid the truth that a human being had done this. That someone in their village had pushed Mary Beth into her nightmare.

"Thank you," Mary Beth whispered. "Thank you for finding him."

Too late.

"I will help you carry him home," she said. "Whenever you're ready."

Mary Beth only needed a few minutes to collect herself enough to let her father go. Rowan lifted him once more and led the procession out of the forest toward Elderglen.

Mary Beth's home was near the outskirts of the village, and they reached it with little time wasted, though passers-by witnessed the somber group. Word began its rapid spread that another villager had died in the woods.

Wil offered to speak to the carpenter about a prepared casket as Jean came with Peter, several villagers in their wake.

"We were in the tavern, waiting for news," Jean said. She looked at

Mary Beth with kindness. "Stay with me tonight, love, after we get your father settled."

"I don't want to leave him." She sniffled, looking at him in Rowan's arms. "I don't want him to be alone."

"Then I'll stay with you." Jean patted her shoulder. "Let's go, love. Let's make some tea while you tell me your favorite memory of him."

Rowan laid him on his bed and moved aside as Mary Beth fussed over his clothes and shoes. She wept as she smoothed his hair, apologizing for not realizing he'd gone.

"I closed my eyes for just a second," she said, another wave of emotion crashing down. "Just for a second."

As she dissolved into tears, Jean held her and nodded for the others to go.

They said nothing as they left Mary Beth's home and walked toward the heart of Elderglen, where whispers circulated quickly.

"It's wounded," Rowan muttered, eyes tracing the shape of the mayor's home before scanning the faces around her. Once the mayor knew—

Rowan stopped, spotting Halie among the villagers milling around the thoroughfare, pedestrians navigating around horses and carts to trade. Halie spoke with the village florist, shaking her head and sharing a laugh. Someone as bitter as Halie, *amused*.

"—more money than I can spend!" She guffawed, the sound offensive and over-the-top. "A new patron loves my embroidery, and—"

Halie's voice returned to a normal volume, but Rowan couldn't be bothered to adjust her hearing to listen to anymore. But as Halie walked away, her gait was uneven with a limp favoring her right leg.

Was she limping from a wolf bite? Halie's skirt was long and thick, offering no glimpse of whatever wound would be there, potentially staining her socks or stockings. She would had to have wrapped it well to keep any trace from surfacing. The thickness would be the tell-tale sign.

Thoughts flew through Rowan's mind, recalling the vitriol she shared with her brother over Rowan, her guardianship, and her place on Sentinel Hill. Had Halie made some dark pact? Did she give herself over to dark magic to threaten all that Rowan's grandparents had built?

"Does she even know—" But Rowan's whispered thought remained unfinished as she followed Halie.

"What?" Fen asked. "What is it?"

This magic was beyond Rowan's skill, but Jean may know how to face soul magic.

Soul magic mingled with blood. *Necromancy.*

"Rowan?"

Halie entered the tailor's, and Rowan continued around to the nearest window where she could listen and watch. Fen and Wil moved with her, silent observers with concern digging deep lines between their brows. Rowan put her finger on her lips and gestured toward her eyes before looking through the window.

Halie passed a load of spun wool, not yet dyed or treated.

"Halie," the tailor said, eyeing her with concern. "By the gods, what happened?"

"I fell off of the back step," she said with a nonchalant giggle. "Trying to take the clothes out to dry."

Falling from her back step. A clever lie. One that wouldn't be suspicious.

"Gracious, that's awful." The tailor passed her a small pouch of coins. "Hurry home and rest up. I can have the apothecary bring you something."

"I've already seen to it," Halie said with a charming smile. "But thank you. I'll be alright."

She turned to go, and Rowan waited to follow, tracking the leg she favored, imagining the wolf's bite tearing through flesh as Halie tried to escape. How was she able to walk, let alone see to chores?

"Rowan?"

She turned at Wil's voice before glancing back at Halie, who limped toward home. She hadn't turned around. Was she aware of Rowan's watchful, knowing eye?

Fen cleared his throat quietly. "Why are we following her? What's going on?"

"Not here." Rowan navigated around the shop, avoiding the thoroughfare. They'd walked far enough from the marketplace to avoid any eavesdroppers, but Rowan pulled both Fen and Wil close. "The wolves bit the killer on the leg. And your arrow," she said to Fen, "shot her. But I don't know where."

"*Her*." Wil looked from Rowan to the village. "You think it's Halie?"

"The killer screamed when Fen shot her. The voice was definitely female. But Winter and I couldn't catch her scent."

"You mean she masked it on purpose?" Fen asked. "She *knew* to mask it?"

Rowan nodded slowly, relieved they came to the same conclusion. "The wolves described dark magic, saying she consumed the wolf with her breath. Like a soulwitch."

"A soulwitch in Elderglen?" Wil narrowed his eyes. "How—?"

But Rowan wasn't listening, her mind working fast. "Has she really been right there this entire time?"

"Rowan—"

"All the trouble she's given us, and to think that it was *her*."

"*Rowan*." Wil took her shoulders. "Halie fell down the steps this morning."

"That's what she told the tailor, but—"

"I saw it happen," he said. "She and Braithen were having an argument, and he shoved her."

Rowan stared, disbelief trying in vain to hold up the false truth she needed, that crumbled like cracking stone.

"Gods," Fen said. "He hurt her?"

"I didn't think he could be more of a bastard, but here we are." Wil's concern didn't lighten as he read Rowan's face. "You alright?"

She didn't answer, bringing a hand to her forehead. Wil's arms wrapped around her, bringing her firmly against his chest.

"I thought—" Her voice wavered, returning his embrace. "I really thought—"

He stroked her hair, careful of the wild curls. "We all want this killer found. We all want this nightmare to stop."

She said nothing, half of her wanting to accept Wil's comfort while the other wanted to rip the forest apart to find the true monster.

"Let's go," Fen said. "A crowd is forming."

"I have to see the mayor." She rubbed her temples, the headache blooming with a rhythmic pulse. "If only I could crawl into bed and never get out again."

"Soon," Fen said, looking up toward Sentinel Hill. "I'll stand guard by your door if that's what it takes."

Wil raised an eyebrow, impressed. "She'll take you up on that if you're not careful."

Fen's dark eyes met Rowan's. "I wish she would."

CHAPTER 40

Rowan didn't send word before going to the mayor's front door and knocking, giving no thought to the schedule laid out before him. But as she waited, a slight pang of remorse tingled in her core. The mayor and his wife had more than Elderglen weighing on their shoulders. In memory, Rowan heard Gran and Jean asking about Derin, and Suna always offered the same response that tried to show the face of hope to hide the fear that likely gnawed at her core.

The butler answered and stood aside for Rowan's entry. "Come in, ma'am."

He led her down the familiar path to the mayor's office, up the stairs and down the hallway to the right. The sunlight brilliantly illuminated the space through the tall, open windows, but both Frederick and Suna looked pale as Rowan entered.

"I hope I'm not interrupting," Rowan said, the sentiment half-meant.

"We expected you," Suna said, her smile thin but soft. "Your days have been busy, Guardian."

Rowan always liked Suna's use of her chosen title. *Guardian*. Not Watcher. One chosen, the other inherited, both still to be earned.

"Death is rampant," Mayor Frederick said. "Our hearts are freshly broken from the farm, only to have another one of our own found dead." He shook his head. "We're fighting a war on two fronts, Rowan."

She hadn't thought of it that way. From cultists to a mysterious killer targeting Elderglen villagers, they balanced on the edge of a precipice, the cliff leading to the fathomless dark.

"How is your son?" Rowan asked. "I haven't heard anything since we last spoke."

Frederick and Suna shared a look. She pressed a hand to her mouth, muffling a quiet sob.

"He worsens," Frederick said. "Everything we've tried. Everything we've done—"

He stopped himself, looking down at his desk.

"I'll prepare some tea," Suna said, averting her eyes, turning to leave.

"Not on my account," Rowan said. "Please. I beg you to rest. I won't be here long."

She reached a hand for Suna's shoulder to guide her to the door, but Suna cried out, jerking her body away from Rowan's touch.

"I'm sorry," Rowan said quickly, recoiling her hand. "I meant no offense."

Suna gathered her composure, embarrassment twisting her features. "I'm the one to apologize." She edged toward the door. "These days have held little rest, and the chair in my son's room has ruined me, I'm afraid."

"There's space enough for a small bed." Frederick's tone suggested this wasn't the first time he'd said it. "But we'll see where the days lead."

Suna excused herself once more before leaving the room, latching the door behind her.

"We are distraught," Frederick said, not bothering to mask his vulnerability. "As you can imagine. Powerless. And the *waiting*." He pinched the bridge of his nose. "And I've never seen my wife so frail."

"And the world, folding in around you," Rowan whispered. She hadn't expected kinship with the mayor of Elderglen. "Our people are suffering, Mr. Mayor. Yourself, among them."

He heaved a sigh. "Inaction doesn't suit me, Rowan, but I know of nothing to do. Other than write to as many outposts as I can, to the Wolf Seat itself, and beg for aid."

"Have you?" Rowan didn't hide her surprise. "Have you reached out?"

"Twice." He glanced at his desk again, gesturing vaguely toward a half-written letter. "This will be my third. But resources are thin everywhere, with the Wandering Order preying on innocent people."

Which reminded her...

"Mr. Mayor," she prefaced. "One of my friends saw you speaking with a Preceptor."

Frederick's eyes widened, but he didn't back away. "Cut right to the chase, Miss Watcher. Yes, I spoke with him, not realizing he was cultist scum." He rubbed his forehead, closing his eyes to calm himself. "He wanted to use Elderglen to house a few of his members while they worked on exploiting one of the mines of arcana crystal. He even promised a considerable cut from their yield."

"But you refused." She gave the words as a statement rather than a question, gauging his mood. She needed him amenable to continue to speak with her, to tell her whatever he could about the Wandering Order's silver-haired, devilish Preceptor.

"If I'd realized how close that family's farm was to the mine, I'd have done something. Reached out. Sent villagers to help." He ran a hand through his hair, the normally tended locks more haphazard than Rowan had ever seen them. "Hells, I would've had Braithen and a few others patrol their perimeter, since they're so in need of something to do. But I—"

He pressed a fist to his mouth, taking a breath.

Defeated. The Mayor of Elderglen was *defeated*.

"I didn't think," he said. "Geography never entered into my reckoning, and look at what's happened. Because of my ignorance and neglect. Look at what I've done."

What have I done? The same question Rowan asked herself when she stared at the bodies.

"You're not the only person who could have acted," she said, "but I wish you would have told me about him."

"I was ashamed, speaking to a Preceptor and not even realizing until I looked down at his boots. Gods, how stupid—" He stopped himself again. "Be that as it may, we have a killer preying on villagers and a cult laying siege wherever they can." He met her gaze. "What would you have me do?"

"Send for reinforcements," she said. "A mayor's seal will go farther than my paltry letter, but I will happily include a message from one of Rhiann's chosen."

Saying the words left a bad taste in her mouth, but perhaps the Wolf Queen would respond with both an elected official *and* a god-touched asking for help.

He nodded. "I'll see it done."

Rowan left, the butler in her wake as her focused stepped carried her out of the house. A part of her was tempted to find Suna, to see Derin and pray for his healing. As far as Rowan knew, Jean hadn't been called to lend any help, though Suna was close with the village apothecary.

"They're doing everything they can," she muttered to herself, descending the front steps. She looked up toward Sentinel Hill, the climb taller and steeper than before.

But smoke feathered from Jean's chimney. Her body guided her there as though beckoned, Jean's wisdom and insight needed.

She would be with Mary Beth, helping to guide her through grief and anger at such a tragic loss. Mary Beth needed Jean's soothing presence more than Rowan. Rowan could wait.

Climbing the hill, Rowan found Fen working on Jean's fence, pulling rusted nails from the posts to add new ones in place. There were even new boards to replace the old, warped, and weathered ones that had survived the years, all lying at his feet.

When their eyes met, Fen set his hammer down and walked toward her. His steps were long and determined, the distance between them closing fast.

"I don't want to disturb your work," she said.

"Disturb me." Then, laughing, he said, "You're not interrupting anything."

"Could we talk?"

"Of course." Then, looking down at himself, he gestured toward Jean's. "May I clean up first?"

"Sure." She gestured toward her home. "I'll make us some tea."

"You're a goddess."

He turned, thinking nothing of the compliment that warmed her cheeks. Her steps were lighter as she returned home, preparing herself for the words she was about to say.

CHAPTER 41

Fen's timid knock came moments after Rowan pulled the kettle from the fire. She poured the hot water into the teapot before letting him in.

He'd changed clothes, the dark blue fabric flattering his skin tone, hair, and eyes. His hair was towel-dried, the curling ends still dripping on his shoulders.

"I'm sorry if I kept you waiting," he said.

"You didn't." She latched the door behind him and gestured toward the table. "Would you like a cup?"

"Yes, thank you."

He'd been in her home before, but this time was different. There wasn't a crisis or grief, no urgency or danger. There were only the two of them, with Winter lounging by the window.

He turned, startling her. "How did—"

He must not have realized how close she was behind him. She reached for his arms to brace herself as she leaned back. His arms found her waist in an instant, keeping her from falling.

"Gods, I'm sorry." He helped her to stand straight, his hands slow to leave her side. "I'm not normally so clumsy."

"Though the gesture is vaguely familiar." A shadow of a smile toyed with her mouth, remembering how she'd caught him before.

It was easy to look at him, to read the softness around his eyes and mouth, to see her reflection in his dark irises.

"Are you alright?"

"I'm fine," she said. "You caught me before I fell."

He took her hands, the gesture gentle, his grip loose and fingers open, as though to give her room to refuse. "That's not what I meant."

She looked down at their hands, his calloused and warm. "I hardly know. It comes in waves."

He ran his thumb across her knuckles. She enjoyed the way it felt, his touch gentle, showing she was precious.

The sweet floral fragrance of the tea filled her home, mingling with the honeyed scent of the soap Fen had used. She edged closer, drawn to it. Drawn to him.

"Tell me," he whispered. "You can, if you want. You can tell me anything."

Somehow, he'd unlocked the door to her cage and waited for her to step through.

She held his hands tighter, an offering of encouragement before the words came at last. "I have received extraordinary gifts. Rhiann, herself, has transformed my body to bear strength and power not many humans possess."

She paused, the ambiance around them calm. Rhiann listened, along with Fen, but lying would shove the emotional thorn deeper into Rowan's soul. Saying the words out loud would offer the truth to a goddess who already knew the deepest corners of Rowan's heart.

"I hate it," she whispered, furthering the confession from before, baring her vulnerability to a man whose heart was also on display for her. "Guardian. Cornerstone. Watcher of Elderglen." She clenched her teeth, the bitterness souring to an emotional wave she didn't want to release. Her throat tightened. Anger was easier than the emotion that welled within.

"When my parents were killed," she said. "I couldn't find the strength to breathe. I was so *hollow*." She closed her eyes. "Any good within me dissolved to nothing."

"That's not true." Fen pulled her closer, bringing her knuckles against his chest. "That's not true, Rowan. You are good. You are whole. But your heart is broken."

You are whole. Even when it felt like the opposite was true.

He brought a hand to her hair, sweeping errant strands behind her ear. "You are good, Rowan. And you are strong. But that doesn't mean you have to carry this alone."

She studied his eyes, the shape of his brow, the way his mouth moved when he said her name. *Rowan,* with his deep voice soft and lips poised to kiss. As though her name shaped his mouth specifically for her. *Rowan.*

"May I..." His thumb glided across her bottom lip. "Would it be alright if I—"

When she kissed him, the air stilled, the world taking a breath as she learned the softness of his mouth. His stubble was pleasant against her skin. She touched his jaw, gliding her fingers up his cheek, feeling the vibration of a low moan rumble in his throat.

He gripped her hair, his hold gentle, fingers flexing as he massaged her scalp. His other hand slid down her throat and along her side until it reached her waist. He pressed his palm against her back, bringing her closer. Her arms found his shoulders, resting there as their kiss deepened. When his tongue swept over hers, lightning cascaded down her spine in a dance of energy, but the sensation didn't linger. He pulled back only once, eyes eager as they searched her face before kissing her again with promises unspoken.

She eased back, staring into his eyes. "Are you teasing me?"

"I want you to enjoy our first kiss," he said, rubbing her nose with his. "And our second. And our third..."

Rowan was careful with him, her strength itching to surface and surround his body. She eased her hold on him, afraid of hurting him.

"Rowan?"

He searched her face, noticing the flush painting itself across her cheeks.

"I don't want to hurt you," she whispered, resting a hand against his chest. "I said I can be too much at times. I—"

"Don't remove any part of yourself for me." Fen's quiet voice bore a low timbre that rumbled in his chest, its vibration reaching her finger-tips alongside the rhythm of his heartbeat. "Your wildness. Your rage. Your passion. I want it all." He pressed her hand firmly against his chest, willing her to feel his sincerity. "I'm strong enough to take it. There is no part of you I cannot carry." He brought her fingers to his lips, his kiss tender. "I want all of you."

Elation flooded her bloodstream, her heart fluttering to keep up with the rush beneath her skin. Her hands gripped against his sides as she walked him back, his look curious until he read the mischief in her gaze. When he landed against the front door, his shock dissolved to plea-sure as her touch skated down his arms to his hands, interlacing their fingers. She pressed a gentle kiss to his mouth, trailing across his cheek, smiling to herself as he bent at the knees to help her reach him.

"You never cease to amaze me." He smiled, dark blue eyes glistening. "Pity I'm taller than you."

"Why is that a pity?"

His knee moved between hers as he pivoted, using his height as leverage to spin her. She cried out, thrilled by his strength and the mischief that framed his eyes and mouth.

He leaned to her, their smirking mouths inches apart. "Gods, that look. It's intoxicating."

"What look?"

"Like you've just met an intriguing challenge. The defiant tilt of your chin. The gleam in your breathtaking eyes. They tell me how beau-tifully you're going to win."

"And how spectacularly you're going to lose?"

"Oh, no. I won't lose, love." *Kiss.* "No matter the outcome, I will win." *Kiss.* "And so will you."

"An interesting game for us to play." She enjoyed the pressure of his hands and the shape of his mouth. "Challenge: accepted."

HOURS PASSED before Jean returned home from Mary Beth's, the night shrouding the village in its star-speckled reprieve from what the day had wrought. The moments spent with Fen held the world at bay, yet Rowan lamented their parting as they watched Jean make the short trip home.

"Let's pray we both get some rest," he said, cupping her face and kissing her forehead. "You'll need it, Guardian."

"I wish this could wait until morning," Rowan said. "But so much happened in just a few hours."

"Cornerstone and the Veil," Fen said. "She'll want you to talk to her."

So she did, walking with Fen to Jean's as the night bugs chirped and buzzed around them.

"I'll work outside for a bit," he said. "I won't go inside until you're done."

She thanked him, squeezing his hand before they separated. Rowan moved to Jean's front door and waited, hand poised to knock. But she hesitated, imagining Jean seated at her dining table, shoulders hunched in mental and physical fatigue.

"It's open, Rowan."

Rowan stared at the door before turning the handle, timid as she stepped in.

"I caught you and Fen heading this way." She offered Rowan a small, tired smile. "Things are progressing beautifully, aren't they?"

"It feels wrong," Rowan admitted. "Feeling this happy when the world is breaking."

"We need to hold our happiness as tightly as we can," Jean said. "The number of breaths we're promised is not a guarantee." Her smile was warm as she placed two steaming cups on her small, worn dining table. "Sit down and tell me everything."

"You were expecting me?" Rowan took a seat, wrapping the warm cup in her hands. "I thought you'd be exhausted."

"I am, but I expect you every day. Just in case either you, Rowan, or you, the Cornerstone, need me."

"Either, or?" Rowan lifted a brow. "Aren't I both?"

"You are Rowan, but the *Cornerstone* isn't your identity. It's a title you bear, among others. They exist because of you and those who came before. You don't exist for them."

Rowan stared, steam feathering around her face, warming her

cheeks. Immediately, without prompting, Jean knew exactly what to say, her words reaching the tender, frightened corners of her heart, wrapping them in protective hands.

"Cynthia had moments of crisis," Jean went on. "Not saying that you're—"

"No," Rowan interrupted with a light laugh. "I am. There is so much."

She didn't have to elaborate. Jean rested a hand on Rowan's arm, her thumb stroking its curve. The gesture was loving and maternal, soothing Rowan from the inside out. But with it came a flood of emotion long suppressed.

"I asked Mayor Frederick for a letter with his seal. One to join a message from me, the wolfkind Watcher of Elderglen. For what good it will do." She paused before asking, "What's the best way to call for aid?"

"Other than running there yourself?" And Rowan knew Jean meant literally. "His seal is the best and fastest."

"If they arrive. How do we ready Elderglen for any soldiers?"

"*If.*" Jean chuckled. "You sound like Cynthia."

Comfort reached through Rowan's hands and arms, through to her heart.

"The tavern will need rooms ready, depending on how many we get." Jean regarded Rowan with a raised brow. "But this isn't what we need to discuss."

Confused, Rowan sat up straighter. "What do you mean?"

"You're stepping into a role," she said. "You must wear the mantle. It's understandable that it overwhelms you."

"I would throw it into the Sea of Kings if Gran hadn't made it with her own hands." She traced the curve of the cup handle with her index finger. "The feel of it is comforting to me still, even with the responsibility it brings."

"And that's why it should be yours." Jean's soft, pleased expression held pride. "Because you don't want it."

Rowan let her words sink in, stubbornness leading to snark. "A pleasant sentiment from those who don't want it, themselves."

Jean pinched Rowan's little finger, smirking. "We can both be right." After a beat, she added, "Look at Mayor Frederick. Hells, look at

Braithen. Both seek power, believing they have none. And neither of them should ever get it."

"I don't have power, either," Rowan countered. "I'm thwarted and denied at every turn."

"By those who are intimidated by you." The hearth fire complimented Jean's hazel eyes. "Because they're afraid of you."

"Why in the name of—" She exhaled sharply, firing herself to calm down. "Is it because I'm so angry all the time?"

"No—well, that's likely part of it." Jean laughed, the lines around her mouth deep. "You know your value and your worth, and that intimidates people who would like to use that against you. But they can't."

"It doesn't feel that way," Rowan said. "Not when I'm so powerless to stop this. To change it. To make us stronger."

"You already have power, my love. You've given it to yourself."

"But Rhiann—"

"Your gifts as guardian aren't your power. You may draw strength from them, and they may add to your resilience, but your *power* is all your own."

Jean's truth touched her where she was afraid, shedding light on areas long kept in shadow.

"The family that they killed." Her hand was gentle on Rowan's arm. "The monsters who killed them wanted to reach you, to hurt you in a way no weapon could. To make your power falter."

"It nearly did," Rowan admitted, her voice raw. "If it hadn't been for Fen..."

A breath of quiet passed over them.

"Your anger can become your weakness," Jean said, "but its energy is invaluable. Finding the balance to use it is one of the hardest things you can do. It hides itself well beneath your fears and self-doubt."

"And loathing." The word escaped Rowan's mouth before she could think to stop it. "I hate carelessness and the catastrophes it brings. I hate selfishness and greed. And I hate those things in myself." She roughly prodded her chest for emphasis, stabbing the truth of it into skin and bone. "I want my parents back. How could they die and leave me behind?" Her voice tore through her throat, the muscles too tight to allow passage. So she forced her way out, defying her own body to set herself free. There was no more holding back the river. "How could the hand that killed them go on without punishment? Without judgment?"

"What would you give them, Rowan?" Jean's quiet question was a cacophony. "Would you kill them?"

Yes. She pressed a trembling hand to her mouth to keep the word caged where it belonged. She could almost feel their flesh rend beneath her claws.

"Their darkness does not belong to you." She touched Rowan's hair, stroking gently. "Do not take it from them."

Would that she could take everything from them.

Their darkness.

Their breath.

Their beating heart.

Would that she could devour them all.

"Rowan." Jean's hand never ceased in applying steady, rhythmic pressure. "Talk to me."

"I—" She gasped, her lungs desperate for breath. "I can't—"

She rose quickly, the chair scraping loudly against the floor. Somehow, it didn't topple as Rowan rushed past, heading for Jean's back door.

"Rowan."

She stopped, her hand resting on the door handle, her breath catching in her chest.

Jean's hands turned her, and, without a word, her arms wrapped around Rowan's shoulders. She said nothing, bringing Rowan's head to her shoulder as her hands stroked soothing lines down her back. Rowan's breathing quickened, her heart fluttering so fast that her blood raced.

"I'm here," Jean whispered. "I'm not going anywhere."

A thorn had pulled from Rowan's heart, the wound gushing blood.

Neither woman spoke. All of Rowan's effort went into breathing, pushing her body to comply with her need for air despite its descent.

"I've got you," Jean said. Her hold tightened. "I've got you."

"I'm sorry." Tears warmed and stung Rowan's eyes. "You have to be everyone's comfort."

"You are my comfort," she said. "Thank you for letting me take care of you."

Another thorn broke free from Rowan's heart, each beat stronger than the one before.

"When will I be whole again?" Rowan asked. "I don't want to be a monster."

"You're not a monster." Jean ran a hand over Rowan's hair, the rhythm and pressure soothing. "You're already whole, my love."

"I've lost so much." Rowan shook her head against Jean's shoulder. "There are dozens of holes inside of me. My soul feels paper thin."

"That's how your anger filled you," she said. "It fills us all when grief leaves us hollow. But it isn't lasting. And it isn't satisfying."

"Then what is it?"

"Sustaining."

Rowan said nothing, the pressure of Jean's embrace helping her breathing to level and balance.

"Anger sustains us, but it does not complete us. And it will not keep us for long. Every flame will burn out, Rowan."

"But this has burned for so long."

"And you're losing fuel for it, aren't you?"

Shorter tempers. Hastier actions.

Jean had summed everything so succinctly.

She was losing fuel.

"We love you," Jean said. "And we are here beside you. Trust us. Trust *me*."

"I do."

But even as Rowan said the words, she felt the weakness within them. Her trust in Jean and the others met a point, then it recoiled from fear of the tether not reaching its anchor.

But it never would if Rowan didn't try.

She cleared her throat. "I will."

Jean kissed her temple, studying her face before returning to her cup of tea. Rowan took a tentative sip, the liquid still steaming.

"When are you going to tell me about Fen?"

Rowan sputtered, the hot tea splashing inside her mouth and down her throat. She coughed, the pain lingering as her eyes watered. But Jean, unaffected, sat at her table and waited.

"You waste no time." Rowan wiped her mouth, clearing her throat before laughing. "You and Wil didn't have a bet going, did you?"

"Of course not." Jean sipped her tea. "But Peter and I did." She grinned. "And I won."

"Gods help us." Rowan chuckled. "What was the bet?"

But instead of answering, Jean took another sip.

CHAPTER 42

Rowan relished the cool touch of moonlight as she strode the field toward the forest.

The last of her patrols for the day lay before her, but the lightness of her heart and mind made each step easier. Trusting Fen. Trusting Jean and the others. Knowing she wasn't alone.

She reached down to pet Winter, her companion's fur soft, her eyes warm, her ears back in happiness.

"Let's see what the night brings."

She shifted, padding quietly into the trees, moving through to burned brush and bark before crossing into the untouched part of the forest. Voices carried, a woman speaking. Rowan followed the sound.

She picked up their scents before she saw their shapes. Patchouli, lavender, and citrus. *Mirelyn.* Vetiver and pine. *Marc?* Had she captured his scent before?

Then, a third. Leather, salt, and cinnamon.

Her heart fluttered as she shifted, walking as a human toward Mirelyn, Marc, and Fen. They were speaking quietly, Fen standing a few feet from Marc, who remained close beside Mirelyn. While the brothers weren't at odds, there was still a rift between them, one based in fear.

But Marc seemed more relaxed than before, the shadows beneath his eyes almost gone.

Their eyes found her as she moved in, her smile small and tentative. Fen's smile spread wide, highlighting his relaxed demeanor. Even Marc looked happy to see her, much of his color returned.

"Sorry to interrupt," she said. "I was on patrol, and I heard voices."

"You're not interrupting," Mirelyn said with a kind, maternal smile. "Fen stopped by, and we're so glad he did."

She looked at Marc, who agreed. "I feel much more like myself now. Ever since that crystal." He showed his hands, turning them over in front of them to show the absence of their infernal glow. "I don't feel like I'm going to set the world on fire anymore."

Set the world on fire. She smelled the singed woods behind her. She recalled the burned farmhouse and barn and the family who lay in front of it, dead. Had the latter been a part of Marc's control? Or did his anger dictate his actions?

Not that I am different from him, she thought. *If I had fire magic—*

She pushed the thought aside before it could finish, a tinge of cold fear rattling her nerves as it settled in her core.

"I'm glad," Rowan said. "I'll finish my patrol and let you continue."

Fen moved as though to stop her, but she smiled. "I'll finish soon."

She felt him watch her leave, even as she shifted and trotted beside Winter.

"He smells like that poison," Winter said, sneezing. "How can you bear it?"

"It's easier when you're a human," Rowan said, a sting in her heart nearly pulling her to turn back. Traces of mist arcana came to her nose, but she didn't follow its trail. Marc's use of mist arcana wasn't her battle to fight. It was his, and she prayed he would come out the other side.

But worries over his addiction dissolved at the sound of someone crying.

"A human?" Winter's ears perked at the sound. "Over there."

As they stepped forward, a familiar metallic fragrance pulled Rowan's attention. And her fear.

Blood.

Its scent came from the other direction, opposite to the sound of someone crying.

"Rowan?"

"I smell blood," she blurted. "Someone could be hurt."

But the stone in her core settled hard, fearing a worse fate had befallen them.

And the stone was right.

The woman was on her back, mouth agape, eyes wide, her bandaged ankle visible from the disturbed skirt of her dress.

Halie.

What blood remained had pooled around her, staining grass and soil. Her wide eyes showed tiny pupils, giving Rowan a glimpse of how afraid she'd been before her heart stopped beating.

"Murder!" a crow cried, alerting the others to call in echo.

"Murder!"

"Murder!"

"What did this?" Rowan asked. "Did you see?"

"A shadow with claws!"

Wings fluttered, and branches whispered as they left and returned.

"They're restless," she told Winter. "Something's not right."

"Crying woman," Winter said. "She could be hurt."

"A woman?"

"I caught her scent."

A woman.

A shadow with claws.

Darkness given human shape, hollowing Halie of blood and life, taking her soul and leaving her a husk on the forest floor.

Who would have command of the shadows like that? Who in Elderglen would lean into Chaos, summoning Aishlin's power?

Bloodless bodies, eyes devoid of light...

She and Winter moved slowly toward the weeping woman, both careful of their footsteps. Leaves and twigs were abundant, making a quiet approach almost impossible.

But the crying was heavy, the woman's breathing labored as she struggled to fill her lungs. Rowan continued, moving around trees, seeing a hunched shape nearly on its knees, shoulders wrapped in a dark shawl. Her dark hair was unbound and loose around her face, which she hid in her hands as she cried.

Rowan nearly whispered her name aloud—*Suna?*—hoping to be gentle to keep from scaring her. But her eyes alighted to the tendrils of shadow around Suna's feet, feathering out as though made of fog.

No. Gods, no.

"Winter," Rowan said gently. "She's a soulwitch."

"What—"

"Go." Rowan couldn't waste time explaining. If Suna wasn't in control, it was dangerous for them both. "Stay with Jean."

"Rowan—"

"Promise me." Rowan met Winter's beautiful eyes. "Stay with Jean. Get away from her. She's already killed so many. *Please.*"

Winter's hurt radiated from her, stinging Rowan's heart as her companion turned and stalked quietly away.

Only then did Rowan shift, but her heel pressed a twig, the dried wood breaking with a resounding crack. Suna gasped, whirling as her wide, reddened eyes stared at Rowan. She faltered and fell.

"Are you alright?" Rowan's hands reached for her, alarmed by the state of her. Small, frail, *defeated.* Suna's hands were cold as Rowan helped her to her feet. "Has something happened?"

She wanted to give Suna a chance to explain. Approaching her with the veneer of ignorance would be safer than throwing accusations to make her defensive. Her shadow magic would lash out, singing its dark hooks into Rowan's life thread. Rowan had to be careful.

Suna's pupils were pinpricks, her limbs trembling as though freezing. She didn't answer, shock and trauma locking her in place as she shook.

"Suna?"

She struggled to breathe, hyperventilating, clawing at her throat and chest. Instinct brought Rowan's hands to Suna's wrists, trying to keep her from hurting herself, but she shrugged Rowan off, stepping away, shaking her head. She struggled to speak, her voice breaking.

"Breathe," Rowan said, her voice low and soothing. She held her hands as though to soothe a spooked animal, maintaining a calm presence to balance Suna's chaos. "You're alright. Deep breath. Slowly."

Rowan modeled the slow, steady breathing through her nose, which Suna mirrored. Several seconds passed before she was well enough to speak.

"I'm sorry, Guardian." Suna, panting, pressed a hand to her forehead. "I don't seem to be myself at the moment."

"Is it Derin?"

Suna shook her head. "No. He lives, thank the goddesses. But—" She clenched her teeth, lips trembling, and pressed her fingers to her mouth.

"Suna." How could she ask her? "Suna, I saw—"

"I know," she said, turning her face away. "How long have you known?"

"Not long." It wasn't untrue, even if *not long* was within the last few minutes. Suna, possessing the capability to commit to such darkness... Rowan would never have fathomed it, had she not seen that darkness with her just now. "My suspicions were on Halie."

The laugh that came from the mayor's wife was severe in its bitterness, a projectile of sound as sharp and pointed as a blade. "She had a darkness of a different kind. If she'd have just left me alone—" Suna stopped, biting off her words.

"Why?"

The simple question was the hardest to answer. Suna met Rowan's eyes with heartbreak. "Derin."

"You killed them for your son?"

Suna nodded. "His life thread is so thin. But this isn't helping anymore. It's not making him stronger."

Anymore. Whatever soul magic Suna had done no longer sustained the frail life of her only child. Her guilt and grief must have been limitless, a chasm of dark, chilling loneliness.

"And Halie?" Rowan licked her lips, static in the air as anticipation and fear kept her hackles raised. "Why did you kill her?"

"She saw me." Suna wiped her cheeks, her hand leaving a streak of dirt in its wake. "Threatened me. Made my life hell." Suna chuckled, once again devoid of mirth. "If that's possible."

"You've been collecting souls." Rowan didn't understand soulcraft and how witches practiced dark magic. Necromancy repelled Rowan on a deep, instinctual level. "How does that help your son?"

"Transference." She made it sound simple, though its simplicity eluded Rowan. "Arcana crystals act as conduits, and I move the power I pull from the living to give it to Derin."

"But it's not working."

Suna shook her head. "Not anymore."

"You're losing him all over again."

Suna's eyes welled with tears.

"Suna." Her name came out as a whisper. "You have to let him go."

"*No.*" The utterance was low, almost feral. Suna would cling to him with tooth and claw, no matter the cost.

"His soul needs to rest," Rowan said, thinking of Gran, thinking of the peace she'd earned after decades of fighting. "He deserves peace."

Suna screamed before pressing her fists to her mouth. Her body trembled as she tried in vain to hold herself together. "I can't, I can't!" She repeated the words over and over into her knuckles.

"Suna—"

Overhead, the ravens cried a cacophony from the boughs, shaking branches, bringing leaves fluttering to earth.

"What—"

Rowan saw them fluttering their wings, hopping, screaming out. Suna looked up with her, the emotional tide ebbing quickly as her focus found another emergency.

"Something's wrong," Rowan said.

She shifted without another word, hearing the ravens' cries at last.

"Wanderers! *Wanderers!*"

"Where?" Rowan drew a long breath through her nose, desperate for any traces of foreign scents that could lead her to the Wandering Order.

"Here!"

"At the Hill!"

"Jean! *Jean!*"

Ice flowed through Rowan's veins. "They found Jean?"

"Wagon!"

She ran, several ravens flying above her as guides.

"Wagon!" they cried. "Jean!"

Rowan ran hard, her paws pounding against the earth. Her lungs and throat burned with cold air, her breath coming fast.

"Rowan!" Winter's voice, full of panic. "Rowan!"

"Don't follow them!"

"Please!"

"If you get hurt, I'll murder every single one of them," Rowan said. "Promise me!"

"Gods damn it, Rowan!"

Hurt and pride mingled all at once at the sound of Winter's frustration.

"I love you," Rowan said. "Please, stay back."

She felt Winter's obedience.

"Peter and Wil are hurt," Winter said. "I will guard them."

Peter and Wil. *Gods.* "Thank you."

Rowan ran harder, no longer hearing Winter's voice, but the ravens continued to cry overhead.

There! A wagon leaving Elderglen at break-neck speed, the driver whipping the horses while two men held Jean's arms in their unrelenting grips. Her captors had gagged her, the cloth tight around her face, and her wide eyes found Rowan's running form.

Jean shook her head vehemently, her hair falling around her face and eyes. One man jolted her, laughing cruelly, glancing over his shoulder to the driver. Jean screamed through the fabric.

Fire surged through Rowan's blood, her vision hued red as she locked eyes with the man beside Jean.

"Here she comes," he said, her god-touched ears catching his voice on the wind. "Right on schedule."

CHAPTER 43

The horses pulled hard, hooves pounding against the earth as their driver whipped them on. But their load was heavy, with two grown men and one woman on a large wagon. The driver cracked the reins, the horses' high-pitched whinnies laced with terror.

"Stop the wagon!" But Rowan's voice didn't break through their panic. "They stole my friend! Stop the wagon!"

The horses thundered on. Rowan pushed harder, forcing her legs to move faster and faster. Jean screamed through her gag, trying to call, trying to warn her, telling her to stop.

Jean's captor threw something, glass shattering on impact. A cloud of white puffed out, swelled and swept by the breeze, feathering around Rowan as she ran.

A sharp scent. Citrus laced with sulfur.

Rowan sneezed, gasping, her lungs filling with poison.

Her vision blurred, but she didn't stop. Her steps came faster, her heart pumping hot blood through eager veins.

She was magnificent. Unstoppable. She was fury given blood and bone. She was wrath given breath and skin.

Rowan leapt for the wagon, her body powerful, her legs strong. The eyes of the man widened, the shadow of his mistake giving way to fear.

His hands reached her, futile, his strength paltry compared to hers. He couldn't stop her as her jaws reached for his throat.

Her teeth met his flesh easily, sinking in, tasting salt and copper and iron. Her jaws ripped sinew, sinking deeper. He gurgled a scream as he died, his blood coating her fur and the wagon floor.

Jean screamed.

The driver was swift in defense, reaching back and stabbing Rowan in the side. Rowan's agonizing howl pealed through the air, her agony reaching heavenward as the driver yanked the long dagger free. He then shoved hard, with more force than Rowan expected. Her body rolled across the moving wagon to its edge. She landed hard against the solid ground, all breath forced from her burning lungs as Jean kept screaming.

"Rowan!" Fen, fear in his voice. She didn't like its sound with his natural baritone, throwing off its pitch. She didn't like him afraid. "Rowan!"

The wagon drove on, the horses beating the earth into submission, galloping their frenzy beyond her sight.

Rowan stood and shifted, the pain excruciating, the mist arcana playing hell with her senses. She cried out before screaming Jean's name as hands reached her.

Fen. *Fen.* She could smell him, even with her human nose. The colors of the world were brighter, its sounds louder, and he smelled like everything she wanted. Salt and cinnamon and heat.

"Rowan."

But Fen recoiled as she whirled on him, her eyes wide and wild. Every muscle pulled tighter than a bow's string.

"Gods, your eyes." He stared, reaching to touch her arm, his movements skittish.

"You're afraid of me?" Her voice mingled hurt with a challenge. The world spun, focus difficult, but she locked onto his beautiful eyes. Deep and dark as the secrets of the ocean and just as promising of adventure.

"Never." He told the truth. Everything about his body language showed resolve and strength. "I don't want you to be afraid of me." He touched her arm, gently at first, his fingers curling around her wrist. "I will take hold of you only if you want me to, Rowan of Elderglen. And I would like you to let me. Gods—" He stared at her arm, where he touched her. "You're burning up. What did they—"

"Run." She closed her eyes, fury tangling with her senses in a combination the Sea of Kings couldn't cool. Brena's forge would rival the furnace inside her.

"Rowan—"

"Run," she repeated through clenched teeth. She still tasted the villain's blood. Her fingernails pressed into her palms, threatening to break the skin. "Run, Fen."

"Never."

"I'm so—" Her chest heaved, breathing a labor. There wasn't enough air. "I'm so *angry*." She focused on every inhale, every exhale. "He threw mist arcana. I can't—"

I can't stop. But she had to.

"I'm not leaving." He touched her face. She jerked away, ashamed, her sins far too exposed beneath the sun and his eyes. "Wil and Peter are alive. They were knocked unconscious, but they're alright."

"I killed one," she said, the confession necessary before time and shame sealed her lips. "Gods, Fen. I could kill them all."

He wiped her mouth, his fingers coming away red. "Both of us have blood on our hands, Rowan."

She closed her eyes, letting him inspect her wound.

"Gods," he said, his thin voice carried on an exhale. "You're losing a lot of blood."

"I can't tell. I feel—"

The world spun once more, faster and darker and—

"Rowan." Fen touched her face. "*Rowan*."

His voice echoed as she moved her lips to respond, but the rush of blood in her ears had deafened all sound save the pounding of her heart.

She was weightless, the star-studded sky surrounding her as she sailed through infinity.

Her side ached, the pain progressing to burning, the flames in her muscles and skin rivaling that in her blood. The hands that touched her were cool, fingers and palms gentle, even as bees stung her over and over. She reached for them, her side plagued with sting after sting, her head flaring, but someone held her, a voice whispering to her, telling her everything would be alright, that she would be fine and the worst was over.

The worst? Over?

Fog swept in, her sinuses congested, her limbs far too heavy. Darkness, stillness, slow and steady breaths. She hadn't known such deep rest in years. *Years.* From her parents to Gran to Elderglen to the Wandering Order to Moonblade to—

Fen.

Her rest. Her peace.

Fen.

"Rowan?" Fen's voice was just above a whisper, close to her ear. His hand cupped her forehead, stroking back, repeating the motion with his gentle, soothing touch. "Can you open your eyes?"

Cool breath passed through her nose, filling her lungs, but her eyelids were far too heavy, the congestion behind them far too dense.

"Open your eyes, love." He kissed her forehead. "Look at me."

His hand massaged hers, bringing life back into her skin, her blood flowing faster. She took a deep breath, eyes adjusting to the sunlit room. Unfamiliar. Until—

Wil and Peter's home. The spare bed they had for Jean when storms raged in summer.

The broad window, with both curtains drawn, allowed sunlight to pour upon her. Mid-morning sun, by her drowsy reckoning.

Winter whimpered, resting her head on Rowan's chest, tail thumping on the bed. Rowan touched the wolf's crown, scratching near her ears.

"Are you in pain?" Fen hadn't let go, one hand holding hers as the other rested on her forearm, thumb drawing a vertical line at her wrist. "I did what I could to stitch it closed."

Stitch it closed. Stitch—

Flashes of Jean's capture. Rowan's anger. The man she killed.

She attempted to sit up, her body punishing her with a wave of bladed pain.

"Stay still." His hands were gentle on her shoulders even as he insisted she remain where she was. "You're still healing, Guardian."

Guardian.

One who failed to save Jean.

One who ripped a human being's throat out.

Guardian.

"Jean," she said, her throat coarse, her voice ragged. "We have to—"

But she collapsed on the bed, defeated, flames licking her side as the wound flared.

"Peter is with Avenith, doing what they can."

"What can they—" Her chest and throat tightened. Her burning eyes welled, the saltwater stinging. Pain pulsed out through her chest and core, but it wasn't enough. It didn't match her fluttering heartbeat, her quickness of breath.

"Hey." Fen cupped her cheek, his fingers sweeping away a tear that had fallen. "How badly does it hurt? I have—"

She wouldn't let him turn, taking his arm and holding on as though she would drown without him as her lifeline. He sat slowly, studying her.

"I killed him," she whispered. "Jean was screaming. My teeth sank in and—" A sob choked her.

"There was mist arcana, Rowan." He spoke without hesitation, the words ready, said with conviction. "You were protecting Jean."

She shook her head, the excuses too thin. Too easy. "I am no guardian. Rhiann was wrong to give me this power."

"She wasn't." He kissed her knuckles. "I don't know anyone else strong enough to even bear the title and all that it comes with."

"I wanted him dead." Rowan pressed a trembling hand to her eyes, every inch of her fevered. "Gods, what you must think."

Her lips quivered, the corners pulling down with more force than she had the strength to fight. The quiet room granted space to breathe, to let the swelling tide consume before it receded. But its leaving was slow, inching back to make the suffering linger.

"Would that I could show you the dark within me." He pressed the back of her other hand to his cheek. His beard pleasantly scratched her skin. "You would know that you don't stand there alone."

She wiped her face, selfishly grasping the line he threw to pull her from the tumultuous sea. "What dark, Fen?" She met his gaze, truly seeing his fatigue—the shadows that hung beneath his bloodshot eyes, the slack around his mouth, the bow of his shoulders. "Gods, haven't you slept?"

"You've been unconscious for two days." He turned her hand over and pressed his lips against the soft line of her wrist. "I felt for your pulse almost every minute the first night. I was so scared, Rowan."

"What of Wil or Peter? They could have stayed so you could sleep."

"I wouldn't let them," he said. "They were both recovering from head injuries themselves, and Wil couldn't stomach watching me give you stitches."

She rested a hand on her side, wincing beneath its weight.

"As for your other question..." He paused, studying her. "I took my first life when they came for my brother."

She waited, giving him time to tell her, reading the eyes that held hers without wavering.

"It was the cultist that grabbed me." His voice remained steady. "Then it was my father. With his own knife."

How many times had he relived this moment, either through words or memory?

Horror chilled her to the bone, imagining him betrayed by his parents, fearful for his and his brother's lives. She tightened her hold, feeling him return her meager strength with a firmer press between his hands. He wouldn't slip away. She wouldn't let him.

His sadness drove the depth of his sorrow into her heart.

"That darkness wasn't yours," she said. "It was theirs."

"I wanted him gone," he whispered, looking at their hands, opening her palm to trace its lines. "I wanted him gone long before that moment, but I never imagined it would be murder that did it. He was a terror long before the Order came into their lives. He and my mother."

Rowan brought his hand to her mouth and kissed his fingers.

"I don't remember much after that. Flashes. The knife at the cultist's belt, within my reach." He swallowed. "There have been others. Some in Runa. Others at sea. A threat to life and limb and everything they say to help you feel better, but those people remain dead because I ended them." He grimaced, looking away. "I understand, Rowan. I understand every agonizing second. The platitudes might be right, but it doesn't stop the churning in your stomach."

She attempted to turn to face him better, shifting slightly for better comfort. The stitches tugged, the sharpness stabbing through tender skin and muscles.

"Here." He stood, reaching for the pillows behind her head and shoulders. Then, with care, he slipped one arm behind her shoulders as the other carefully took her waist. "Together. Push gently with your feet."

She obeyed, grateful for his strength to help her sit up. But she didn't let go, holding him tighter, bringing him to sit beside her. She buried her face against his neck as he stroked her wild, tangled hair.

"You're not alone in the dark, either, Fen."

His sigh was heavy, his cool breath sweeping over her hair and shoulder. "Thank you for trusting me."

"Thank you for not fearing me."

"I want to be a safe space for you, Rowan. For you to lay your burdens down, to give them to me." He leaned back to look at her face, smoothing her cheeks with his thumbs before he kissed her. "Thank you for letting me in."

Their tender moment lingered, Fen leaning his forehead against hers. The urge to make him smile surged within her, a streak of mischief bringing her to pull back and meet his gaze.

"Thank you for sewing me closed."

He laughed then, her own chuckles joined with groans.

"Gods." She pressed a hand to her side. "How long will this bloody thing take to heal?"

"Not long," he said, rocking slightly as he held her. "Wil knows of a healer not far from Elderglen. He said to expect him back tomorrow evening."

She closed her eyes, not eager to let him go yet. "How are we going to find Jean?"

"With Moonblade," he said. "Peter and Avenith left last night. We'll have Valera and her resources behind us."

The news should have given Rowan more relief than it did. Their reliance on such a variable was too risky. The foundation wasn't stable.

But what other options were before them? With Moonblade's

strength in skill and numbers, they were their best bet to reach Jean before—

Rowan bit her lip, blocking her thoughts from progressing. She loosened her arms, allowing Fen to straighten and relax.

But he held her tighter.

"Not yet," he whispered. "I'm not ready to let go yet."

Her heart surged as she held him closer. "That's all I needed to hear."

CHAPTER 44

Rowan awoke with a start, the dream invisible but for the sensation it left behind.

Panic. Escape. Hope fleeting. No way out.

She sat up, the stitches tugging with a sharper ache than before. The curtains were closed over the window, giving her no idea how long she'd slept, how long she'd been without medicine. She'd never envied godborn until this moment, longing for their rapid healing.

"She should eat something," came a voice through the open doorway. Wil had returned.

His footsteps soon approached, hands laden with a wooden tray. Porridge steamed from a bowl, as did freshly brewed tea from its cup.

Wil beamed, seeing her awake. "Good afternoon, sleepyhead." He set the tray on the nightstand and looked her over. "Feeling up to some lunch?"

"Lunch." She glanced at the window. "How long—"

"Just a few hours," he said, rightly guessing the rest of her question. "Fen said you woke up early this morning."

Peter's sweet porridge filled her nose with its tangy fragrance, her mouth watering. "Lunch sounds great."

Wil put the tray of food on the nightstand and helped her sit up. He took her head in his hands and kissed her crown.

"Thank you," he said, his lips pressed against her hair. His voice quivered. "Thank you for trying to save her."

Hot tears stung her eyes, the emotion in his voice pulling every string of her heart.

"You nearly died." He stood straight and passed her the tray. "You're not allowed to do that ever again."

"A promise I cannot keep." She took his hand. "We'll get her back, Wil."

"You shouldn't—"

She took his hand, squeezing his fingers. "You know better. There's nothing that could keep me from going after her."

"Even with the hole in your side?"

"It's sewed closed."

He rubbed his face, muffling a chuckle. "You're stubbornness would rival Gran's."

Pride, not grief, made her smile. She took her first bite.

"Peter and I were here alone," he said. "We didn't hear the back door open. Gods, Peter nearly broke the table when he fell."

"He was standing up?"

Wil nodded. "We still don't know how they reached that high to knock him out."

"A slingshot?" Rowan was only partially kidding.

"With damn good aim? Maybe."

"I was in the woods," she said, remembering the wolves. Remembering Suna. "I have news. The others should know."

"And Avenith and Peter have word from Valera. After the healer, are you up for it?"

She nodded. "We've already lost so much time."

"Your healing is vital, Ro. Not a single minute has been wasted, so get that out of your mind."

"I—"

"No arguments." He nudged the bowl. "Eat, heal, and then we'll talk. And don't eat too fast."

She couldn't help but smile, the slightest tug of her mouth evidence that his love had reached her. "Yes, sir."

But urgency filled her spoon, her grumbling stomach making demands of its own. Wil was quiet company, their silence comfortable until her last bite.

"Send them in?" Wil asked, getting to his feet.

"You're a good guard, Wilhelm."

He winced at his proper name. "Gods above, that was unnecessary."

The healer entered alone, her presence gentle and her magic strong. The ache in Rowan's side lessened until it was gone, and she inspected the stitches that held her skin together.

"Beautiful work," the healer said. "Who did this?"

"Fen," Rowan said.

The healer was gentle as she snipped the thread and pulled it free. Rowan groaned at the stinging, the sensation of it unpleasant as it left her. When relief settled, she breathed easier.

"Once more," the healer said.

Rowan didn't argue, the healer's hands gentle and consistent as magic flowed through them. Tension eased throughout her body. If she closed her eyes and allowed herself to give in, she would sleep for days.

"There." The healer stood. "Wil told me what happened. I would recommend you rest for a few more days, but I don't imagine you'll have time for that."

"More like the patience," Rowan said with a small smile. "Thank you."

"Be kind to yourself," she said. "Your body needs to recover."

As she stepped out, Wil entered. "Ready?"

Rowan nodded, touching her side, relieved to feel only slight discomfort. "Ready."

The others entered at Wil's beckoning, Avenith and Thenik among them. Fen's shadows lingered beneath his eyes, though lighter than before. Peter suffered a bruise near his left eye, and his knuckles were red.

But worse was Avenith, her skin pale and body slack with exhaustion. Rowan's eyes held hers, concern exchanged between them. Avenith gave the slightest shake of her head—*don't ask*. But Rowan would as soon as they were alone.

"The fierce warrior awakens." Peter was careful as he kissed her forehead. "How's the pain?"

"Nearly gone. Nothing lady's ivy won't remedy."

"Valera wanted you to have this." Avenith held up a small glass jar, the lid sealed with wax. "A fresh batch of merfolk balm."

Rowan knew the value of what she held, the diameter of the jar barely larger than a gold coin. This far north and inland, magical remedies from the merfolk were well beyond Rowan's coin purse.

"I will thank her when this is over." She glanced over every face, lingering on Fen's the longest. "I learned who killed the villagers."

The silence of the room was tangible, Rowan's ears nearly ringing.

"When I was in the woods, before Jean was taken, I found Suna."

Peter gasped while the others stared in disbelief. Then their stunned silence broke into a cacophony of "*She's* the killer?" and "Are you sure?"

Wil, speaking above the others, asked, "She has magic?"

Rowan nodded. "Soul magic. And mist arcana."

"Necromancy," Avenith said with disgust.

"For her son," Peter said. "It was to heal him, wasn't it?"

Rowan nodded.

"Why blood?" Fen asked. "I know next to nothing about soulcraft other than they devour souls."

"Powerful soulwitches can consume souls and use their energy for magic," Peter said. "For some spells, blood is required. Most often, it deals with significant healing or resurrection."

"She's living her worst nightmare." After a beat, Rowan looked at Wil, Avenith, and Thenik. "News from Moonblade?"

"She's preparing a team as we speak," Avenith said. "They're likely to leave at dusk."

Rowan hid her grimace. Movement at night was better, but that would mean another six to eight hours of Jean in the hands of evil.

Dark thoughts circulated in her mind. *Why would they keep her alive? What purpose could she—*

Rowan's core froze in panic. *Mist arcana.* And they've captured an earthwitch, prime for any depraved experiment.

"Do we know how many we're dealing with?" Peter asked. "Fen said the wagon had one."

"*One.*" Rowan swallowed, refusing to let the weight get heavier. There simply wasn't time. "I would guess at least a dozen if the last few encounters are any indication."

"I would say closer to two dozen," Thenik said, speaking up for the first time since entering.

Wil jumped. "Gods. You were so quiet, I forgot you were there."

Thenik shrugged, his expression remaining stoic. "I like to listen."

"We'll need more help," Avenith said. "There's no telling how many Valera can muster on short notice, though they're eager to shed cultist blood."

"The wolves will help," Rowan said.

"You're not shifting," Wil said, reading her mind. "Out of the question."

"I—"

"The healer is earthborn, and her magic is precise," Wil said, "but you almost died. Changing your shape?" He shook his head. "Don't do it. Please."

She didn't argue, but she didn't agree, either. She'd have to reach the wolves somehow, though doubt whispered that her human voice wouldn't be enough.

"You should rest," Fen said, his quiet tone authoritative to the rest of the group. "I'll return to change your bandage soon."

They turned to go, but Rowan said Avenith's name, prompting everyone to freeze in place.

"Can we talk?" she asked, eyes roving to the others. "You all are dismissed."

Wil chuckled. "She's sounding more and more like Gran with every passing second."

Her guests shuffled out of the room, leaving Avenith to face her alone, slipping her hands into her pockets. Her signature posture feigning nonchalance.

"What's wrong?" Rowan asked. "Is it Valera?"

"No." The longer Avenith regarded her, the weaker her veneer became. Worry presented itself in the lines between her brows, in the tightness of her mouth. "It's not Valera."

Rowan gestured for Avenith to sit, adjusting her legs to give her space on the bed. Surprisingly, Avenith obeyed.

"You almost died." Her voice was meek, almost childlike, her fear such a rare thing to see. "I didn't handle that very well."

Avenith worried the skin around her thumb until Rowan took her hand. "I'm alive, Av. Those bastards didn't kill me."

"Thanks to Fen."

Rowan waited, sensing the coming storm as Avenith closed her eyes, controlling her breathing.

"It was the tavern first," Avenith said. "I don't think I'm allowed back."

"What did you do? Start a fight?"

Avenith's silent look gave her the answer.

"Gods, how drunk were you?"

"I wasn't."

She tightened her hold on Rowan's hand, the gesture full of apology.

"This was what broke us apart," Avenith said, her words barely above a whisper.

"What?"

"Our tempers." She exhaled a breath of a laugh, her mirth laced with sadness. "Grief and anger."

"It wasn't our tempers," Rowan said. "It was your absence."

Avenith met her gaze, accusation pointed before the truth dulled its edge.

"You left," Rowan said. "You joined Moonblade, and I never saw you again."

"I couldn't let it rest." She drew a circle on the back of Rowan's hand. "Every moment I wasn't pursuing that bastard was a moment my family died in vain."

Both of them, victims of hatred, orphaned by malice. Both of them angry and lost in grief. And Avenith took power for herself, saturated with vengeance. Rowan's reach for power started out in violence, but becoming wolfkind had healed the still-bleeding cuts in her heart, granting her passage through a layer of the world unknown to anyone else.

"It's taken such a large part of you," Rowan said. "It didn't leave any room for me."

Avenith looked away, lips trembling, nodding. "I'm sorry, Rowan."

"I am too. But I'm alright." She meant it. Every word. "The hurt has healed, Av. Our paths weren't meant to stay joined."

"But I am so thankful we met."

"Me too."

Avenith exhaled, the relief in the room palpable. "I'm still going to bring his end. I know that's not what you want to hear."

"I hate he still has his hand around your throat."

Avenith's expression flashed offense, the lift of her lip almost a snarl. But she couldn't deny Rowan's words.

"I know where you are, Avenith," Rowan said. "I know what you feel. There's nothing that compares to it, nothing that can dissolve it. Nothing except time and love."

"And I have had one but not the other."

"You've had both." Rowan squeezed her hand again before releasing her. "I can do nothing about the path of revenge you choose to follow, but I will not let you diminish what I felt."

Rowan shifted her legs, delicately pushing Avenith to stand as she turned, bringing her legs over the edge of the bed.

Avenith scowled. "What are you doing?"

"To see the wolves." Rowan pushed herself up, her side catching. She winced with a groan, glad when Avenith's hands braced her arm.

"Are you insane?"

"Probably." Rowan grinned despite the flair of heat in her muscles. "So, I'm in good company."

This made Avenith laugh. "Wil is going to hate this, you know."

"Wil is going to help me get there."

"I've missed your stubbornness, Ro."

"I'm sure you have."

With one hand on Wil's arm, Rowan walked, the woods in her sights with Jean's scarf in her hand.

"Thank you," Wil said, "for not shifting."

"I promise I'm fine. The healer's magic was thorough."

"I heard her tell you to be kind to yourself. Her magic may have sewed you shut beyond what Fen's stitches did, but you're still recovering in ways we can't see."

She hugged his arm tighter, resting her head on his shoulder for a moment.

"Thank you for giving me your mother's scarf." Rowan held the blue and green silk in her other hand. "This will help."

"It will have to since I made you promise to stay human."

She prodded his side. "I'm always human, Wil."

"You know what I mean."

Walking brought out the ache in her side, but the motion offered optimism when staying in bed would have given shadows instead. She was doing something, taking literal and figurative steps toward finding Jean and giving the Order hell for what they'd done. And when she and Wil crossed through the trees, her sense of accomplishment grew. Even if they couldn't understand her, maybe they would pick up the scent. Maybe they would help lead her in the right direction.

"How will this help?" Wil asked quietly. "What if they trail her now when we're not ready to leave?"

"This isn't their fight," Rowan said, "and I don't expect them to put themselves at risk. But I hope the wolves will learn where they are and tell the ravens. Then the ravens can call to me."

"Call to you," he said, understanding, "when you're a wolf."

She squeezed his arm. "I have to shift, Wil, but I promised not to yet."

He said nothing, disagreement radiating from him as they continued further in.

The wolves were close, judging by the rustling of the brush and the calls of the ravens. Rowan waited, steadying herself with Wil's help, glad to still have her feet under her.

The matriarch's eyes appeared first, watching with their amber light as the rest of her blended into the scenery. Two other wolves joined her, their presence steady.

"I was wounded and should not shift," Rowan said, bending to offer the scarf. "My friend was taken by the Wandering Order. You probably already know." She let the scarf fall to the earth. "This is hers."

"My mother," Wil added. "We need to get her back."

"This is not your fight," Rowan said, watching the matriarch sniff the scarf. The others with her did the same. "If you would help to find her, to tell the ravens where she is, it would help guide our steps. We will take care of the rest."

The matriarch shared glances with the other wolves before blinking up at Rowan. Hope surged through her throbbing heart, though she had no real way of knowing the matriarch's thoughts or words. But she would swear she saw sympathy in her fire-like gaze.

"I am honored to call you friend," Rowan said. "Whatever your decision, I am proud to know you, to bear your trust."

She winced as a flaring ache, not so much pain as it was discomfort. The sensation was strange, pulsing through the wound, in one side and out the other.

"You need more medicine," Wil said, retrieving the scarf. "Let's go."

Rowan bade the wolves farewell before another voice came. "Rowan?"

They stopped as Marc stepped through the trees, followed by Mirelyn. His was a look of trepidation, even shame, while hers was serene empathy.

The wolves slipped away, understanding, leaving the humans to talk.

"I tried to stop them," Marc blurted, gesturing with his hands. "Even with the help of the crystal, I could feel my power taking over."

"I felt the same," Rowan said. "They hit me with mist arcana."

Rowan looked from Marc to Mirelyn, finding understanding in her gaze.

"The magic pulled from the crystal restored much of what was taken," Mirelyn said, her smooth alto voice comforting. "But there is still much to do."

"We're seeking the camp where they took her," Rowan said. "I've just asked the wolves for their aid. Moonblade is doing what they can."

"When will you go?" Marc's question carried hope, as though seeking permission to join them. He was a variable, and he knew it.

"Tonight," Wil answered.

Marc glanced at Mirelyn, something unspoken passing between them.

"We'll leave you to prepare," Mirelyn said.

"If you choose to go," Rowan blurted, "we will welcome the aid. But if you choose to stay—" She met Marc's gaze. "Please don't feel guilty." She touched her side. "My body is healing. So is yours. We owe them the time they need."

A sad, half-smile graced his features. His resemblance to Fen had never been stronger. "If only my heart would agree."

She understood, her own at war with her mind as every hour passed.

Rowan and Wil turned to go, her movements more natural and eased as her feet carried her.

"We go," she said. "We fight. We get her back."

But he could sense what she wasn't saying. "I'm afraid too, Rowan. Afraid of what we'll find."

"And I'm—" She took his hand, squeezing his palm, grateful for his warmth and strength. "I'm afraid of what I'll do."

"Your vulnerability isn't weakness, Rowan. You're human," he said, as though it was that simple. "Something awful happens to someone you love, and you want to rip the world apart. That is something every human shares."

"But I'll actually try," she said. "I don't know if I'll have reason enough to stop."

"Your reason is your heart. Your kindness."

"All life is precious," Rowan whispered, "but I can't bring myself to see them as anything but monsters."

"And that is a fault they bear."

She stared ahead, desperate to cling to a hope that seemed fleeting. "This is a war, isn't it?"

"Fought one battle at a time."

They returned to Wil's home, Peter preparing tea as Fen waited with balm and bandaging.

Wil squeezed her shoulder. "One battle at a time."

CHAPTER 45

The group had gathered in Wil's home, waiting by the warmth of the hearth.

Each looked at her as she entered with Wil, silently assessing the state of her as they prepared to raid a camp of Wandering Order cultists to rescue someone beloved. But none of them voiced the concerns she could read on their faces. They knew how useless their attempts would be.

Wil settled at the dining table with Avenith and Thenik. Peter and Fen stood by the hearth, Fen handling clean strips of linen. Rowan moved to Winter, bending to scratch behind her ears. The discomfort in her side pulled but didn't ache.

"We should change your bandage," he said, winding the fabric around his fingers. He glanced at the others.

Thenik was the first to rise, waving a hand as he made for the door. "I'll get some jerky at the tavern. Avenith?"

"Jerky?" She stood, following him. "Why jerky? We're not traveling for weeks without food."

"Because I like it. The salt helps me think."

"What a load of—"

The door closed before the others could hear the rest.

"Let us know if you need anything." Peter took Wil's arm. "Let's give them some privacy."

"Why?"

But Peter didn't answer, dragging his husband to their room and closing the door.

"Don't lift your arms," Fen said, placing the linen and the merfolk balm on the table. "If you want to lift your shirt and hold it—"

But she removed it halfway with her other arm, resting it on her shoulder with her arm and side exposed. Her undergarment remained, and the bandaging at her waist let very little skin show. But a faint touch of pink painted Fen's cheekbones.

He blinked, brows raised. "Alright, then."

He knelt beside her, careful as he began unwrapping the soiled bandage. She glanced down. "I still feel a pull sometimes when I move."

"I would imagine that's normal." He touched the wound at her back, his fingertips cooling through the linen. "These were what I was worried about—the stitches on your back. I didn't know how well you'd sleep, but the healer did well."

"You did well, too, Fen."

The flush deepened, but he didn't look up from his work. Slowly, with practiced fingers, he pulled the end of the linen and peeled the bandaging away. Rhythmically, he leaned toward her as his arms surrounded her, hands passing the fabric back and forth until the rest fell. His closeness, his arms and hands, his focus, his breathing—she found it difficult not to take his face into her hands and kiss him.

He looked up at her, eyes glancing at her cheeks, seeing her own blush there. "What?" He blotted the remnants of medicine with the linen before throwing it into the fire. "Did I do something?"

He pulled the waxed seal from the jar, the cork releasing with a satisfying pop. The salty seaweed smell overtook her senses immediately, and she scrunched her nose before she could control her face.

"Yeah, the smell is strong," he said, scooping some onto his fingertips. "I've never used this before. It's supposed to help you heal faster."

"It had better, as payment for its stink."

He grinned, walking on his knees to her side. "Scoot forward and lean back for me."

She did, reclining fully with her shoulders on the back of the chair as chilling medicine made her catch her breath.

"Sorry, love. It'll warm up."

Her heart fluttered, lips pressing into a smile. After the sensation lessened, she said, "I like it when you call me that."

She glanced down from the corner of her eye, pleased to see his smile.

"I like calling you that."

"Weeks, Fen. *Weeks*. And so much has changed."

"I'd like to say it will get easier after this is over. But this won't be over." Her skin prickled to goosebumps at his steady touch. "And it won't get easier."

He guided her forward, repeating the process on her back. She was ready for the cold this time, containing her response with a shiver.

"We have our loved ones," she said. "And we have each other. I—" She smiled through her shyness. "I look forward to learning what that means."

"I do, too."

The balm worked at relieving the ache in minutes, such that Rowan helped Fen wrap the clean linen around her waist.

"Don't take this as permission to move and shift as though you weren't run through two days ago."

"I know, I know." She waited, arms raised, as he tucked the bandage in place. "I don't want to do anything that could risk Jean."

Fen, from behind her, rested his palms on her shoulders, guiding his hands toward her arms as he lowered them. Her bare skin enjoyed the fullness of his touch, his fingers curling around her bicep, his thumbs stroking gentle lines.

"Those monsters will fail in keeping her," he said, his voice low. His breath swept over her neck. "And they will pay for taking her."

He brought her shirt over her arm and guided her arm through the sleeve. She turned, crushing her lips against his, pressing their chests together with such strength that they gasped for breath. But he met her force and energy, matching her every move, parting her lips to deepen the kiss. When they parted, she clung to him. His arms surrounded her, his face buried against her neck.

"That felt like a goodbye," he said, his voice muffled. "We're getting through this, Rowan. We'll make it through."

She held him tighter, squeezing her eyes shut. "It's not goodbye. I want you here. If you want to stay."

The icy hand wrapped its fingers around her heart, its frost familiar. Fen may leave. That was life, the world passing forward day to day as people moved in and out of her life. But it would be alright. *She* would be alright.

"I would like to stay if you'll have me."

Shouts broke out, their cries outside coming from the village. Rowan leaned from Fen's arms, glancing toward the door as Wil and Peter stepped out and passed through the front door, Rowan and Fen at their heels.

"What in the hells…"

But Wil's question was unanswered, but the crowd gathered at the mayor's house, the legion breaking through the front door and pouring in.

"SEVEN HELLS," Fen exhaled, his mouth agape. "It's like they're raiding the place."

"What brought this on?" Peter asked.

"Suna," Rowan said. "It has to be."

Then the pieces fell into place as Braithen shouted from among the crowd.

"We know you're in there, Frederick!"

Villagers poured in, their shouts carried on the autumn breeze.

"Gods," Wil said. "They're going to kill him."

"No—" But Rowan couldn't be sure, not with Braithen fanning the flames.

Rowan rushed over, her ears ignoring the calls from the others.

"Move," she said, shouldering her way through the crowd. Someone laid a hand on her arm, which she shrugged off. Another grabbed her. She returned with a vise grip of her own and turned the arm sharply. The man cried out.

"Not me," Rowan growled. "And not now."

But she was met with another, then another. Sneers and jests surrounded her—*Elderglen's faithful Watcher, the mayor's favorite watchdog*—

Anger welled, boiling within her core until her body shoved them aside. She shifted, her snarls and barks frightening them, forcing them back. She hurried inside, baying viciously, commanding them all to go. They understood her well enough, nearly tripping over themselves to get out of her way.

"You know better than to lay your hands on her," Wil said, his voice commanding. "Do so at your own peril."

"Please," Fen said, his hand resting on his knife. "All I need is a reason to make sure you never touch her again."

Peter looked at each of them, shocked, but concern and frustration shadowed his glare as he looked at the whole of Elderglen up in a frenzy.

"Get out!" Frederick's voice thundered as he pushed through, grabbing a man by the throat. "You dare touch my son's things!"

Rowan became herself, calling out his name. But rage consumed him, his bloodshot eyes wide and manic, veins protruding in his neck and forehead.

"Mayor Frederick!" She repeated. "Don't!"

"They think they can dismantle my home, disturb my son. My son —" Rage gripped him as he gripped the man, his face turning purple. "How dare you touch his things?"

"Your son," Rowan said, realizing. "He's—"

"Dead." Mayor Frederick's lips quivered, grief softening the sharp lines of anger.

"So is my sister," Braithen said, sauntering in. "So is her son." He pointed to one villager, then another. "And hers."

All of Suna's victims.

"Ignorance won't save you," Braithen went on. He was bloodthirsty and saw the mayor as vulnerable prey. "Your wife did this."

"Have you known all along?" Rowan asked.

"My sister learned the truth, and it cost her her life!"

"But only after she blackmailed Suna," Rowan said. "All that money she was freely spending in town, the way she bragged about her new patron." Rowan shook her head. "Your sister's crafts weren't worth the gold she'd earned."

Every eye turned to Braithen.

"She knew," Rowan said. "And so did you. And you said nothing."

The murmurs grew. Braithen shook his head feverishly. "No. You don't believe—"

But hands reached for him, shoving him out of the mayor's house. The crowd needed their target, their person to blame. Now, they had Braithen.

"You all should go," Rowan said, her voice full of authority. "Leave a father to grieve in peace."

Several argued, but Rowan cried, "Enough! Your anger yields nothing. Put it to better use than this."

"How?" One meek female voice asked. "I can't even think straight."

"Start with who would make a good mayor." Rowan looked at Frederick with sympathy. "We're going to need one."

The crowd dispersed, Frederick falling to his knees, hands now clutching a beautifully made teddy bear. He wept openly, and Rowan left him, the others following close behind.

"Well done, Watcher," Wil said, taking her under his arm. "*Cornerstone.*"

She looked up and offered her friend a small smile, one that bore both sadness and relief. "I suppose so."

Fen glanced at her side. "Did anyone hurt you?"

She shook her head, her hand feeling the slight warmth from her injury. "I'm fine. Even after shifting. Which means..."

She let the thought dangle unfinished as she glanced at each of them, understanding already in their eyes.

"Let's get Jean back."

CHAPTER 46

Rhiann showed her full beauty with the sunset.

Rowan always loved sunsets. The day's ending, the world slowing, the demands of her time evaporating. And with that came her freedom. Her senses opened, mind relaxed, everything favored and familiar.

As soon as Rowan fastened the cloak of the Cornerstone around her neck, the team set out to find where the cultists were hiding, leaving Sentinel Hill and Elderglen behind. Winter fell in step with her, ears perked and eyes at attention.

Thenik, true to his word, bought jerky for everyone. Avenith chewed as she contemplated their next move. "Should we tell Marc?"

"He knows," Rowan said. "Mirelyn, too."

"Control is vital," Thenik said. "After what they did to him..." He shook his head. "I wouldn't be alright if it was me. I don't blame him one bit if he stays behind."

Walking down the clay road, memories of Jean's kidnap lined the horizon as Rowan stared ahead, seeing the wagon racing off as she stared into Jean's wide, frightened eyes.

"Wheel tracks," Fen said, eyes focused on the road. "There's your blood."

He pointed to a dark spot on the clay path.

"*There's your blood*," she repeated. "I'm more unsettled because I'm *not* unsettled, hearing those words said."

"We have our work cut out for us," Wil said, following the tracks into the distance. "There are plenty of settlements along this road."

"They'd keep her close enough to pursue," Avenith said. "She's bait. They can't make the stick too long for the carrot to break."

"I love and hate that analogy," Peter said. Thenik grunted in agreement.

"What do they want from her?" Rowan asked. "What do they want from *us*?"

"Power," Avenith said. "Control."

The others regarded her without speaking.

"Could be hours," Thenik said, passing out more jerky. "Good thing we came prepared."

"My blades are sharp," Avenith said, glancing at Rowan. "I stopped by the smithy after leaving yours. Before the mayor…"

She didn't need to finish her sentence.

"Is the smithy missing Naelor?" Wil chuckled. "I'm surprised he lasted as long as he did."

"Speaking of," Fen said to Thenik. "Any word from him?"

"None."

Thenik was accomplished at masking, but Rowan caught the slight squint as he answered. His lack of communication left Thenik unsettled.

"Here." Fen crouched, tracing his hand over the wagon track. It veered off-road, heading west. "This just got more complicated. Wait here."

"It's already complicated with the sunset," Wil said, glancing up. "Those clouds are going to shield too much light."

Fen jogged ahead several paces, following the road before doing the same into the grass. "They went west." He pointed down the off-road line. "The tracks further up the road stop."

"They think they're so clever." Avenith toyed with her knife, spinning it on her index finger and catching the handle.

"It is clever," Fen said. "He had to have pulled the wagon back by hand after detaching the horses. I saw hoof prints that looked out of place—easy to miss if you're not looking."

"With Mom in the back?" Wil's furrowed brow carried anger as he thought through what could have happened. "Unconscious? Somehow unable to fight?"

Rowan rested a hand on his arm. "They will feel every one of her bruises tenfold."

"I will temper myself to make sure they stay alive for every second of it," he said.

Winter kept pace with Fen, watching the ground with her nose as he did with his eyes. *A lovely pair*, Rowan thought with pride.

"When we get close, we should split up." Avenith's suggestion garnered looks from each of them, save Winter. "Surround the camp. Make them fight on two fronts."

"I don't like it," Rowan said. "What you said makes sense, but we're already the few against the many. I don't want two of us to get surrounded and killed while the others don't know or can't help."

"That will probably happen anyway if we stay together," Peter said. "Surround us in a small group, or surround us in a larger one?"

Wil blinked at him. "You're supposed to be the optimistic one. I'm the doom-sayer in this marriage."

"We can't escape reality," Peter said. "We lack numbers and magic. They likely have both, with mist arcana."

"And the poor magic folk used against their will," Thenik said. "It's crossed my mind a lot."

"That we're going to die?" Avenith asked.

He nodded. "The one thing that cult has in common with Moon-blade is they are relentless."

"But you still came with us," Avenith said. "That means the world, Thenik."

Even with her jovial, teasing tone, he took her words as genuine. "It will mean more if we survive."

Rowan and the others silently agreed.

HOURS SPANNED between them and Elderglen, moonlight beaming intermittently as clouds passed. If a storm loomed, Rowan couldn't smell it, but the sounds of night were still. The group collectively walked with careful steps, remaining vigilant in the eerie quiet.

Winter's ears perked, standing still for two breaths before easing forward. The group matched her gait and caution, conscious of every rustle of grass and wildflowers. Rowan longed for the cover of trees, for a dense forest to shield her movements from enemy eyes. But the only cover on their path was a thin copse of trees, still several yards in the distance.

"There could be a scout," Rowan said, lifting her hood. "Winter and I will go ahead."

No one verbally objected, though Fen and Wil's expressions were clear enough. She shifted, the cloak shading her fur like night, and edged forward with Winter.

"No scent yet," Winter said, "but there are sounds. Quiet and far, but the night carries them."

The stillness, the silent world. A subtle blessing from Rhiann, helping them on their mission to rescue Jean.

Thank you, Rowan prayed. Gratitude bloomed within. Her goddess was by her side, despite everything.

"Tree!" A raven, its caw piercing the air. "Tr—"

A whistle preceded the sound of the bird's death, its body landing with a subtle thud. Pain stabbed Rowan's heart at the raven's sacrifice, adding to the simmering heat in her core.

She shifted and told the others.

"They shot a raven in the dark?" Avenith's brow raised. "I hate being impressed by a cultist."

"If he reveals his position," Rowan said, eyes locked on Fen's. "Could you make the shot?"

"Rowan—"

"Could you?"

Wil cleared his throat. "There's probably more than one."

"I can," Fen said. "But Wil's right."

"Then we make them adjust to follow us." She subtly pointed down the tree line. "They may know that we know, but we won't make it easy for them."

She shifted without another word and led Winter down through the grass, circling the copse before veering toward it.

"As stubborn as Gran," Wil said, shaking his head.

Then they followed.

CHAPTER 47

The shrouded sky offered cover as they slipped through the trees. Rowan and Winter's eyes and ears were alert, every whisper through the trees a potential sign.

"No crows," Winter said. "Too quiet."

"One was killed for calling out. They may fear the archer's aim looking for them next."

"A swarm would blind. They may fall from their cowardly perch."

Rowan couldn't argue with her logic, but she understood the unrelenting grip of fear left little room for reason.

Wood creaked. Rowan and Winter froze, ears attuned, their wolf eyes seeing through the dark to the branches that shook.

Rowan and Winter studied shadows and shapes, seeking the source of the disturbance. "Where?"

An arrow whistled, and Rowan rolled, bracing for the shot. But a considerable weight fell, hitting the ground and landing among roots and flowers.

Fen moved close, each step silent. "How many others?"

Rowan shook her head.

"On your lead." His eyes shone like black glass in the dark, the intermittent moonlight illuminating before the clouds draped the world in shadow.

Wil and the others moved quietly behind as Avenith crept to the body, looting each weapon. She passed Fen the arrows and kept the long dagger and throwing knives for herself.

Creeping forward yielded no other signs of cultist scouts, the wind combing through the boughs like gentle sighs.

"There has to be another," Thenik whispered. "They wouldn't send only one."

"Unless they did," Peter and Avenith both said, each regarding the other in shock.

"Knowing we'd take caution," Avenith continued. "Knowing we'd move slowly."

Wil offered Peter half of a smirk, not saying a word.

Their insight made sense, but Rowan couldn't bring herself to move faster. As soon as she lost focus, as soon as she made haste, the delicate thread she followed would snap.

"I don't smell them," Winter said, concerned. "Masking their scent?"

"That's very likely."

"Cowards."

Rowan chuckled, the sound a quiet rumble in her wolf throat.

"There," Fen whispered, pointing ahead. "Another one."

"Gods," Wil exhaled. "How can you tell?"

"Notches in the tree." He readied his bow. "His boots stabbed into the bark to help him climb up."

"Impressive trick," Avenith said with a grin. "Do another."

He aimed his arrow up, eyes squinting as he worked to see in the dark. It was difficult to discern dark shapes in tall trees, even for Rowan's magical eyes. But the clouds parted, and she glimpsed a flicker of eye shine.

She shifted, extending a hand to Avenith as she kept her eye on the trees. "Pass me a knife."

"Say *please*." Rowan heard the smirk in Avenith's voice, then felt the handle of the knife in her hand.

Throwing a knife differed from throwing a hatchet. Rowan didn't consider that difference as she hurled the blade. The grunt preceded the stumble, and the man fell from the branches. The knife lodged in his arm above the elbow, all the way to the hilt.

"Nice shot," Fen said.

Avenith grinned. "And I get the knife back."

The cultist got to his feet, short sword drawn, and cried out as he ran for them. Fen landed an arrow in his throat as Avenith threw a second knife, piercing his chest. He crumpled to the ground, gurgling until his body stopped moving.

"Safe to say he's dead," Peter said.

"Can't be too careful." Avenith yanked both knives free, wiping them on her trousers. "These bastards are—"

She groaned, an arrow piercing her shoulder. Fen reacted quickly, but the assailant already shifted to hide.

"Last one?" Wil asked. "Our luck comes in threes?"

Thenik seized Avenith and pulled her back before shoving a hand-kerchief in her mouth. He snapped the arrow shaft and yanked it free. Her scream ripped through her throat, muffled by the fabric. Thenik had reacted purely on instinct and muscle memory. This was far from his first recovery.

Rowan shifted and ran, going in a fast zig-zag pattern to keep the archer guessing.

"Last!" One raven cried. "Last!"

"The last in the trees?" Rowan asked. "They're the only one left in the woods?"

The ravens cawed in affirmation.

One arrow missed her, followed by another. Fen fired, his arrow finding its mark at last. The man hit the ground as more shouts sounded from beyond the trees.

The Wandering Order was on high alert, leaving them little time to recuperate and tend to Avenith's wound.

Rowan took her human form. "Gods, Avenith."

"Your heartfelt concern warms me up inside." Sweat beaded at her hairline. "Leave me here. Go, before we lose our chance."

"It may already be lost," Peter said.

"I need to bind this." Thenik already had linen ready.

Avenith scoffed, doing her best not to grimace from the pain. "It's not like the Order can smell blood."

"He's right," Wil said. "That's your throwing arm, isn't it?"

She grinned. "What kind of assassin would I be if I couldn't throw with both?"

"It's your dominant, though," Thenik said, wrapping her wound tight. She grunted in pain. "Almost done."

"The plan is still on," Rowan said.

Steps moved quickly toward them. They armed themselves, bodies bracing for a fight. Winter whined, jogging where they'd come through the trees, her tail wagging.

"Wait," Rowan said, lowering her hatchet. "Is that—"

The answer came as a pair of amber eyes, the matriarch leading a pack of nearly ten wolves.

Rowan changed her form, approaching in reverence. "You're here."

"Of course." Her warm voice was full of love. "Our guardian needs us."

Rowan walked to her and bowed, Winter doing the same beside her.

"Matriarch." Fen took a knee. "You honor us."

The others, save Avenith and Thenik, matched Fen's pose.

"He speaks well." The matriarch glanced at Avenith. "You have injured. That will not be the only blood shed. You keep strong company, Guardian, to have those face this darkness alongside you."

"I am very blessed."

The matriarch glanced at her pack. "We follow the guardian and offer tooth and claw."

"End the Wanderers," one cried.

"They must rescue their friend," the matriarch said. "They risk their lives to save her. We will help."

"Wanderers," one raven said. "Many Wanderers."

"Silver hair," another said.

"Elias," Rowan said. "A Preceptor."

"Which means danger," the matriarch said.

Another wolf repeated, "End the Wanderers!" And more wolves bayed and barked.

"Stay alive," Rowan said. "Don't risk your lives for this. There is no cowardice in running. You are doing me a great service, and I would have you live to tell about it."

"You have us, Guardian." Her eyes burned like embers. "We are ready."

CHAPTER 48

The plan was straightforward.

Scout the camp.

Find Jean.

Get her to safety.

But Rowan knew it was far from simple. Her hands would not come away clean.

Forgive me, she prayed, knowing that Rhiann would hear.

The camp was modest, likely from the Order being itinerant, but every tent was the same in size, shape, and color. There was no larger tent here, nothing marked where the Preceptor would be or where they would keep Jean.

"No scent of her," the matriarch said, smelling the air as they studied the camp. "They've hidden her from us."

It was to be expected. Even Rowan and Winter had to follow a physical trail to get this far.

Thunder rumbled quietly overhead, static energy charging through the air.

"Let's use the storm," Wil said. "Mask our sounds."

"Glad it came now when we aren't tracking," Fen added. "The goddesses are on our side."

At this, Avenith smiled. "Erys always takes care of her own."

Another rumble released the steady trickle, the light patter of rain increasing with each passing second. Their approach was steady over wet grass and damp earth. Rain dripped from Rowan's fur, slowly soaking through and cooling her warm skin.

Thenik slipped into the first tent they reached. The cultist couldn't cry out, his death sounds muffled through fabric and rain. But there was a second, on the brink of a shout before Thenik silenced him. Rowan exhaled sharply through her nose, assailed by the salty metallic perfume of fresh blood. When Thenik emerged, the rain ran through the blood on his face and hands, washing it away.

"Two down," he said. "Twenty to go."

Rowan's stomach flipped, the violence reminding her of the invisible line she was preparing to cross. Something should separate them from the monsters they faced.

"Unclench your jaw," Fen whispered to her, crouching to reach her. "Remember to breathe."

Wil smirked at Peter. "Why don't you ever tell me to unclench my jaw?"

"Because it won't work."

Rowan exhaled, grateful she wasn't alone.

"This kept Gran from peaceful rest," Rowan said. "How did she carry it?"

"She had to," the matriarch said. "She was strong enough. And so are you."

The wolves remained close, keeping quiet as Thenik and Avenith dispatched another pair in a tent.

"I don't like it," Wil whispered. "I have no alternative that ends well, but I still don't like it."

"They don't play fair," Thenik said. "Neither do we."

In the next tent, one cultist stepped out, empty water skin in hand. He didn't hesitate, crying out, "They're here!" He ducked inside for his weapon. Wil and Peter charged in as lights bloomed around them, the camp coming to life.

"Avoid the archers," Rowan told the wolves. "Stay alive."

"As our guardian commands," the matriarch said, pride in her voice.

The fray swelled in seconds, cultists appearing with blades and hatred. One charged Rowan, his sword ready, his boots fast against the wet ground. She dodged, feinting one way as she pivoted to another, and her attacker slipped. His momentum carried him over and down, his back slapping the ground. Rowan blinked as Fen ran an arrow through the cultist's throat, shoving it in and yanking it free before nocking it, bloody, for a second target.

Glass shattered, and flames erupted, consuming pieces of a broken lamp as oil spread over the grass. The wolves bayed, one yelping, before they charged.

Rowan shifted, hands finding the handles of her hatchets, and she wove through the onslaught, her sharpened blades offering no mercy. Her cloak took the rain, balance adjusting to let the added weight work with her. She flanked one cultist facing Wil, helping to make short work of his attack until one faced her, his pair of short swords an adequate match against her.

"Wolfkind," he said with a satisfied grin. "He was telling the truth after all."

Rowan didn't ask, having neither the time nor the care to let this man speak. Instead, she clanged one hatchet against his nearest sword and swung with the other. He countered well enough but hadn't accounted for Rowan's force as she pushed her way into his space, disrupting his balance. As he faltered, her hatchet found purchase in his chest at his shoulder, a nonfatal wound but debilitating enough. She kicked hard, her heel meeting his hip and shoving him to the ground. He curled up from shock and pain.

"Rowan!"

Fen's arrow was nocked, aimed at her. She ducked, rolling swiftly as he fired at the cultist behind her.

"Good shot," she said, breathless.

He helped her to her feet and switched to his long daggers, standing with his back to hers. "I had a dream like this."

"Of us fighting?"

"It was like the goddesses, themselves, willed it. We moved as one."

She liked that, imagining Fen moving with her as though he knew every step and every gesture. It was a rare trust, more precious than gold.

A pair of cultists raced for them, their feline movements as graceful with their thin swords as trained dancers as they struck and dodged. One pirouetted as the other kicked, their arms and legs as precise in their strikes as Fen's arrows.

"The Carnival?" Fen asked, amused. "One of their acts?"

"Court performers," one said with a grin as she moved to strike Rowan, the hatchet blocking and sweeping up the sword. "From Storm Seat."

"Sword dancers," Fen said. "I'm impressed."

"And you?" The other woman nearly stabbed him, feinting a strike to mislead. His block barely made it in time. "Where did you train?"

He used his sword as a distraction, sweeping a leg. She faltered but corrected quickly, pivoting back on the balls of her feet.

"On a ship."

Rowan's opponent swung, offering the length of her forearm as she did. Rowan's hand gripped it easily, fingers curling around the thin, delicate bones and muscles, and pulled hard. Her forehead slammed against the woman's nose, the cartilage breaking. The crack was loud, and blood flowed quickly.

The dazed woman was defenseless against Rowan's strike, the heel of her hatchet slamming hard at the base of her skull. Her opponent collapsed like a discarded doll.

She and Fen rejoined, their backs against one another's, more opposition surrounding them. But the camp had thinned, the scales balancing.

Hold on, Jean. We're coming.

But a desperate scream ripped through the air seconds before a tendril of fire whipped toward the tents, creating a cloud of steam and catching the canvas ablaze.

"No—" But Fen's breath caught, eyes wide in horror as Marc, feral and untethered, conjured still more fire. His hands worked fast as he approached, chest heaving.

"Where is she?!" His question tore through his throat, growling each syllable. "Where is she?!"

Wolves bayed and yelped, steering clear of the fire, their movements compromising their attacks.

"Go!" Rowan cried, praying the wolves could understand. "Go! Run!"

A knife landed in her arm, the small blade long enough to pierce through to the bone above the crook of her elbow. She screamed, the pain burning like the seven hells, as the cultist pulled the knife to turn her. She punched him hard, her uninjured arm providing incredible force behind her fist. When his body crashed to the ground at her feet, she holstered one hatchet and yanked the knife free. The blade was black beneath a steel hilt, the leather-wrapped handle worn from many hands. The Wandering Order had commissioned iron knives. If Rowan had been godborn, this wound would have crippled her.

"She's here," came a voice rich with smugness. Elias sauntered toward her, his movements casual, his abyssal eyes more fathomless in the dark. "Your precious chaosborn."

Before him, brought by two cultists, were Jean and Mirelyn, bound and gagged. The men forced them to their knees, holding beautiful black-bladed daggers to their throats. Mirelyn trembled, grimacing as though to hide how weak she'd become. Pallor had swept over her otherwise beautiful skin, the man holding her shoulder the only thing keeping her upright.

Godborn, Rowan realized, eyeing the black metal at her throat and around her wrists. *Iron sickness.*

"Avenith—"

Naelor dragged Avenith behind him, his meaty hand nearly tearing the collar of her shirt. She struggled, her weak attempts futile with the iron bonds.

The rain slowed to a mist, the overcast casting a hazy shield against the moonlight. Even still, Elias's silver hair made him a beacon as he combed it back. He was all angles and darkness, hatred coloring his soul like pitch.

"Hello, wolfling."

CHAPTER 49

"Naelor." Fen's glare was lethal, his deep blue eyes like the unforgiving depths of the sea. "You've actually surprised me."

Avenith and Mirelyn, weak from iron. Jean upright, though bruised and bloody. Elias, unarmed with his sword still sheathed at his side. Two with knives on Jean and Mirelyn. The others that still surrounded them, armed—maybe ten?

The wolves had gone, from what Rowan could tell. A quick glance showed none dead on the makeshift battlefield. A small relief.

"I like to keep you guessing." But when Naelor's eyes met Thenik's, his bravado faltered. "Sorry, old friend."

"This isn't sorry, Nae." Betrayal carried through every note of Thenik's voice. His hurt ran deep. "You did this on your own, knowing what you know. How—" His lips pulled back in a sneer. He didn't finish, the words burned away in anger.

Elias watched both men with surprising interest. What had Naelor told him about Rowan and the others? About Moonblade? What price did Naelor have to pay to buy his way into the Wandering Order?

Two godborn was a steep entry fee. Avenith and Mirelyn's irons clung to their wrists, and Mirelyn suffered an iron blade pressed to her throat. How could Rowan give them distance from the poison so that Jean could help them heal?

There isn't time. There isn't—

Rowan inhaled deeply, forcing cold, damp air into her aching lungs. Her arm throbbed, the stab wound still oozing blood. The pulsing ache became her focus, centering her mind away from panic toward action. She tallied the threats again.

Ten armed men surrounded them, two with knives to Mirelyn and Jean's throats.

Naelor, a betrayer. Elias, a variable Rowan didn't know. But the depths of his depravity left nothing to the imagination.

"It wasn't personal," Naelor said.

But Thenik wouldn't have it. "It was to me." His eyes fell to Avenith. "It was to her."

"Bit of luck, finding out she has magic." Naelor chuckled. "She was always a pain in my ass."

"And she's right here." Avenith shuddered a gasp, shivering, the iron sickness likely pulling the cold of the misting rain deeper into her bones.

"You didn't know?" Thenik's teasing was knife-edged, the amusement acting as a gateway for his ire. "Gods, it was obvious. How she never sat close to the cook or to a kitchen in a tavern. Where they cook with cast iron..." He let the sentence hang on purpose, his eyebrows raised to mock.

"What magic?" Naelor kicked Avenith's legs. "What magic, then?"

"She's stormborn," Elias said, looking down at her. His lordship over their fall was a dangerous, flammable agent too close to Rowan's anger. "Aren't you, Avey?"

Mustering what strength remained, Avenith lashed out, growling and kicking. Pride swelled in Rowan's chest at her fighting spirit until Naelor struck her hard, the back of his hand colliding with her cheek. Avenith landed on her side in the mud.

"You'll die for this," Thenik said. "I still hold the oath you abandoned."

"I would expect nothing less, old friend."

"Isn't *old friend* pushing it?" Despite her fatigue and agony, Jean smirked. Blood lined her gums and teeth. "I think that ship has sailed.

"She makes a fair point," Elias said. "Now, getting to matters at hand..."

As though on cue, the cultists with Jean and Mirelyn brought their blades higher, tucking them beneath their jaws. Wil and Marc each reacted, but Peter and Rowan held firmly to Wil while Fen struggled with his brother.

"Gods, your skin is on fire," Fen muttered. "You have to control this. Breathe."

"You're quite valuable, wolfling," Elias said. "Almost as valuable as the chaosborn I caught." He chuckled, the sound more pleasant than it had any right to be. "Charis was *furious* when I brought her in. She's a bit too competitive for her own good."

Marc moved a half-step back, fists balled too tightly, his knuckles white.

"She's the one, isn't she?" Rowan's question was a whisper, reading Marc's confirmation in the pallor of his face. "The other Preceptor?"

"Marc and Charis have an interesting relationship," Elias said, eyes fixed on him. "She learned a lot from you. Just as she will learn from her." He rested a hand on Jean's shoulder. "Unless..."

Rowan growled.

"There she is," Elias crooned, pleased. His smile was bright against the night's darkness, as though it radiated a light of its own. "All forest and moonlight."

"I prefer tooth and claw."

Fen smirked.

"My proposal is this." Elias walked from Jean to Mirelyn. "You come with me, and you choose which one to save."

To what end? Experiments with mist arcana? What could Elias and the others hope to gain by capturing her?

Mist arcana. A precious commodity, likely in short supply.

Could she bluff a Preceptor into believing she possessed magic that didn't exist?

"That's your offer?" Jean's snark earned her a wince as the knife bit into her skin.

"I will kill you slowly," Wil said, Peter forcing him back. "You will be conscious for every second."

"Looks like the village healer is a fan favorite." Elias bent next to Mirelyn. "Any friends out there who'll bid for you?" After a pause, he added, "How's your son?"

"Counteroffer," Rowan said, thoughts racing.

She felt Wil, Peter, and Fen close in ranks, but she was undeterred. Elias's brow raised in interest.

"We speak alone," Rowan said, large stones settling in her core. "No harm comes to my friends."

"Are you out of your mind?" Naelor asked with a laugh. Other cultists voiced the same mocking words and tone.

"Rowan." Wil's voice bore a warning. "No."

"Absolutely not," Jean said.

"Trust me," Rowan said, looking at her loved ones. Of their concerned looks, Wil's was the most severe, though Fen's was a strong rival. When she turned back to Elias, she said, "Take those knives from their throats while we speak. They're not going anywhere."

"Trust the wolfling?" Elias's amusement rivaled his malice for the gleam in his eyes. "I will agree. We'll speak privately." He nodded to the two holding Jean and Mirelyn, and they dutifully withdrew their knives. His gaze passed over each of the Order that remained armed and unmoving. "If they flinch, they die."

"If they make the first move," Rowan said, her voice full of authority. "Rip out their throats."

"I like how you play, wolfling." Elias slipped the vial of mist arcana into his breast pocket and approached the nearest tent, holding the soaked canvas open. "After you."

***

ALONE.

Lantern light offered a cozy, warm ambiance that conflicted with the cold touch of fear that pulsed in Rowan's core like a second heartbeat.

"What do you bring me, wolfling?" Elias's voice was low, the tone almost soft. Rowan heard his deception, the silk in every syllable placed with crafted intention. "I'm all ears."

Rowan drew a slow, deliberate breath. "I can see how much you want to know exactly what being wolfkind means."

His grin was predatory. "Can you, now?"

"Going with you means giving up everything I love."

"So you can *save* everything you love."

The sugar-sweet cadence of his words made her stomach turn. She fought to hide her grimace. "You'll need a lot of arcana crystal for whatever hell you intend to put me through."

"That is a relative perspective," he said. "I wouldn't put you through anything I wouldn't do to myself."

She met his eyes then, reading into the abyss. "What do you mean?"

"Mist arcana is an incredible, *invaluable* gift." He shifted his weight to one foot, relaxing the other as he crossed his arms. "What it does to those with magic, what it does to those who are human..." Reverence brightened his features, warmed by the lantern's flame. "I understand its strengths and uses. Fully and completely."

"You..." Shock slowed her body from reacting to what sent her mind reeling. "You use magic."

A Preceptor of the Wandering Order, giving himself access to arcane power...

No wonder he and others like him were hellbent on experiments, gathering knowledge and information for their depraved ends.

"I use a weapon to even the playing field."

"*Playing field.*" She sneered. "This isn't a game."

"And your offer has me interested." He tilted his head, reading every curve of her face. "Tell me."

"I can find arcana crystal."

A simple lie, but Elias wasn't a mindless brick of a human. Cunning thrived behind those eyes.

"Are you prepared to prove it?"

"Only when my loved ones are safe."

"That's an unfair offer, wolfling."

"It is what I can give."

"Was this merely a distraction?" He glanced at the canvas wall as though to see through it. "I don't hear the sounds of a struggle outside. If you'd planned on backup arriving, it doesn't appear they've come."

"There isn't any backup," she said. "There is only you and me and the offer I give. I can find arcana crystals. When you let my loved ones go, unharmed, free to return to their homes, I will go with you."

The corners of his eyes pinched in scrutiny, temptation flickering across his face. He wanted her proposed power and all that would come with it. "I wonder how effective your arcana hunting skills would be with mist arcana to aid you."

"Absolutely not."

"I'm not sure you're in a position to refuse." He took a half-step toward her. Sound erupted outside, voices shouting for someone to stay back. "It seems we have an audience."

"The earth talks to me," Rowan said. "I have no need for that poison."

"No, but I do." The deal had settled in his mind by the glimmer in his eyes. "That is the offer. Both prisoners returned, all of your loved ones safe to go home without further injury, in exchange for you working for me under whatever conditions I set."

She balled her fists tighter, palms stinging with her fingernails stabbing the soft flesh, muscles and tendons aching from pulling beyond their normal limit.

"Do we have a deal, wolfling?"

"I'll never let you go," Rowan said. "Avenith would never forgive me."

"Her opinion of you matters?"

"More than I care to admit."

From outside, again, "I said stay *back*!"

He quirked an eyebrow, knowing Rowan's answer, knowing he'd get what he wanted. "We should see what your friends are doing."

They stepped out of the tent, Fen being held back, the cultist's broad hand firm against his chest.

"It's alright," Rowan said.

The others looked braced for war, hands on weapons ready to draw, Marc with hands poised to cast.

"We've reached an arrangement," Elias said.

"I never said yes, Preceptor."

"Your eyes spoke what your pride could not." He smirked. "You know this is the best possible outcome."

"Rowan." Jean's voice, rich with heartbreak. "Don't."

"What did she promise?" Naelor asked, chuckling. "To help you sniff out magic folk?" He mocked her with exaggerated sniffs.

"One better," Elias said. "It seems the Watcher of Elderglen has a nose for arcana crystal."

Rowan couldn't look at Jean and the others. The weight of their disappointment made it hard to breathe.

Naelor narrowed his eyes. "What a neat trick."

"It's not a trick," Rowan said.

"But you're the Cornerstone," Naelor said. "Your maps mark the mines."

Gods damn it all. Rowan thought fast, feeling Elias's curiosity process quickly in his calculating mind. "Which do you think came first, *cultist*? Those maps or my ability to find them?"

Naelor sneered at the nickname but said nothing more.

"I'm interested in your *maps*," Elias said. "This may alter the terms of our deal."

"There are no more," Thenik said quickly, his defense of Feather and Claw surprising everyone. "They were destroyed."

Naelor reached behind himself, pulling something from his back pocket. The folded, waxed parchment had cracked from many hands. He unfolded it carefully, passing it to Elias.

"My, my," the Preceptor said, eyeing the parchment as the overcast moved swiftly across the sky, a break in the clouds unveiling moonlight. "What a useful traitor you turned out to be."

On the back, the watermark for Feather and Claw was visible, as was a brown spot where candlelight had singed it.

"That—" Fen looked from the map to Naelor. "That map—"

Elias grinned, folding the document and slipping it into the back pocket of his trousers.

"Bought it from a scamp in Runa." Naelor grinned. "She asked a fair price, eager to get rid of it." He locked eyes with Fen, every word uttered with scathing intent. "Some mad sailor was on her tail, eager to get it back."

The map, stolen from Fen and sold to Naelor.

When Feather and Claw had searched.

When Rowan's parents had died.

"All this time?" Rowan didn't blink, reality filling her like stones, piling until there was nothing left. "You had it?"

"Why?" Naelor chuckled. "Were you and your gran crying over getting it back?"

"A man and a woman," she said slowly, eyes stinging, her skin too hot, her blood flowing too fast. "At a mine in Sudor."

Naelor's grin flickered, confusion awakening to realization as he remembered. "Lass—"

Her fingers lifted her hatchet before her mind had awakened her taking it. She pulled back, stopping at the cries of her name, pleas for her to stop. Naelor's pupils shrank, hands extended in supplication.

Behind her, Elias chuckled.

"No," Naelor said, hands shaking. "Please."

"Is that what they said?" Rowan's question came as the wind stilled, as though the earth longed for Naelor's answer. As though it longed for an answer to Rowan's rage. "You dare seek mercy from me, you coward?"

"I didn't know," Naelor said quickly, shaking his head. "I swear, I didn't know."

"You didn't know that they were my parents?" she whispered. "Or that someone would kill you for what you've done?"

"I didn't know—"

"Why would that make any difference?" Thunder rumbled overhead. "*Murderer.*"

"How she hasn't killed you yet is either a miracle or proof that she has no spine," Elias said. "Don't tell me I've bartered for a wolf who has no teeth."

Naelor's breath caught, eyes going wide from shock. He collapsed to his knees and fell forward, the hilt and handle of the dagger familiar as it stuck out of Naelor's back.

Behind him, Avenith glared, her breathing labored and eyes aflame with vengeance. Her manacled arms remained poised after the throw, one of her beautiful daggers between Naelor's shoulders, just to the left of his spine. The blade was long enough to pierce through muscles and ribs to the vital organs protected within.

"A wolf with no teeth." Elias clicked his tongue. "What a shame."

CHAPTER 50

Thenik ran to his former ally, none of the cultists stopping him as hurried and fell to his knees.

"Serves me right, eh?" Naelor's breath rattled with blood.

"Guardian of Elderglen," Elias taunted. "All bark and no bite."

Rowan stared at Avenith, disbelief mingling with selfish gratitude, the kind laced with shame. The taste of vengeance was not unfamiliar on Rowan's tongue, but Avenith had spared her the agony of what comes after, of choice and its aftermath.

"I didn't set out to kill them," Naelor said. "If it matters."

"It doesn't." Rowan had no room for sympathy, even as he bled all over Thenik's hands. "They're still dead."

"The goddesses will have a time with you," Thenik said, sadness heavy in his voice. "You have a lot to atone for."

Naelor couldn't laugh, the smile barely visible as he rasped through his final breath.

"You saved me the trouble of killing him later," Elias said. "So, my little magical wolfling." He pursed his lips as he regarded Rowan. "You were saying about our deal?"

"Let them go." Rowan's tone managed a blend of irritation and confidence, a bravado she hoped Gran would be proud of. "This isn't what you want."

"And what do I want?" He moved closer, prompting Wil and Fen to raise their weapons.

Intrigue painted itself across Elias's handsome face. His dark eyes held fathoms Rowan could reach if she dared to search them, but she already knew what darkness she would find.

"Power." The word came from Rowan, but she heard Wil's voice echoing in memory. "That's why you're fascinated with mist arcana."

"Because it gives me power?" Approval highlighted his features. "How insightful."

The clouds shifted once more, moonlight shimmering on everything, casting the grim, bloody scene in its ethereal glow.

"At last," he said, eyes piercing. "All the better to see you with."

Rowan's hackles tingled, alarm tugging at her muscles, skin prickling to goosebumps. He was evil masking as human, the body merely a disguise of flesh and bone and blood. Funny how certain truths relied upon the sun while others, born of darkness, unveiled themselves beneath the moon.

"I'm afraid I cannot agree to your terms," Elias said. "I can only give you one."

"Because of the chaosborn," Rowan said. "Because you think I won't choose her."

"I have learned a lot about you, Watcher." The Preceptor tilted his head, his body language remaining casual despite the mounting tensions of those around him. "The way you care for your village. How deeply you love your friends."

Rowan didn't glance at Naelor, avoiding his death gaze. He'd told Elias everything.

"The earthwitch is like a second mother to you," Elias said. "A strong bond, especially in the wake of loss and grief."

Rowan couldn't be sure if he'd meant her parents or Gran.

"If you choose neither," he said, "I won't kill them."

It hadn't occurred to her to refuse completely. She waited, sensing his villainous speech would continue.

"I haven't experimented on them yet." He pulled the small corked vial of bluish-purple powder, moonlight glimmering off the glass. "An earthwitch and a chaosborn. Though I won't make the same mistake as my colleague." He turned to call over his shoulder. "Right, Charis?"

As though waiting for her summons, a blonde woman emerged from another tent. She was a striking beauty, her thick hair braided over one shoulder, her blue-green eyes illuminated by the moonlight. One of her hands was bound in wood and leather, the other cradling another vial of mist arcana.

The second Preceptor studied their faces, her eyes lingering on Marc's, then Avenith's.

"Good to see you both." Her voice. She was the person Elias was speaking with that day Rowan eavesdropped. Both Preceptors, speaking of Naelor having a heart that matched their own, hoping for more arcana crystal from the map he'd hoarded.

A map that Elias still held.

To Avenith, Charis quirked an eyebrow. "How's the family?"

She growled, the sound nothing more than an exhale. Still weak, the iron sickness taking its toll, the metal on her wrist slowly burning her skin.

Jean glared from Charis to Elias. "Heartless cowards."

"My heart aches for a world divided by magic," Charis said, her tone cool. "It longs for the peace that will follow once our work is done."

"You mean murder," Rowan said. "The blood on your hands will never wash away."

"A price I'm willing to pay." Charis turned the vial over in her hand. "So much to learn. So much to gain..." She met Rowan's gaze, curiosity aflame.

Mirelyn and Avenith would die. Shallow breathing. Pale skin.

Jean would die. Elias would kill her simply out of spite.

"It's alright, Rowan," Mirelyn said, forcing her voice despite her fatigue. "Trust me."

"How gallant." Elias snickered. "So eager to self-sacrifice."

Trust me.

"Rowan—"

Marc's voice broke through, agony in each syllable. She stepped forward, wincing, fearing he wouldn't understand.

Rowan wouldn't give anyone up to such darkness. No matter what it took, no matter how much blood she would have to pay to bargain for them, no one would be at the mercy of the Wandering Order.

"I think we have a volunteer," Charis said. "I've never tested wolfkind before." Her sneer fell to Mirelyn. "I had the pleasure of the might of a chaosborn, his power unbridled and magnificent. He put on quite a show."

"Did he?" Amusement found its way to Mirelyn's tired mouth and eyes. "How's your hand?"

Charis held the vial up, the moonlight reflecting off the glass. "Still capable of pouring this down your gullet."

"I don't understand the use of mist arcana on those with magic," Wil said, his tone conversational while his body language remained aggressive. His shoulders angled forward as his hand rested on the handle of his sword, ready to draw. "Why grant them more power?"

"Did you learn nothing from that chaosborn you're so quick to brag about?" Fen scoffed. "Rumors say you barely made it out alive."

Rowan caught the glimmer of pride on Mirelyn's face, a corner of her mouth ticking up.

"You both make excellent arguments," Elias said. "I should like to use two members of your own beloved party as examples of our mission with mist arcana." He gestured to Marc and Mirelyn. "One, a human with learned skill in fire magic. The other, her godborn son with the power of chaos. Each with different ways of channeling and controlling their magic, with very different responses to magical stimuli." He drew the vial of mist arcana from his pocket. "A single, small dose on the tongue gave one incredible power. For one, shadows gathered at his feet as though worshiping a god. For the other, flames coursed through his veins, every inch of his body begging for that power's release."

Marc struggled to control his anger—shaking hands, unblinking eyes. He was a captured predator pacing, waiting for the cage door to burst open. It would only take a word, a gesture, a flicker of light for Marc to unleash every ounce of rage that swirled in his blood. How he contained it at all was a feat of unimaginable strength.

No one grabbed or bound Rowan, but the bonds that caged her

were in the men with iron knives too close to Mirelyn and Jean. One misstep...

The cultist threatening Jean howled in pain, the knife twisting in his grip. But there was no sign of anyone or anything attacking. No knife's blade or magic. Still, the man fell to one knee screaming.

Rowan wasted no time, the confusion offering an opening she had no leverage to bargain for. She loosed her hatchet at Mirelyn's captor as she dove for Jean's captor, bringing him to the ground before her fist drove into his gut again and again. A rib cracked beneath her knuckles, the sickening pop barely audible over the sounds of fighting around her.

Glass shattered, but Rowan didn't stop, bringing her fist to his face and breaking his nose. She leaned back, panting, staring at his motionless form before the stench of citrus-laced sulfur nearly made her sneeze.

Charis's hand, the uninjured one, was empty. The vial was gone, its pieces shattered beside a white stone that shone in the moonlight. Jean cackled, the earth responding as roots surfaced through the mud. Cultists cried out, trying to jump away from capture. Most didn't escape, their footing unbalanced and bodies falling.

Rowan's trembling hands itched with the driving urge to shift. Her rage bloomed with fuel from the mist arcana she'd breathed. Her fingers ached to rip and rend, to tear every cultist to shreds. She white-knuckled her hatchet, control a desperate lifeline in a sea of flames that burned beneath her skin.

"Rowan."

Fen. The only person to douse the flames within her. Where others had soothed the burning, Fen had erased it completely.

Mirelyn rose to her feet, the iron sickness affecting her stability while the mist arcana boosted her adrenaline. Her conjured shadows made short work of the iron manacle around her ankle. The cuff was devoid of its chain, the poison enough to keep Mirelyn in check. But no more, as the iron fell away and she moved.

Mirelyn took a cultist's arm and pulsed shadowed terror through his skin. His scream pealed through the night, matching his ally as Jean, even with hands bound, summoned the earth to bind him in root and vine.

"Rowan." Fen's hand touched hers. Her shaking had worsened. "Look at me."

She didn't, closing her eyes and turning her head. Shame hollowed her.

"The beast wants out, love," Elias said, his voice like velvet, his abyssal eyes eager. "Don't become its cage."

"You're the cage." Speaking was a struggle. Rowan's voice strained through taut muscles. "Every word is another bar of iron."

"Such is the power I wield."

Peter blocked a cultist's strike before kicking his stomach. He tumbled to the mud, breathless. "Your Preceptor's smugness is infuriating."

"Show us." Elias edged closer, ignoring Charis's hand as she tried to pull him back. "Show *me*."

"You bow to no one," Fen said, touching her face, kissing her forehead. Shame within her grew, but she selfishly accepted his love. "Your power is yours, no matter what happens."

Rowan flexed her grip on her hatchet, expecting Fen to hold her back, to guide her to control what mist arcana did to her blood. But his hand slipped free of her arm. With it, he picked up a fallen sword and moved to stand at her side. "I am with you, Rowan. At every step."

The cage door was open, with Fen waiting patiently for Rowan to step out on her own. The choice was hers.

She tore her eyes from Fen, regarding Elias with fury blazing. And with it, *hope*.

"This ends now."

CHAPTER 51

The poison of iron rivaled the Wandering Order in its greed, siphoning the life and magic from anything it touched.

Rowan closed the distance between herself and Avenith, moving closer to the iron-bound woman ignited by mist arcana. Jean continued to manipulate the earth, though her bound hands limited her power. But iron had no effect on her, where Avenith's hold on consciousness remained thin.

A few cultists groaned as they fell to their knees—two, then three, then five. Elias and Charis's eyes were wide and watchful as they backed away. Where was their attacker?

Rowan looked to Mirelyn, the chaosborn's power over the shadows greater than it had ever been. Was she manipulating their life threads?

But there wasn't time to think or stop. As Rowan knelt beside Avenith, the pair finding the ground to regain some of what they'd lost, Elias drew his sword.

Fen engaged, giving Rowan what he could so she could aid unhindered.

"This is agony," Avenith whispered, resting her head on Rowan's shoulder. "No power left, but I feel like I can burn the world. Pulled in two directions. To sink into the earth and finally rest. To rise to the sky and rain death upon them all."

"Stay with me, Avenith."

The metal was slick beneath Rowan's fingers as she pulled one of Avenith's throwing knives from her belt and forced the blade into the lock. "How many of these things do you have?"

"Plenty," Avenith whispered with a weak smile. "An arsenal."

"You're going to need them."

She was careful not to cut Avenith but not so with herself. The blade slipped, slicing through her palm.

"He loves you," she muttered in Rowan's ear. "Or at least he's starting to."

Rowan didn't respond, forcing her hands to work with the pain as the tip of the throwing found purchase in the lock. Rowan pushed and twisted, the manacle breaking open.

"I think your muscles caught his fancy." Avenith chuckled, letting Rowan take her bruised wrists, her skin bloody from Rowan's wound. "They certainly caught mine."

"Go somewhere safe," Rowan urged. "Stay alive long enough for me to forgive you."

"The earth isn't ready to take me yet, and Erys sure as hell isn't." Avenith kissed Rowan's hand. "Go to Jean. I'll be alright."

But a cultist met Rowan as she rose, his battle cry her only warning to raise a defense. She caught his sword arm by the wrist, the throwing knife a weak barrier against the blade of his sword.

Her feet moved quickly and kicked at his knee, making her body a living barrier between the enemy and Avenith. As his stance faltered, she leveraged his weight to bring her strength upon him. The throwing knife, though small, was enough to inflict considerable damage as she raked it across his middle, the soft flesh of his stomach giving easily. She let him fall to the ground, giving Avenith one more look before crossing to Jean.

Mirelyn's shadows had moved on to Charis as Jean manipulated the earth around the cultists who tried to intervene.

"You give your lives freely," Jean said. "Offering your blood to those who don't deserve it."

The cultists responded by trying to fight, but Jean's control of the ground beneath their feet did not yield.

Fear cascaded ice through Rowan's blood at the thought of what this magic would cost. Jean, a human, mist arcana coursing through her veins...

"You fed this poison to my son." Mirelyn's voice was otherworldly, shadows licking around her feet with every step. Her eyes had gone black, shadows becoming her.

Rowan pulled her hatchet from the chest of the man she'd killed and closed the distance between herself and Elias. His grin was one of victory, as though she'd unleashed the rage he was so eager to see.

But Rowan hadn't given an inch. She would yield to no one.

Mirelyn struck without mercy, bringing Charis to her knees. Elias moved to intervene, but Rowan met him with bladed fury.

"You asked for this," Rowan said, her will pushed closer to the edge. Any second, and she would fall. "This is what mist arcana can do, Preceptor."

He shoved her back, their weapons singing as metal scraped against metal.

"Your control is remarkable," he said, studying her, arcing his sword with an impressive flick of his wrist. "A light dose does nothing to you, it would seem. But how much would be *too* much?"

A throwing knife sang in its spinning arc before Elias's sword swatted it away like a pesky insect. Avenith slowly rose to her feet, her beautiful eyes glowing with the dangerous light of heaven, the angry, burning blue deadly as she stared at the man her vengeance sought.

"Rowan's control always made me jealous," she said, her voice bearing a similar power to Mirelyn's. But where Mirelyn's was a deeper, shadowed layer, Avenith's was an aeolian echo. "I've never had such temperance. Or patience."

Avenith lifted her hands as storm clouds reformed, lightning forking above their heads. Thunder rattled Rowan's bones.

"She's magnificent," Fen whispered, drawing close to Rowan.

"Yes, she is."

Rowan took in the wonder on Elias's face as it bloomed into terror.

"You called the thunder," Avenith said, static flickering around her hands and arms, within her eyes and mouth. She didn't conjure the storm. She *was* the storm. "Now, you've got it."

Blood, rain, sweat, earth—Rowan smelled it, heard it, tasted it. And Avenith's power made all of her senses sing.

Rowan took Jean's hands carefully and cut away the rope.

"How much did you breathe in?" Jean asked, force behind her words. She had to focus, to maintain control. The mist arcana demanded her attention every second it moved within her. "Gods, I feel like I'm young again."

"I can still think straight," Rowan said. "So, that's something."

She helped Jean to her feet, the woman crying out as she put weight on her left ankle.

Understanding slammed into Rowan's mind, remembering Jean's abduction. "Your ankle wasn't injured in the wagon."

"Rowan—"

"What did they do?"

"Rowan—"

Rather than be blinded by rage, Rowan's vision narrowed onto Elias as she loosed the throwing knife, the blade meeting his ankle above the joint. His agonized howl gave Avenith an opening to bring a long dagger to his throat. But Charis ran screaming, colliding with Avenith and landing hard on the soaked earth.

Charis. That means—

Rowan hurried, supporting Jean as they found where Mirelyn lay. The iron knife pierced beneath her right clavicle, moving up and down as she breathed.

"You're alright, Mir," Jean said. "Rowan, put me down."

She obeyed, helping to ease Jean to the ground.

"Gods, I—" Mirelyn shivered. "I haven't had—iron sickness in so—"

Jean pulled the knife free and threw it hard. Rowan lost sight of it in the dark.

"Tell me more about your son," Jean said, pressing her hands to the wound. "What's he like?"

Mirelyn blinked slowly. "He's perfect. Kind. Loving."

"Handsome?" Rowan asked, keeping Mirelyn focused.

Jean hummed, taking one hand and pressing her palm firmly to the earth.

"Very." Mirelyn smiled, though every inch of her was tired. "He has my eyes and his father's devilish grin."

"Sounds like a heartbreaker." Rowan knelt at her other side as Jean continued to sing.

"His love is more than a match for him. I met her not long before Marc came to me. Beautiful girl. Practically made of sunlight."

Strength returned to her voice, color to her cheeks.

"No!" The agony of a woman in horror. "Elias!"

Avenith stood, barely upright, her breathing labored. Bloody. Alive. And Elias and Charis were at her feet.

"Two Preceptors on the ground." A voice from the shadows. A woman, appearing among the tents. Darkness lined her eyes and mouth, shadows feathering from them like veins dyed with ink.

"S—Suna?"

The mayor's wife, kindhearted, a loving figure within Elderglen...

Now her body was a vessel for darkness.

She reached her hands toward the Preceptors, shadows feathering around her fingers.

"Two Preceptors on the ground," she repeated. "Two souls, ripe for the picking."

Gone was the woman weeping in the wounds, broken by shame and guilt and grief. Replacing her was a warrior of shadow and vengeance, hands extended and eyes alight, eager to consume.

The cultists who had fallen, their attacker unseen.

It had been Suna, her soul magic primed for killing.

"She's a soulwitch?" Charis looked from Elias to Rowan. "A *soulwitch*?"

What few cultists remained gathered themselves, figuring out the best approach. But Suna didn't wait for someone to strike. Charis and Elias both choked a gasp, their breath pulling from their lungs. Avenith stepped back, lightning eyes wide as her power flickered, fading. She collapsed to her knees, vulnerable, and one cultist saw.

He ran for her.

"Avenith!"

Rowan struggled to run, rising from her knees as her feet sank into mud and soft earth. Avenith barely missed the arc of his sword, pulling her remaining dagger from her belt and burying it in his stomach.

More charged, finding the weak spots of the group, several going to Elias and Charis's aid while others stormed Jean and Avenith. Wil, Peter, and Thenik met them blade for blade, protecting Jean and Mirelyn, as Fen rushed to Rowan's side, helping her protect Avenith.

"Suna was an unexpected surprise," Fen said, taking the first hit against his sword and pushing his foe back.

"An unexpected variable," Rowan said.

She threw one hatchet at a charging cultist before lowering her hand to Avenith. "Is there a sword or something close by?"

Avenith filled Rowan's hand with her own. "Better. There's me."

No. Not with iron sickness. "Av—"

Lightning crackled overhead, the boom of thunder deafening as tendrils of light reached down and touched the three cultists around them. As Avenith's fingers slipped from Rowan's hand, fear dripped ice down her back, pooling in her core.

Avenith lay in the mud, eyes open, chest barely lifting with each breath. But the immediate threat was over. All that remained were those fighting Wil, Peter, and Thenik, their spirit faltering as their comrades either died or ran.

Suna breathed heavily, bracing herself on her knees, bloody, a hand pressed to her chest.

Two more cultists died before the others broke for the trees, their boots slapping the wet ground loudly in their panicked retreat.

Elias and Charis were gone, the rain pelting the grass and mud where they'd been.

"Aided by their blinded followers," Suna said, wincing. Shadows swirled around her, the wound in her chest slowly healing.

"A death blow," Wil said. "She survived a *death blow*."

"Soulwitches can perform remarkable magic," Mirelyn said. "But the cost of such power is steep."

A life for a life. Rowan understood well enough the souls Suna's magic had consumed to fuel her rage and hatred, her grief and shame. Now, what remained kept her alive, shielding her body from death.

"Come, Suna." Jean reached her arms down to help her stand. "Let's go home."

"I cannot." Suna stood with Jean's help, her rueful smile full of goodbye. "My path to redemption is long, and this war is far from over."

"Suna—"

"If I am damned to Chaos for what I've done, so be it." She gripped Jean's hand with affection and reassurance. "But, so help me, I'll take as many of them with me as the goddesses allow."

Suna rose and left in silence, the hole in her dress the only sign that she'd been stabbed, that she'd escaped death with the power of darkness fueling her life. She left them to gather and reclaim, the living cultists having fled, the battlefield around them filled with death.

"They can't be far," Fen said, looking to Rowan. "Elias and Charis are both hurt. We could pursue them."

But Rowan looked to Mirelyn and Avenith, to her loved ones, bloodied and bruised but alive. "We will see them again, I'm sure of it. But we have more pressing matters now. No one should face them alone, and taking others to confront them leaves the wounded vulnerable."

"He still has the map," Wil said, the situation's weight and severity rich in his voice. "We can't—"

Avenith pulled the document, still folded, from the front of her tunic and held it aloft with a weak hand. "Never fear. I have done my guild proud this day." She coughed, groaning. "Gods, I feel like death."

"You clever woman." Rowan knelt beside her, taking the map and the hand that held it. "Can you stand?"

"In your arms, I could fly."

Rowan rolled her eyes, though her smile broke through, and helped Avenith to her feet.

"What will you do now?" Wil asked, looking at Thenik.

"Back to the guild," he said with a shrug. "Valera will be pissed over Naelor. There's no telling what he told those cultists about us."

"This does put all of us in an interesting situation," Jean said, still kneeling beside Mirelyn. The chaosborn breathed better, more deeply and steadily, but she remained weak. "I think our leaders should discuss where this leaves us."

Her eyes met Rowan's, and the Cornerstone nodded. "We stand a chance if we fight together."

She looked at her friends, her loved ones, her gaze lingering on Fen. His soft smile captured her, disarmed her, welcomed her, bloodied and bruised and raging and strong. He hadn't shied away, not once, embracing every part of her.

"I'm glad we're together for the coming days," she said.

His smile widened. "And for what comes after."

Wil looked from Fen to Rowan, playfully rolling his eyes. "Gods, get a room."

CHAPTER 52

Elderglen was quiet upon their return.

In the days that passed, the mayor's house remained empty once Frederick buried his son. He settled outside of the village, begging only to live near his son's grave. The villagers had no qualms with such a request, his loss considerable.

Braithen was gone, his tannery empty. No one knew where he'd gone, but the atmosphere of the village improved with his absence.

Which left Rowan at Sentinel Hill, unofficially resuming her role as Watcher of Elderglen. No one voiced an objection or asked questions, though the blacksmith inquired about another assistant at the forge.

"That idiot from Moonblade didn't know his own ass from an alloy, but an extra set of hands was nice to have around."

With the blacksmith in need of aid and Braithen's home in need of a resident, Rowan knew the perfect person to recommend for both.

"Would that make you happy?" Fen asked. "To have me so close?"

She answered by embracing him, resting her head upon his shoulder. His quiet presence soothed her, reaching deep within her heart, her muscles, her blood, filling her with peace.

"I'm afraid you're stuck with me, Alden Fen." Her chin rested perfectly on his chest as she looked up at him. "You don't get a say in the matter."

"That's fine by me." He kissed her forehead, holding her as tightly as she held him, reaching an aching need that had been long dormant within her. "If you get sick of me, that is the bed you made."

"One we will fill."

His shock had her laughing, a sound so rare that the villagers had to look twice to see if it was really their Watcher.

Rowan only allowed herself one day of rest before venturing to the Moonblade hideout, seeking their leader. Moonblade and Feather and Claw had much to discuss.

"I'm glad to see you're alive," Valera said, sitting with Rowan at the small wooden table in their base underground. "Facing two Preceptors and coming out alive is no small thing, Guardian."

"I had strong allies with me," she said, glancing toward Avenith and Thenik. The pair sat across from one another at the long dining table, sipping their ale as they surreptitiously watched Rowan and Valera. "Which brings me to one point I wish to discuss."

Valera raised an eyebrow. "I think I have an idea what that point may be."

"You knew," Rowan said, her voice calm while maintaining her accusation. "Since he first arrived at your doorstep, you knew."

Valera leaned back, assessing what Rowan wasn't saying, likely trying to find a loophole to exploit.

"The map was too good to pass up," Rowan continued. "The temptation was too strong. So what if the Cornerstone's daughter and husband paid the price?"

"I didn't know they were the ones," Valera said. "I never lied about that."

"You didn't know until you *did* know. And you still protected him. And you had the audacity to make me feel terrible about destroying your load of mist arcana."

"You cost me a lot of money that day, Cornerstone, yet I had my people pay *you* a debt."

From *Guardian* to *Cornerstone*. Valera's veneer was slipping.

"Don't act like you've done me any favors," Rowan countered.

"You should watch your tone," Valera said, her voice low. Nearly half a dozen pairs of eyes watched them. "You'll regret making an enemy of us."

"Our guilds are not enemies, Valera. But you and I? Whatever friendly terms we'd managed have dissolved. You protected the man who murdered my parents. The man who nearly killed Avenith and Jean."

Valera crossed her arms. "I have my reasons."

"And they're terrible."

Avenith choked on her ale, trying in vain to be quiet.

"Imagine having to fight a war on two fronts," Rowan went on, "because the corrupted leader of an assassin's guild would compromise her own people for a bottom line."

Valera's expression turned sharp, but Rowan stopped her. "You made a mistake. You know exactly the wrong you did, but you would do it again without batting an eye."

"Make sure Thenik and Avenith have my regards," Valera said, leaning forward, a predator's gleam in her eyes. "They'll regret abandoning the guild."

"They'll regret nothing, and you'll leave them alone. Unless you want to know what my vengeance feels like."

"No one turns their back on the guild."

"*You* turned your back on *them*." Rowan scoffed. "To think I had respect for you. You're no worse than the cultists we fight against."

Valera snarled, rising fast to reach for Rowan across the table, but Rowan shifted and pounced in one motion, her paws pressing hard on Valera's chest and shoulder.

Several chairs toppled as bodies rose, blades sliding free from their sheaths. But Rowan didn't break her gaze from Valera's, snarling and snapping her jaws before becoming human again.

"Remember this moment, Valera," she said. "If you hadn't let your selfishness win, we'd have had a very different conversation."

"Take care not to cross me again, Cornerstone," Valera said. "Our protection will not reach your guild."

"Your protection leaves something to be desired." Rowan studied Valera's expression briefly. "And I think, deep down, you love the challenge."

Rowan winked before rising, helping Valera to her feet. But the assassin reached a hand for Rowan's side quickly, prompting her to catch Valera's wrist. With one smooth motion, Valera had loosed a small knife from somewhere on her person, its short blade aimed at Rowan's ribs.

Rowan spun Valera, gripping her small wrist without mercy. Valera cried out, the blade dropping from her fingers.

Low in her ear, Rowan whispered, "Play nice, Valera."

Valera grinned. "I see why Avenith liked you."

Rowan released her, nodding to Avenith and Thenik to leave. The assassins waited for Valera's signal, which never came, so they remained ready to strike as the trio ascended to their exit.

"Well," Avenith said, rubbing her palms together. "That went well."

"How did you know about the knife?" Thenik asked. "You moved like you knew it was there."

"Being wolfkind has its perks."

The trio walked on, and the days that passed held much the same responsibility and duty as the days before. Soon, Elderglen sought Rowan's recommendation for another mayor, a post that shouldn't remain empty when the world was turning in on itself, and small villages would be consumed first.

"What about Jean?" one villager asked. "Or Wil?"

"Jean first, then Wil," another said. "She knows Elderglen better than most of us, *and* she's served on the Hill."

Rowan smiled to herself, knowing exactly what Jean would think of such high praise and distinction.

"She'll hate this," Rowan muttered to Fen. "Being recommended for responsibility."

He smiled to himself, turning his face so only she would see. "What about you?" He studied her, sweeping strands of hair from her face to tuck behind her ear. "Do you wish to remain Watcher?"

"I do." And she meant it for the first time since bearing the title.

"I would have you unbound and unburdened." He kissed her, holding her lips for several breaths before pulling away. "Whatever you wish, I will see it done."

"Whatever *we* wish," she said. "Together."

EPILOGUE

"He wasn't there."

The Storyteller read over the final pages, her heart aching for the sign she sought in every memory.

"He wasn't there, but he was close. So close."

She could hear his voice. She could feel his breath. One of them had said his name, leaving her heart to thrum in anticipation of the stories to come.

She closed the book of wolves, the ferocity burning within its pages.

"Save your rage," she whispered, running a soothing hand over the book's cover and spine. "I will have need of it in the coming days."

Both Preceptors had escaped the wolf's fury, but their time would come. And the Storyteller had yet another story to tell, pages ready to be filled. Her hands and eyes ached, but the tales wouldn't stop simply because she was tired. They filled her to the brim.

The only way out was *through*.

She slipped the book onto the shelf, where room remained for the next and the next and...

"Don't get ahead of yourself."

She could almost hear him answer. "What's ahead of me if not you and our future together?"

Whatever we wish, together, the wolfkind had said.

An inky tear fell onto the parchment, black touching a new, clean page. So she began.

Acknowledgments

Once more, this book came into existence thanks to the loving grace of my Lord and Savior. Thank you, Jesus, for the path that led me to loving my writing journey all over again. (And thanks a million for the delicious coffee to drink along the way.)

My family and friends have offered unyielding support, for which I am eternally grateful. Mom, Dad, and Kelly, your fierce protection of my writing time, your unwavering encouragement, and your listening ears have been essential in me surviving the drafting and revising processes. Thank you for loving me so much.

Frank and Laura, thank you for always checking in and supporting my writing from day one.

Anne and Misty, you have helped me push outside of my comfort zone to broaden my bookselling horizons, and I will be forever grateful for your guidance, patience, and friendship.

Bridget, Sue, Terry Anne, and Laura, your encouragement has filled my heart to the brim. You have been incredible cheerleaders. I am so grateful to have you all in my life.

Amanda, your enthusiasm at beta reading made my heart soar. Thank you for your notes, your reactions, and for always being my hype queen.

Charlie, your patience and professionalism are incredible, and I truly appreciate the time you've taken to help me shape this manuscript into the book it's become. I am so blessed that our paths have crossed. THANK YOU.

To my beloved friends at Salient Books and The Crafty Bookstore, your virtual companionship has been so much fun and so encouraging.

From rants to raves to everything in between, our Discord and Instagram DMs are chaos incarnate, and I am loving every minute of it.

Thank you to Georgia and Wendy for book-related chats and an unending stream of pop culture references and musical enthusiasm. I find kindred spirits in you both, and I am so glad the indie publishing world brought us together.

And thank YOU, my dearest reader, who took the time to read *The Book of Wolves*. If this is your first book from *The Dark Library Series*, I am so thrilled you've stepped into the library to read its collection. If this is your return to the library, welcome back, weary traveler. I hope the book offered you space to breathe, to feel seen, and to feel loved.

About the Author

When Morgan's not writing, she's playing video games. Find her on social media @morganreallywrites (except X, which insists on being DIFFERENT — @morganrlywrites).

Find all of her stories on Kindle Unlimited:
amazon.com/author/morganreilly

Stay up to date by signing up for her newsletter at
https://subscribepage.io/gQ6p2Z

Website: https://morganreallywrites.com/

facebook.com/morganreallywrites

instagram.com/morganreallywrites

tiktok.com/@morganreallywrites

threads.net/@morganreallywrites

amazon.com/author/morganreilly

goodreads.com/morganreallywrites